"So what do you say, Miss Carrington? Are we cool?" He extended a huge hand to her, palm up.

"We're cool," she said, reluctantly reaching for it.

"Good. Let's kiss on it."

God, I hope so, she thought just as her palm met his and he used the leverage to bring her skipping toward him. Halfway there, the tip of his tongue peeked out from between his open lips in a silent invitation that she went up on her tiptoes to greedily accept, sinking into his mouth so deeply that she felt his tongue touch the back of her throat. It was the wettest, thirstiest, most invasive kiss that Olivia had ever experienced, so raw and uncivilized that her face flamed with embarrassment even as she gripped his shoulders and let him take her head back on her neck. He gripped her waist possessively and groaned into her mouth, and a rush of liquid pleasure drenched her thong. He glided a hand up her back to press her closer, and she purred.

D0285557

Terra Little has been reading romance novels for decades and falling in and out of love with the heroes between the sheets for just as long. When she's not in the classroom teaching English literature or desperately trying to keep up with her energetic grandson, you can most likely find her tucked away somewhere with her laptop and a dog-eared romance novel. To share feedback, yummy recipes and suggestions for great reads, drop Terra a line at writeterralittle@yahoo.com and visit her online at www.terralittle.net.

Books by Terra Little

Harlequin Kimani Romance

Beneath Southern Skies
Road to Temptation
Journey to My Heart

Visit the Author Profile page
at Harlequin.com for more titles.

TERRA LITTLE
and
BRIDGET ANDERSON

Journey to My Heart &
The Sweetest Affair

HARLEQUIN® KIMANI™ ROMANCE

If you purchased this book without a cover you should be aware that this book is stolen property. It was reported as "unsold and destroyed" to the publisher, and neither the author nor the publisher has received any payment for this "stripped book."

ISBN-13: 978-1-335-43304-6

Journey to My Heart & The Sweetest Affair

Copyright © 2019 by Harlequin Books S.A.

The publisher acknowledges the copyright holders of the individual works as follows:

Journey to My Heart
Copyright © 2019 by Terra Little

The Sweetest Affair
Copyright © 2019 by Bridget Anderson

Recycling programs for this product may not exist in your area.

All rights reserved. Except for use in any review, the reproduction or utilization of this work in whole or in part in any form by any electronic, mechanical or other means, now known or hereafter invented, including xerography, photocopying and recording, or in any information storage or retrieval system, is forbidden without the written permission of the publisher, Harlequin Enterprises Limited, 22 Adelaide St. West, 40th Floor, Toronto, Ontario M5H 4E3, Canada.

This is a work of fiction. Names, characters, places and incidents are either the product of the author's imagination or are used fictitiously, and any resemblance to actual persons, living or dead, business establishments, events or locales is entirely coincidental.

This edition published by arrangement with Harlequin Books S.A.

For questions and comments about the quality of this book, please contact us at CustomerService@Harlequin.com.

® and TM are trademarks of Harlequin Enterprises Limited or its corporate affiliates. Trademarks indicated with ® are registered in the United States Patent and Trademark Office, the Canadian Intellectual Property Office and in other countries.

Printed in U.S.A.

CONTENTS

JOURNEY TO MY HEART   7
Terra Little

THE SWEETEST AFFAIR   229
Bridget Anderson

To the little girl they used to call "Booty-Boo."
Hello there, Sunshine. Long time, no see…

JOURNEY TO MY HEART

Terra Little

Dear Reader,

Just when you thought you'd heard the last of the Carrington twins, Olivia Carrington finds herself next in line for a nip from Cupid's arrow. Of course, being the independent, carefree sort, both Cupid and Cooper Talbot—the relentless FBI agent from hell…or heaven, depending on how you look at it—have their work cut out for them.

Never one to be easily intimidated, Olivia is the perfect match for Cooper's disarming Southern charm. So much so that talking her way out of potential legal problems is a piece of cake. It's the risk of being talked out of something else that keeps her awake at night.

Should she or shouldn't she?

That's the million-dollar question, but you'll have to discover the answer for yourself. First, though, settle in, grab a cool drink and put up your feet. This is one journey that I hope you'll be glad you took!

Bon voyage!

Terra

Chapter 1

The Wi-Fi call was on its fifth attempt to ring through, splitting the calm morning air with one last shrill-sounding, eardrum-scraping melody that finally managed to accomplish the seemingly impossible task of rattling Olivia Carrington's resting nerves and startling her awake. Up until that very moment, she'd been asleep for exactly three hours, a fact that she planned to remind her caller of as soon as she could think clearly. Cursing viciously under her breath, she kicked her feet loose from a tangle of covers and punched a pillow before turning her head, zeroing in on the culprit—the open MacBook on the nightstand—and reaching out to press a button on the keypad.

"This had better be good," she snarled.

"Don't worry, it is," a cheerful feminine voice immediately replied. Triggered by the exchange, the screen flickered to life, giving Olivia an unobstructed view of plump, plum-tinted lips and even white teeth, curved into a gracious smile. After a few seconds, the camera zoomed out and the face belonging to the dazzling smile came into view. Unlike Olivia's, it was flushed with happiness, perfectly made up and runway ready. "Oh, damn. Did I wake you?"

"Uh, yeah," Olivia said, barely restraining herself from adding *duh*. "So if you're calling to swoon in secret over some new trick that your husband just learned, that you don't want him to know that I know about, could I please, *please* hear about it later?" The last few words came out on a whine as her head sank deeper and deeper back into her pillow and her eyes started drifting closed again.

"For your information, I'm not calling to talk about Broderick. Although now that you mention it, there was this one incident yesterday—wait a second. You don't...you're not...is there a *man* in bed with you? Is *that* why you're in such a hurry to hang up?"

Olivia's head popped up from the depths of her down-filled pillow just in time to catch a close-up and grossly distorted view of the other woman's eyeball as it peered suspiciously into the camera. For a second, she was stunned into speechlessness and could only stare at the screen blankly. The call had come in all the way from the other side of the world—Abu Dhabi, to be exact—where it was probably early evening right now and at least seventy-five degrees in the shade.

She knew firsthand that it was impossible to visit the tropical oasis and not be both physically and mentally seduced by its balmy breezes and panoramic seascapes, so she didn't give a thought to envying the other woman's glowing caramel-brown skin or the lively sparkle in her eyes. Coveting her thick lashes and naturally arched, bushy brows was an exercise in futility as well, since they, along with her dimpled cheeks and the tiny beauty mark in the center of her chin, were birthrights that she'd come by naturally. Neither the surf, sand nor sun was to blame for enhancing the other woman's good looks. But the perpetual glow of blissful cluelessness in her laughing eyes was something else altogether. Apparently the surf, sand and sun had joined forces to make her delusional.

The poor thing had only just acquired that annoying trait a little over a year ago, when she'd given up her lifelong membership to the single ladies' club to elope with her Prince Charming. The problem was that, in the process, she had seemingly forgotten that the rest of the world, and every happily-single-by-choice woman in it, including Olivia, still had to work for a living. *And* that they required sleep to do it.

When Olivia found her voice, it roared. "No, I don't have a man in bed with me, you sex fiend! It just so happens that I was up late, working!" The entire bed shook with the force of her outrage. "Some of us still have to do that, you know!"

The oversize eye crinkled with humor and then withdrew to normal proportions. Minus the artfully applied makeup, purposely wind-blown hairstyle, and a freckle or two here and there, it was an exact replica of Olivia's face, right down to the beauty mark in the center of her chin and the secret third dimple in each of their right cheeks. The woman on the other end of the camera was Elise Carrington, her identical twin sister.

Which, Olivia mentally reasoned, was the only thing keeping her from going through the phone.

"Wow," Elise Carrington said. "Someone's angry." Clearly not in the least bit put off by Olivia's hysterical tone, she sat back in her chair and scratched her fingers through a wild mane of curly, bronze-streaked brown hair and shook it loose around her bare shoulders. "Good morning to you, too, sunshine."

It was Saturday, barely seven o'clock in the morning, and her first day off in weeks. Olivia was exhausted—not to mention overworked—and hardly in the mood for small talk. As far as she was concerned, she'd seen and heard enough. "Elise Monica Carrington, I swear to God," she warned as she reached across the mattress for the MacBook's blinking power switch. "I closed three cases last week and took on two new ones just yesterday, which means that I have work to do and I need sleep to do it. I'm hanging up now. I'll call you back later."

"Wait!" Elise cried just before Olivia would've hung up on her. "I have some news that I'm pretty sure you'll want to hear."

Olivia froze. "What is it? Are you pregnant?"

Elise's expression turned admonishing. "I've

asked you to please stop speaking things like that into the universe. It gets less and less funny each time you do, you know."

"So that's a *no*?"

"That is most definitely a *no*. As a matter of fact, my dear, that is a definite *hell no*." Elise's head dropped back to the pillow heavily. "I called to give you a heads-up. Live coverage of the robbery at First Federal Credit Union, there in Clayton, has been streaming all morning. They think it's connected to a string of heists that have happened across the country over the last several months. Your friend—what's her name? Shannon something-or-other?—and one of the tellers were both there when it happened." Elise raised her head, staring at the screen incredulously. "They've been detained by the FBI for questioning about their possible involvement."

"Oh my God! The last time I talked to Shannon, she'd just been promoted to branch manager and seemed happy. Why the hell would she be involved in a bank heist, of all things? It doesn't make sense."

Elise shrugged. "It does if you recall that I have always said she was a very strange person."

"Elise—"

"What?" The look on Elise's face was innocence personified. "She's always been weird and secretive, and you know it. That's all I'm saying."

"She's my friend."

"Which is why I figured you'd want to know. Google it. See for yourself."

Olivia leaned forward and pressed a series of buttons on the MacBook's keyboard to split the screen.

She searched the web for up-to-the-minute news about the incident and clicked on the first credible link that popped up in search results. "What in the world?" she wondered aloud, midway through watching the live feed that was plastered across the top of the web page. Police helicopters circled the air above the credit union, and on the ground, a swarm of law enforcement officers and media foot soldiers milled around the building.

"I can't imagine what Shannon must be going through right now," she said just as the coverage shifted to a recap of earlier events and an image of Shannon being escorted off the premises by two somber-looking agents flashed across the screen. She gasped in shock. "Wow!"

"I know," Elise said somberly. "She looks terrible, doesn't she? After all this, her mug shot has to be worse than Nick Nolte's."

An errant giggle bubbled out of Olivia's mouth. "Only you would notice her looks at a time like this."

"Well, it's certainly something to consider, isn't it? What are you going to do? And before you answer that question, I would just like to go on record as saying that I think the correct and appropriate answer to that question is, absolutely nothing."

"She's my sorority sister, Elise, and from the looks of things, she's in serious trouble. The least I can do is make sure she's okay." Olivia had been so busy with work that she hadn't seen or spoken to Shannon Bridgeway in more than a year. But they'd been close in college and had regularly kept in touch over the years. She'd never forgive herself if something terrible happened to Shannon and she hadn't at least attempted to check on her friend's well-being. "It won't hurt to have Eli do a little poking around," she added, referring to Eli Seamus, the ex-CIA agent who dabbled heavily in private investigations, now that he was retired.

"Olivia…"

"Relax. I said a little poking around, and that's exactly what I meant. Trust me, with everything else going on around here, the last thing I need is more work. I don't know if you've gotten the memo yet, but running a private-investigation agency all by myself is pretty exhausting. Poor Harriet is on the verge of going on strike, and frankly, sis, so am I." Harriet was Olivia's part-time office assistant who had been working full-time at an intense pace for the past several months. "But not before I make sure that Shannon is okay," she declared as her head hit the pillow again and she snuggled in. "After that, I can't make any guarantees. Thank you for the update. I'll take it from here. Now can I sleep, please?"

"I'll be home soon. I promise."

"Yeah, yeah," Olivia drawled into her pillow. "That's what you said last month and the month before that. Meanwhile I'm here, sinking deeper and deeper into an abyss of case files and wearing the soles off my Jimmy Choos while I wait. I don't think I believe you anymore."

"That's cold, Olivia. Really cold. Even for you."

"Yeah, well, I'm too sleepy right now to care." Her gaze landed on the time stamp in a corner of the screen and she sighed long and hard. The downside was that she'd lost several minutes of potential sleep time, but the upside was that if she drifted off in the next couple of minutes, there would still be plenty of time to sleep like the dead before noon rolled around and Eli turned his ringer on. Now if she could just get rid of Chatty Cathy. "Was there something else you wanted?"

Elise had the nerve to look hurt. "Well…no, I guess not, but—"

Olivia snuggled inside a mound of pillows and covers. "Okay, well in that case, sis…"

"Well, damn. Will you at least call me later?"

"I will. I promise."

"Today?"

"Yes, Elise," Olivia promised sleepily. "Now, for God's sake, goodbye."

For ten blissful seconds after she pressed the end button, absolute quiet reigned. Grateful for the reprieve, she wrapped her arms and legs around her body pillow, buried her face in the dark, chilly space between it and the mattress and willed herself to drift off to sleep.

Then, far off in the distance, a lawn mower roared to life.

"Oh, no…" The sound came closer, or at least Olivia imagined that it did. "Oh, nooo…" Curled into the fetal position now, with a pillow clamped over her head, she tried to block out the noise with sheer willpower. When that didn't work, she tossed the pillow aside and flopped onto her back in defeat. "Damn you, Elise," she growled at the vaulted ceiling.

As hard as it was to begrudge her sister her luxurious new globe-trotting lifestyle, the longer she was away, the more Olivia was tempted to put her foot down and insist that Elise come home immediately. Running Carrington Consulting—the boutique private-investigation agency that they had started together five years ago—solo was becoming more and more chaotic by the day. Even with Elise working a small portion of the firm's incoming cases remotely, the demand for their services was currently experiencing the kind of spike that made physically sustaining a two-woman operation all by herself nearly impossible. Olivia was all for true love and never-ending honeymoons, but after a year of jet-setting, Elise had to return to the real world sometime, didn't she?

Not that she didn't absolutely adore her brother-in-law, Olivia hastened to remind herself, because she did. How could she not? Broderick Cannon was tall, dark and gorgeous, and he was rich enough to whisk her sister off for an exotic getaway at a moment's notice, which was always a plus in Olivia's book. As a former navy SEAL and the CEO of Cannon Corp—an underground securities firm that did most of its work in classified overseas locations—his fearless, larger-than-life personality was the perfect complement to Elise's reserved, look-before-you-leap demeanor, and his professional expertise had come in handy countless times.

In more ways than one, theirs was a marriage made in heaven, except that Olivia hadn't quite counted on Elise practically handing over the reins to Carrington Consulting and disappearing in the process. The idea of hiring a part-time associate was sounding better and better every day. Until now she had purposely avoided thinking about it, but if Elise didn't come home soon, she just might have to start.

But not today.

Today, she thought as she rolled back onto her stomach, plopped the nearest pillow over her head and reached for her body pillow again, not even the steady growl of a nearby lawn mower was strong enough to beat back her fatigue. Determined to get at least a couple of hours of sleep before she had to get up and hit the ground running again, she closed her eyes and imagined that one of the Chippendales was outside, mowing the lawn naked, and that she had a front-row seat for the event.

In no time at all, she felt herself dozing.

Chapter 2

"Are you out of your mind?"

Olivia thought about the question for a second and then nodded at the open MacBook in her lap. "Possibly," she admitted, thinking *probably*. Then again, if you considered the fact that she had gone down to the federal courthouse first thing this morning to bail a college friend out of jail and then brought that friend home with her, then *definitely* was more like it. "But keep your voice down, will you?" She leaned closer to the screen and stage-whispered. "Shannon will be back down any minute now, and she's already anxious enough without you making her feel unwelcome."

The frown on Elise's face deepened. "Shannon's not the one I'm worried about here," she went on, completely ignoring Olivia's request for quiet. "You were friends with her in college, but how well do you really know her right now? You have no idea what she's capable of but—*hello!*—here's a hint—she was just accused of taking part in a bank robbery! What were you thinking, inviting her to stay there with you, alone?"

Cringing, Olivia darted a glance at the doorway and wilted in relief when she saw that it was still empty. But that didn't mean that Elise's voice wouldn't carry out into the hallway, or worse, the foyer, where the stairs were. Suddenly the idea to pass the time chatting with her sister while she waited for Shannon to join her for tea in the study was the worst she'd ever had.

"What was I supposed to do, Elise? Let her sit in a jail cell with seven other women and one community toilet, while the powers-that-be sorted everything out? Besides, her court date is Wednesday, the day after tomorrow, so what's the harm? It's actually kind of nice to have some company around here, for a change."

"You should have left her in jail, where she could be supervised at all times!" Elise cried.

"Why? She wasn't accused of anything, only questioned, which—" she held up a finger for patience when Elise would've interrupted "—is standard procedure for any employee who's present during a robbery. The teller who was also there when it happened was questioned, too, as a matter of fact, so that's a moot point."

"Well then, what *is* the point? And why in the world does she have a court date if she was cleared?"

"Apparently she kicked an FBI agent after she claimed that he shoved her from behind. He charged her with misdemeanor assault."

"Violent tendencies," Elise sputtered incredulously. "Oh, well *that's* nothing to be concerned about, is it?"

Olivia giggled. "As usual, you're overreacting." She leaned sideways and scooped up a floral-print bone-china teacup and saucer from the end table next to her, bringing the cup to her mouth to blow gently on the steam rising from it. "Relax," she suggested, sipping carefully. "Everything will be fine. You'll see."

"You're sure?" Elise looked and sounded less than convinced.

"Yes, I'm sure."

"I don't believe you, and don't think I didn't catch your little comment before, about having some company for a change, because I did."

Olivia rolled her eyes to the ceiling and stifled a sigh. "She's my friend, Elise. That's all I meant. She has no family and she's been through a traumatic event. And as if that wasn't bad enough, at around eight o'clock this morning, her mug shot went viral. I think there are even a couple of very unflattering memes floating around cyberspace, too. After all that, I figured that Shannon could use a shoulder to cry on right now, and what else are old friends good for?" She sipped again and then hummed with appreciation. Sweetening her freshly steeped orange pekoe tea with a few drops of her homemade apricot-peach marmalade had been a stroke of pure genius. "And you were right, by the way—her mug shot does look worse than Nick Nolte's."

"Don't make me laugh right now, Olivia. Let's just hope that's the only thing I'm right about," Elise snapped. "Promise me you'll be safe."

"I will," Olivia promised. "I am."

"And you're sure she's only staying there for a couple of days?"

Olivia set down her teacup and saucer and held up three fingers, close together. "Scout's honor. There's nothing to worry about, sis. I promise." She caught a flash of movement in her peripheral vision and looked up at the doorway just as a tall, willowy blonde woman walked through it. To the screen she said, "Shannon just walked in. I'll call you back."

"All right, but…"

"I will."

"Okay. I love you."

"I love you, too." They traded air kisses before Olivia ended the call and closed the MacBook. Setting it aside, she unfolded her legs and sat up to pour a second cup of tea from the antique sterling-silver serving tray on the coffee table. "Did you find everything okay?"

"Yes, I did, thank you." Freshly scrubbed and dressed in jeans and a tank top that Olivia had borrowed from Elise's closet, Shannon Bridgeway dropped into a seat at the other end of the sofa and murmured her thanks when Olivia passed her a steaming cup of tea. An uninterrupted nap and a long, hot shower had softened the worry lines around her eyes and mouth, and two helpings of Olivia's eggplant Parmesan during dinner had put a little color back into her cheeks. "I know I've said it a hundred times already, but this house is amazing. I remember you mentioning to me that you'd moved but I had no idea that it was into this place. I feel like I'm staying in a luxury hotel. Your parents gave up all this to move to—where was it, again?"

"London. Apparently my father was homesick and my mother was ready for a new adventure."

"I see," Shannon said, though it was clear that she didn't.

After thirty years of dominating courtrooms around the country, Lance Carrington had announced his plans to retire from his lucrative criminal-law practice and enjoy the fruits of his labor. In addition to the trust fund that he'd inherited as a child, his aggressive courtroom prowess had amassed him a sizable fortune over the years. The house, which had been built and furnished to Yolanda Carrington's exact specifications, was a tangible reward for his life's work: phase one of his and his socialite wife's transition into their golden years. Among the list of lifestyle amenities that the two-story, Colonial-style home offered were a sunroom out back, a music room on the west wing of the second floor and a wine cellar just steps away from the state-of-the-art kitchen. Her father had insisted on crown moldings, hand-laid hardwood and Spanish tile floors throughout; her mother, recessed lighting and an indoor wading pool.

It had taken months to fully decorate the place, because most of the furniture had been purchased from overseas estate sales, and every piece had been carefully placed for maximum effect. Then, seemingly overnight, her parents had decided to chuck it all and fly off into the sunset, leaving their post-retirement showplace standing empty and their twin daughters baffled.

Fortunately Olivia had managed to recover quickly from her shock.

Never one to pass up a golden opportunity, she hadn't wasted any time taking her parents up on their offer to trade in her South St. Louis County condo for their extravagant West County residence. Elise was a little harder to convince, but once Olivia pointed out that the pros in favor of the idea far outweighed the short list of cons against it, she had eventually come around. For her levelheaded sister, it had all boiled down to simple economics. While it was true that there was more than enough room for them to peacefully coexist under the same roof, what had ultimately sold Elise on the idea of giving up her townhouse in nearby Clayton, Missouri, was the fact that, with Carrington Consulting still in its infancy, living together made working together that much easier. And with a few minor adjustments, it completely eliminated overhead expenses. Put that way, it was a win-win situation for everyone involved.

Four years ago, neither of them could've predicted just how successful Carrington Consulting would be, but in hindsight the move was a self-fulfilling one. Ironically enough both she and Elise had walked away from their respective careers because they'd grown weary of glass ceilings, bureaucracy and red tape, only to stumble their way into the field of professional private investigations, a field that was riddled with the very same bureaucracy and red tape that they despised. But this time around, their perspectives were different—a little more unorthodox—and so were their approaches.

And so were most of their methods for getting results, Olivia thought as she topped off her tea and stirred in a generous dollop of marmalade. But that was neither here nor there, because Carrington Consulting was operating firmly in the black, with an impressive client list and an enviable success rate, and the house, with its stately exterior and sumptuous interior, was partly responsible for that.

"Was that Elise's voice I heard just now? Is she off somewhere, working a case?"

"I guess you could say that. She's in Abu Dhabi right now, with her husband. He's working a case there and she's assisting, but it's looking like she may never come home."

"Well, I hope you don't mind me saying this, but I'm glad she isn't here. I heard what she said about not wanting me here, and I know I wouldn't be here if she were. And honestly I don't know what I would've done if you hadn't shown up when you did. I still can't believe you did." Shannon's face creased with gratitude and a watery smile curved her lips. "Olivia, I can't begin to thank you for everything you've done."

"Please." Wanting to avoid a mushy exchange,

Olivia flapped a dismissive hand and then focused on stirring her tea for a few seconds, to give Shannon time to compose herself. "Don't give it another thought. Harriet—that's the lady you met this morning—and I were starting to run out of things to talk about anyway, so it's good you're here to shake things up a little bit. I think we could both use the company, even if it's only for a day or two. Oh, that reminds me…" She settled back into her corner of the sofa and sat crossed-legged, cradling her cup in her hands and sipping carefully. "While you were napping, I put a trace on your missing cell phone. It's inside your car, which will be delivered here tomorrow morning. Until then, I'm sure I have a spare around here somewhere that you can borrow, if necessary."

Shannon looked as if the weight of the world had just been lifted from her sagging shoulders. "Oh my God, thank you so much."

"Yeah, well don't thank me just yet. It was pretty short notice, with your court date being just two days away, so the attorney that I hired to represent you isn't all that pleased with either of us right about now. She has a wait list a mile long, but she owed me one, so she'll be here tomorrow, too, after lunch, so brace yourself. Her name is Sabine Barnes and her reputation for being a bitch more than precedes her. The bad news is that you're on your own when she gets here, because as it turns out, I have a meeting in Collinsville around that time."

Shannon's blue eyes narrowed suspiciously over

the rim of her teacup. "I'm almost afraid to ask what the good news is."

"The good news is that Sabine is the best at what she does, so you're in very good hands. We go way back to grade school, and if anyone can make this mess go away, she can."

"I hope so, because if I never hear the term *FBI* again, it will be too damn soon."

Olivia smiled at her friend. "Trust me. By this time Wednesday night, you'll be home, sleeping in your own bed and the FBI will be a distant memory." She reached for Shannon's hand and squeezed it reassuringly. "Everything is going to be fine. You'll see."

It was after eleven when Shannon decided to turn in for the night, but it was closer to 2:00 a.m. when Olivia took off her glasses, shut down her workstation and emerged from behind a false wall in a corner of Elise's bedroom closet. She sidestepped a rack of coats as the panel secured to the other side of it shifted and clicked into place, and then rearranged a stack of shoeboxes to fully conceal the small touch-ID screen near the edge of the panel, before she left the closet and the bedroom.

Working in what she and Elise had affectionately termed the *war room* wasn't her usual MO, but both of her most recent cases were, at least by Hollywood's and the media's fickle standards, highly classified. With Shannon in the house and Harriet not due in for hours yet, she hadn't wanted to risk even the slightest breach of client confidentiality. Usually reserved for top-secret casework only, the war room was both light and soundproof, outfitted with a highly sophisticated technological desk and absent from any blueprint of the house in existence—all of which was serious overkill in this instance—but given the nature of one case and the severity of the other, it was better to be safe than sorry.

In her own bedroom, Olivia closed and locked the door and made a beeline for the adjoining bathroom. Stripping along the way, she walked into the shower as soon as she crossed the threshold and switched on the spray full blast. Determined to get at least a few hours of sleep before her alarm clock went off, she soaped herself quickly and then skipped the search for a fresh nightgown and climbed into bed naked. It wasn't until the moment that her head hit the pillow, her eyelids drifted closed and her cell phone vibrated on the nightstand that she gave a thought to what she might've missed throughout the evening hours. Switching her cell phone to Vibrate or—God forbid—Silent to entertain house guests, even after business hours, wasn't her usual MO, either.

She pushed her hair out of her face and sat up, reaching for her cell with one hand and her glasses with the other. The glaring new voice-mail notification was the first thing that caught her eye, so she touched a finger to the screen to access the most current message and waited.

"This message, along with all of the others that I've left," a deep, authoritative voice promptly informed her, "is for Olivia Carrington. Once again, my name is Cooper Talbot, Special Agent in Charge here at the FBI field office in Knoxville, Tennessee.

I'm attempting to reach Shannon Bridgeway and I was told that she was released to your custody earlier today. If this is true, then I would appreciate a call back as soon as you get this message." He paused to release an impatient-sounding breath. "As a matter of fact, even if it isn't true, I would still appreciate a call back, letting me know that as soon as you get this message. I can be reached at—"

Having heard enough, she closed the voice-mail app and navigated to the incoming-calls log. Surprised to see that she'd missed a total of five calls over the course of the evening, and all from the same anonymous caller, she reopened the voice-mail app and settled in to listen to each of the resulting messages, starting at the beginning. By the time she was done, she was wide awake, several minutes had passed and her mind was racing.

It was nearly three o'clock in the morning, she reminded herself as she listened to Cooper Talbot's callback number once more and committed it to memory. Way past the proper time to return a phone call, no matter how crisp and impatient the caller's voice had been. To do so now, at this hour, would be beyond inconsiderate, she told herself as she touched the callback button. But then again, she'd been given explicit instructions to call back as soon as she received the message, hadn't she?

Settling back underneath the covers with her cell to her ear, she listened to the phone ring on the other end, praying that it was his cell-phone number and that the thing was lying right next to him at this ungodly hour of the morning.

"Cooper Talbot," a deep, gravelly voice barked into the phone a few seconds later. She smiled at the urgency in it. He'd been asleep and the ringing phone had startled him awake. Good.

"I'm sorry to bother you at this hour, Agent Talbot," Olivia said in her sweetest voice. "But your message said to return your call immediately, so that's exactly what I'm doing. I just received your message and now I'm returning your call. This is Olivia Carrington, sir. What can I do for you?"

Chapter 3

Five hundred miles away, in Knoxville, Tennessee, Cooper Talbot took his cell phone away from his ear and stared at it in disbelief. It was almost three o'clock in the morning and his caller—Olivia Carrington, had she said?—was talking to him as if it were the middle of the day and she wasn't talking to a *special agent in charge* with the FBI. Was the woman insane?

Possibly, he thought as he glanced at the bedside clock, rolled over onto his back in bed and scrubbed a hand across his face. Except for the sheet that was tangled around his hips and legs, he was naked and, up until about thirty seconds ago, he'd been deep into his first night of uninterrupted sleep in months. "I'm sorry, who did you say this was?"

"Olivia Carrington, sir. You called me five times this evening, leaving a message, ordering me to call you back as soon as possible after each call. You sounded so insistent that I didn't think it was wise to wait a second longer than necessary to do as I was told." She chuckled nervously, as if she was fully aware of just how ridiculous her reasoning sounded. "Did I wake you?"

The question pissed him off, even more than her insolent tone already had. "I think you know damn well that you did. It's three o'clock in the morning, Miss Carrington, so I think a better question would be, what can *I* do for *you*?"

"In your messages, you said you were looking for Shannon Bridgeway."

"I am." He found a pillow and bunched it underneath his head, thinking that if she wasn't already, she could easily make her first million in the phone-sex industry. "Is she there with you now?"

"She is, but she's asleep right now."

He sighed. "As we should *all* be. Do you make a habit of returning phone calls that should be returned during business hours in the middle of the night, Miss Carrington?"

"Only when I receive a few voice-mail messages, suggesting very strongly that I do so."

"You keep mentioning that—the fact that I called you several times last evening and left messages. Is that your way of eliciting an apology from me? Because if it is, I should probably tell you that you're wasting your time."

"No, it's my way of asking if you were raised in

a barn," she shot back, and his eyebrows rose in the darkness of his bedroom. "Who does that?"

Tongue in cheek, Cooper considered Olivia's question for a second. Then he thought of a few questions of his own that were suddenly more important. "Isn't it past your bedtime? Why are you even awake at this hour?" He glanced at the bedside clock again and sat up, swinging his legs over the side of his king-size bed and dropping his size-fourteen feet to the chilly hardwood floor. After six hours of hibernation, his mouth felt like a dust bowl. Thinking that a glass of ice-cold sweet tea would hit the spot, he rolled to his feet and ran a lazy hand around the back of his neck as he padded, barefoot and naked, out of his bedroom and down the stairs, to the kitchen.

Olivia's insistent voice buzzed in his ear as he walked. "Oh, no you don't. Don't try to change the subject, Agent Talbot. Explain yourself, please."

"Now, see, the beauty of this situation is that I don't have to explain myself to you. Nor do I see the need to apologize, so I won't." In the kitchen, he tucked his cell between his head and shoulder and opened the refrigerator, taking out a pitcher of iced tea and bumping the door closed with his hip. "You have something that I want and I intend to get it," he said as he located a glass, filled it with ice from the dispenser on the outside of the refrigerator door and then followed up with iced tea.

"Shannon Bridgeway."

"Bingo," Cooper said and downed half the full glass in one long gulp.

"Now, wait just a minute, Agent. I was under the

impression that Shannon was cleared of any possible involvement in that bank robbery."

"The investigation is still ongoing, but my interest in her has nothing to do with that, except that I have a suspect in custody on another robbery in Missouri and I believe she might be able to offer some insight. I'd like to interview her as soon as possible, which—" he paused to down the other half and then refill "—is why I've been trying to reach you. Bridgeway's release paperwork lists you as her emergency contact."

"And is this an emergency?"

He leaned back against the nearest counter and slowly ran his tongue around his teeth. Thanks to the dim, under-cabinet lighting, his own ghostly reflection stared back at him in the window over the sink, reminding him that he was too damn old to be up, poking around the house in the middle of the night, especially when he had to report to work first thing in the morning. "Don't be coy, Miss Carrington. You called me at three o'clock in the morning, so you tell me. *Is* this an emergency? And by the way, it's *Special Agent in Charge* Talbot."

"Wow. Somebody sure is important."

"What—" He paused so that the incredulous chuckle that suddenly filled his mouth could escape. "So you *were* doing it on purpose." She chuckled, too, a low, mysterious sound that stirred his dangling sex. Scratching the top of his head with his free hand, he shifted against the counter, crossed his ankles and rattled the ice in his glass idly. "I should've known. When can I speak with Bridgeway?"

"She doesn't want to speak with you or anyone

else from your agency, Agent Talbot. You people have scared her half to death already and enough is enough. Now she just wants to clear up the bogus arrest that you people have slapped her with, which she will do in court tomorrow morning, and move on with her life."

"You know, if Bridgeway is as innocent as she says she is, then I would think she'd want to help law enforcement out as much as possible."

Olivia snorted sarcastically and Cooper took a breath for patience. "Yes, well, think again."

"Look, Miss Carrington, as I said, I have a suspect in custody here in Knoxville and—"

"Knoxville?" Olivia cut in, sounding surprised. "Is that where you are right now?"

"Yes, it is," Cooper snapped. He hated being interrupted when he was speaking. "We have evidence that points to his having strong ties to the group that we believe is responsible for the bank heist there in Missouri, as well as for a string of other similarly executed heists across the region in recent months. So as much as I'd like to let Miss Bridgeway get on with her life in peace, at this point in our investigation, it really is important that we meet with her, if for no other reason than to eliminate her as a potential witness."

"The answer is still no, Agent Talbot."

"Are you sure about that?"

"Positive. Your new case has nothing to do with Shannon and she'd like to keep it that way."

"And she can't tell me all this herself?"

"No."

"Because she's afraid." It wasn't a question, more like a mocking drawl.

"Exactly. So if you wouldn't mind, Shannon and I would both appreciate it if you'd stop calling."

He rolled his eyes to the ceiling and thought about going through the phone. "You do realize that I don't actually need your permission to access or speak to Shannon Bridgeway, don't you? This is merely a courtesy call, Miss Carrington." She chuckled—a fluttery, mysterious sound that stroked the shell of his ear like a lover's breath. His dangling shaft tingled and he frowned down at it in disgust. *Traitor.*

"Fine," she chirped. "Thank you for the courtesy, Agent Talbot, but—"

"There you go not addressing me properly again," Cooper snarled before he could think better of it. She burst out laughing and suddenly his sex felt ten pounds heavier. "Listen, Miss Carrington—"

"No, you listen, Agent Talbot. It's very late—or very early, depending on how you look at it—and I'm tired. I need sleep." *And he didn't?* "I can't help you and neither can Shannon, so please just leave us alone." Apparently taking his silence to mean that he intended to comply with her ridiculous request, she was gracious enough to offer him a soft "thank you" before ending the call. He stood there for several seconds afterward, holding his cell phone, staring down at his swooning penis and cursing viciously under his breath, before it occurred to him to go back to bed.

He was late for work.

Thanks to Olivia Carrington's outrageous timing, he'd slept right through both his bedside alarm and his cell phone's backup alarm, only managing to crack open his heavy eyelids when a passing early-morning thunderstorm had unleashed a clap of thunder that shook his entire house. He had bolted upright in bed, taken one look at the time and cursed so dramatically that by the time he was done, he'd given himself a headache. On top of that, he had damn near broken his neck, stumbling around in his bathroom, trying to wake himself up and get dressed at the same time, and now that he was thinking about it, there was a very real possibility that he'd forgotten to close his garage door after he'd burned rubber backing out of the damn thing at 8:45 a.m.

Cooper thought about the vintage 1989 Porsche 930 Turbo that was currently parked in his three-car garage and felt a momentary punch to the gut. Just this past weekend, his precious baby girl had been hand-waxed to a high-gloss, metallic-silver shine and her black, butter-soft leather interior had been lovingly cleaned and conditioned. He knew because he'd done both himself, just as, over the years, he'd done most of her restoration work himself. As a result, she was primed and ready for the next time that he had an urge for a midnight joyride, which sadly hadn't been the case in weeks. Her tinted windows were halfway down and the keys were dangling on a hook in the garage, leaving her vulnerable to his neighbor's pain-in-the-ass teenage grandsons, one of which he'd caught ogling his baby just yesterday.

Great. Just great.

A car horn blared, intruding on Cooper's darkening thoughts, reminding him that the time was now 9:30 a.m. and he was officially an hour late for work. Spying the endless line of bumper-to-bumper cars beyond the windshield of his black Audi A7, as well as the trail of cars visible in his rearview mirror, he sat back in the driver's seat and frowned as he thought of Olivia Carrington.

Besides being incredibly inconsiderate, the woman clearly had no idea whom she was dealing with. Calling her and trying to play nice was nothing more than his attempt at promoting positive public relations between the bureau and the community at large, because positivity was the name of the game these days. But had he known that Olivia was going to be so uncooperative, he'd have followed his first mind, skipped the phone calls altogether, and saved himself some time and aggravation by sending a team of agents to ring her doorbell instead. Preferably at three o'clock in the morning, he added bitterly, because playing nice was clearly highly overrated.

He tried to picture her answering the door at that hour of the morning, perhaps in curlers and a sensible nightgown, with fuzzy slippers on her feet and a pair of glasses sitting lopsided on her face. A ringing doorbell at that time of the morning or night would bring her running, her thoughts as scattered as the hair on her head, and she'd be pissed.

Almost as pissed as he'd been early this morning.

After she had hung up on him, it'd taken him over an hour to settle down and doze off again. His thirst quenched, he had climbed back into bed and collapsed on the mattress, fully intending to capitalize on whatever time he still had left to sleep. But his quivering penis had other ideas, which, as much as he hated to admit it, was the *other* reason that Olivia Carrington was now at the top of his hit list.

His rational mind had quickly decided that he disliked her, but his penis—traitor that it was—hadn't wanted to get on board with the plan, as hypnotized as it seemingly was by her sultry, breathless-sounding voice. He'd lain in bed for long minutes afterward, replaying the sound of it in his head, trying to imagine what she looked like one minute and then telling himself that he couldn't have cared less in the next. All the while his penis had been on the verge of a self-induced nirvana, bouncing against his abdomen like an insistent guest and refusing to be ignored. After the twelve months of forced celibacy that he had intentionally inflicted upon it, it had apparently grown tired of behaving and decided to stage an uprising. And all it had taken was an absurd phone call from a strange, faceless woman with a sex-infused voice and an orgasm-laced giggle.

Nice, he thought and mentally kicked himself in his own forty-year-old butt. Would he never learn?

Unbidden, an image of his former fiancée flashed before his eyes, and just as quickly as it had come, he banished it. Blythe Nunley was the only child and sole heiress to the Knoxville-based Nunley Pharmaceuticals brand. She was also spoiled, impulsive and used to getting her way—all characteristics that he had dismissed as relatively harmless, since she was over thirty, living on her own and halfway through a pediatric residency at Knoxville General when they were introduced by mutual friends. It had taken him three years and returning home a day early from an out-of-town speaking engagement to figure out that he'd been played for a lovesick fool.

In more ways than one, he qualified, recalling the scene that had unfolded when he'd walked into the condo they shared and interrupted a pretty intense lovemaking session between his then fiancée and his then best friend. For six months their affair had been going on right underneath his nose, and all he'd been able to see the entire time was the incredible beauty that was Blythe, which, he realized in hindsight, was by calculated design. Blythe was a master manipulator. Discovering in the aftermath that his best friend hadn't been the first man Blythe had cheated on him with bruised his ego even more.

But, hey, at least he wasn't bitter, right?

Aside from being a colossal waste of time, the three years that he'd spent with Blythe had also taught him a valuable lesson. Sex was one thing, but relationships were something else altogether. In the eighteen months since he'd kicked Blythe out of the condo, sold the damn thing and bought himself a new bed, he had gone looking for sex a few times but always with the understanding that relationships weren't an option. Once bitten, he wasn't just shy. As far as he was concerned, he was completely over it.

Still, though.

Not counting the first nineteen years of his life, twelve months was the longest he'd ever gone without sex. He was usually so busy working that it was easy to forget about satisfying his flesh, but every once in a great while, a subtle reminder crept up on him and tapped him on the shoulder. Olivia Carrington's

X-rated voice had done exactly that, and at the worst possible time—at the witching hour and, if he was being honest, at the onset of a fantastically erotic wet dream that his ringing phone had rudely interrupted. So while it did occur to him that his problem really wasn't so much with Olivia Carrington as it was with the fact that he needed to find time in his busy schedule to get laid, the fact remained that, either way you spun the situation, her timing sucked to hell and back.

And somehow, some way, he was going to make her pay for it.

Acutely aware that time was something that seemed to always be in short supply, Cooper glanced at his watch and sighed gratefully when traffic slowly began moving forward. Minutes later he was finally clear of the three-car collision that had caused the traffic jam. Accelerating to just under the posted speed limit, he drove the rest of the way to the Knoxville FBI Field Office in deep, calculated thought. For a second, as he parked his car, grabbed his leather attaché case from the passenger seat and slammed the driver's door in his wake, he considered cutting Olivia Carrington some slack. Then he recalled the exact number of times that she had purposely called him *Agent* Talbot and thought, *nah*.

He had called her to ask nicely and she had returned his call at three o'clock in the morning, only to turn him down flat and not-so-nicely. She had balls—he'd give her that. But damned if he was going to let her add *his* balls to her collection. He considered calling her again during business hours, when she might've been more willing to hear him out. Then he remembered that she had asked him if he'd been raised in a barn and thought, *hell nah*.

Suddenly he had an even better idea.

"Good morning, sir."

"Good morning, Amelia." Cooper glanced at his assistant on his way past her desk, noticing without breaking stride that her naturally brunette hair was no longer arranged in a hot-pink bouffant, as it had been when he'd left work yesterday evening, but was now deep purple and framing her heart-shaped face in a sleek pageboy style. He had inherited her with his promotion five years ago and, while all of her various eccentricities had initially thrown him for a loop, he had quickly come to the conclusion that she was exactly the kind of assistant that his type A personality needed.

"Did you get my text?" he asked as he walked into his office and dropped his attaché case on his desktop. He shrugged out of his suit jacket, hung it on the coat rack behind the door and then returned to the doorway to lean against it. She swiveled around in her chair to face him and he saw that her lipstick was black and extra glossy.

"You mean the one you sent me while you were driving?" she asked, sniffing with disapproval. The hoop in her right nostril quivered as she exhaled.

Cooper waved a dismissive hand, silently refusing to entertain her attempt at chastising him. Then he saw her eyes narrow and said, "I was sitting at a red light when I sent it, all right? Did you get the text or not?"

Apparently satisfied with his answer, she smiled graciously. "Yes, I did and I even managed to track down Judge Sheppard to sign the arrest warrant. The paperwork still has to be processed and filed, but it should be here by lunchtime," she said. "Late afternoon at the latest. In the meantime, I booked you on a nine-thirty flight to Missouri, which puts you there at around eleven o'clock tonight. Shannon Bridgeway isn't on the federal docket there until ten o'clock tomorrow morning, so you have a little time to prepare beforehand."

"Does the Missouri field office know I'm coming?"

"They've been notified and I also requested a vehicle loan, which—" she paused to swivel back around to her desk and tap a few keys on her computer's keyboard "—was just approved. There will be a car waiting for you at the airport. Pick up the keys from airport security."

"What would I do without you, Amelia?"

"Let's hope I never win the lottery and you have to find out," she quipped. "But if you were looking for a way to show your appreciation, coffee would be nice, sir."

He pretended to think about the request for a second. "You still take it with two sugars and three creams?"

"Yes, and did I mention that I also cleared your schedule for the rest of the week, just in case?"

"Ah, and since good help is so hard to find, why don't I bring you a doughnut, too?" he offered as he straightened from his perch against the doorway.

She grinned as she adjusted the wireless headset on her head and tucked her legs underneath her desk. "That sounds lovely, sir. Chocolate, please."

"Coming right up." *Since the mountain refused to come to Mohammed,* Cooper thought as he strolled down the corridor toward the staff lounge, *then Mohammed was going to the mountain.* With any luck, not only would he score a sit-down with Bridgeway but he'd also discover the answer to the question circling around in his head: *Did Olivia Carrington's face match her sensual voice?*

Chapter 4

Court was in session.

Late, Olivia ended her call, dropped her cell phone inside of her clutch and snapped it shut. After hopping down from her corner seat on the vanity, she checked her makeup one last time in the mirror over the row of sinks in the fourth-floor ladies' room, then unlocked the door, swung it open and hurried down a long corridor, toward a bank of elevators. Thankfully she caught up with a small group of people waiting at the far end of the corridor just as two elevator cars arrived. She glanced at her watch and hurried toward the empty one.

She'd been gone for twenty minutes, which, given Shannon's current mental state, wasn't necessarily a good thing, but it couldn't be helped. Her cell had

rang at the worst possible moment—in the middle
of the courtroom, just as the bailiff was giving the
order to rise for the judge's entrance. But sending
the call to voice mail wasn't an option. In the first
place, she'd cashed in way too many favors in exchange for the callback to start looking a gift horse
in the mouth now, no matter how bad its timing was.
In the second, she was getting desperate.

Settling Shannon's legal issues with the FBI was
definitely a top priority, but as far as Olivia was
concerned, so was solving the mystery of where her
friend would live after the dust settled and her life
was her own again. The FBI had searched Shannon's
South City duplex apartment immediately following
the heist and, for a variety of reasons, she hadn't gone
back there until the day before yesterday. The problem was that, sometime between then and yesterday evening, when she and Shannon had gone there
to gather a few of Shannon's things for court this
morning, the place had been completely ransacked.
Ripped clothing, pieces of shredded furniture and
shards of broken glass were everywhere, in every
corner of every room. In her line of work, she'd seen
her share of search scenes, certainly enough of them
to know that, even without the FBI's vehement deni-
als of responsibility, what they were looking at was
most likely not the work of any law-enforcement
agency that she'd ever heard of.

Under the circumstances, sending Shannon back
there to live was out of the question. But the alter-
native—taking her back to Carrington Consulting
headquarters to stay—didn't hold much appeal for

Olivia, either. She hadn't counted on the limitations that Shannon's presence would place on her daily workflow or the amount of personal attention that Shannon would require. Since Shannon had been staying with her, Olivia had given Harriet more time off in the past few days than the retired school principal had apparently known what to do with. Harriet was ready to get back to work and, truthfully, so was Olivia. But if they hoped to get any real work done in the near future, Shannon had to go.

She'd been up half the night last night, coaching Shannon through her latest anxiety attack and making phone calls. Wondering about the *whos*, the *whats* and the *what the hells* behind the break-in, and convincing herself that she was better off not knowing, especially since Shannon seemed to have no clue as to who might be responsible or why. Frankly she was exhausted, but as of a few minutes ago, her mission had been accomplished, so the bags underneath her eyes were worth it. A new apartment had been rented in Shannon's name—Olivia had called in the mother of all favors in order to pull that one off so quickly—and a team of cleanup technicians was on location at her old one, dealing with the disaster there. By the time Olivia delivered Shannon to her new address later today, her personal effects, along with what could be salvaged of her furniture, would be there waiting for her.

Everything was under control.

Or at least it would be, once Shannon's pending charges were resolved.

Alone in the elevator car, Olivia breathed a sigh of

guilty relief, pressed the button for the fifth floor and stepped back to wait for the doors to close. When five long seconds passed and they still hadn't moved, she frowned at her watch and pressed the button again. It figured that everyone else had chosen the second car, which of course was long gone by now.

"Thank God," Olivia murmured when the car suddenly jerked as if it had just received a surge of energy and the doors began slowly gliding closed. Relieved, she tucked her clutch underneath her arm, glanced at her watch again and leaned a hip against the nearest handrail to wait out the rise. A moment later, she scowled as a large hand and then a giant, wing-tipped foot appeared in the space between the doors just before they would've closed. The doors froze in place, vibrating ominously for several seconds, and then slowly began reversing directions. "Oh no! Look what you did!" she shrieked as she watched first the doors disappear and then several of the buttons on the operating panel light up, one by one. She was so busy staring at the thing in horror that she barely noticed the body attached to the offending body parts breez-ing past her and joining her in the car.

"Ma'am, if I had time to look, I would," a deep, honey-dipped voice drawled from somewhere be-hind her. "But I don't, so…" It came closer. "Do you mind?"

She jumped a full foot when one long arm reached around her from behind and pressed the button for the fifth floor. Ironically enough, it was the one but-ton that should've already been glowing but wasn't.

Olivia's voice, when she finally managed to find

it, was crisp. "As a matter of fact, *sir*, I do mind—"
But the moment that she whirled around to confront her offender, anything else that she might've said died an instant death on her plum-tinted lips. As if she'd just run face-first into an invisible wall, she came up short and then instinctively took a step back. Suddenly the elevator car seemed much, much smaller and she couldn't quite remember exactly how pissed she was supposed to be. Or, for that matter, about what specifically.

"Oh..." she heard herself say and then felt her face catch fire. Several tense seconds passed as she stared up at the man standing in front of her and tried to think of something else to say. In the end, all she could come up with was: "My God, you're huge." Which of course only made her face burn hotter and his eyebrows disappear into his hairline. She was staring and she couldn't seem to make herself stop. It was just that he was quite literally the adult version of every childhood nerd that she'd ever seen, with a dash of post-pubescent Harry Potter thrown in for good measure, and the visual was...interesting.

Above his silk bow tie and matching suspenders— both of which were a conservative blue paisley print— and the discreet leather pocket protector that was neatly tucked into the breast pocket of his soft blue dress shirt, his Adam's apple bobbed prominently in the column of his neck. A little higher up, his ears protruded slightly from the sides of his close-shaven head, expressive brown eyes blinked down at her from behind rounded, metal-rimmed lenses and the ghost of a unibrow filled the space between his thick, naturally arched eyebrows.

Instead of a cape, his suit jacket was neatly folded and draped over one arm, and in place of a magic wand, there was an ion-plated watch on his wrist, tasteful gold cuff links in his French cuffs and stylish derby shoes on his long feet. He looked like his areas of expertise were quantum physics, vintage action figures and, possibly, Impressionist art. Like he'd grown up wearing head-gear, collecting pet rocks, watching Saturday-morning cartoons and building model spaceships.

Back then he would've been cute, maybe even adorable, but in the here and now, given his towering height and booming voice, he was almost…mythical. Except that both his suspenders and his bow tie were Hermes, his high-tech watch was a Bvlgari master-piece and the way his tailored navy blue suit fit his frame positively screamed Brooks Brothers. She rec-ognized good taste when she saw it, and she didn't quite know what to make of the air of bourgeoisie surrounding him, but at the moment, nothing about it was especially hard on the eyes.

You're staring, Olivia.

"I'm sorry," she said, forcing herself to blink first and then look away. He was much larger than she was and she wasn't under any illusions about her ability to overpower him, if it came down to that. "That didn't come out right. Wh-what I meant was—"

"I know what you meant." He waved a giant, dis-missive hand and then reached around her to press the button again, this time a little impatiently. "Look, in a few minutes' time, we'll part ways and in all likeli-hood never cross paths again. So it doesn't really mat-ter what you meant to say, does it? I, for one, would just

like to get to where I'm going before the day is out." He
reached for the button again. "Does this thing work?"

"Maybe it would if you'd stop randomly pushing
buttons and give it time to catch up with itself. It's
not a keyboard."

"Gee, it isn't? I didn't know."

"Please don't ask me why I find that hard to believe." She caught herself just as she was about to
swat his hand away when he would've pressed the
button again and immediately threw up her own in
defeat. Physically assaulting perfect strangers was
a clear sign that it was time to come up with a plan
B. "Okay. You know what? Why don't I just step out
and let you have the elevator to yourself? I'll catch
the next one." But the car chose that exact moment to
kick into gear, the doors gliding closed at her back.

Dammit.

"Too late," he murmured as she spun around to
see for herself.

Tight-lipped, she re-tucked her clutch underneath
her arm and cleared her throat. Neither of them spoke
as the car lifted off and began a shuddering journey
to the floor above it. The bell signaling their arrival
to the fifth floor rang and, a few seconds later, the
car jerked to an unsteady stop. After several more
seconds of staring at the closed doors expectantly,
it occurred to Olivia that they should've opened by
now. Now it was her turn to reach for the button and
press it repeatedly. "What the hell?" she wondered
aloud when nothing happened.

"I knew I should've taken the damn stairs."

She glanced back at him over her shoulder. "Yeah,

well, it's too late for that, too, isn't it?" She reached out to press a button on the operating panel, only to snatch her hand back when the floor began vibrating underneath their feet. Thinking that the elevator was about to kick into gear once again, she pressed the button for the fifth floor once more. In response, the floor of the elevator suddenly dropped several feet beneath them. Shaken, she reached for the nearest handrail and held on for dear life. "I'm going to die in an elevator? Really, God?" She looked up and shook a fist at the ceiling. "A freaking elevator?"

A dark chuckle floated across the width of the elevator, and Olivia's eyes swerved over to its owner in silent reproach. "I'm glad you think this is funny," she practically spat at him. "You obviously haven't been to the movie theater lately," she went on, feeling herself getting more and more worked up. "Because if you had, and you'd seen the same movie that I saw, then you wouldn't be laughing right now."

"You mean the cheesy, cinematic train wreck that's supposedly loosely based on actual events? Please. I saw it last week."

"Then I'm sure you can understand why I'm concerned." How was he not seeing the similarities between the two of them being trapped together on an obviously demon-possessed elevator and the scene in the movie in which a group of people were trapped together on an elevator that had eventually caught fire and burned its occupants alive?

"Actually, no, I can't." She gaped at him. "If you recall, the elevator fire in the movie was caused by a ball of fire being hurled at it by a minion from the dark side, who'd been sent to planet earth by aliens who intended to take over what was left of the planet's natural resources. Somehow I don't think that scenario applies here. Unless of course—" he added, spreading his arms diplomatically and cocking a brow at her "—you happen to be the Catholic nun with secret supernatural powers that the minion was after, in disguise."

Put that way, Olivia could hear the silliness of her own argument. "You're right, of course," she conceded, pressing a hand to her chest and taking a deep breath. She hated closed spaces. "I'm being silly."

"A little," he conceded with a shrug. "I think a much more rational explanation is that we're just stuck between two floors. Are you all right?"

"I'm fine. Just a little caught off guard." Honestly, she had passed *caught off guard* a few terrifying seconds ago and was now firmly planted in the middle of *shaken the hell up* territory, but she wasn't about to admit that to a complete stranger, especially not one whom she was trapped alone inside of an elevator with. "What about you? Are you okay?"

"I'm fine," he said, removing his cell phone from his trouser pocket and pressing a button. "I'm going to send my colleague a text, asking him to alert building maintenance." She watched him begin texting, completely unprepared for the moment that he paused in the middle of typing and his gaze flickered up to hers over the rim of his glasses. "You aren't in any danger of fainting or hyperventilating, are you?"

For the second time in as many minutes, Olivia found herself at a disadvantage. But for his generous mouth and his thick, curly, reddish-brown hair, he might've been mistaken for a white man. In fact when he'd first stepped into the elevator and she'd caught a glimpse of him in her peripheral vision, that was exactly what she had thought he was. It had taken a second or two of staring at him to notice that his curls were coarser than most and springy, valiantly fighting against the confines of his low-cut, trendy hairstyle and *this* close to winning the battle. To notice that his skin was more the color of sweet milk than skim, more butter-cream and honey than alabaster, and that it was infused with the slightest hint of mocha. She wondered which of his parents was responsible for it, and if it was the same parent who'd given him his incredible mouth. Which, she realized with a start, was moving right now.

Snap out of it, Olivia.

She shook her head to clear it. "I'm sorry, what?"

"I was asking if you needed an ambulance."

"No…no, I'm fine."

My God, he's good-looking, she thought as her nipples hardened to pearls inside the lace cups of her bra and the beginnings of arousal simmered in her belly. But…oh, come on now. Really? No way in hell was she attracted to him. She couldn't be. Could she?

No way. If ever there was a poster child for the type of man that she was definitely *not* attracted to, this man was it. What was the matter with her?

On second thought, maybe she did need an ambulance.

Chapter 5

Or sex, a little voice in the back of Olivia's mind interjected. *Maybe a hot, sweaty round of great sex is what you need. It's been a while, hasn't it?*

She quickly calculated dates and times, and then stifled an incredulous groan when she realized that a little over a year had passed since the last time she'd had an encounter of any kind, let alone one that had ended with an orgasm. With Elise away so much, finding time for anything other than work was becoming more and more difficult. She hadn't been on so much as a date in how many months—six? Eight? Ten? How pathetic was it that she'd lost count? To make matters worse, the only reason she was able to pinpoint the last time she'd had sex with any degree of accuracy was because the date just happened to coincide with the last time she had visited her parents in London. Which, coincidentally, was right before Elise and Broderick had eloped.

Well, at least one of them was getting some. The other one, Olivia mused ruefully, was clearly losing her damn mind.

"You're sure about that ambulance?"

"Positive."

Cooper wasn't so sure about that. She looked like she was about to hurl any second now, and her purse didn't look like it could hold much. He debated moving closer to check on her but then changed his mind when his cock threatened to show its support for the idea with a standing ovation.

Done texting, he put away his cell phone and glanced at his watch. A second later it chirped, signaling an incoming text, and he took it out again. "They're saying that it's going to be at least a half hour before maintenance can get to us."

"What? Why?"

"Apparently ours isn't the only stuck elevator in the building today," he drawled, setting his attaché case down on the floor, at his feet, and then squatting down next to it. "They'll get to us as soon as possible."

"I'd better text my friend and let her know what's happening."

Expecting to wait at least twice as long as the estimate that he'd been given, Cooper pinched the creases in his trousers and lowered himself to the floor to sit. There, he stretched his legs out in front of him and crossed his ankles, relaxing against the wall at his back. A second later he threaded his fingers in his lap and watched her over the rim of his glasses as she took out her cell phone and began typing as she paced back and forth across the width of the elevator. Several minutes into it, after she had finally finished texting and put away her phone, he cleared his throat. "Something tells me that you're not a fan of closed spaces."

She froze in place, staring down at him as if she were just now realizing that he was there. "I'm not." She resumed pacing. "When I was eleven, I accidentally locked myself in a closet and it was hours before anyone found me. Then, when I was fifteen, a group of bullies locked me in a dark supply closet at school, and if it hadn't been for the night janitor, who didn't report to work until eight o'clock that evening, I'd probably still be there." She cut him a look when he snorted. "Then, in college, I hid in the trunk of a friend's car as part of a prank gone wrong, and she didn't remember that I was in there until the next morning, so—"

Cooper took off his glasses, dropped his chin to his chest and pinched the bridge of his nose to keep from laughing out loud.

"Are you laughing at me? Seriously?" His shoulders shook with silent laughter. "I was traumatized." He laughed harder.

"I'm sorry," he said between rounds. "But it doesn't seem like the problem is closed spaces. It sounds like you might be jinxed and also you have bad taste in friends."

The giggle that came out of her mouth was both self-deprecating and sexy as hell. "In my friend's defense, we were both drinking, but…" She stopped short and waved a dismissive hand. "Oh, who am I kidding? In my defense, too, but that's beside the point. The point is, you're probably right. I do seem to be the common denominator, don't I?"

"Unfortunately, yes." They shared a chuckle. "And you know, as much as I'm enjoying watching those lovely legs of yours strut back and forth, since you are the common denominator, I'd feel much better about being stuck in an elevator shaft, on a *haunted* elevator, if you would please sit down."

"I'm not sitting on the floor," she shot back, still pacing. "And stop looking at my legs."

As if that were possible. He was a man, and really, what else was there to do right now but look? She was a gorgeous woman and he had a sneaking suspicion that she knew it. Built like a brick house, with jiggly, palm-sized breasts, a two-handed grip of a waistline and a butt that jiggled almost as much as her breasts, she obviously dressed to be seen and admired, so he looked his fill. On another woman, the simple wrap dress that she was strutting around in would've been appropriate for Sunday-morning service. But on her, it might as well have been flesh-toned Saran Wrap because it matched her creamy caramel complexion nearly perfectly and left very little to his suddenly lurid imagination. Honestly, as far as things to look at went, those smooth, shapely legs of hers were just the tip of the iceberg.

Wondering what the chances were of this woman

and Blythe somehow being related, possibly even long-lost sisters, he slipped his glasses back over his eyes and sighed. "You're joking, right?" She dimpled prettily, and behind his lenses, he rolled his eyes to the ceiling. The move was classic Blythe Nunley.

"Weeellll," she drawled, obviously pleased with herself as she stopped to strike a pose that turned out a stiletto-clad heel and showcased her taut calf muscles. "Not to toot my own horn, but—"

"Of course not. Why would someone like you toot your own horn?" Her head snapped back on her neck and her eyes widened, but whatever she'd been about to say in response was abruptly cut off by his chirping cell phone. "Excuse me," he said, unclipping it from its holster and turning his attention to the oversize screen. "Good news. We're next in line to be rescued…within the half hour." Irritated all over again by the delay, he returned the phone to its holster and met her eyes. "Now, what were we talking about?"

"I think you were just about to finish insulting me." Shifting to face him, she crossed her arms underneath her breasts and took a step in his direction. The pointed toes of her stiletto pumps stopped just shy of his crossed feet, and her gaze narrowed in on his. "Am I right?"

Secretly swooning, Cooper tipped his head back and stared up into her frosty, amber-colored eyes. He was wondering if she was aware that her nipples were hard and straining through the fabric of her dress. "Trust me, ma'am, insulting you is the last thing on my mind right now." Certainly not when getting the hell away from her as soon as possible was the first.

In his current state of mind, she was a sensual distraction that he could've definitely done without. Lack of sex had his eyes wandering to places that they shouldn't be, that ordinarily they wouldn't have—from her breasts, to the play of muscles in her calves when she moved and the perpetual pucker of her ridiculously suckable, plum-tinted lips. To her bare ring finger and the tiny, sparkling diamond piercing her left nostril.

From where he was sitting, she was lit from behind by the overhead florescent lighting, casting a glow around her shapely silhouette and an angelic halo around the shock of wild, curly, copper-streaked hair framing her stunning face. Yet every time she flicked her jewel-toned, feline eyes at him, his cock growled and alarm bells went off in his head. Nothing about her suggested piety or vows of chastity; instead he was instantly reminded of the insanity of his weakness for beautiful women.

The woman standing in front of him wasn't Blythe Nunley, not by a long shot, but something told Cooper that she was just as—if not even more—dangerous to his drama-free way of life. Once bitten, he was definitely twice shy.

Thanks, but no thanks.

Still, though. She was pretty, like a trinket that was nice to look at but best admired from a safe distance.

"Good, because you don't know the story behind

these legs. I worked hard for them and I earned them fair and square."

He thought about what she'd said and grinned. "Zumba classes?"

She stopped short and sucked in a deep, seemingly fortifying breath. "No. Spin classes," she admitted sheepishly as her shoulders slumped guiltily and a shy smile took her mouth. Charmed despite himself, Cooper—his cock tightening—returned her smile. "And maybe a few water-aerobics classes, too. But it was still intensive, backbreaking work."

"And it definitely paid off, if I may say so."

"Coming from someone like you, Harry Potter, that really means a lot."

Zinged right between the eyes, just as she had no doubt intended, his brows shot up just as the car shuddered and then stabilized, and the panel lit up again. A few seconds later, his cell phone chirped and he reached for it blindly, still holding her amused gaze with a slightly offended one of his own. It rang in his hand, surprising them both. He touched a finger to the screen. "Hold that thought." Putting the phone to his ear, he said, "Yes?" He was so busy watching her take out her own cell phone, try to make a call and then curse when she couldn't that he barely heard a word the agent on the other end was saying to him. Something about them working on the elevator right now and having them out soon. "Okay, thanks for letting me know," he said and ended the call.

She looked worried. "I'm sure everything is fine," he said, rolling to his feet and straightening his clothes. "Your husband is probably standing in the corridor right now, sweating bullets and praying nonstop for your safe return."

She dropped her cell back in her clutch, snapped it shut and tucked it once more underneath her arm, chuckling pitifully. "Is that your way of asking me if I'm married? Because if it is, I have to say, it's pretty terrible. But for the record, I'm not."

He shook out his suit jacket and shrugged into it before picking up his attaché case and slinging the leather strap over his shoulder. She had turned away to give him some privacy when he'd gotten to his feet and began adjusting himself, and now he stepped up next to her, where she stood facing the doors, and slipped his hands into his trouser pockets. Even in heels and with big hair, the top of her head just barely cleared his shoulder. She was shorter and curvier than the women he was typically attracted to, and, based on her attire, much more free-spirited, but none of that stopped him from wondering if she tasted as delicious as she looked.

Okay, so obviously you've lost your mind, right, Talbot?

"You know, that Harry Potter remark stung a little bit," he told her, staring straight ahead. "And here I thought we were becoming friends."

She giggled. "You thought no such thing. But if it helps, I really didn't mean to insult Harry Potter, even though you really do remind me of him."

"Oh? How so?"

"I think it's the bow tie and suspenders," she mused softly. "And you both have nice lips." Cooper felt her eyes on the side of his face and turned his head to look down at her.

Big mistake, Talbot.

"Yours are nicer, though," she added, seemingly as an afterthought, and he flushed to the roots of his hair.

"Thank you but that doesn't help." She lifted a brow, then opened her mouth to speak, and he put up a hand. "*Buuut*… I'm willing to give you another chance to redeem yourself."

"Oh, really? And just how might I do that?"

"Well, since I'm here on business and this is my first time visiting St. Louis," he said just as the car shuddered again and then slowly began ascending. "Maybe you could show me around the city a little bit and then join me for dinner afterward."

She looked surprised. "Are you asking me out?"

"You know I am." She was a good actress, but she wasn't that good. She'd been staring at his lips for so long that he knew the answer to his next question long before he asked it. "Are you interested?"

"Um…" The bell signaling their arrival to the fifth floor sounded again, and she jumped as if she'd been caught doing something naughty. They were still staring at each other when the doors slid open.

"Dr. Talbot!" a deep, frantic voice boomed as soon as they did. "Over here, sir."

And just like that, Cooper thought cynically, their captivity was over and his chances of talking her into wrapping those lovely legs of hers around his neck went up in smoke.

Back to reality you go, Romeo, the little angel on his right shoulder drawled.

Kiss my ass, the one on his left snarled back.

As soon as they stepped off the elevator, Agent Bearden cleared a path through the small crowd that had gathered in the corridor outside the elevators and hurried toward him. He was one of the two rookie officers that Cooper had brought along to Missouri with him, as part of their field-training experience. He spotted the other one, a petite blonde with multiple food allergies, several feet away, and nodded with satisfaction when he saw that the show had gone on in his absence. This one, he recalled as he met Bearden halfway and took the lead, had an annoying habit of ending almost everything that he said to him with *sir* and was currently on the fence about whether or not to get rid of his dreadlocks. He had talked nonstop about it during the flight, until Cooper was ready to grab a pair of scissors and chop them off himself.

"Glad you're okay, sir," Bearden said, reversing directions. "As you can see, we've already detained the subject but she hasn't been formally Mirandized yet. I thought it would be best to wait until you arrived with the arrest warrant."

"Good work, Bearden," Cooper said, reaching into an inside breast pocket and taking out a copy of the arrest warrant. "I'll take care of Mirandizing her. Good work, Agent Bidwell," he told the other agent as they approached. Then he turned his attention to Shannon Bridgeway. She didn't look very happy about the handcuffs around her wrists or the restraining hand around her forearm, but both were standard procedure. "Shannon Bridgeway, I'm—"

"What in the hell is going on here?"

Cooper stopped short, surprised to find the woman from the elevator shooing him aside and positioning herself between him and Shannon like a human shield. When both of his agents moved to block her, his gaze left hers long enough to silently order them to stand down before zooming back to hers and locking in. "What are you doing?"

"I was just about to ask you the same thing!" she raged up at him. "What are *you* doing and why is my friend in handcuffs?"

"Your friend?"

"Yes, my friend! Why is she being arrested?"

He reached up and scratched a spot on the back of his head thoughtfully, took a breath for patience. "I'm sorry, but what did you say your name was again?" Like he didn't already know. *Talk about bad luck.*

"My name is Olivia Carrington. Who are you?" He knew the second she realized what was happening, because her eyes widened in shock and the expression on her face turned thunderous. "Agent Talbot?"

"In the flesh, except it's *Special Agent in Charge* Talbot, and I have a warrant to detain Shannon Bridgeway."

Her eyes popped. "On what grounds?"

"On the grounds that she may be in possession of information that is material to an active federal case. Information, I might add, that could possibly have been obtained days ago, and without all of this fuss, had you just handed Miss Bridgeway the phone when I called, Miss Carrington." They stared at each other and, in her eyes, he saw his fantasy of bedding her crash and burn.

He sighed.

"I told you that she didn't want to speak with you." Sparks were shooting out of Olivia's eyes when she folded her arms underneath her breasts and closed the short distance between them, putting herself in his personal space in a silent challenge that he motioned for his interning agents to ignore, if for no other reason than from his new vantage point, he could see straight down the front of her dress. She tipped her head back to look up into his eyes and he sucked in a sharp breath. "I told you when you called that she had nothing to say to the FBI."

"And I warned you that this would happen if you insisted on blocking access to Miss Bridgeway. As a matter of fact, I was tempted to bring along an obstruction warrant for your arrest as well, but now that we've met, I'm glad I didn't. However, I am going to have to insist that you step aside."

Chapter 6

Speechless, Olivia watched helplessly as Cooper and his minions whisked a shell-shocked Shannon away from the growing crowd of spectators in the elevator atrium and rushed her down the corridor in the opposite direction. Left with no choice but to follow them, she fell in step behind Cooper and kicked her stilettos into overdrive to keep up with his long-legged stride. Before long she was practically skipping to keep pace.

"Is all of this really necessary, Agent Talbot?" she hissed under her breath at his back. He didn't break stride, nor did he acknowledge that he'd heard the question; instead he turned a corner abruptly and sent her into a skid. "Very funny," she murmured when she caught up to him again. "I almost broke my neck back there!" Still nothing. She picked up her pace. "Seriously, Agent Talbot? Just a moment ago you were complimenting me on my lovely—" He stopped short and she plowed into him from behind, planting a lip-gloss-laden kiss right between his shoulder blades before bouncing off him and steadying herself. "Oops."

"Seat Miss Bridgeway in interview room three," he barked at one of his minions. Then he was reaching for a doorknob along the wall to his immediate right. "I'll join you shortly," he said, swinging the door open and spinning around to confront Olivia. "You. Come with me, please."

As if she really had a choice in the matter, Olivia thought as Cooper ushered her inside a dark room and slammed the door shut behind them. A second later the overhead florescent lights flickered on, illuminating a small, windowless office, two wooden desks that were set up to face each other and barely enough room left to move around in. They locked eyes and stared.

"Look," Cooper began gravely, pointing one long, stiff finger in Olivia's direction. "You're pissed, I get that. But this isn't some high-end fashion boutique, where you can just stamp your feet and pout, and magically get your damn way. This is a federal courthouse, Miss Carrington. What the hell were you thinking, following me around like that?" She opened her mouth to speak and he sliced the air for silence. "You know what? On second thought, I don't even want to know. Here's how this is going to go down from here on out. I'm going to go back out there and interview Shannon Bridgeway, and you're going to calm the hell down, keep your mouth shut and stay out of my way while I do it. Is that clear?"

It took some serious effort for Olivia to look away from the finger pointed at her face, but she finally managed it. "You can't tell me—"

"Is. That. Clear?" he cut in, still pointing.

"Get your finger out of my face!" she exploded, slapping his finger down and replacing it with hers in the air between them. "And what was that, anyway? Another one of your little sly digs about my looks? You think I spend all of my time wandering around in fashion boutiques and staring at myself in the mirror?"

"That's not what I said."

"Good, because you would be wrong. And you know what? Screw you anyway, Agent Talbot. Funny how you didn't seem to have a problem with my looks when you were drooling over my legs."

"Drooling?"

She dropped her clutch on the nearest desktop and crossed her arms underneath her breasts. "You heard me."

He shook his head as if to clear it, and the movement was so smoothly executed that she didn't notice him moving closer to her until he was just *there*, and her nostrils were suddenly filled with his intoxicating scent. "I'm sorry, but when exactly did you notice me drooling over your legs, Miss Carrington? Was it before or after you stopped staring at my lips?" His expression turned thoughtful. "How was it that you described them? Oh yeah, that's right. I believe you said they were 'nice.'"

"*Nice* is a very generic word, Agent Talbot. Plenty of people have nice lips."

"You're staring at them right now. Did you know that?"

"No, I'm not!" But she was and she couldn't seem to make herself stop. "Okay, maybe I am, but not because I find them—or *you*—attractive," Olivia quickly added. He cocked a brow at her and she dug herself a little deeper. "Not really anyway, because honestly you're not my type. It's just...been a while since I've seen such nice lips on a man and I was curious about your ethnicity. I wasn't trying to offend you."

"No offense taken, especially since I happen to be a leg man and that's the only reason yours caught my attention. Like you, it's been a while since I've seen such a nice pair on a woman, so I commented on them." He slipped his hands into his trouser pockets, rocked back on his heels and shrugged nonchalantly. "If it seemed like I was hitting on you before, don't worry, I wasn't. Because you're not my type, either."

"I bet you like women who are simple and follow orders," she sniped, because his words left a salty taste in her mouth. "Do you grow them like that in Kentucky, Agent Talbot?" She saw his eyes narrow behind his lenses and the witch in her smiled.

"I wouldn't know, because I live in Tennessee, Miss Carrington. But tell me, are all of the women here in Missouri so feisty and obnoxious, or are you the only one? And for the last time," he barreled on without waiting for a response. "It's *Special Agent in Charge* Talbot. Get it right, would you? As a matter of fact, it's *Doctor* Cooper Talbot, to you."

"Oh, *doctor*, whoo-hoo," she drawled mockingly. "So you really *are* a nerd. I wondered about that."

Cooper sucked his teeth as his gaze flicked over her from head to toe. "Yeah, okay, I've got your nerd," he said, stepping back and taking a hand out of his pocket to reach for the doorknob. "Let's get this interview done, shall we? I'm sure you need to get back to taking selfies of yourself doing absolutely nothing, day after day, and posting them to your Instagram account."

She sucked in a mouthful of air and nearly choked on it. "You know what, Agent Talbot? I don't think I like you very much."

"Frankly, my dear, I don't give a damn," he snapped back, yanking the door open and stepping aside. "Are you coming or would you like to go clothing shopping?"

"Please," Olivia purred dismissively as she picked up her clutch and tucked it underneath her arm. "Your comment is so shallow. I think you've just done bow ties and pocket protectors everywhere a grave disservice."

"Hmm, I must've missed that in the nerd handbook. Can I ask you a question?"

"Sure."

"Why are you so flushed? Are you nervous?"

"Dealing with you makes my pressure rise. Which reminds me," she said, smiling sweetly. "I accidentally smeared my lip gloss on the back of your jacket.

I was going to offer to have it dry-cleaned for you, but now I hope it stains permanently."

He chuckled darkly. "Oh, now that's a low blow, Miss Carrington. Even for someone like you." With a flick of his wrist, the door closed again. "And here I was, just about to suggest that we stop taking shots at each other and let bygones be bygones. I was just thinking that I'd hate to leave Missouri tonight, knowing that I made an enemy while I was here."

"You made an enemy the second that you arrested my friend, whom I refuse to leave here without."

"Good, because I'm only holding Shannon Bridgeway on a material-witness custodial order, which means that after I'm done interviewing her, she'll see a judge, who I'm sure will release her under her own recognizance. So it's actually a good idea that you do stick around. She's going to need a ride home and I have a plane to catch. And to answer your earlier question about my ethnicity, I'm half black and half Irish."

"Oh." She blinked. "Well, that's a relief. About Shannon, I mean. Not about your ethnicity—"

"I know what you meant."

They stared at each other.

"So, what do you say, Miss Carrington? Are we cool?" He extended a huge hand to her, palm up.

"We're cool," she said, reluctantly reaching for it.

"Good. Let's kiss on it."

God, I hope so, she thought just as her palm met his and he used the leverage to bring her skipping toward him. Halfway there, the tip of his tongue peeked out from between his open lips in a silent invitation that she went up on her tiptoes to greedily accept, sinking into his mouth so deeply that she felt his tongue touch the back of her throat. It was the wettest, thirstiest, most invasive kiss that Olivia had ever experienced, so raw and uncivilized that her face flamed with embarrassment even as she gripped his shoulders and let him take her head back on her neck. He gripped her waist possessively and groaned into her mouth, and a rush of liquid pleasure drenched her thong. He glided a hand up her back to press her closer, and she purred.

A knock at the door had them springing apart like guilty teenagers. "Sir, we're ready to begin whenever you are," Bearden called through the door.

"We'll be right out," Cooper called back. He took off his glasses long enough to drag a hand down his face and pinch the bridge of his nose. Then he put them back on, cleared his throat and buttoned his suit jacket. "Here," he said, producing a neatly folded handkerchief from an inside jacket pocket and handing it to her. Touching the pad of his thumb to the center of her bottom lip, he watched his finger and then his gaze flickered up to hers. "Fix your lipstick," he suggested, reaching for the doorknob and pulling the door open. "I'll see you next door."

The interview was already underway when Olivia joined Cooper in the small conference room next door. He was alone, standing in the middle of the tile floor, frowning intently at the one-way glass panel in the wall in front of him, while the other two agents interviewed Shannon in an adjoining room. Glasses pushed up to the top of his head, suit jacket flung open and his arms crossed, he was watching them like a hawk.

Relieved to see that Shannon was sans the handcuffs and that she appeared significantly more relaxed than she had just a few minutes ago, Olivia closed the door and stepped up beside him at the panel, subconsciously mimicking his pose. They watched the interview progress silently for several minutes.

"They're still in training," Cooper eventually explained, nodding his head toward the glass. "But I think they're doing pretty well and look, ma, no handcuffs."

"I can see that, and I can also see that someone was nice enough to get her a Coke, but for all the trouble you went through, it doesn't seem like she's very much help to your case."

He shrugged noncommittally. "Maybe, maybe not. I'll know more after I review the tape," he said, glancing at her. "What took you so long? What were you doing in there, taking selfies?"

"You would love that, wouldn't you, Benjamin Button?" He snorted. "No, I wasn't taking selfies, which, in case you hadn't noticed, is a very offensive assumption. Not that it's any of your business, but I was on the phone with my assistant. Thanks to you, I had to move some things around on my schedule for today."

"I didn't think to ask before, but what exactly do you do...for a living, I mean?"

"Why? Are you worried that you might've just kissed a criminal, Agent Talbot?" She caught the uncertainty on his face and rolled her eyes to the ceiling. "Seriously?" Cringing, he reached up and scratched a spot at the top of his head.

"Weeelll…"

"Well, you can relax, hot lips. I'm a private investigator. I run my own firm and I'm very good at what I do, which is why I have to ask if we're watching the same interview. Shannon is all over the place. Maybe she recognizes your guy, but then again maybe she doesn't. It could be the same guy, but then again maybe it isn't. I'm confused just listening to her. How can this possibly be of any help to you?"

"You'd be surprised."

"Or maybe you wasted your time, in which case I hate to say it, but I believe I told you so." She felt his gaze on the side of her face and refused to allow herself the luxury of returning it. Encouraging what could only be described as a colossal lack of judgment on both of their parts was a bad idea. A very, very bad idea, she reasoned as the memory of his hungry mouth taking possession of hers flashed across her mind and spiked her body temperature. "And stop looking at me like that." She saw him smile in her peripheral vision.

"Why? Does it make you uncomfortable?"

After today they would never see each other again, so what did she have to lose by being honest? "No, it arouses me."

"And that's a problem?"

She looked askance at him. "I think it is. Don't you?" He turned his attention back to the trio on the other side of the glass and remained silent. Uncomfortable with the void that his silence left, Olivia rushed to fill it. "I mean, if you think about it, the only reason we kissed is because we were both a little shaken up after the near-death experience we had in that elevator. Obviously I don't make a habit of kissing complete strangers, and forgive me but you don't strike me as the type of guy who finds himself in these kinds of situations very often, either. How else would you explain what happened between us?"

"It was complete-and-utter insanity," Cooper readily replied.

"Exactly!" Thank God he understood what she was saying, where she was going with this.

"An exciting prelude to what I'm positive would've been some of the best sex that either of us has ever had," he continued as if she hadn't spoken, and she froze in place, with her hands clasped underneath her chin in joyous relief and her mouth hanging open. He glanced at her and chuckled knowingly. "What? You know it's true."

"Th-that's beside the point."

"You're blushing," he pointed out quietly. "I wonder why?"

Because she could see it clearly—his mouth on her breasts, his tongue busy between her thighs, her thighs riding his hips as he thrust into her over and over again—all of it. Every frantic, sweaty, nasty second of it, and even in the land of make-believe, it felt incredible. Because it galled her to admit to herself that, had it not been for a knock at the door, she'd have likely been happily bouncing up and down on a perfect stranger's shaft right this second, and enjoying every second of it.

Which was how she knew with 100 percent certainty that she had temporarily taken leave of each and every one of her senses. The elevator incident had obviously traumatized her.

Facing the glass again, Olivia cleared her throat. "It doesn't matter why. The point is, the best thing to do in this situation is to forget that the kiss ever happened. It was a mistake, one that I'd like to put behind me as soon as possible."

"If you say so."

"I do. Thank you for understanding." *Stop talking, Olivia.* "I mean, some men would completely misread the situation and think—"

"That you might be interested in meeting me later for dinner and drinks and then, if we're both drunk enough, maybe breakfast?" He shrugged nonchalantly, shaking his head. "Nah. Never crossed my mind."

Her eyes closed on a long-suffering sigh. "Exactly. I'm glad we understand each other, because the sooner we can put this behind us, the better."

"We do," Cooper said, glancing at his watch. "Sounds like they're wrapping up the interview now."

She started visibly when he suddenly sprang into action, breezing past her and heading over to the door in a series of surprisingly fluid movements, given his towering height and thin build. He reached for the doorknob and pulled the door open, glancing back at her over his shoulder. "Which means that, if I hurry, I might even be able to catch a flight back to Knoxville this evening, rather than tomorrow morning. Would that be soon enough for you, Miss Carrington?"

Chapter 7

Over the next two days, Cooper watched Shannon Bridgeway's interview video several times, and each time he did, he walked away from the experience that much more certain that she was hiding something. At first glance she seemed relatively stable, despite her obvious fidgeting and nervousness during the interview, but because he knew precisely what to look for, his second glance was much more revealing. Shannon Bridgeway was a good liar, but she hadn't succeeded in making him believe half of the lies that she'd told to both his agents and the investigating agents in Missouri.

Her body language was off, he realized after he'd finished watching the video the first time. Her eye contact was overly deliberate, he noticed during his second viewing, and during his third, he saw that her pulse was thumping erratically. By the time he had finally grown tired of watching the video, which was somewhere around the sixth or seventh time, he was convinced that something was seriously off with her and he was determined to find out what. Quietly, of course, because technically the agency's interest in her was a thing of the past, and on his own time, because there was no telling what he might find once he started peeling back the surface.

Well, mostly on his own time, anyway, Cooper conceded as he jogged up the steps to the US Prison Bureau in downtown Knoxville, paused just outside the entry door to collapse his umbrella and then swung the heavy steel-and-glass entry door open. Stepping inside from out of a steady summertime rain shower, he checked his weapon in at the security desk and then took an elevator to the third floor. Earlier today an underground copy of Shannon Bridgeway's sealed juvenile court records had fallen into his lap, courtesy of his contact in the Knoxville Child Protective Services Offices, and it'd made for some very interesting late-night reading.

According to court records, Shannon Bridgeway's birth name was actually Karen Lewis and she'd been raised in Peoria, Illinois, by a single father. With no other known family on record or in evidence, she had been placed in state custody after he was killed in a motorcycle accident, just a few months past her twelfth birthday. Over the next six years, she'd been assigned to live in a residential group home, but the reality was that she'd spent nearly half of that time sitting in local juvenile jail cells, either awaiting arraignment or serving out a sentence for one or another of the many theft charges that she had steadily accumulated.

Eventually, though, by some miracle, she managed to straighten herself out about a year shy of her eighteenth birthday and convince a judge that she was a new person. Along with her custodial release at age eighteen, her request to have her record expunged was granted and she was free. Free to legally change her name and start a new life, which was seemingly exactly what she'd done.

Except that her juvenile offender MO had almost always included the help of a co-offender, a partner in crime, who was typically another female and usually attractive. Shannon had hardly ever worked any of her many con jobs or petty thefts alone. *Not then*, Cooper conceded ruefully as an image of Olivia Carrington immediately came to mind. *And just as likely, not now.*

He thought about the kiss that they'd shared and wondered just how far the lovely Miss Carrington would have actually gone to keep his cock hard and his attention diverted. Naturally, running into her on an elevator and then having the elevator get stuck was an unforeseen fluke, but even that seemed to have worked in the dynamic duo's favor. It had given Olivia more time to hypnotize him with the spicy floral scent clinging to her skin and the sight of her gloriously round, jiggling butt. More time to seduce him with her mysterious, jewel-toned gaze and her masterful ability to blush like a virgin on cue.

Ironically enough she'd had no way of knowing that, though she claimed that he wasn't her type, she was exactly his, making him especially susceptible to her charms. But in the broad scheme of things, that didn't really matter, either. Because, frankly, in one way or another, she was every red-blooded, heterosexual man's type.

Cooper couldn't imagine any sane man being completely unaffected by her sexiness. Not even a priest was that immune. Her sex appeal was a living, breathing, palpable thing, and she knew exactly how to work it to her best advantage. So much so that if she was in fact Bridgeway's modern-day partner in whatever criminal enterprise they were currently involved in—and he strongly suspected that she was—then she was an excellent choice on Bridgeway's part. He hadn't yet received the results of the background screening that he'd requested on Olivia Carrington, but when he did, he fully expected its findings to confirm his suspicions.

If she was a professional private investigator, then he was the damn Duke of Wales.

In the meantime, while the jury was still out on Olivia, he didn't see the harm in shaking a few trees and seeing if anything fell to the ground.

He had used a public-access elevator, which put him off at the entrance to the third floor's visitor's area. Afternoon visiting hours hadn't yet begun, so the room was empty, which was just fine with Cooper, because he wasn't planning on staying long. Access to inmates was restricted to a series of thick, bulletproof glass panes, with a plastic stool and a telephone headset at each window. He made his way down one long row and then another, and then took a seat on a stool at a window along the far wall. The inmate whom he'd come to see—a thirty-five-year-old father of three, who worked as a truck driver by day and then used his job to traffic underage children by night—was already seated on the other side. His name was Malcolm Johnson, this was his third offense, though unrelated, and if Cooper had his way, very soon he'd be going away for a long time.

They stared at each other, both picking up the headset on the wall to their respective rights simultaneously and putting it to their ears.

"Man, you know damn well that I'm not supposed to talk to you without my attorney present," Malcolm immediately growled into the headset. He looked as if he hadn't slept in days, and there were at least two new knots upside his head. It looked as if someone or possibly several someones—if the angry-looking bruises dotting his sun-tanned face were any indication—had used his face for a punching bag.

Cooper smiled. He detested child abuse in any form. "Calm down, Mr. Johnson," he advised good-naturedly. "I'm not here in an official capacity. I was actually just passing by and thought I'd stop in and check on you."

Malcolm's beady brown eyes narrowed suspiciously. "Yeah, right. What kind of game are you playing, Agent? Ain't this a violation of my civil rights or something?"

"Not at all." Cooper's tone was easy, laid-back.

"In fact, what I'm about to tell you might just help your case in some way. You never know."

"Well, spit it out, then. What is it?"

"I thought you might like to know that my witness picked you out of a lineup. She's not positive but she thinks you might be one of the suspects who robbed that bank in Missouri a few weeks back. The one you mentioned when you were first arrested," he added, seemingly as an afterthought. "I believe you intimated that you had some knowledge about that robbery, some knowledge that could lead to an arrest in the case. Last I heard, your attorney was interested in making a deal."

"Hmph." Johnson sucked his teeth for several seconds. "Now, why would I find that interesting, Agent?"

"I don't know, Johnson. Maybe you wouldn't. Maybe I was wrong. If so, then I'm sorry I wasted your time," Cooper said and dropped the headset back into its cradle on the wall. Ten minutes later he was back in his car, headed to his office. *Mission accomplished*, he thought as he glanced at his watch and pulled out into afternoon traffic. *Now let the chips fall where they may.*

Later that night, when Olivia Carrington's name flashed across his cell's screen, he couldn't help thinking: *and so it begins...*

He touched a button to accept her incoming call and put the phone to his ear. "Cooper Talbot."

"It's Olivia Carrington, Agent Talbot. Did I catch you at a bad time?"

"When has that ever stopped you?" Cooper drawled as he unlocked the door to his house and stepped inside, out of the rain. "In any case, no, you haven't caught me at a bad time. I'm actually just getting in from a date, so if you were hoping to catch me in a good mood, this is probably as good as it's going to get. What's up?" He scooped up his mail in the small entry foyer and dropped his briefcase on the couch as he passed through the living room.

"A date, huh?" Olivia purred in his ear. His cock went on full alert. "Is she there with you now?"

In the kitchen, he stuck his head inside the refrigerator and emerged a few seconds later with a cold beer in his hand. "If she was, you wouldn't be."

"No, I guess not, huh?" She giggled devilishly. "Well, at least tell me if you kissed her good-night or not."

"A gentleman never kisses and tells. You should know that, Miss Carrington." But he chuckled into his bottle anyway, enjoying this. "But if you must know, yes, I kissed her."

"Oh."

He tipped the bottle up and drank deeply, smothering a belch. "Oh?"

"Yes, *oh*. Does she kiss better than I do?"

Cooper almost choked on a mouthful of beer. "Are you serious right now, Olivia?" he asked when he could talk.

"Yes, Coop, I am. Is it okay if I call you Coop?"

"No, it's not, and none of your business. What did you say you wanted again?"

"Oh, so you're going to be like that?"

"Yes, I'm going to be like that."

"Then she probably doesn't," Olivia decided and Cooper roared with laughter. "It's only eleven o'clock. Why are you home from a date so early?"

"It's almost midnight here, it's a weeknight and some of us have to go to work in the morning. Do you usually stay out all night on a date?"

"Well, now that depends on the date, doesn't it? What are you wearing right now?"

He looked down at his jeans, Nikes and blue short-sleeved polo shirt. They had gone bowling. "Uh, jeans and a shirt. Why?"

"Because it explains why you're home so early, without your date, and therefore without a good story to tell the guys tomorrow at the watercooler."

Actually, it didn't, but he wasn't about to disabuse the lunatic woman on the other end of the phone call of her stereotypical notions about him. She seemed to be enjoying her perception of him as an over-grown, clueless nerd and he wasn't in the mood right now to square off again with her about it. "Whatever, Olivia."

"Okay. Don't say I didn't try to warn you."

"Are you going to tell me why you called or…?"

"Yes, I'm going to tell you why I called, Cooper. You're awfully uptight, which is probably because—"

"Today, Olivia," Cooper cut in, rolling his eyes to the vaulted ceiling.

"All right, fine. You've probably already heard, but your prosecuting attorney called Shannon today to set up a meeting. From what I gathered, she saw your tape and apparently read your notes, and now she wants her to view an in-person lineup and sit for a formal interview, under oath. She thinks Shannon's sworn testimony could help nudge the grand jury toward an indictment when the time comes. I suppose Shannon has you to thank for that?"

"Not really, no," Cooper said, setting his half-empty beer bottle down slowly on the kitchen counter and then leaning back against it. He tucked his cell between his head and shoulder and crossed both his arms and his ankles. "This is news to me. Has she agreed to the meeting?"

Olivia chuckled incredulously. "Does she really have a choice? I mean, look what happened the last time she tried to duck you people. She's still too traumatized from that experience to even think about refusing. Honestly, are you *trying* to push her to the brink of insanity?"

He wasn't touching that question with a long-handled spoon; instead he asked one of his own. "When are they meeting?"

"I'm not sure—maybe next week sometime. They're flying her to Knoxville. Coach, of course," she drawled disgustedly. "Anyway, I was just wondering if you were aware of the mess that you caused."

"No, I wasn't, but thanks for letting me know. Are you going with her?"

She was silent for several seconds. "I don't know," she finally admitted. "I hadn't really thought about it. It seems like she'd be better off bringing along her attorney, even if they didn't exactly hit it off the first time they met. I think Shannon wants me to come along, though, in case they need a referee."

"Hmph."

"Hmph?" she parroted. "What does that mean, hmph?"

"Nothing. Just…hmph. Have you ever been to Knoxville, Miss Carrington?"

"No, but then again it's not exactly on my bucket list of places to visit before I die. Why, am I missing something?"

"Only the best barbecue you've ever tasted and some of the greatest country-music house bands in the world. I'm just saying…it's something to think about."

"Mmm…maybe."

"Maybe," he replied and picked up his beer.

"Well, I guess I'll say good night, then."

"Good night, Olivia."

"Good night, Coop."

"I could've sworn that I told you not to call me Coop."

She smiled and hung up the phone.

Chapter 8

"Is that everything?"

"I think so," Olivia said, shuffling through the stack of file folders in her hand. When she came to the last one, she peeked up at her MacBook's screen and cocked a brow at her sister. "Wait, are you sure you're okay with me turning down the McMillan case?"

"God, yes." Elise rolled her eyes to the sky. "Debra McMillan is a nutcase. Do you remember how she behaved the last time we took on a case of hers?"

How could Olivia forget? Phone calls at all hours of the night. Spontaneous drop-ins at the most inconvenient times imaginable. Outrageous demands and ridiculous temper tantrums. And that had only been the first week.

"Back then we were just starting out and we

needed the money," Elise continued. Behind her, the view of a sunny, cloudless sky and the calm water below it went on as far as the eye could see. While Olivia was surrounded by paperwork, Elise was in the middle of the ocean, sailing on her wealthy husband's luxury yacht. "That's nowhere near the case now, so…" She waved a flippant hand at the camera. "I say let someone else prove that her third husband faked his own death. If the poor guy is still alive, which we both know could very well be the case, he's probably lying on a beach somewhere, sipping daiquiris and soaking up the sun. And really, after being married to the woman for ten years, hasn't he earned a little peace and quiet?"

"Yes, but I don't think she wants him back so much as she wants back the five million dollars that her accountant hasn't been able to account for since just before the poor idiot kicked the bucket. And honestly, I can't really say that I blame her."

"Well, if you ask me—and you did—he's earned every red cent. Run, man! Run like the wind!" Elise turned and shouted to the wind in question. Turning back to the camera, she said, "You know, someone should find him and warn him that she's coming for him."

Chuckling, Olivia set the stack of files aside, took off her glasses, dropped them on the tabletop and then reached for her coffee mug. "I'm inclined to agree," she said, relaxing back in her chair and sipping the hot liquid carefully as she eyed a laughing Elise over the rim. "It won't be me, though, because for the first time in months I have a little downtime ahead of me and I plan to enjoy every minute of it."

"Where's your strange friend these days?"

Now it was Olivia's turn to roll her eyes to the ceiling. "If by strange, you mean Shannon, then I'm happy to report that she's settling into her new apartment very nicely and she likes her new job. So far, so good."

"Any news on the break-in at her old apartment?"

"None yet, and she doesn't seem too worried about it."

"And that doesn't strike you as a little odd?"

"Of course it does, but how she chooses to handle the situation is her business. Besides, she's probably too preoccupied with the fallout from her latest run-in with the FBI to concentrate on much of anything else right now."

"What about you? You've been a little preoccupied with the fallout from your latest run-in with the FBI, too. Have you decided if you're going to sleep with the fallout or…?"

"Uh, no." Olivia rolled her eyes at the camera. "And I'm not preoccupied. You of all people should know that Cooper Talbot would hardly be the first man that I've ever slept with. I've played this game before, you know, so please spare me the lecture."

"I'm not trying to lecture you. I'm just saying, maybe this Cooper Talbot guy is exactly what you need right now. Hasn't it been a while since…?" She paused to wriggle her eyebrows suggestively. "Well, you know."

"Cooper Talbot couldn't be any more *not* what I need right now, if he tried."

"You said he was a great kisser."

"Yes, and the price of gas is up by a dollar this week. What's your point?"

"Weeelll," Elise drawled in a tone that put Olivia on alert instantly.

"Oh, God, here we go," she murmured, dropping her head in her hand and shaking it sadly.

"Now that you mention it," Elise continued as she sat up on her lounging chaise and pulled her Mac-Book closer. "I took the liberty of looking up your Cooper Talbot," she explained as her fingers began flying over her keyboard.

"He's not *my* Cooper Tal—"

"Here's what I have so far."

"Elise—"

"He's forty and single, no kids, and you're right, he does appear to be a nerd, or at least he used to be. He graduated from Columbia with a law degree, as well as a graduate degree in psychology, when he was twenty-two, and then worked as a public defender for a few years before joining the FBI fifteen years ago. Since then—and here's the part I really like— he's written a dozen post-secondary textbooks on criminology—most of which either have or are being used in college classrooms around the country—and one highly successful true-crime book about the—"

"The Charleston Child Abductions," Olivia supplied, referring to the year-long reign of terror that a child abductor and murderer had subjected the city of Charleston, South Carolina, to between the summer of 2005 and the fall of 2006. A total of eighteen children, ranging in ages from seven to sixteen, had been abducted and never seen or heard from again, and a suspect hadn't been arrested in the case until early 2010. The resulting trial was televised, capturing the country's attention and holding it raptly right up until the defendant had been found guilty and sentenced to death by lethal injection. "Yes, I know."

"Dr. Cooper Talbot was a profiler on the case."

"I know that, too."

"I read somewhere that his input was instrumental in narrowing down the suspects."

Olivia sighed. "Yes, I think I heard that."

"His book was on the *New York Times* bestseller list for weeks," Elise chirped. "And even more importantly, did you happen to notice that the brother is *fiiine?*"

Olivia blushed to the roots of her hair, just as she did every time Cooper Talbot crossed her mind, which he seemed to be doing quite often lately. Nearly a week had passed since they'd spoken last, and in that time she'd caught herself trying to think up excuses to call him more often than she cared to admit. Found herself wondering where he was and what he was doing at odd hours of the day, and constantly checking her cell for missed calls, just in case. Of course she wasn't about to admit any of that to Elise, though. She recognized the signs of Cupid Fever, otherwise known as married people's tendency to match-make for their single family members and friends, often with disastrous results, and didn't want any part of it.

Thankfully Elise didn't seem to notice her flaming face.

"I mean, I know that he's the antithesis of everything you've ever stood for where men are concerned, but still. As hard as you've been working this past year, you deserve a little rest and relaxation. What would be so wrong with getting a little of both with Cooper Talbot—I'm sorry, *Doctor* Cooper Talbot? From what you've told me, I think he's made it pretty obvious that he's interested. The question is, are you?"

Olivia thought about the question long after she'd hung up with Elise and sent Harriet home for the day. Alone in the house, she fixed herself a simple dinner, poured herself a glass of Chardonnay, and took both her plate and her glass with her out onto the screened-in deck at the back of the house to enjoy.

Later, in her bedroom, she put on Bach's Cello Suite no. 1 in G Major, lit scented candles, set them around the perimeter of her spa tub and drew herself a frothy bubble bath. A second glass of wine in hand, she soaked and sipped until it was well after midnight, the water was cold and it was time for bed.

And all the while Cooper Talbot's liquid-brown eyes and picture-perfect smile occupied her thoughts.

It wasn't like she'd never had an affair before, because God knew she had. Of the two of them, she had always been the adventurer, the explorer. Elise was the one who preferred the company of a good book and a mug of chamomile tea over the excitement of breaking rules and pushing limits. Growing up, those were Olivia's domains, and she had not only excelled in them but she had owned them. As far as she was concerned, an affair between two single, consenting adults wasn't exactly front-page news. Instead, when done right, it could be exciting and rejuvenating—just what the doctor ordered when a pleasant but temporary distraction from everyday life was called for.

It had taken Elise thirty-plus years to discover what Olivia had known since her senior year in high school—that sex really was better than chocolate. Elise's response to the discovery had been to marry the first guy who finally succeeded in rocking her world, which was typical Elise. But Olivia was content to live her life on her own terms, and nowhere in the contract was there room for any such nonsense. Elise was right: it had been a while since she'd been on a date, much less been kissed senseless by an attractive man, but she wasn't so sure that getting any more involved with Cooper than she already was would be the right move.

Aside from the glaring discrepancies between the men that she was typically attracted to and Cooper Talbot, there was something about the man that made her hesitant to let her guard down. Flirting with him was one thing, but sleeping with him was something else altogether. For one thing he was an FBI agent and there were times when Carrington Consulting wasn't exactly a poster firm for law and order. There were times when successfully closing a case required one or both of them to operate in a gray area, times when it was necessary to engage in the kinds of back-room deals that could only be made in secret and under the cover of darkness. Times when, in the interest of plausible deniability, even Harriet was kept out of the loop.

The last thing either she or Elise needed was a hyper-vigilant, uber-intelligent G-man in their midst, no matter how surprisingly strong his grip was or how deliciously nimble his tongue. If Carrington Consulting somehow found itself in a professional jam because of him, the means wouldn't even begin to justify the undoubtedly disastrous end.

Olivia was and had always been a bit of a free spirit, but one thing she'd never been was a fool, especially not where matters of the heart were concerned.

Self-control, she decided as she finished up her bedtime routine and left the bathroom, was the name of the game and, except for the time back in high school when she'd almost eloped with her first love, she wasn't unfamiliar with the concept, not completely, anyway. Possibly a refresher course was in order, she thought as she visualized Cooper's broad shoulders, taut butt and long legs, but she wasn't overly concerned about failing, because…

"Everything is under control," she assured herself, crawling into bed and burrowing into a cave of six-hundred-thread-count-sheet-and-down-filled-duvet heaven. Her head had no sooner hit the pillow before the wine, the quiet and the bubble bath began working their magic and she was drifting off.

Five minutes later her cell phone rang somewhere in the room and her head popped up from the depths of her pillow. Half asleep, her eyes darted around her dark bedroom frantically, until she spotted lights flashing on her nightstand and cursed under her breath. In her line of work, late-night calls usually brought either bad news or an important break in a case. Either way, not answering wasn't an option.

She cleared her throat of all remnants of sleep and put the phone to her ear. "Olivia Carrington."

"It's Friday night, Miss Carrington," Cooper drawled into the phone. "I thought all of the popular girls had hot dates on Friday nights, so why are you home and, from the sound of things, in bed alone?" He sucked in a sharp breath and then chuckled darkly. "Wait, you *are* alone, aren't you?"

"If I wasn't, I wouldn't have answered the phone." She squeezed her thighs together and smiled in the darkness. "Or maybe I would have, and you could've taken a break from your stamp collecting to listen in." He chuckled but said nothing. "Do I even need to ask why *you* don't have a date tonight?"

"You can ask but I'm not promising an answer. What do you know about breasts?"

Her eyebrows shot up. "Excuse me?"

"Chicken breasts, Miss Carrington. Get your mind out of the gutter."

"You called me at one o'clock in the morning to ask me about chicken breasts?"

"As ridiculous as it sounds, yes, I did. I found a recipe online that I decided to try whipping up tonight and…" The sigh that floated through the phone sounded so dejected that Olivia melted a little. "Well… I'm calling you for help, aren't I? Do you really want me to go into detail about the tragedy that's taken place here over the last four hours? Because it isn't pretty."

"Since you put it that way, I guess not. What's the name of the recipe?"

"I'm trying to make golden chicken with cilantro-cashew pesto and coconut rice on the side. Sounds simple enough, right?"

"Uh…right. So what's the problem?"

She listened to his tale of culinary chaos and mayhem with baited breath, giggling when he admitted that he was currently on his third tray of chicken, having burned the first two beyond recognition, and then apologizing profusely for bursting out laughing when he revealed that he had mistaken sugar for salt once and pickle relish for pesto base twice.

"I'm glad you think it's funny," Cooper snarled when she couldn't stop laughing. "Could you have done any better?"

"Yes," Olivia panted between guffaws. "Yes, I could have. Tell you what, Coop," she said, sitting up and scooting to the edge of the mattress. She tucked the phone between her head and shoulder and grabbed her MacBook from the nightstand. "Stop what you're doing and give me the website's URL, so I can pull up the recipe that you're using. We'll take it step by step."

"Okay, but does it matter that I've already seasoned the chicken with salt and pepper?"

"Probably not, but don't touch anything else until I tell you to."

"Agreed," he said, rattling off the URL in the next

breath. "You know what I just realized, though? I didn't think to ask before, but can you even cook?"

"Oh, Coop…honey, you have no idea. Now, pay attention," she instructed as she began walking him through the recipe, one step at a time.

Two hours later she hung up with a smile on her face and waited for Cooper to follow her parting instruction—to send her a picture of his breasts. It landed in her inbox a few seconds after she'd hung up, along with a text.

Now you. Send me a picture of your breasts.

In your dreams, she texted back.
Several minutes passed before his rebuttal came.

Well, at least allow me to thank you properly for your help. Will I see you next week? If so, dinner? I promise I won't make it.

Shannon was scheduled to fly to Knoxville on Tuesday to meet with the prosecuting attorney there. Until that very second, Olivia had managed to avoid thinking about the possibility of accompanying her, but now that Cooper had brought it up again, it was suddenly the proverbial elephant in the room. There was really no reason for her to go—none at all. But…

Still undecided, she eventually texted back.

But was she really? Maybe Shannon really did need her to tag along for moral support, in which case she sort of had to go, didn't she? And if she just happened to run into Cooper Talbot while she was there, well, that couldn't be helped, could it?

Admit it, Olivia. You want to see the man again.

All right, fine. Okay. She did want to see him again. But that was all and, really, what was the worst that could happen?

She texted Cooper a short time later.

I'll come. But I have no intention of showing you my breasts.

His reply was an innocent-looking smiley-face emoticon, but the sizzle of anticipation that zinged through her in response was anything but.

Chapter 9

A lamp crashed to the floor with a loud thud. "Shit!" Cooper growled as the sound of shattering glass filled the room. "Be careful," he murmured just before he caught a corner of the couch with his knee and cursed like a sailor.

Undeterred by the minor casualties, he moaned with approval when Olivia promptly plopped down on a corner of the end table that he had just accidentally cleared, leaned back and parted her thighs for him. Unwilling to release his hold on her, his legs buckled beneath him and he went with her, his hands riding the slope of her thighs like a blind man's.

As if she were reading his mind, she hiked up the hem of her denim sundress and tilted her smooth, bare sex up to him in invitation. He had bared it himself just a few minutes ago, backing her into a corner of the elevator downstairs as soon as the doors had closed them inside and it had lifted off from the hotel lobby, and reaching underneath her dress to drag her lacy snow-white thong down the length of her stunning legs. Just before the doors opened again, he had pressed his wispy prize to his nose and inhaled the vanilla-laced aroma of her sex, and then tucked it in his pocket to keep as a souvenir.

At the door to her suite, he had reached around her from behind and slipped his fingers into her slick folds as discreetly as possible, pressed his stiff cock into her butt cheeks by degrees and whispered into her ear all the nasty things that he planned to do to her. *Starting with this*, he thought as he gripped her thighs, pinned them back further still and slowly parted the thick, slippery lips between them with the very tip of his tongue.

She cried out when his tongue glided over her engorged clitoris and swam down into the pool at the entrance to her pulsing walls. Reached down to cup the back of his head and hold him in place when he slid one long finger inside of her and stroked her with it, while he tongued her clitoris like a starving man. He heard himself moaning ecstatically, almost gleefully, as he devoured her and was helpless to curb his enthusiasm. She tasted even sweeter than he'd imagined she would, and her lack of inhibition was the ultimate turn on. He loved a woman who could set aside the structured mechanics of sex and simply enjoy a good fuck.

"Oh God, oh God, oh God," she chanted like a

prayer as he sucked and licked at her dewy lips one at a time and then opened his mouth over her entire sex like a suction cup. "Aaahhh... I'm coming!"

And she did, noisily and trembling violently, in the perfect position for him to mount her and drive his cock into her over and over again, hard and fast. Resisting the temptation of quick release, he rolled to his feet and licked his drenched lips as he stepped out of his shoes and reached for his belt. The sound of his zipper lowering in the darkness punctuated the chorus of their heavy breathing. He understood that she was on her knees before him when he felt her hands pushing his aside and reaching down into his boxers to free his anxious cock with a grip that sent his eyes to the back of his head. Pumping him softly, she dragged his pants and underwear down to his ankles so that he could step out of them.

"Damn, Coop," she murmured up at him, her lips riding his length as she spoke. "You're just full of surprises, aren't you?" His long cock spasmed in her hand and a bead of pre-cum bloomed on the very tip. Cooing with pleasure, she found it and smeared it into the skin there with the pad of her thumb.

"Mmm, and just think, in a few minutes you can have as much of it as you want." Following the cut of her sundress with his fingertips, he found the zipper in the back and lowered it. She shrugged out of it and let it fall to her lap, exposing her fluffy breasts to his greedy hands. He fingered her jutting nipples gently. "I can't wait to give it to you." She could barely wrap her fingers around him and even then, they didn't meet. The anticipation of slowly sliding his erection inside of her and watching the play of emotions on her face as he stretched her wide and drove deep was starting to mess with his head. He couldn't remember the last time that he'd been so aroused. "Suck it," he murmured quietly and pushed his fingers into the curly hair at the back of her head and brought her mouth closer to his shaft.

Seconds later her head was bobbing back and forth, meeting the rhythmic stroke of his hips. Her hot, wet mouth was wrapped around his straining flesh and, inside of it, her tongue was busy dancing up, down and around and around his length. "Awww, Liv, that feels so good." He loved oral sex, both giving and receiving it, and the discovery that she obviously enjoyed it as well was damn near hypnotizing. The sounds she made as she pleasured him pushed him closer and closer to the brink of exploding in her lovely mouth, ultimately forcing him to withdraw from her greedy suction and take an unsteady step back. Reaching down, he hauled her up against him, chest to chest, and rooted around for her mouth with his own until he found it.

She tasted like brown sugar and barbecue sauce, like mustard potato salad, baked beans and the Irish ale that they'd both drunk with dinner. Like the candied yams and homemade macaroni and cheese that they had gorged themselves on. Her hair smelled like smoke, because he had taken her to a ramshackle little juke joint that was set back too deeply in the woods to be on any map, where the men grew their beards long and scraggly and chain-smoked, and the women wore tight dresses and too much lipstick and filled the place with the sound of belly laughs. He had promised her the best barbecue that she'd ever tasted, and by the time they had finally pushed back from their table near the makeshift stage, she was in agreement that he had fulfilled it.

And he'd been on his best behavior the entire time.

He wasn't much of a dancer, but the house band's slow mix of country and jazz gave him the perfect excuse to touch her, and for a few short songs, he had taken it. Later, when she had looped her arm through his and leaned against him during their after-dinner stroll around the lake out behind the juke joint, he had dutifully kept his thoughts from straying into the gutter then, too. But the moment that he pulled into the hotel parking lot and she leaned across the armrest and offered him her tongue for a good-night kiss, he had bid a fond farewell to what little self-control he still possessed and snatched Olivia up the way an addict snatched up his next hit.

Just once, he'd promised himself, mentally licking his chops. If she was playing games with him, pretending to be something that she wasn't, then just this once he'd given himself permission to be the sucker that she believed him to be. *I'll make her come just once—okay, maybe twice*, he qualified as one of her pampered-looking hands had crossed the divide, found the tent that his cock was making inside of his trousers and closed around his thumping flesh as if to soothe it. *Then it's back to business as usual*. If it turned out that she and Bridgeway were working together, then he was completely prepared to arrest her, even if it meant taking a little heat himself for temporarily thinking with the wrong head.

But that hadn't been established yet, and technically he was working off the clock anyway, so as far as he was concerned, in the here and now, she was fair game.

At least, that was the justification that he was prepared to give, if one should ever become necessary.

Too far gone now to check himself, Cooper picked up his pants from the floor and brought them along with him as he walked her backward through her suite toward the bedroom, with his tongue busy in her mouth. There, she toppled over onto the king-size mattress on her back and scooted across its width until she was in the center of it. Somewhere in the room, a nightlight cast a soft, rosy glow and, as his eyes slowly adjusted to the sudden light, the picture she made came into focus. He watched her stare at his stiff cock while he found his wallet and removed a condom from it. Braced on her elbows, with her legs spread wide for his viewing pleasure and her dark, bulbous nipples pointing up at the ceiling, she tracked his progress as he slowly walked across the mattress on his knees toward her, sheathing himself as he came.

"Ahhh…such pretty tits," he murmured just before he braced himself above her, opened his mouth over one swollen, elongated tip and proceeded to inhale the delicate morsel. At the same time, he relaxed his knees on the mattress, allowing them to slowly slide from beneath him while his cock sank into her tight velvet tunnel, inch by excruciatingly tight inch, until he was planted to his balls.

As soon as Cooper's hips began dancing against hers, she stiffened and cried out, instantly coming around him like a contracting velvet fist. He threw his head back and growled at the ceiling, picking up the pace of his strokes until the mattress shook underneath them and Olivia's breasts were bouncing around on her chest. Aware of the almost painful thumping at the base of his spine, he shifted and sucked her other nipple deep inside of his mouth, feasting on it as he tilted his pelvis and deepened his hard, fast strokes.

The last thing he remembered seeing before his vision went blurry and his mouth went slack was the sight of Olivia, stroked into orgasmic silence and gazing up at him through sightless eyes as she bucked beneath him like a fish out of water. Unable to deny himself any longer, he turned his lips and tongue loose on the column of her neck and gave in to a toe-curling climax that stole his breath.

Several minutes later Cooper finally mustered up enough energy to roll off Olivia. Flopping back against the mattress beside her like a lead weight, he dragged a hand across his damp face and stared up at the ceiling. It was a toss-up as to which of them was panting harder.

"That was good," he eventually managed to get out.

"Yes, it was," Olivia agreed. "But you know this can never happen again, right?"

"Absolutely not. This was totally a one-time thing. We agreed."

"Totally."

He scratched a spot low on his abdomen and stretched. "Right."

"Should we pull the covers back and get in?"

"Totally," he said, yawning.

Getting out of bed and hitting the ground running the next morning was easier said than done for Olivia. She'd only been asleep for a precious few hours when the 7:30 a.m. wake-up call that she had requested at check-in yesterday rang her bedside phone and startled her out of the deepest sleep that she'd had in months. Expecting to find Cooper still lying next to her, she rolled over and reached out for him. Coming up empty, she threw the covers back and cracked one eye open to look around the room. She might've missed the note that he'd scrawled on a sheet of hotel stationery and left lying on the pillow next to her if she hadn't rolled over and landed on it with her face.

You were sleeping so soundly, didn't want to wake you. Later.
Coop

Later.

In the light of day, Olivia was dreading *later*. The memory of precisely what they'd done and exactly how many times they'd done it singed her skin with embarrassment. The realization that she'd been way off base about Cooper's sexual prowess had hit her like a punch to the gut sometime during the wild night that they had just shared, sometime between a third orgasm that had left her legs trembling for several minutes afterward and a fourth one, later still, that had reduced her to little more than a drooling puddle of quivering matter. She was confident that she had given just as much as she'd taken from the exchange, but still. The man's stroke game was seriously on point.

She pushed her hair back from her face and stared up at the ceiling as if it could provide her with the answer to the question swirling around in her head. *What have I done?* A vivid image of something very specific that she'd done flashed across her mind and she groaned. *You know what you did.*

A pitiful-sounding sob tumbled out of Olivia's mouth as she pushed herself up on all fours and, after three tries, mustered up the energy to crawl out of bed and make her way to the adjoining bathroom, against the advice of her screaming thigh muscles. Conscious of the time, she brushed her teeth and showered quickly, padding back out into the bedroom several minutes later, feeling a little less comatose, but still nowhere near bright-eyed and bushy-tailed.

Praying that the morning passed quickly, she dressed in an off-white linen pantsuit and scraped her hair up into a bun at the crown of her head. After dusting her face with a light layer of translucent powder, she finished her makeup with mascara and a sheer pink lip gloss that coordinated perfectly with both the rose-colored silk shell that she wore underneath her blazer and the multicolored scarf accentuating her bun. She found her shoes and stepped into them quickly, and then checked her cell for missed calls. Shannon's meeting was scheduled for ten thirty, which was a little over an hour and a half from now. Plenty of time for them to find the nearest Starbucks and then get to the downtown Knoxville law-enforcement complex in time to meet Sabine Barnes before the meeting was scheduled to begin.

Speaking of Shannon, she thought as she glanced at her watch and went in search of the color-block Kate Spade tote bag that held all of her business-on-the-go essentials. She had purposely reserved a suite on the opposite side of the hotel from Shannon's room and sneaked out with Cooper only after she was positive that Shannon was asleep for the night. But now, with it getting closer and closer to showtime, the distance concerned her, mainly because of the dramatic anxiety attacks that Shannon was prone to but also because she was starting to feel guilty about sneaking out to begin with. Olivia tried to picture Shannon having an anxiety attack while she was surrounded by FBI agents, and she couldn't see it ending well, no matter how she spun the story in her head. Any way you looked at it, she came out looking like a selfish, absentee friend who had used the trip to Tennessee as an excuse to hook up with a man and engage in a reckless one-night stand.

Which was exactly what she was.

But that part of her trip was over now, and her head was officially back in the game. Snatching up her purse and room key from the sitting-room coffee table, Olivia headed for the door with a new resolve. She and Shannon had agreed to meet in the hotel lobby at nine fifteen, and she didn't intend to be late. From here on out she was committed to focusing on being there for Shannon. There was always a chance that she might run into Cooper at some point during the morning, but she was prepared for that possibility, too. She dug her Chanel sunglasses out of her tote, slipped them over her eyes and cleared her throat. *There.* Grateful that she'd had the foresight to request a late check-out when she made her reservation, she left her suite and went in search of the elevator.

She spotted Shannon immediately. She was sitting alone in a chair in the hotel lobby, next to a window that looked out onto the street. Olivia didn't notice until she was halfway across the lobby that Shannon was also in the middle of a very intense-looking conversation.

Wait a second. Olivia slowed to a stop and stared. *With herself?*

She hadn't gotten close enough to hear any of what Shannon was saying, but fortunately she'd gotten pretty good at reading lips over the years. *There's nothing to worry about,* Shannon was saying to the invisible person sitting next to her. *After today, it's all over. They don't know... No one does.*

Advancing more cautiously this time, Olivia waved her arms and called out to Shannon while there was still enough distance between them to pretend that she hadn't noticed her talking to herself. "Shannon! Good morning!"

Shannon's head whipped around and, while her eyes widened in alarm, Olivia exhaled with relief because the move revealed the cell phone in Shannon's other hand. "Olivia, hi. Good morning. You're early."

Olivia glanced at her watch as she approached. "Only by a few minutes. Did you eat breakfast already?"

"No, I, uh…" She pointed to the cell phone pressed to the side of her face and flashed an apologetic smile. "I was just wrapping up a call." Into the phone, she said, "I have to go. I'll call you back." She ended the call abruptly and tucked the phone inside of her purse.

Olivia frowned. "That looked pretty serious. Is everything all right?"

"Everything's fine. That was just an ex-coworker from the bank, checking up on me."

She was lying, Olivia was sure of it, but after last night she wasn't going to be the one to call her out on it. If Shannon wanted to keep secrets, that was her prerogative. God knew that Olivia was keeping enough secrets of her own.

"Oh, okay. The car that they're sending for us should be here any minute. Did you remember everything?"

Shannon slung her purse strap over her shoulder and got to her feet. She was wearing a knee-length sundress, with a matching shrug and sensible flats. "I think so, yes, but if you're hungry, we might have time to grab something to eat on the way."

"Right now, all I need is coffee," Olivia said, waving away Shannon's suggestion of food. She paused to inhale slowly. "Real coffee, because, if that's supposed to be coffee that I smell in the air right now, it doesn't even begin to qualify."

"So… Starbucks?"

"There has to be one around here somewhere."

Chapter 10

They both started when the heavy wooden door swung open and a brunette head popped out into the hallway. "Miss Bridgeway?"

Shannon jumped to her feet and Olivia stood too, reaching for her hands and squeezing them reassuringly. "I'll wait for you out here." On the other side of Shannon, Sabine cut the text message that she'd been composing short, put away her cell phone and stood, as well.

"This shouldn't take long," she advised Olivia. "As soon as we're done here, you and I can discuss the myriad of ways in which you now owe me, friend."

"Pretty big, huh?"

"Oh my God, so big," Sabine said, winking saucily as she ushered Shannon through the doorway and followed behind. Settling in to wait, Olivia resumed her seat on the padded wooden bench across from the door and crossed her legs. A few seconds later, she glanced at her watch and reached for a section of the day's newspaper that someone had been thoughtful enough to leave behind. She was perusing the editorials when her cell phone vibrated in her blazer pocket. Fighting a yawn, she set the paper aside and took it out.

Meeting started yet?

She smiled. Why was she smiling? *Stop it, Olivia!* She looked both ways down the corridor, saw that she was alone and reread Cooper's text. She texted back.

Yes, just now.

What are you doing?

Waiting. Their car had been late arriving to pick them up, so there hadn't been time to find a Starbucks on the way there. As a result Olivia was suddenly struggling with a bout of mid-morning drowsiness, so she added to her previous text.

Trying to stay awake.

Have you had breakfast?

No time and not really hungry. Would kill for coffee, though.

A winking emoticon flashed across her screen first and then he responded.

Got you covered. Meet me downstairs in the lobby in five minutes?

Absolutely not. She wasn't ready to see him again so soon.

See you then.

She told herself that she'd only come because she was in a strange city, she didn't know anyone else and she desperately needed coffee. But the moment that Cooper walked off the elevator, with his cell phone pressed to his ear and a wrinkle of concentration in his forehead, her nipples tightened with awareness and she flushed involuntarily. She forgot all about her craving for coffee as, from behind her dark lenses, she watched him look around the lobby for her and then change directions when he saw her standing near the exit doors. He continued his phone conversation as he strolled toward her but she was too busy appreciating his loose, long-limbed stride to even think about trying to read his lips.

"Hi," Olivia said when he was close enough to reach out and touch. She was tempted to do just that, but she managed to resist.

"Hi, yourself," he replied, glancing at his watch

as he snapped his cell back into the clip on his belt. She noticed that there was a Glock holstered next to it today.

"What are you doing here?" The third time they'd made love, she had instigated it, awakening him with a long, leisurely blow job. She flushed now, just thinking about it. "I thought you worked on the other side of town?"

He pushed his hands in his trouser pockets and smiled down at her. "Believe it or not, I've answered that very question about ten times already this morning. Up until now I've basically pleaded the fifth, but the truth is, I've been hanging around here, hoping to see you again before you left. You look great, by the way."

"Thank you. So do you." The longer she stared at him, the more she realized that truer words had never been spoken. Sans suspenders and a tie of any kind, the first few buttons of his pristine white dress shirt were unbuttoned and his cuffs were rolled back from his wrists, giving him a casual air that, together with his height, shouldn't have meshed so well with his authoritative carriage but somehow did. Spectacularly.

"Feel like taking a walk?"

"Sure, but do we have time?"

"I left word upstairs for someone to call me on my cell when the meeting wraps up, so we should be good. We won't go far."

"Okay, then let's go. I did mention that I needed coffee, didn't I?" Olivia asked as she walked through the exit door that he held open for her and was immediately hit with a wall of warm, humid air. "On second thought, I think I'd better have iced coffee," she said, pausing to shrug out of her blazer and drape it over her arm. It wasn't even noon yet and the temperature outside was already approaching the triple digits. "Is it always so hot here in the summertime?"

"Please. Like Missouri's so much better?" He took a hand from his pocket, waved it dismissively and then casually rested it on the small of her back. "I grew out of my childhood asthma thirty years ago. Haven't had an attack in at least that long. Then I made the mistake of visiting Missouri in the middle of July—the hottest month of the year."

"You had an asthma attack while you were in St. Louis?" Why was she just now hearing about this?

He chuckled at the concern on her face. "No, but I thought I was going to. Let's cross here at the light. There's a corner store just down the block." They joined a group of people crossing the street at the stoplight and hurried across the busy intersection. Back on the sidewalk, their pace slowed to a leisurely stroll again and the group quickly passed them by. "So, have you always lived in Missouri?"

"For the most part, yes. My father is originally from London, so I spent a lot of time there when I was growing up, too. But Missouri has always been home. What about you? Did you grow up here in Knoxville?"

He shook his head. "I was born in Los Angeles. My mother was sixteen and an honor-roll student when she got pregnant with me. She was black and poor, my father was white and from a wealthy family, and it was the seventies…" He shrugged as they approached a sidewalk food cart outside the store and joined the short line. "So you can probably guess how it all went down. She worked her ass off during the day and took college courses here and there at night, until she earned a nursing scholarship to the University of Tennessee and we moved here. I was ten at the time and I hated it here." It was their turn in line. He stepped up to the metal counter and looked at Olivia expectantly. "What would you like?"

"Just an iced coffee, please," Olivia said. "Black."

"Are you sure you don't want something to eat?"

"I'm sure."

Three minutes later, she was eyeing his hotdog greedily.

"Stop staring at my hotdog, because I'm not sharing," he warned as they settled at a tiny sidewalk table in front of the store and he passed her the coffee that she'd requested. "You should've gotten your own."

Thanks to her growling stomach, which hadn't started making a fuss until *after* she'd set eyes on his mouthwatering hotdog, she was well aware of her mistake. She set her coffee down and scooted her chair closer to his. "You know, your mom sounds pretty great. It's a shame she didn't teach you to share with your friends."

Cooper snorted. A few seconds later he picked up his cholesterol-packed, Chicago-style hotdog and made a fourth of it disappear inside of his mouth. "Yeah, well, we're not friends," he said after he swallowed. "And don't talk about my mama." Besides his foot-long hotdog, he had also ordered a basket of cheese fries and a large Dr. Pepper. He turned his attention to the fries next, picking up one long, golden, cheese-soaked fry and biting into it dramatically. "Aw, damn, that's good."

She caught herself watching the play of muscles in his squared jaw as he chewed, the coordinated bob of his Adam's apple when he swallowed, and forced herself to look away.

"You're staring."

But obviously not soon enough.

"Penny for your thoughts?"

She picked up her coffee cup and sipped carefully. "It's…nothing… It's just…you surprise me, that's all."

"Oh?" His thick, reddish-brown eyebrows shot up and his eyes swerved over to hers. "How so?"

"You just do, that's all. I can't explain it."

He took another bite of his hotdog, studying her curiously as he chewed. "Try."

"I wasn't expecting to be attracted to you," she said after a few seconds of silent contemplation. "But you've got this Barack Obama kind of thing happening that turns me on." She popped the top off her cup and reached for the sugar dispenser. "And it shouldn't, because—"

"Let me guess, he's not your type, either."

Aware that her face was burning, she stirred her coffee. "Right." She treated herself to a refreshing sip before daring to look at him again. "Sorry."

"No worries. Since we're being honest, can I tell you a little secret?"

"I'm all ears." Well, if not all, then at least half ears, she conceded as he slid his hotdog and fries across the tabletop to her and then handed her the plastic fork that he hadn't bothered with. She inhaled two cheese-soaked fries, sighed with contentment and then wiped her mouth with a paper napkin. Then she took a huge bite of the hotdog and blushed to the roots of her hair when she caught Cooper staring at her mouth as she chewed. "Stop that," she whispered when she could talk again.

"You're a very beautiful woman, Olivia Carrington. It's hard not to stare."

What could she say to that? She couldn't think of anything just then, so she blushed even harder and looked away from him. "Thank you."

"You're welcome." A beat passed before he spoke again. "I lied before about you not being my type. Women like you are precisely my type. I seem to always go for exactly what I don't need, where women are concerned." He held up one huge hand and ticked off his points, one by one. "Beauty, drama, games and hidden agendas. When my last relationship ended over a year ago, I swore off women with trust funds and decided that, if and when I was ready to date again, I'd find myself a potential soccer mom."

The coffee that Olivia had been swallowing almost went down the wrong way. She coughed her throat clear and slowly sucked in a deep breath. "I'm sorry, a potential soccer mom? What does that even mean?"

"I know, right?" Cooper drawled, rolling his eyes

to the sunny sky. "But I'm forty and my mother wants grandchildren before she's too old to enjoy them."

"You're an only child? Her only hope for grandchildren?"

His expression turned adorably sheepish. "I'm afraid so. Problem is, I haven't quite made up my mind about whether or not she'll ever actually *get* any grandchildren. What I do know is that, if I keep chasing self-absorbed, runway-model types—which clearly the hound in me is prone to do, or else we wouldn't be sitting here together right now—chances are she won't."

"Excuse me, but did you just insult me?"

He winked at her. "Sorry."

"Go to hell, Harry Potter. You could always marry a runway-model type who's ready to settle down and be*come* a soccer mom." He was certainly good-looking and successful enough to pull it off.

"Do you want children, Miss Carrington?"

That stopped her in her tracks. "Um…well…"

"My point exactly. Here," he said, taking pity on her and gently wiping her mouth with a paper napkin. "As far as what happened between us last night is concerned, it was good. Damn good. But it would never work between us, and the good thing is, we both know it. It was just one of those incredibly random and incredibly irresponsible things that happens every once in a great while. And to top it all off, it was also pretty damn incredible."

He caught the droll look that she shot him and chuckled. "Please, Miss Carrington. You aren't that good of an actress. You enjoyed yourself. You know it. I know it. The people in the room next to yours know it. And so do most of the night staff at the hotel, thanks to the three-o'clock-noise-complaint call that the front desk received while you were sitting on my face. That was all you, Olivia. Enjoying yourself."

Even as she racked her brain, trying to think of a strong rebuttal, Olivia's face burned. He was right. That particular time, she had come long and hard... and very, very loudly.

But still.

"I wasn't alone, Agent Talbot. If my memory serves me right—and you know it does—you were every bit as loud as I was." She thought about it for a second and then took another hefty bite of his hot-dog. "Well, maybe not *as* loud," she qualified after swallowing. "But still loud."

"There you go with that *Agent Talbot* shit again," he griped and she cracked up.

"Payback for calling me self-absorbed. Sorry."

"No, you're not, but are you sorry about last night?"

She didn't even have to think about it. "Not at all. I mean, you're right. What we did was very irresponsible, and now that I think about it, it was also probably against some vague rule in the FBI employee handbook. But we're both adults and there was some chemistry between us, so we acted on it and it was..." She trailed off, unsure where she was going or how she planned to get there.

"Amazing. Sort of like two ships passing in the night," Cooper finished for her. "A couple of months from now, we probably won't even remember each other's names, let alone the fact that we weren't each other's types."

"Probably not," she agreed and picked up her coffee again.

They were walking back to the courthouse complex when she remembered something else that she'd meant to ask him earlier. "Where's your mom right now? Does she still live in Knoxville, too?"

"Yeah, she does." He glanced at his watch. "This time of day, though, she's probably on shift at the hospital."

"Does she enjoy being a nurse?"

"I'm sure she did when she was a nurse. She's a doctor now. She's been the head of oncology over at Knoxville General for years. What about you? Any brothers or sisters?"

"Actually—"

His cell phone rang. "Excuse me," he cut in, sliding it out of the clip on his belt and shifting away from the sun's glare so that he could read the screen. "It's the district attorney's office. I'm guessing the meeting's over." Touching a button to the screen, he put the phone to his ear with one hand and held the other out to her. "Dr. Talbot." He listened for a moment. "Great, thanks. We'll be there in five." He ended the call and looked down at her. "Come on. I know a shortcut."

Olivia hurried to keep up with Cooper's long-legged strides, but in four-inch heels, her efforts ended up being more comical than functional. Twice, she almost skidded out into oncoming traffic when they turned a corner, and once, when her heel got stuck in a manhole cover, she almost dragged Cooper down to the ground with her when she stumbled. By the time they finally reached a side entrance to the courthouse and Cooper swiped his ID card to unlock the door there, they were both out of breath and he appeared to be slightly afraid for his life.

"Are you all right?"

"Are *you*?" he shot back, gaping at her as if he were surprised to find that she in fact was. Motioning for her to precede him, he stepped inside the building after her and leaned back against the door to finish catching his breath.

"I'm fine."

"Good. At least one of us is. They're waiting for you upstairs," he told her. "The elevators are down at the end of this hallway, to your right."

"You're not coming with me?"

"Nah, I'm parked on the lot right outside. This is where we say goodbye, Miss Carrington."

"Oh…okay. Well, thanks for the coffee, Agent Talbot."

He pushed his hands deep in his front pant pockets and studied her. "Don't mention it. See you around?"

"Two ships passing in the night, right?"

Smiling, he lifted a hand in farewell and backed out of the door. She was still standing there when it closed with a soft *swish* in his wake.

"So?"

"So, nothing. It was…nice."

"So nice that you've hardly said a word about it

since?" Elise queried with a wrinkle of concern in her otherwise smooth forehead. "Did something happen in Knoxville that you're not telling me about, Olivia?"

"Of course not."

"You two were careful, weren't you?"

Olivia's eyes bugged. "Yes! What kind of question is that?"

"A logical one, and if that's not what's bothering you, then what is? You haven't been yourself since you got back, which was almost two weeks ago. You're starting to worry me."

"I'm fine, Elise, I promise. I'm just busy with work. I've said it before and I'll say it again. If you don't get your ass back here soon, I'm going to fire you and hire an associate to take your place."

"You can't do that!"

"I love you and I love Broderick, but I've about had it with the two of you and your ongoing love affair with being in love. If I were you, I really wouldn't try me on this."

Speechless, Elise stared at the camera on her side of the globe incredulously. "My God," she whispered at the screen several seconds later. "What the hell happened to you in Knoxville?"

"Goodbye, Elise," Olivia replied as she reached for the disconnect button. "I'm working right now. I'll call you back later."

"Wait—"

She pressed the button.

"Was that Elise?" Olivia swiveled in her chair just in time to see Harriet cross the threshold into the study, carrying a stack of file folders in each hand. She brought them over to the antique wooden Duncan Phyfe conference table, where Olivia had set up shop that morning, and held them out to her sides, as if she were a human scale. "Which do you want first, the good news or the bad news?"

"Give me the good news."

She set the stack in her left hand down on the tabletop in front of Olivia. "These are all closed cases. As soon as you sign off on the invoices, I can process the electronic transfers and archive the files."

"That is good news," Olivia joked. "Got a pen?" Harriet reached up, slid an ink pen out of the nest of hair on her head and passed it to her. Taking it, Olivia flipped through the papers in each file, quickly checking figures, dates and times before signing the necessary documents and setting them aside. "There," she said, closing the last one, adding it to the stack and handing the whole thing back to Harriet. "Now for the bad news."

Harriet presented Olivia with the stack of folders in her right hand with a flourish. "These are the files that you requested from Dr. Batiste, Florida Memorial University's provost. They arrived this morning, along with your plane ticket, the keys to your new apartment and a copy of your new-hire personnel file."

Olivia peeked inside each of the file folders and nodded in approval. They were packed with, among other things, photocopies of receipts, signed documents and personnel information, and everything was neatly sorted and categorized. "Sweet. What about the paperwork for my new identity?"

"Eli should be sending it over by courier later today."

"Let me know the minute it arrives, will you, Harriet?"

"Sure thing. Can I get you anything else? Lunch, maybe? When was the last time you ate?"

"This morning," Olivia said, waving away Harriet's concern as she reached for her coffee mug and sipped. "I had eggs Benedict and toast. Go check the kitchen if you don't believe me," she shrieked when Harriet tsked suspiciously. "Really, Harriet? If you need proof, the dishes should still be in the dishwasher. Look, please don't start with me. It's bad enough that Elise is on the warpath—'why haven't you been eating? Why are you so tired? Why are you so cranky?' and on and on. Now you, too? And don't think that I don't know that you've been feeding Elise information about me behind my back, because I do," she charged, pointing an accusing finger at Harriet. The older woman had the grace to flush guiltily. "This new case couldn't have come at a better time, because I'm starting to feel like a prisoner in my own home."

"We're just worried about you—that's all."

Olivia's eyebrows disappeared into her hairline. "Why, Harriet? I missed a couple of meals a couple of days ago. So what? I'm tired, that's all. Plus you keep buying those fake eggs that come in a milk carton, which you know I hate, so I don't eat them. Oh, and also, I need a vacation—a real one. The next

time you report to Elise, tell her I said that, and also
tell her that you need a vacation too, because I don't
know about you, but I think we've both earned one.
Tell her that it's our turn now, that you would like
to have some time off to go visit your grandchildren
before they go away to college, and that maybe, just
maybe, I might want to take a soccer class. Okay?"

Harriet appeared to be shocked into silence.
"Uh…" The doorbell rang, saving her from having
to say anything else. "I'll get the door," she said and
hurried out of the room.

"Good idea."

After she was gone, Olivia snatched her glasses
off her face and dropped them onto the tabletop noisily. Okay, so maybe there was something to Elise's
working theory that she wasn't acting like herself.
Truthfully, she had been a little distracted lately and
possibly a little short-tempered. But if she wasn't eating properly or getting enough rest, it was only because she was too busy working herself to death to
get around to doing either. There were only so many
hours in the day, and unlike Elise, she wasn't really
in a position to wile any of them away, scuba diving
and lying on sandy beaches.

Promising herself that she would have her travel
agent set up something tropical and luxurious for her
as soon as she returned home from working her next
case, Olivia scrubbed a hand across her face, took a
deep breath and put her glasses back on.

In the meantime, she thought as she took a folder
from the stack on the table and opened it, *working
undercover on a co-ed college campus for the next*

couple of weeks might not be the worst assignment in the world, after all. A few days from now, she'd be flying to Florida and filling a job vacancy in the secretarial pool of the university's finance department. Officially her job was to investigate the as yet unsolved theft of millions of dollars in university endowment funds, but unofficially she planned to enjoy the hell out of Miami Gardens, every spare minute that she got while she was there.

In keeping with the rank and pay scale of her new job, Dr. Batiste was putting her up in a small, one-bedroom garden apartment that was within walking distance of the campus. And as if walking to work every day wasn't going to be enough of a lifestyle adjustment, she'd also have to do without her designer clothes for the next little while. But even the obvious drawbacks, of which there were many, couldn't overshadow the fact that the beach was nearby and the ocean nearer still.

If her brief romp in Knoxville had taught her anything, it was that she was sorely overdue for more of them. All work and hardly any play apparently made Olivia Carrington a very cranky girl.

Chapter 11

Already loaded down with his attaché case and the carryall that he'd taken on the plane with him, Cooper grabbed the handle of his suitcase as soon as it reached him on the luggage conveyor belt and emerged from the crowd of weary travelers who were gathered there. He set his suitcase down on its casters and navigated through the airport terminal, avoiding clusters of emotional families, restless children and departing soldiers as he made his way to the nearest exit with an ease born from years of practice.

Because he'd never been able to stomach airplane food, he was starving, so he stopped at a folding table that was set up along the wall in the concourse and let himself be charmed by three excited Summer Scout girls into buying a box of peanut-butter-sandwich cookies to keep him company during his drive home.

He tore into the box as he walked and was halfway through the first sleeve of cookies by the time he reached the last gate standing between him and freedom. A plane was in the process of disembarking when he cut through the gate area, so he used the time that it took to step aside and allow a throng of passengers to file past him to finish off the first sleeve and start in on the second. A profiler by nature, he watched the people around him curiously, his eyes randomly darting from face to face as he chewed and analyzed.

The first time they landed on Olivia Carrington's profile, they bounced on to the next one without registering. She'd been on his mind for days now, consuming his thoughts during the day and haunting him between the sheets at night, playing the kinds of tricks with his eyesight that had him randomly approaching strange women, mistaking them for her, and then apologizing profusely when he realized his error. He'd done that three times now—thought he had spotted her in a crowd and made a complete ass of himself, and he wasn't in a hurry to repeat the experience anytime soon.

The second time his gaze landed on her profile, he lingered, taking her in by degrees. He stared at her as if transfixed, suddenly remembering all sorts of odd little details about their lovemaking. Like the fact that her clitoris was unusually plump when she was aroused. Like the fact that she liked the juicy little morsel sucked the same way that she liked her nipples sucked, which also happened to be the same way that she kissed—with loose, lavish swipes of her tongue and plenty of greedy suction. It was also the same way that she had sucked his cock, he recalled, just as an image of her lips wrapped around his length flashed before his eyes.

His cock stirred and Cooper blinked to clear his thoughts. *Focus, Cooper*, he told himself and was almost successful at taking his own advice.

Then he realized that he was no longer staring at her profile because sometime during his trip down memory lane, she had turned her head and caught him in the act, and had apparently decided to return the favor.

His feet were moving in her direction long before his brain had cleared enough to give the command. She switched off the mini-TV that was attached to her chair and rose to meet him when he walked up. "Hey."

"Cooper! What are you doing here?"

"I live here." It was early, barely 6:00 a.m. In deference to the early hour, she wasn't wearing a drop of makeup and her hair was pulled up into a giant Afro-puff at the top of her head. Thin tendrils of curly hair framed her oval-shaped face, and tiny freckles dotted the bridge of her caramel-brown nose. How had he missed those before? "I could ask you the same thing. What are you doing here?" He noticed that her eyelashes were the same color as her tawny-brown hair and they were almost translucent because of it, and then it occurred to him that he'd missed her.

"Just passing through on my way home. I'm about

five minutes into what started out as a two-hour lay-over, but thanks to unexpected flight delays, is apparently now going to be a four-hour layover," she explained, waving a hand wearily to indicate the other people milling around them in the gate area. Then she waved it in the direction of his suitcase. "What about you? What's your story? Are you coming or going?"

"Coming. I just got in from Portland a few minutes ago." He'd been there for the past three days, facilitating a criminal profiling workshop by day and meeting with the subject of a true-crime novel that he'd recently been contracted to write by night. Part of his time there had been spent teaching law enforcement professionals about the nuances of profiling criminals, and ironically enough the other part had been spent in the region's super-max prison, huddling over notes, crime scene photos and trial transcripts with a death-row inmate who could've written the textbook on serial killing. Sleeping or, for that matter, eating between the two extremes was damn near impossible. He was wide awake now, though.

Dressed as she was, in ankle-length skinny jeans that fit like a second skin and a flowing, sleeveless white top, Olivia Carrington was a breath of the sexiest fresh air that he'd ever had the pleasure of inhaling. He reached up and scratched a spot at the back of his head, thinking. "Four hours, huh?" The whatever-will-I-do-with-myself? face that she made was so cute, so appealing that he suddenly had a brilliant idea. "Why don't you come and hang out with me while you wait?"

"With you?" She looked skeptical as she glanced at the delicate gold watch on her wrist, and his cock stirred again. "I don't know, Coop…"

"I promise to have you back in time for your flight," he lied with a straight face. She still didn't look convinced, so he held up a hand and arranged his fingers accordingly. "Scout's honor."

"Where would we go, back to your office?" She looked amused by the prospect but quickly sobered when he didn't return her smile. It took her a second, but he saw in the slant of her gaze the exact moment that she started to get a clue.

"I'm actually on my way home. My car is parked in the airport garage." He spied a designer carry-on sitting on the floor near her feet. Then he spied her white canvas sneakers and realized that she was wearing flat shoes. "Is this all the luggage you have?"

"Um…yeah." She bent down and picked it up, slinging the strap over her shoulder and hefting its weight. "I sent everything else ahead of me yesterday." They stared at each other. "So…" She reached for the cookie box and he willingly handed it over. He watched her teeth sink into a cookie. "You got any food at your place?" she asked as she chewed.

He reached out to relieve her of her bag and she handed it over just as willingly. "Would you like to come and see for yourself?"

They talked about work during the twenty-minute car ride from the airport to the private, gated community that he called home. She told him about her work and the case that she'd just closed for the provost of FMU, about the month that she had ended up pretty much living in Miami Beach while she followed a complex and corrupt financial paper trail that had led to the arrest of at least two tenured professors, one high-ranking member of the alumni board of trustees and all but one member of the university's finance office staff. And he told her what it was like to sit just a few feet away from a convicted serial killer and listen to him recount his crimes, in great detail and with little remorse, and about how difficult it was to eat or sleep afterward.

After they passed a satellite campus for the University of Knoxville and she commented on the colorful landscaping, they began trading college war stories and he pretended to be shocked all over again to learn that she'd majored in Chemistry, of all things, after all of the crap that she had given him about being a nerd. The first time that he'd read that about her, which was actually a little over a month ago, when the results of her squeaky-clean background check had come back, the discovery really had shocked him. Possibly later he would think about it again and it would floor him then, too. But in the here and now, he was so distracted by the mesmerizing scent wafting off her silky-looking skin that he could hardly think straight.

Shortly after they arrived, he sent her off on a self-guided tour of his house, while he called in an order for enough breakfast food to feed a football team, shuffled through his unopened mail and set a chilled, newly opened bottle of champagne on the counter to breathe. When the unmistakable sound of liquid filling a glass reached her ears, she cut her exploration of the outdoor Jacuzzi deck short just long enough to come inside and claim the frothy mimosa that he poured for her, and then she was off again, seemingly content to wander around in his personal space, barefoot and completely oblivious to the spell that she was casting on his cock.

In addition to four bedrooms, the kitchen and the great room, there was a den, a home gym and a private lap pool. The split-level floor plan was open and airy, enabling him to stand at the granite breakfast counter in the kitchen and track her progress with his eyes as he sipped his wine and leaned. As near as he could tell, she had seen every room in the place, a few of them twice, but she hadn't yet wandered into the first-floor master-bedroom suite. He wondered if she was purposely avoiding it and was just about to ask her when the doorbell rang. Seeing that she was headed in that direction now, he traded the delivery man a couple of folded bills for the bags in his hands and pushed the door closed in the man's face as soon as the exchange was done.

Five minutes passed, and then ten, while he set out two place settings, refilled his mimosa, dimmed the lights and put on his favorite CD—*Beethoven's Greatest Hits.*

"Liv?" he called out at the fifteen-minute mark. "Babe, breakfast is here. Come and eat something."

"In here!" she called back and, like a hunting beagle, his cock sprang to attention and led the way down the hallway.

Halfway there, the sound of the shower running

clashed with the music streaming through the house's built-in surround-sound system, and something like a growl rumbled in Cooper's throat. Shedding his clothes as he walked, he was completely naked when he deposited his watch, glasses and champagne glass on the armoire just inside the bedroom doorway and padded into the adjoining bathroom with his throbbing shaft in his fist and a Magnum condom packet sticking out from between his gritted teeth.

"Bend over," he said, stepping inside of the steam-filled walk-in shower and closing the glass door behind him. She had activated all of the jets, raining water down on her from all sides and from a variety of different angles. He joined her in the midst of it, his hands riding her butt cheeks as she swept her wet hair from one shoulder to the other and slowly bent over. By the time she had completely turned her butt cheeks up to the spray, he was on his knees on the tile floor behind her, ready to bury his face in the sensual divide between them. Appreciating her obvious enthusiasm, he spit out the condom packet and dragged the tip of his tongue back and forth across her flesh, teasing her until she screamed that was she coming.

Then he sucked her dangling clitoris deep into his mouth from behind and underneath, spread his thighs wide and forced her to watch him pleasure himself while he pleasured her.

Olivia's mind was officially blown.

Over a month had passed since they had last slept together, and if it was good the first time, then it was even better now. She hadn't realized just how much she'd been craving Cooper's fullness inside of her, his weight on top of her, until the moment that she was pinned underneath him in the middle of his king-size bed, writhing helplessly as he held her trembling legs aloft and drove his thick shaft into her over and over again. The bed alternated between thumping against the floor and the wall, and the sounds coming out of her mouth could've been a foreign language. She couldn't control the drama playing out on her face any more than she could control the ripples of sensation that his powerful strokes set off inside of her. Her nipples were tight, her throat was raw and every cell in her body begged for release.

He was a stunning lover. Unrestrained and instinctively responsive. So damn good that the erratic and unpredictable rhythm of his strokes was dizzying, the angle and depth electrifying. Wherever his mouth happened to land—on her breasts, the small of her back, the soles of her feet, between her thighs—it was undisciplined and greedy, wanton. The faces he made were raw and unflattering, and the sounds shooting out of his mouth hit the air like canon blasts. He did what felt good, when it felt good, and in the process made her come harder than she'd ever come before in her life.

Ever.

Physically spent and struggling to catch her breath, Olivia collapsed face-first onto the twisted landscape of bed covers and groaned with contentment. One of her arms rolled off the edge of the mattress and dangled over the side limply, and her eyes drifted closed. "Okay… I just need to know one thing."

"What's that?" He was breathing just as hard as she was.

"How in the *hell* are you so good?"

From somewhere behind her, Cooper chuckled wickedly. "I'm going to ignore the negative implications about nerds that's behind that statement and take it as a compliment, anyway. Would you believe that I was inspired?" he asked, first pressing a soft kiss to each of her butt cheeks and then kissing his way up the middle of her back. Understanding that it was a rhetorical question, Olivia lay still and quiet, enjoying the sensual treat. He lingered at the nape of her neck, tonguing the sensitive skin there leisurely before moving away again. She missed his warmth as soon as it was gone. "I think you missed your flight."

She caught herself drooling and shook herself awake. "I'll call the airport and reschedule for a later one…as soon as my eyes uncross."

"Or you could just stay here tonight and catch a flight home in the morning," Cooper suggested, as if it were the most natural thing in the world for her to stay the night at his house.

Olivia's head popped up from the mattress. "Is it safe for me to stay here?"

"I'm not sure I understand the question." She didn't have to look at him to know that he was frowning.

"Cooper, I saw the swamp that you keep out on the sun porch," she accused around a teasing laugh. Rolling over onto her back, she propped herself up on her elbows, found his heavy-lidded gaze and stretched a leg out to playfully nudge his thigh with her toes. He was sprawled out at the foot of the bed. "There are like thirty frogs out there—"

"Two," Cooper corrected. "And their names are Caesar and Othello."

"Seven icky lizards—"

"Only two and they're chameleons, Liv. Not lizards—*chameleons*. Their names are—"

"So many turtles that I tried to count them and kept losing count—"

"Antony and Cleopatra," he finished dryly. "And there are only three turtles out there, which I'm sure you already know."

She cocked a brow. "Oh, really? And what are their names?"

"Snap, Crackle and Pop," he said quietly, and Olivia promptly threw her head back and roared with laughter. A full minute passed before she was capable of speaking coherently.

"Are you kidding me?" Secretly she thought it was adorable, but she'd cut her tongue out before she ever admitted as much. His pets, if they could be considered that, were obviously well cared for, and the faint blush on his face told her that they were his babies. "It's like Hogwarts up in here!"

"Okay, so I'm a nerd. I'm not ashamed of it." He reached out and toyed with the tips of her toes, eventually looking up from his play and locking eyes with her. "Stay."

"Is there a snake out there in that aquarium some-

where? Because if there is, that's a deal-breaker."
The expression on his face was unreadable when he
shook his head. "Then, okay. I'll stay, but you have
to promise me that you'll get me to the airport as
early as possible."

"I'll drop you off on my way to work."

"Okay."

"Okay," he said, rolling off the bed and padding
out of the bedroom butt naked. "Let's go eat. I'm
starving."

She scrambled off the bed and followed him.

Chapter 12

Her layover in Knoxville lasted for four charming days and three passionate nights, during which time she and Cooper toured the city and surrounding countryside extensively, and made love in so many different positions and in so many different places that she'd lost count.

Harriet's face was the first thing that Olivia saw when she walked through the front door of her house on day four and set her carryall and small suitcase down at her feet in the foyer. Surprised, she stopped short and did a double take. "Oh my God, Harriet!" she shrieked, clutching her chest where her heart was pounding inside of it. "You scared me to death!"

"Sorry," Harriet said, sounding anything but. "You looked like you were in your own little world."

"I guess I was." She'd been thinking about the kiss that Cooper had laid on her at the airport. "What are you doing here? Is everything all right?" It was Sunday afternoon and Harriet rarely worked weekends, and never in a tracksuit and sneakers, with a moon-shaped Afro framing her round pecan-brown face and neon-pink earbuds sticking out of her ears. "Did something happen?"

"Nope," Harriet chirped, switching off the digital music player that was clipped to her waistband and removing one of the earbuds. "I was just finishing up some paperwork. So…" Looking pleased with herself, she leaned a hip against the centerpiece of the foyer—a round, French baroque-style marble pedestal table that Yolanda Carrington had bought at an estate auction and imported from the south of France—and folded her arms underneath her breasts. "Did you enjoy your two-hour layover in Knoxville?"

Olivia looked up from the stack of mail that she'd just picked up and started flipping through, meeting Harriet's knowing gaze and flushing to the roots of her hair. "Harriet, please don't start. As usual, you're imagining things."

"Oh, Olivia, please. You walked through that door a few seconds ago, humming, with a giant feather hanging out of the side of your mouth," Harriet said, giggling like a schoolgirl. "Been a long time since I've seen you do that. He must be fine."

Refusing to be baited, Olivia rolled her eyes to the ceiling and then took them back to the mail. "As a matter of fact, he is fine, but Cooper and I are just friends, so let's not get carried away."

"Oh, *Cooper*, is it? Well, that's certainly a name." Seemingly speechless, she stared at Olivia for several seconds as her face slowly creased into a wide smile. "Well, I'll be damned," she finally said. "You didn't have to go all the way to Knoxville just to fall in love, honey. You could've done that right here in Missouri."

"Really, Harriet?" Olivia cried, tossing the mail back down on the tabletop and throwing up her hands in disbelief. "This is why I never tell you anything, because you always take everything and run away with it. Before you know it, something as simple as the fact that Cooper and I are *just friends*, who happen to enjoy each other's company, gets blown way out of proportion. Like now, actually. That's exactly what's happening now, so just stop it, okay?"

"Uh-huh," Harriet said and then grunted.

"And another thing, Harriet. For your information, there are still some women left who aren't interested in marriage, kids and a white picket fence, and as you very well know, I happen to be one of them. So to answer your questions, *yes*, I did enjoy my layover in Knoxville, very much so, and *yes*, Cooper is handsome. If you need a visual, think Barack Obama meets a younger Tom Selleck. But none of that even matters, because that's all that it was—a layover—and layovers, if you recall, are by their very nature usually very brief in duration. We're just friends. Period. Now, can we please be done with this topic?"

"Sure we can, but what about the other thing that I mentioned?"

"Which was?"

"The thing about you going all the way to Knoxville and falling in love."

Olivia thought about the question for a second. That was about as long as it took for her false bravado to crumble and her heart to pop back out on her sleeve. "Dammit, Harriet." She stamped her foot and whined, sounding pitiful even to her own ears. "I don't know." What was she trying to say? "I mean, I'm not…" What *could* she say? "Okay, look…here's the thing…there is a strong possibil—"

"I knew it!"

Olivia put up a hand. "I haven't finished yet, Harriet."

"Well, spit it out!"

"All right! All right!" Olivia snarled, feeling cornered. "Probably. That's all I'm prepared to say right now. Okay, Harriet? *Probably*."

"Okay. Probably," Harriet repeated, as if testing the word out on her tongue. "Probably. We can work with probably."

"We're going to have to work with probably, Harriet, and listen to me—" She stopped short and waited for Harriet's eyes to meet hers. When they did, the hand that she'd put up slowly turned into a fist, with one finger pointing at Harriet. "Not a word of this to Elise."

"But—"

"*Harrriiieeet.*"

"You know that's not—"

"I mean it, Harriet. You're like a second mother to me and I love you dearly, but if you breathe a *word* of this to Elise, I'll never trust you again."

Harriet sighed long and hard. "Okay."

"Okay? It's in the vault?"

"Okay," she said again. "It's in the vault. I won't say anything to Elise. It's not really my place, anyway, but I'm surprised that you're not going to tell her. You two are like two peas in a pod. What's going on?"

"Nothing's going on. It's just a fling, that's all. I don't want to make a big deal out of it. Now, can we please be done with this conversation?"

Harriet seemed to hesitate but she eventually nodded.

"Thank you." Relieved, Olivia snatched up her luggage and hurried toward the stairs.

Harriet has a point and you know it.

Shut up. Upstairs, she swung her bedroom door open and set her bags down inside the doorway, thinking, *Does she?*

You know she does.

Had she gone all the way to Knoxville to fall in love? *No.* But could she pinpoint the exact moment she realized that she was half in love with Cooper Talbot, anyway? Of course she could. Right down to the millisecond. But still. It wasn't like she was an expert in matters of the heart, so she wasn't in a great big hurry to share her suspicions with anyone else just yet. You know, in case it turned out that her emotional compass was in such a state of disuse that it was simply way off base here. Because, really, stranger things had been known to happen.

Much stranger things.

They hadn't spoken in ten days, not since the morning that he'd kissed her at the gate, she had thanked him for his hospitality and they'd parted ways—him heading to work for the first time in four days and her boarding a flight back to St. Louis, Missouri. He had asked her if it would be okay if he called her some-time and she'd said yes; he'd invited her to call him sometime, too, and she'd said that she would. But ten days had passed now and so far neither of them had bothered to pick up the phone.

Cooper wasn't sure how he felt about that, nor was he crystal clear on why it even mattered, but somehow it did.

You could always call her.

Tempted to do just that, he picked up his cell from his desktop and hefted its weight in the palm of his hand. Then a second later he set it down again. *Remember the agreement, Talbot*, he reminded himself. *Two ships passing in the night.*

His intercom buzzed, breaking into his thoughts. "Excuse me, sir?"

"Yes, Amelia?"

"I have Rick Rhinehart on line one for you."

Cooper glanced at his watch and sighed. If his frat-brother, who just happened to be an assistant district attorney, was calling him on what was usu-ally a busy court day, at almost three o'clock in the afternoon, whatever it was that he wanted couldn't be good. He reached for the telephone on his desk-top, pressed the button for line two and snatched up the receiver. "Talbot."

"Your suspect is ready to talk deals," Rhinehart said straight out of the gate.

"In exchange for?"

"Information about the recent string of bank heists in the Midwest. I know you've had some input on the case, so I thought you might be interested in sitting in on the interview. Plus Cheryl told me to invite you over to the house for dinner next weekend," he said, referring to his wife. "Be forewarned, though. Her mother and sister will be here from Houston."

Cooper froze. "Which sister?"

"The ugly one," Rhinehart deadpanned. "I guess you want me to tell her that you'll be out of town… *again*?"

"What else are frat brothers for, mate?" Cooper queried, chuckling. "Omega Psi Phi 'til the day we die, right?"

"Whatever. You're not the one who has to listen to her fussing because you keep dodging her attempts to hook you up with your future-baby's mother."

"The woman is way out of line," Cooper decided, shaking his head sadly. He and Rhinehart had been good friends since their high school robotics-club days—good enough friends that they had both chosen Morehouse for their undergraduate studies and pledged together their freshman year. After graduation they had both been accepted into Columbia and, as the years passed and life happened, they'd grown even closer. Cooper was the best man at Rick's wedding over a year ago and he supposed that, if he had a best friend, Rick was the closest thing to it. Still, though. He loved Cheryl like a sister, but she had to be stopped.

"Exactly," Rhinehart readily agreed, laughing, too. "But she might be persuaded to chill the hell out with all the matchmaking schemes if she were to, say, find out that you slept with her mother."

Cooper's laughter died an instant death. "You wouldn't."

"Hey, don't get me wrong, bruh. Cheryl's mom is fifty and fine as hell, so I can't say that I blame you for tightening her up a little bit, especially since she was the one doing all the pursuing. But if you don't accept at least one of my wife's dinner invitations over the next couple of months, it might just have to slip out...to save my own ass, of course."

"Of course," Cooper drawled. "Your pussy-whipped ass."

They both cracked up.

"Tell you what," Cooper continued after their laughter had tapered off. "Tell Cheryl to cut a brotha some slack for the time being and we'll set something up next month. Definitely by the end of the summer." He was thinking of plausible excuses with which to lure Olivia back to Knoxville when he said, "And I might just bring my own date. How about that?"

"That might just buy us some time," Rhinehart mused, sounding thoughtful. "So, who is she and exactly how fine is she? I have to live vicariously through you these days."

"She is none of your business. You talk too damn much."

"Oh, it's like that?"

"Now you know a gentleman never kisses and tells."

"Whatever, dude. Are sitting in on this clown's interview or what?"

"You know I am," Cooper said, swiveling around in his chair and reaching for his suit jacket. He tucked his cell between his head and shoulder, and shrugged into it as he got to his feet. "What time?"

"Four o'clock, over at the lockup, so haul ass. Sixth floor. Let's go get some beer and wings afterward."

"Hooters," they both said at the same time.

"You bet. See you in a few," Cooper agreed.

"Cool, but listen, I can't stay out too late. You know how Cheryl—"

Cooper hung up.

The federal lockup was a thirty-minute drive away. Cooper had driven his Porsche to work today, so he made it in twenty. He parked in the employee lot and entered the facility through the employee entrance, flashing his badge at the entry checkpoint and then signing the departmental visitor's log before being buzzed through a series of steel doors that led to an interior corridor. There he took the elevator up to the sixth floor and made his way to the guard station. Rhinehart and one of his associates, along with the suspect's public defender, were already standing there when he walked up. After greetings were exchanged, the group was led to the interview room that Malcolm Johnson had been placed in for the meeting.

Cooper hung back for most of it. His agents were responsible for taking Johnson into custody, so he was already familiar with Johnson's charges, which included multiple counts of human trafficking, child endangerment and kidnapping, among other things.

He didn't need a recount of the circumstances leading up to them, especially since, as it stood, they had enough evidence of Johnson's guilt to put the man behind bars for the rest of his natural life. Their case was pretty much airtight, and now that he'd been indicted and was fully aware of the predicament that he was in, Johnson was ready to make a deal in exchange for singing like a bird.

If Cooper had his way, the man would be singing from behind bars for many years to come, deal or no deal. But first things first.

Straightening from the corner that he'd been leaning in with his arms crossed, he rounded the table and set a digital recorder down on the table-top, in front of Johnson. Now that Rhinehart was done wheeling and dealing, Cooper was ready to get down to business. "What is your relationship with Shannon Bridgeway?"

"I know her from back in the day," Johnson said, and Cooper noticed that, with the promise of a deal on the table and with life in prison officially off the table, the man's demeanor was much less confrontational. "You want me to tell you all about her?"

Cooper pulled a chair away from the table and sat down. "You understand that this interview is being recorded?"

"Yes."

"And you've been read your rights, which you also understand?" Johnson nodded. "I need you to speak clearly for the camera," Cooper instructed, pointing to the video camera that was set up on a tripod in a corner of the room. "Yes or no?"

"Yes."

"You should also understand that, in the event that any charges—criminal or otherwise—arise as a result of this interview, you will be expected to cooperate with prosecution efforts, up to and including testifying on behalf of the prosecution. If at any time you change your testimony or decide not to cooperate, any deals that you have been or will be offered become null and void."

"Man, I get all that," Johnson sniped, trying to wave one of his shackled hands dismissively. Cooper cocked an amused brow at the attempt. "You want to know about Shannon or whatever she's calling herself these days, or not?"

"Yes, I do." He opened the file folder that he'd brought with him and took out Shannon Bridgeway's mug shot, sliding it across the table toward Johnson. "For the record, Mr. Johnson, is this the woman you're referring to as Shannon Bridgeway?"

Johnson studied the photo. "Yeah, that's her. I've been knowing her since we were kids in the group home together." He slid the mug shot back across the table, toward Cooper. "Where should I begin?"

"Let the record show that the defendant, Malcolm Johnson, has positively identified Karen Lewis, also known as Shannon Bridgeway, via her most recent mug shot, which will be cataloged as evidence," Cooper said, facing the camera. To Johnson, he said, "Why don't you start at the beginning?"

Two hours later Rhinehart caught up with Cooper as he was leaving the building. "Coop, wait up."

"Seems like you should have enough to at least

bring formal charges," Cooper speculated as they fell in step together, pushed through the exit doors and walked out into the employee parking lot. The change in temperature, from cool to hot and humid, was both immediate and extreme. Cooper reached up and loosened his tie to accommodate his suddenly dry throat. "She needs to be picked up before she absconds."

"Already on it," Rhinehart said. "I sent my associate back to the office to make contact with the Missouri field office and get the ball rolling. Johnson's cooperation with their case will help him on ours, but not very much, because if he's convicted, this'll be his third strike. And as such, I plan on throwing the book at him. Subtly of course," he added, seeming to realize that he'd spoken that last part aloud. "After all, I did promise the man a deal and I do intend to offer him one, but I never promised him that the deal would be especially generous. And speaking of generous, Missouri's prosecuting attorney has a reputation for not only having a prick, but also for being one. He's old-school, so be prepared for him to drag Johnson all the way to Missouri for an in-person deposition, when a video conference would work just as well. Your team has more rookie agents right now than most. Who have you got that's seasoned enough to escort him?"

"I'm not sure yet. Maybe I'll send Bearden and Bidwell again. They seem to work well together," Cooper said, thinking, *Who else?* He'd always avoided being a third wheel but this was one instance when he would happily make an exception.

"That's because they're screwing."

Cooper's eyes popped. "What?"

"You didn't know?" Rhinehart queried, chuckling at Cooper's cluelessness. "Man, what rock have you been hiding under?"

"The question is, how do *you* know?"

"I'm an assistant district attorney, man. It's my job to know things like this. Plus me and Bearden use the same barber."

"Wait a minute, you and I use the same barber, so why haven't I heard about this before now?"

Rhinehart looked at him like he was crazy. "Because you're the boss. Put yourself in Bearden's place. Would *you* tell you something like that? Now," he said, before Cooper could offer a response. "In light of the fact that this next case will ultimately be another notch on my impressive professional belt, I think a beer-and-hot-wings celebration is in order. What do you think?"

"I think I'm going to have to have a talk with Bearden and Bidwell."

"Uh-huh. Remember that the next time you start wondering why no one ever tells you anything. And I meant about the beer and wings, Coop." They looked at each other.

"Hooters," they said at the same time and made a beeline for Cooper's Porsche.

Chapter 13

Cooper texted Olivia as soon as his plane landed in Missouri.

Just got here. Pick me up at my hotel?

He had advised her of his pending arrival as soon as Amelia had finalized his travel itinerary a week ago, telling her only that he was tagging along with some other agents on an escort trip for an unrelated case when she'd questioned his reason for returning to Missouri so soon after his last visit, and then breathing a sigh of guilty relief when she accepted his explanation without pressing for more information. "That, and I'd like to see you again," he had admitted, too, because at least that was the truth.

She texted back a minute later.

Sure. Where are you staying?

They hadn't yet discussed that part of his plans but he did have some thoughts on the subject. With you?

She swung through the hotel lobby doors a half hour later, looking like a million sun-kissed bucks in a sleeveless red sundress that stopped just above her knees and matching stiletto sandals. A colorful woven clutch purse was tucked underneath one of her toned arms, and her signature Chanel sunglasses were dangling from the neckline of her dress by one temple. She saw him and stopped short, smiling from ear to ear. He came away from the wall near the elevators, where he'd been leaning, and closed the distance between them with long strides.

"Hi, beautiful," he murmured as he walked up to her.

She blushed and half of the blood in his body flooded his cock. "Hi."

When he was close enough to reach out and snatch her up in a two-handed grip, that's precisely what he did, cuffing her around the waist and hauling her up against him so quickly that she gasped both in surprise and just in time to make room for his tongue in her mouth. Her arms immediately wound around his neck and he groaned in gratitude, loving the feel of her soft breasts pressed against his chest and the scent of her skin in his nostrils, as her tongue lapped against his greedily. She caught his tongue and moaned as she sucked on it within the cave that their fused mouths created and he shuddered, withdrawing reluctantly as soon as she was gracious enough to relax her erotic suction.

"Mmm," she purred against his lips. "You must've missed me."

The tip of his tongue shot out and licked her luscious bottom lip. "I must have. Take me somewhere private so I can show you how much."

They only made it as far as the hotel's parking garage before Cooper had a bright idea that Olivia was completely down with. They tossed his suitcase in the trunk of her Cadillac and quickly hopped into the back seat together.

As soon as the doors were closed and they were hidden behind tinted windows, Cooper unfastened his pants and pushed them down around his ankles. He slipped his wallet out of his back pocket, found the condom tucked there and ripped the foil packet open with his teeth. After quickly sheathing himself, he reached for Olivia. "Oooh…you're so wet," he whispered as his fingers slipped into the silky folds between her thighs and began playing. Gasping, she settled on his lap, straddling him with her dress gathered around her waist and her bright red thong shifted to one side, revealing the plump lips of her glistening sex to his greedy eyes. He spied the tip of her engorged clitoris peeking out from between them and swore under his breath. Taking his rigid cock in hand, he spanked it once, twice, three times, to her audible delight, and then positioned himself at the entrance to her sex and slowly lowered her down onto his shaft.

They cried out simultaneously as his glans penetrated her slick, pulsing warmth for the first time, and then they both seemed to dissolve into a state of catatonic bliss as Olivia sank down fully onto his length with one deep thrust. Cooper felt himself stretching her tight walls wide, felt her walls contracting around him like a honey-drenched velvet fist, and went limp with pleasure.

Her eyes drifted closed as she planted her feet onto the seat at either side of his hips, braced her hands on his shoulders and began bouncing up and down on him. A second later, her head lolled to one side like she was high on a drug that took her straight to the moon, and her mouth dropped open. Even as his own face tensed and relaxed erratically, and his own breath lit the air like gunshots, Cooper watched the dramatic play of emotions as they crossed her face and listened keenly to the symphony of high notes curling out of her drooping mouth. His hands rode her jiggling butt cheeks lightly, possessively, allowing her full control over her ride and him just enough traction to pace his upward strokes.

He reached up and cupped Olivia's face, bringing her open mouth down to his and sinking his tongue deep and wide. Moaned out a song of worship the entire time that his tongue tangled with hers and his hands cupped her breasts through the material of her dress. She had the sweetest mouth that he'd ever tasted, the softest skin he'd ever had the pleasure of licking, the best sex he'd ever experienced. He couldn't seem to get enough of her.

He could feel her walls caressing every swollen

vein in his cock as he slid in and out of her heat, could see the evidence of her pleasure coating his shaft as she bounced. "Awww…you feel so damn good," he panted just as a sharp zing of pleasure thumped at the base of his spine, seizing every muscle in his legs and hollowing out his abdomen. "Oooh… I'm coming, Liv. I'm coming! Ah!" he shouted as his hips shot up off the seat and surged upward. His eyes rolled back in his head and his head lolled as, deep inside of her, he came violently.

In the middle of an orgasm herself, she continued to bounce up and down on him, torturing him and stroking him into a state of ecstatic frenzy at the same time. When he couldn't take any more, he lifted her off him and pressed his damp forehead into the valley between her breasts to catch his racing breath.

And to mentally kick himself.

Dammit, Talbot. You weren't supposed to fall for the woman. Two ships passing in the night, remember?

Four agents had escorted Malcolm Johnson from Knoxville to Missouri, but after his grand-jury testimony the next afternoon, only three agents went back with him. Cooper stayed behind in Missouri for the next three days and two nights.

The evening before he was scheduled to leave, Olivia took him to the historic Laclede's Landing District on the St. Louis riverfront, where there was a lively and eclectic strip of after-dark entertainment venues and access to a walking trail along the river's edge. They had before-dinner drinks in a dimly lit blues bar and then wandered into a karaoke bar for a dose of comedic hilarity before stumbling upon a tiny New Orleans–style supper club that was famous for its authentic Cajun cuisine, for a late dinner. Afterward they strolled along the lighted river walk companionably, watching the dark, murky water rush back and forth in comfortable silence until it was almost one o'clock in the morning and they were both stifling yawns.

"I've kept you out too late," Olivia said, giggling at his unsuccessful attempt to stifle yet another open-mouthed, audible yawn. "You have an early flight in the morning, which means you should be in bed right now." She moved closer to him and threaded her fingers through his. "Let's turn back."

"Soon," Cooper promised, using the leverage that their joined hands gave him to tug her along with him as he continued down the concrete path. She leaned into him as they walked and, after a few seconds, rested the side of her face against his arm companionably. His thumb stroked hers gently. "I'm scheduled to teach a profiling class at a legal conference later next month, in Indiana," he remarked casually. "I'll be there for five days. If I send you a plane ticket, will you meet me there?"

Speechless, Olivia thought about it for several long seconds, while her head secretly wrestled with her heart. Unless she was mistaken, and she really didn't think that she was, neither of them was interested in anything more than what they currently had. This fling that she was caught up in with Cooper was just that—a fling. They enjoyed each other's company, and God knew the sex was great, but at any given moment he was hundreds of miles away in Tennessee, where everything important in his life was. Meanwhile her life was here in Missouri. Add that to the fact that they couldn't be more opposite if they tried, and a relationship between them, especially a long-distance one, would never work. Still, his offer was very tempting.

"We could rent a car," Cooper murmured into the blaring silence between them. "Maybe get lost sightseeing. Make love all night and sleep in in the mornings." He brought their joined hands to his mouth and kissed the back of hers softly. "Catch a show or two and check out some of the local cuisine. What do you think?"

"I think that, if I keep seeing you, I'm going to gain a hundred pounds."

"Would that be such a bad thing?" he wondered. "If we kept seeing each other, I mean."

She couldn't look at him, couldn't hold his piercing gaze for longer than a few seconds at a time because it made her pulse quicken and her blood heat with awareness. She looked out at the water instead. "What happened to the *two ships passing in the night* theory?"

"Hmm…" Cooper breathed expansively. "I think it was shot to hell the moment that we stopped having just a fling and started doing something else." He stopped walking and waited for her eyes to meet his. When they finally flickered up, he searched them for several seconds and then asked, "Or is it just me?"

"No, it's not just you, but—"

"Is there someone else?"

"No, there isn't, but—"

"No buts," he cut in, squeezing her hand gently. "And there's also no pressure, Liv. Just something to think about, okay?"

A short time later, as if to ensure that she did just that, his lovemaking was intense and deliberate. Spread out on the mattress before him like a sumptuous meal, Olivia could do little to defend herself against his dizzying ministrations except lie there, quivering with pleasure, while he took his time feasting on her flesh as if she were both his first and his last meal.

Again and again his lips, teeth and tongue brought her to the brink of orgasm, only to retreat at the last crucial second, leaving her teary-eyed with longing and whimpering pitifully. Grasping desperately at his hips every time he shifted and the tip of his heavy, bobbing shaft glanced across the opening to her pulsing walls and then flitted away, every time he sucked one of her nipples deep inside of his mouth and lapped at it decadently. Every time he sucked at her engorged clitoris and then let it slip out of his mouth noisily, or bit into the flesh on her neck and shoulders or tickled her curled toes with the tip of his flickering tongue.

She was a sweaty, volcanic mess when her clitoris slipped out of his mouth one last time and he rose over her and braced himself on his palms on the mattress. Frantic for release, her legs were already bowed, her knees already practically meeting her ears when he loomed over her and offered her his still flickering tongue. She took it, sucking on it wildly, delighting in the taste of herself on his lips as she reached down between her thighs and soothed her jittery clitoris with a series of love taps.

"Aww, look at you," Cooper murmured into her mouth as his glans stretched her opening wide and dipped inside of her. "Is this what you want?" Her head snapped back on her neck like a piston and he chuckled wickedly. "*Ahhh*, so this *is* what you want. Here you go, baby." Inch by agonizing inch, he slowly filled her until he was buried inside of her balls-deep and she swore that she could feel him in her belly.

"*Mmm*, you feel so good, Olivia." She cried out when he began stroking her slowly and deeply, turning her inside out. "*Sooo...goooood...*" Every stroke elicited a cry, a shriek or a moan. "Aww, you make me feel so good." His lips found the shell of her ear. "I love the way you take this dick."

His mouth against her ear, the words that he murmured into it like a prayer tipped Olivia right over the edge of insanity, into a free fall of mind-bending pleasure. "Oh God, I'm coming!"

Together with the sharp staccato of his grunts and the steady thump of the bed underneath them, they created a symphony of musical erotic tension that ended with a gut-wrenching sob of gratitude as, once again, Cooper's magic shaft discovered her G-spot and completely annihilated it.

The car service that Cooper had ordered the night before arrived bright and early the next morning to pick him up and take him to the airport. Nerd that he was, his monogrammed suitcase was neatly packed and waiting by the front door, he was meticulously groomed and dressed in a navy pinstripe suit and polished wingtips, and his iPad was working overtime, toggling back and forth on command, between five different live news streams and a video conference with his assistant, when the doorbell rang.

Smiling at the strikingly sexy image that he made, Olivia tightened the belt of her pink silk robe and followed him as he strode out of the kitchen and down the main hallway to the door without once looking up from the device. The quiet authority in his voice when he spoke was as much of a turn-on as his confident gait and unflappable demeanor, especially since she'd been up close and personal with the other side of him—the greedy, savage, carnal side of him. Knowing that it was hiding inside of him and what it was capable of, that she was privy to the secret to unlocking it, made her heavy and wet between her thighs.

She hung back while he opened the door and spoke to the driver. Then, wild-haired and droopy-eyed from a night spent rolling around with that very side of him and loving every second of it, she moved into the circle of his arms when he turned and opened them to her, and went up on the tips of her toes for his kiss.

"Call you later?" Cooper asked after several seconds, when they finally pulled apart.

"You'd better," Olivia replied and sent him off with one last kiss.

Chapter 14

Still half asleep, Olivia watched the car until it was out of sight and then closed the door, leaning back against it heavily. She'd never been a morning person, particularly when she'd had less than two hours of sleep the night before. Cooper, on the other hand, had rolled out of bed at precisely 6:30 a.m., whistling a catchy tune and threatening to scramble his own eggs if she refused to do it for him. Afraid for the shelf life of her Williams-Sonoma stainless steel cookware, she had reluctantly rolled over and eventually mustered up the energy to climb out from underneath the covers, but it definitely hadn't been easy.

Now that he was gone, she planned to make up for lost time by spending the rest of the morning and half of the afternoon in bed. Thankfully Harriet wasn't due to return from her spur-of-the-moment mini-vacation until tomorrow morning, and she wasn't due to video conference with Elise until later in the day, so there was nothing stopping her from doing just that.

She smelled him on her pillow, on her sheets, as soon as she crawled back into bed and slid down into a cave of rumpled covers. *Sandalwood*, she mused, sliding the pillow underneath her head and pressing the side of her face into its down-filled fluffiness to inhale deeply. *And citrus. There are definitely hints of citrus*, she recalled as her eyes drifted closed and her breathing evened out.

Sleep had just wrapped its arms around Olivia when her eyes suddenly popped open and her head shot up from the pillow. Something was off, she thought as she quickly scanned her bedroom. At first glance everything appeared to be in its place, but something was still off. As sleepy as she was, it took her a while to figure out exactly what that something was, but eventually it hit her.

Cooper's beat-up leather messenger bag, the one that he said he'd been carrying since his undergrad days, the one that his absentee father had given him when he had popped up out of the blue at Cooper's high school graduation, was still lying on its side, where he'd left it, on the upholstered bench at the foot of her bed. Meanwhile he was probably halfway to the airport, if not already there, by now.

Olivia rolled across the mattress and grabbed her cell phone from the nightstand. Cooper's cell number was programmed into her cell's speed dial, so she touched a finger to a number on the keypad and put the phone to her ear. "Great," she drawled when his voice mail switched on a few seconds later. She tried to call him two more times, with no success and then, thinking that she could probably find a number for his assistant, who might be able to reach him through other channels, she threw the covers back, crawled across the mattress and picked up the bag. The last thing she was expecting was for the bag to fall open, spilling most of the files and loose papers inside of it across the bench and onto the floor beyond it.

"Dammit!" she hissed, hopping off the bed and hurrying around it. At this rate she'd never get back to sleep. Dropping to her knees on the floor on the other side of the bench, she started gathering up the files and stray papers, stacking each handful neatly before shoving it back inside of the bag. She was three or four handfuls in when her own name jumped out at her from the sheet in her hand. Curious now, she plopped down on the floor and started reading.

Thanks to her clumsiness, Cooper's papers were hopelessly out of order, but she managed to make enough sense of them to find the rest of the file that he had compiled on her, as well as most of the contents in the surprisingly thick one that he had clearly been compiling on Shannon for some time.

Wide awake now, Olivia took the papers and the bag that they had fallen out of with her downstairs to the kitchen. There she switched on the coffee maker and settled on a stool at the center island to read while she waited for the handy little machine to finish doing its job.

And for Cooper to realize his mistake.

To his credit, it only took him a half hour to miss his favorite accessory and send a text her way.

Sorry to wake you, Liv, but did I leave my messenger bag there by any chance?

She sipped her second cup of coffee and considered how best to respond. In the end she decided that straight to the point was best. Yes, she texted back.

My flight was delayed for routine maintenance and refueling, so I have a little time. Okay if I come back and get it?

Yes, I think that would be best.

At least that way, if she suddenly had the urge to throw something, Cooper's head would be a realistic target.

She texted one last message.

See you in a bit.

Then she set her cell down on the granite countertop. A moment later she shifted on the stool and her nostrils were instantly filled with Cooper's scent. It was wafting off her skin, she realized, and she was suddenly struck with the urge to shower.

Just a few minutes ago, she had considered his scent an aphrodisiac. But now that she knew that he'd been lying to her all this time and playing her for a fool—spying on her and sleeping with her while he was doing it—well, that…that certainly changed things, didn't it? Now the scent of him on her skin just made her feel queasy.

She took the time to read one last incoming text, this one from Eli, and then, feeling like an even bigger fool, she headed for the shower.

Cooper noticed the change in Olivia as soon as she opened the door and their eyes met across the threshold. Unsure of exactly what to make of it, he stepped into the foyer cautiously and searched her eyes as he closed the door at his back. "I thought you'd still be asleep," he said, smiling. It was still early. He'd been expecting—no, hoping—to find her still in her robe, still half asleep and grumpy, and still naked and warm from the bed covers. Hoping to kiss her until she was breathless and then talk her into a quickie against the foyer wall. But she dodged his hands when he reached for her the first time and sidestepped them altogether the second time. Confused, he dropped his hands and his eyebrows shot up. "Baby…what…?" He looked for her eyes, but couldn't find them, and took a breath for patience. "What's happening between us right now, Olivia?"

Avoiding his eyes, Olivia sprang into action like she'd just been plugged into an electrical socket, hurrying across the foyer in her bare feet to the marble table and scooping up his bag. "Um…here's your bag," she said, bringing it over to him and pushing it into his waiting hands. Her hands were trembling almost as badly as her voice. "It…um…it actually f-fell open when I t-tried to pick it up and some of the papers ins-side fell out. I s-saw my name on some of them, s-so I read them."

He heard the thickness in her voice and saw the tears standing in her eyes, and cursed under his breath. He reached for her again but once again she eluded his grasp, which only frustrated him even more. "Sweetheart, please stop running from me and let me touch you."

"Oh, trust me, Agent Talbot. Putting your hands on me right now is not a very good idea." She moved to the other side of the foyer and folded her arms underneath her breasts, staring at him mutinously.

"You're upset."

"Wouldn't you be if you discovered that the whole time that I was sleeping with you, I was investigating you behind your back because I thought you were a criminal?"

His eyes slid closed for the space of a second. "Look, I know how this looks…what you think you saw, but if you would just let me explain—"

"Explain what, Cooper? How you pretended not to know anything about me, to be so interested whenever I shared something with you about my childhood or my college days or my sister, and it was all stuff that you already knew? How you thought I was a criminal but you slept with me anyway? What exactly would you like to explain?" He opened his mouth to speak but her face lit up with a new thought before he could utter a single word. "Oh, I know. Why don't you explain to me why it never occurred to you to tell me that I had opened up my home to a dangerous criminal?"

"It's not what you think, Olivia."

"Oh, really? Then what is it? Because what I think is that you have got to be the best goddamn actor that I've ever seen. I mean—" she paused to chuckle incredulously "—you actually managed to get one over on me, and can I just say that, up until now, that hasn't been a very easy thing to do. But you…" She trailed off, pointing one stiff finger across the foyer at him and eyeing him with a twinkle of malicious admiration. "You're good—I'll give you that. It's just…just hard, you know? Admitting to myself that I—the notorious man slayer, Olivia Carrington—got played by none other than a Harry Potter impersonator, with great taste in clothes and a giant dick. My God, it was all an act, wasn't it, Cooper? You and your FBI agent buddies must've really gotten a good laugh at my expense."

"Olivia—"

She paced back and forth on her side of the foyer. "Did you tell them stories around the water-cooler about what I'm like in bed?"

"Olivia—"

"Answer me, Cooper! Is this, like, something that you do all the time? Do you go around routinely seducing the unsuspecting idiot women that you meet while you're working a case? Is it a game for you?"

"You know damn well that none of this is a game for me."

She waved away his words impatiently. "What else do you know about me that you haven't told me?"

Cooper searched his memory. "Baby… I don't

know…" At a loss for words, he shrugged helplessly and shook his head. "Nothing."

"Liar," she snapped. "There is a file in that bag with my name on it and my life story inside of it, Cooper. You're going to have to do better than that."

"I never finished reading the damn thing, if you want to know the truth."

"More lies."

"Look, can we please just sit down and talk about this?" He started around the table toward her and she took off, power walking in the opposite direction, only stopping the impromptu game of ring-around-the-rosy when he did. In new positions around the table now, they stared at each other warily across the width of it. "Olivia, this is ridiculous."

"No, what's ridiculous is the fact that I was actually going to pack my bags and meet you in Indiana next month," she said quietly, locking gazes with him and forcing him to watch a lone tear spill over and roll down her cheek. "I actually thought I was falling in love with you, Cooper. Can you believe that? I mean, isn't *that* ridiculous?"

"Listen to me, babe," he said calmly, even as the impact of what she'd just said threatened to buckle his knees. "I read enough to confirm that you weren't involved in any criminal activity. After that it was all about you and me, and what was happening between us. I didn't need to read any more, so I didn't."

"Should I sweep my house for bugs, too? What about my car? Did you tape us having sex?"

"The focus of my investigation has always been on Shannon Bridgeway, Olivia. Not you. Do you really think you need to go to those extremes? That I would do something like that to you?"

"Honestly, I don't know what to think anymore, Cooper. You've had plenty of opportunities to come clean to me about the background investigation in your bag, but you didn't. And you could've warned me weeks ago about Shannon, but you didn't. I had her sleeping right down the hallway from me and I gave her spare keys to my house. Anything could've happened."

"There was nothing in her adult profile to suggest that she was currently a threat to you or anyone else. By the time my suspect offered up what he knew about her, she wasn't staying here with you anymore, and you said yourself that the two of you had barely been in contact with one another. At that point, whatever I knew about her became need-to-know information, and I'm sorry, sweetheart, but you didn't really need to know."

"She's going to be indicted for taking part in the robbery at the bank that she managed," Olivia informed him curtly. "Did you know that? Wait, what am I saying? Of course you knew that because you know everything, don't you? I only just got a text bringing me up to speed a few minutes ago, so I'm the one who's late to the party."

"Yes, I knew." He'd found out just this morning, as a matter of fact. Less than an hour ago, via a text from Rhinehart. "Who told you? Did Bridgeway call you?"

"I'm a private investigator, Cooper. I have ways of finding out things, too. Maybe if I had used them,

I'd have known what you and Shannon were up to long before now."

"I suppose I deserved that."

"I slept with you. You didn't deserve that."

Another zinger. Saddened beyond words, he took a deep breath and let it out slowly. "I love you, Olivia," he eventually said and meant it. "I hope you believe that."

"Get out," she said, marching to the door. She threw it open and stood back with her arms folded underneath her breasts, waiting.

"Olivia—"

"Please just go."

Elise picked up after the first ring. As soon as the camera flickered on and came into focus, her smiling face filled the screen. "Sooo…how did it go?" she purred suggestively. "Did Mr. Goodbar leave you walking with a limp again?"

Off camera, Olivia was too busy mopping the tears from her face and struggling to control the lump in her throat to venture a reply. When she finally got herself together and turned the camera toward her, Elise took one look at her sister's face and scowled.

"Olivia, what's wrong? Did something happen?"

"Cooper and I broke up." She couldn't seem to stop her bottom lip from trembling.

"Oh my God. I'm so sorry! What happened?"

"Well," Olivia began, just before the floodgates burst open and the whole sordid tale rushed out. "Cooper…" she said with a sob. "He was spying on me…" More sobs. "And Shannon…she's a criminal…"

"What…are you *crying*?" Olivia hardly ever cried. "What in the world is going on there?"

"Everything is a mess…" More tears spilled over and out, until Olivia was sobbing uncontrollably and Elise could do nothing but watch helplessly.

Chapter 15

The next four weeks passed in a blur of activity for Cooper, but for once he wasn't complaining about the extra work that having a team mostly made up of rookies added to his plate. The busier he was, the less time he had to think about Olivia Carrington and the way things had ended between them. She wasn't taking his calls, nor had she responded to any of the text messages that he'd sent her, and at this point he wasn't sure that she ever would. Her silence was as deafening as it was telling, and he had no choice but to accept what it meant.

It was over.

Which, as much as he thought of her and his body ached for her, was probably for the best anyway. They lived in two different states and led two different lives, and his was already jam-packed as it was, with responsibilities to his team and to his writing career, and with the ongoing speaking engagements that he could never seem to get out of. He spent half of his life on airplanes and the other half at his desk, only coming up for air from either extreme to find release when his cock would no longer be ignored and there was time enough in his schedule to accommodate its needs.

For about the space of a heartbeat, he'd been considering trying for something more than a fling with Olivia, but in hindsight he realized that it would've never worked. He'd taken more time off work over the past few months than he had in the entire time that he'd been with the agency, which should've been his first clue that he was trying to force something that just didn't fit. She had obviously figured that out before he had and done the smart thing by ending it the first chance she got.

Deep down, he knew she'd made the right decision.

But that didn't stop him from wanting her. From rolling over in the middle of the night, looking to bury his straining cock deep inside of her as he drifted off to sleep, and then waking up hours later with his stiff cock in his fist, a satisfied groan on his lips and his sheets damp. It didn't stop him from thinking about her constantly and kicking himself for not telling her the truth sooner, or from feeling like shit because he'd made her cry.

"Whatever it is can't be that bad. Penny for your thoughts?"

Cooper looked up from the scotch neat that he was nursing and gazed at the woman standing at the edge of his table. After a few seconds his face instinctively relaxed into a smile. He loved women, all women, and this one was exceptionally pretty, in an athletic, fitness guru sort of way. She ran early in the mornings. He knew because, for the past three mornings, he'd crawled out of bed at the crack of dawn to run with her. And she was a vegetarian, which for just as many evenings now had been a bone of good-natured contention between them during the daily meals that they had gotten into the habit of sharing.

"I'd rather hear yours," he said, rising from his seat and motioning for her to join him. Her name was Alexandra Mason, and she was also smart and funny and easy to talk to. "How was the movie?"

And tempting as hell, he thought as she slid into the chair across from him and folded her espresso-brown arms on the tabletop in front of her. She'd been promoted to Special Agent in Charge a little over a year ago and had come to the conference in Indiana as part of her on-the-job training, to co-facilitate a series of breakout sessions on cultural diversity in the workplace. They had met one afternoon when he had finished facilitating his own workshop a few minutes early and had sat in on the tail end of one of hers. She had come up to him afterward and struck up a conversation. That was on Monday, the first day of the conference. Today was Friday, the last day of it, and he was running out of excuses to avoid taking her to bed.

You could always just tell her the truth, the little angel on his right shoulder whispered in his ear. *That you're afraid you'll call out the wrong name.*

Shut up, the devil on his left shoulder shot back. *Why? It's the truth, isn't it?*

"It was even worse than you said it would be," Alexandra said, laughing. She and a group of other conference attendees had gone to the movies right after dinner, but since he had already seen the cinematic fiasco that they planned to see, he had begged off. "While everyone else was screaming, I was laughing hysterically. You should've come," she said, lowering her voice and leaning across the table toward him. "We could've sneaked up to the balcony and made out."

They had done that once, he recalled, and felt a stab of guilt. Kissed passionately and touched one another with intent, but he had come to his senses and pulled away before things had gone any further. She was attractive and any red-blooded, heterosexual man would be a fool not to take what she was offering, but she wasn't the woman he craved and he had grown accustomed to being able to look himself in the mirror every day. Taking advantage of women, no matter how much either of them stood to enjoy it, had never been his style. And of course there was also the very likely possibility that he actually would mess around and call out Olivia's name at the worst possible time.

"Now I'm really sorry I missed out," he joked. "Why don't I buy you a drink to make it up to you?"

"You're on. I'll have whatever you're having."

After their impromptu petting session the other

day, Cooper had avoided being alone with Alexandra whenever possible. But tonight, as they laughed and talked, and it got later and later, the crowd slowly tapered off and the drinks kept coming, his common sense eventually exited stage left. Somehow he found himself walking her to her hotel room door, even though that was how they had ended up kissing once before, and he found himself doing it at the witching hour, when the hotel corridors were quiet, the lights were dim and his inhibitions were at an all-time low. He knew he was in trouble long before they stepped off the elevator onto her floor and he started walking the green mile.

The devil was back. *This is a classic example of a victimless crime. You know that, right?*

Tomorrow morning they'd both hop on two different planes, fly off in opposite directions and never see each other again, not anytime soon, anyway. And there was a brand-new, unused condom in his wallet, just waiting to fulfill its purpose. Technically the damn devil was right. Who would know? And really, who would care?

"So, does she know?" Alexandra asked quietly as they strolled. Her arm brushed his, and then their fingers touched and lingered in the skinny space between them. He glanced down at her, found her shrewd brown-eyed gaze waiting for his, and realized that he was hovering somewhere between being alarmingly tipsy and dangerously drunk. Too far gone to feign ignorance.

"What? That I'm drunk and tempted to use that as an excuse to sleep with you?" He slipped his hands in his trouser pockets, where he could keep track of them. "Of course not. When did that become the kind of thing that a man tells a woman?"

"That's not what I meant and you know it," she leaned in and stage-whispered. She was leaning toward being drunk, too. "I was asking if she knew that you were so miserable without her."

"Damn, is it that obvious?"

"A little. Have you tried calling her?"

"Only about a million times," he admitted sheepishly. "She's not speaking to me. What else would you suggest trying?"

"I guess you could try standing under her bedroom window and serenading her."

"Yeah, I'm not doing that," he said and she laughed. "Anything else?"

"The only other thing I could suggest—" she said as they approached the door to her room and she slipped her key card into the palm of his hand, "—is allowing me to help you forget her for the next little while."

"Ah, there's that temptation again." Taking the card from her, Cooper slid it into the slot in the door and turned the knob when the light flashed green. The door swung open and the scent of her perfume rushed out of the room at him, stroking his needy senses intimately. "You're a very sexy woman, Miss Mason. Do you know that?"

"But?"

"But," he said, passing her the key card and stepping back from the threshold. "I'd never be able to forgive myself if I did the wrong thing just because no one was looking and I thought I could get away with it. So I think I'd better go back to my own room and sleep it off."

Clearly disappointed, Alexandra leaned against the doorjamb and pouted prettily. "Mmm, that's too bad, Dr. Talbot. Something tells me that you're a great fuck." Her candor rocked Cooper's head back on his neck and flooded his face with burning heat. Speechless, he looked down at the floor and cleared his throat. One wrong word, one wrong move and things would go south really fast.

"Uh… I think I'd better go," he murmured and took the most difficult step of them all—the first one.

Just as all the others had, the call that he tried to place to Olivia a few minutes later went straight to voice mail. But he was drunk and not exactly thinking straight *or* with the right head, so it occurred to him that he was likely dodging a proverbial bullet. What would he have said anyway, if she had chosen *this* call, out of all of the others that he'd made to her with no success, as the one that she would finally answer? That he was weak and getting weaker by the day? That he missed her taste, her touch and her scent, so much that he'd almost let himself sink to new lows just so he could pretend for a little while? That he was on the verge of becoming *that* guy, the one who conjured up images of a woman he couldn't have while he was making love to a woman that he didn't want? Or even better, that he had turned down a very attractive woman's advances because he was pining away for someone who'd made it very clear that she couldn't care less what the hell he did either way?

Thinking of you, he texted Olivia as he stumbled through his dark hotel suite and collapsed on the neatly made bed. He was an idiot. If tonight didn't prove that beyond a shadow of a doubt, then nothing would.

Olivia was sick. She'd caught a cold or the flu or eaten something that her stomach didn't agree with. It was impossible to know which, because her symptoms were a mash-up of all of them and she was experiencing all of them at once. One minute she was hot and sweaty, and the next cold and shivering. Her sinuses were congested, she had a low-grade fever and she couldn't seem to keep anything solid down. It occurred to her that she should get up and drag herself to the nearest urgent-care center for a medical checkup, but the farthest she made it when she did finally manage to climb out of bed was to the adjoining bathroom.

Two seconds after she brushed her teeth, flossed and then gargled with mouthwash, her roiling stomach led her over to the toilet, where she promptly threw up the chicken noodle soup that she'd risked eating for dinner. Back at the sink, she rinsed her mouth, brushed her teeth again and then splashed her face with cold water. Then she padded, barefoot and miserable, back to her bed and collapsed onto the mattress.

Two and a half days, she thought as she tucked her freezing feet underneath the covers and flipped her pillow over to the cold side. She'd been sick and completely alone in the house for two and a half days now, and none of the cold remedies that she'd tried so far seemed to be working. The only good thing to come out of the whole nightmarish ordeal was the fact that, while her condition hadn't improved much, at least it hadn't gotten any worse.

Not that that was saying much, she conceded and sneezed hard enough to temporarily clear her congested sinuses. But all she had to do was hold on until eight o'clock tomorrow morning, when Harriet arrived for work. Eventually Harriet would notice that Olivia was missing and come looking for her. The trail of snotty, used tissues scattered around the house would lead her here, to Olivia's war-torn bedroom, and then Harriet would rescue her.

A smile curved Olivia's lips as she drifted off to sleep again. Harriet would know just what to do to make her all better. She always did.

Two days later Olivia had just dropped a clean nightgown over her head and gotten in bed when Harriet knocked softly at her bedroom door and then threw it open.

"Well, look who's starting to look like a human being again," she said, smiling from ear to ear as she carried a covered lap tray into the room and brought it over to the bed. "Didn't I tell you that a hot bubble bath would make you feel better?" She set the tray down at the foot of the bed and moved to the head to help Olivia sit up against the tufted leather headboard. "Let me see if you're still running a temperature." She smoothed Olivia's still-damp hair back from her forehead and pressed her lips to the center of it. "Your fever's gone," she announced a few seconds later. "I came in and changed your bed linens while you were in the tub and I also set up the humidifier."

Frowning, Olivia looked around the room curiously. "Is that why I smell peppermint?"

"Yep, it's peppermint oil. I put a few drops in the humidifier. It's calming."

"It makes me want a giant bowl of mint-chocolate-chip ice cream."

"Like I said, calming," Harriet said, picking up the tray and setting it down across Olivia's lap. "I brought you some breakfast."

"But it's lunchtime!" Olivia protested. She sounded like a petulant child even to her own ears. "And I wanted pizza today."

"You eat what's on that tray without giving me any lip or hiding any of it in a balled-up napkin, and we'll talk about ordering pizza."

Momentarily pacified, Olivia turned her attention to the covered dish on the tray, lifting the top warily and then groaning disgustedly when she discovered what was underneath it. "Oh, no, not fruit salad and whole wheat toast again! This is all you've fed me since Monday, which was two days ago. What in the hell is happening downstairs in the kitchen, Harriet? Are we poor?"

"First of all, you don't pay me to cook gourmet meals around here, young lady. And second of all, don't shoot the messenger, okay? I'm just following doctor's orders. Now eat."

"What kind of quack doctor prescribes meals like this?" Olivia wondered as she scanned the contents of her tray disdainfully. For the third day in a row, she was being force-fed mixed-fruit salad, with giant hunks of seedless watermelon—which she could barely tolerate the taste of—four whole-wheat-toast triangles, each with its own pat of real butter, and a mug of ginger-honey tea. She hadn't had a slice of bacon in so long that she'd forgotten what it tasted like.

"Your ob-gyn," Harriet informed her. "Three days ago, when I called her and told her that you'd caught a cold."

"You called my ob-gyn?" Olivia was incredulous.

"Yes and stop fidgeting, will you? All I could get out of her was to give you plenty of fresh fruit and lots of liquids. And that she wants to see you in her office in another day or so, if you're not feeling better by then. Now, I have to run out for a while, so stay in bed, eat everything on that plate and behave yourself while I'm gone."

Olivia watched her retreating back with mounting alarm. "Wait!" she cried around a mouthful of watermelon. "You can't just leave me here like this, Harriet! Where are you going?"

"I'm going to the supermarket for more fruit and then I'm going to the drugstore to pick up a home pregnancy test. Don't get out of bed unless the house catches fire," she said and walked out of the room, closing the door soundly behind her.

Chapter 16

Pregnant?

Pregnant?

Oh, hell no. She couldn't be.

Suddenly more energized than she'd been in days, Olivia set the tray aside and scrambled out of bed, hurrying over to her dressing table, where she'd left her cell phone earlier. She snatched it up, navigated to the calendar app and began counting backwards from the day's date. When she realized that over thirty days had passed since her last period, her eyes slid closed and something like a prayer tumbled out of her mouth before she went back to her starting point and began counting all over again.

"Oh no," she whispered to the empty room. "Oh no, oh no, oh no." Breathless and dizzy with fear,

Olivia tiptoed back over to the bed, sank down onto the side of the mattress heavily and dropped her face into her hands. *A baby? What in the world would she, Olivia Carrington, do with a baby?*

She was still sitting there, mentally pondering the question, when Harriet returned from her errands and sent her into the bathroom to pee on a stick. "This may take a while," Olivia warned Harriet as she shuffled into the adjoining bathroom and reached for the doorknob to close the door in the woman's face. "I think I may have to puke first."

"Well, in that case, you'd better take this in there with you." She slipped a thin sheaf of folded papers out of her pocket and handed them to Olivia.

"What is this?"

"A Discovery Summons. The Marshal Service just dropped it off." Harriet stepped back as the door closed in her face. "The prosecuting attorney and that crazy girl's public defender want to talk to you. Downtown. Next week!" she called through the door. "Should I call Sean?" Sean Poindexter was Carrington Consulting's attorney of record and a close family friend. "You know she has a fit when you two don't keep her in the loop."

Unfolding the bundle, Olivia scanned the papers quickly. "No, don't call Sean."

"Well, then I'm calling your parents, because—"

Olivia snatched the door open and stuck her head out, putting her face in Harriet's. "Harriet! Don't you dare call my parents! Why would you do that? Shannon's attorney wants to use me as a character witness for the defense—that's all. This is no big deal, certainly no reason to interrupt my parents while they're on a Caribbean cruise."

Harriet didn't look convinced. "Well, what about Elise? Can I at least call Elise?"

"I just spoke to Elise last night, Harriet. Everything is fine."

"Are you going to tell her that you're pregnant?"

"I have the flu. I'm not pregnant. Get your facts straight."

"Hmph," Harriet grunted, sucking her teeth. "I suppose you want me to keep my mouth shut about that, too."

"If you could, that would be great. When the time is right, I'll tell Elise—"

Harriet folded her arms across her chest and peered at Olivia over the rim of her glasses. "And your parents," she cut in.

Olivia sucked in a deep breath and squared her shoulders. "*And my parents*, myself," she finished tightly. Her father was going to kill her, right after her mother fainted. "Assuming that there's anything to tell. If it's okay with you, I'd like to put all of this Shannon business behind me first."

"It's not looking good for that poor, crazy girl, is it?"

"I don't have all of the details, but no, it's not. And she's not crazy—she's just…in a lot of trouble." That was an understatement, if there ever was one.

It was also a lie. A necessary one, but still a lie. She'd read enough about Shannon's life in Cooper's file to know better, but Harriet didn't need to know that. In all of her retelling, Olivia hadn't even men-

tioned that part of the tragic saga that was her life
to Elise. Nor had she told anyone that she'd visited
Shannon at the federal lockup a few weeks ago,
mainly because she couldn't bring herself to talk
about the experience just yet, but also because she
wasn't quite ready to hear Elise say *I told you so.*

She'd been relieved to see that her friend was
physically okay, but the state of Shannon's mental health was a completely different story. Just as
quickly as her name had changed from Shannon
Bridgeway to Karen Lewis, her personality had
seemingly undergone a drastic transformation, as
well.

Throughout the entire visit, Shannon had talked
in riddles, laughed at her own jokes and repeatedly
asked Olivia for a cigarette, even though, as far as
Olivia knew, neither of them had ever smoked. Seeing her that way had unsettled Olivia so much that she
hadn't been back to visit again since. It was one thing
to understand, in theory, that psychotic breaks were
possible, that they happened to other people, in other
places and at other times, but it was quite another to
watch such a break happen right before your very eyes,
to someone that you knew personally and cared about.
If she never witnessed something like that again for
the rest of her life, it would be too soon.

Frankly she couldn't imagine what she could possibly do or say, particularly on the witness stand,
of all places, that would help Shannon's case in the
slightest.

"At this point all we can do is keep Shannon in

our thoughts and prayers," she told Harriet. "Now, could I please have a little privacy?"

"You've got five minutes," Harriet said, glancing at her watch as she pivoted on her heel and headed for the bedroom door. "That's when my afternoon soaps come on, and you know I don't like to be disturbed when they do," she called over her shoulder on her way out of the room.

In mid-October, Cooper's evening flight to St. Louis, Missouri, landed on schedule at Lambert International Airport. After deplaning and checking in with airport security, he retrieved his suitcase from the luggage carousel, slung the strap of his carry-on over his shoulder and swung through the nearest exit door, out onto the sidewalk. Buttoning his gray trench coat against the chilly fall air, he scanned the busy driveway fronting the gate, his gaze bouncing from one taxicab to the next in the long line of idling vehicles, until it came to rest on a black Buick sedan. Recognizing its driver as the same one who'd picked up his team from the airport once before, he met the man halfway with his luggage. Then he opened the back door himself and got in.

"I'm registered at the downtown Hilton," he said, after the driver had settled in the front seat and shifted into gear.

"Yes, sir." He met the man's eyes in the rearview mirror. "How was your flight?"

"I sat next to a screaming baby the entire time," Cooper quipped, grinning. "You tell me."

"I hear you. I got four boys at home, all under the

age of ten." The Buick eased out of the pickup lane and merged into traffic. "It gets too quiet around there and you better start praying." They chuckled together. "You got kids?"

"No."

"Nieces or nephews?"

"Uh…no."

"Damn, you're lucky. Apparently all I have to do is breathe on my wife and we're pregnant again. But holding my breath isn't really an option, is it?" Cooper understood that the question was a rhetorical one, so he sat back against the leather seat and kept his mouth shut, letting his lopsided grin speak for him instead.

After a stretch of silence, the driver chuckled out of the blue. "I figure we'll slow down when we finally get the little girl we've been trying for." He flipped the visor down against a ray from the setting sun and gave the heavy sedan more gas. "All right, enough of my life story. Let's get you to your hotel. You want the radio on or…?"

"On works for me," Cooper agreed and loosened his silk Hermes bow tie. "Thanks."

When he'd been subpoenaed as a witness for the prosecution at Shannon Bridgeway's trial, he was tempted to contact Olivia to let her know that he'd be in town. But since he hadn't heard so much as a peep out of her in nearly two months, there didn't seem to be any point in stirring up past drama now. And this was just an overnight, quick-turnaround trip, anyway. By this time tomorrow, he'd be back in Knoxville, at his desk. In the meantime, he was determined to keep his impulses under control.

It wasn't long before the Buick pulled into the Hilton's drive-up and rolled to a stop. Cooper thanked his driver with a generous tip and, after checking in and ordering a room-service dinner, went up to his room. His dinner arrived just as he was getting out of the shower. Suddenly starving, he settled down with an expensive beer from the minibar, in front of the flat-screen television in the sitting area. Tuning into an early *X-Men* flick that he'd seen at least a dozen times before, he took a huge bite of the grilled-chicken sandwich that he'd ordered, chased it down with a mouthful of beer and thought about calling Olivia.

When he did, fifteen minutes later, she answered on the second ring, which caught him off guard. He'd been expecting to get her voice mail like he always did, so it took him a second to shift gears. "Uh... hi...it's Cooper."

"I know." She sounded warm and fuzzy and close, intimate. "How are you, Cooper?"

"I'm good. You?"

"I'm good, too."

"Did I catch you at a bad time? If so, I can—"

"No, no, now is fine. It's actually good that you called because I was planning to call you soon, anyway." His eyebrows shot up and a million questions raced through his mind, but he kept quiet and waited. "I, um, I think we need to talk."

"You haven't returned any of my calls or texts for

the past two months and now you think we need to talk? What the hell about?"

She sighed into the phone. "Come on, Cooper. Please don't be like this. You called me, remember? I hope it wasn't to argue, because—"

"As a matter of fact, it was, Olivia, and do you know why?"

"Cooper..."

The pleading in her soft voice stopped him cold. "You're right," he eventually blurted out, catching himself before he could lose it completely and make even more of an ass of himself. "I told myself that I wasn't going to do this, and here I am doing it anyway," he murmured into the phone several seconds later. "I'm sorry."

"It's okay." They were silent for a few seconds more, both holding the phone and breathing into it rhythmically. "This was a bad idea, wasn't it?"

"What? Sleeping with you? Falling for you? Never." He picked up his beer, took a long pull and then set the bottle back down on the tray in front of him with a click. "Calling you when I'm tired and angry and I haven't had sex in damn near two months, well, that probably wasn't the best idea that I've ever had. We can likely agree on that."

"Why don't I give you a call tomorrow evening and we'll try this again?"

"Fine." *I want you. I miss you.* "I guess I'll talk to you tomorrow then."

"Um...okay."

"Wait, what time tomorrow?"

"What?"

"I said, what time tomorrow? You said that you were going to call me tomorrow, so I'd like to know what time you're going to call."

"Ok*aaay*," she hedged. "How about around four?"

"Around four o'clock or *at* four o'clock?" He knew he was being a dick, but he couldn't seem to stop himself. It was hard to think rationally when you'd been walking around with a perpetual hard-on for the past two months. "Which one?"

"*At* four, I guess."

"Fine. I'll talk to you at four o'clock tomorrow." Hopefully by then he would have come up with the words to convince her to take him back. "Good night, Olivia."

He didn't realize until after he'd already hung up that he never got around to mentioning that he was in town.

Four o'clock tomorrow, Olivia mentally confirmed as she set a next-day reminder in her cell phone for the same time and then set it down on the nightstand. Better safe than sorry, she told herself, throwing back the bed covers and sitting up on the side of the bed. Lately she was just as likely to nod off at a moment's notice and sleep most of the day away as she was to walk into a room and forget why she was there. As a result she'd been reduced to making lists for everything, leaving sticky notes all over the house to help jog her memory and relying on scheduled electronic signals to tell her if she was coming or going, like one of Pavlov's dogs. Having to add Cooper's promised callback to an already ridiculously long list of reminders was an embarrassing but sadly necessary evil.

Since pregnancy was apparently capable of scrambling your memory, she didn't want to risk having it turn her into a liar, too. Plus now that she'd finally found the courage to tell Cooper that she was pregnant and planning to move to London next month, she wanted to get it over with before she lost her nerve.

Pushing her bare feet into her slippers, Olivia stood and shrugged into her robe. Then, with visions of the pot roast, honey-glazed carrots and garlic mashed potatoes that Harriet had made for dinner earlier dancing around in her head, she tucked her cell in her pocket and took the rear stairs down to the kitchen, all but skipping over to the subzero refrigerator across the room.

That was the last thing she remembered doing before a sharp pain suddenly radiated across the back of her head and she passed out.

Chapter 17

When Olivia came to, she was lying on her face on the kitchen floor and her head was pounding viciously. It felt like someone was attacking her skull with a jackhammer. Also, her right cheekbone was screaming, having taken most of the impact of her fall. Moaning in agony, Olivia touched a hand to what felt like a wet spot at the back of her head and gasped in shock as a fresh stab of pain radiated across her cranium.

"Get up."

It took three tries before she successfully rolled over onto her back and cracked her eyes open one at a time. As soon as she did, the blinding glare from the overhead lights made her squeeze them closed again. But not before she noticed the gun that was pointed straight at her and the woman holding it.

"Oh, that's bright!" She threw up a hand to shield her eyes and slowly pushed up into a sitting position.

"Don't make me tell you again, Olivia," Shannon warned. "I said, get up!"

With the room spinning the way it was, that was easier said than done, but Olivia eventually managed it. Using first a stool and then the edge of the center island for leverage, she slowly pulled herself up to her feet and wobbled dangerously. "I'm dizzy. I need to s-sit down." Her knees threatened to buckle. "Please."

"All right, fine, but you're going to sit in the study, not in here. Let's go."

"The study?" A sharp pain lanced through her head, stealing her breath, and she sobbed. The hand that she pressed to her mouth was covered with blood. Seeing it, she did a double take. "Oh God, I'm bleeding. I'm not sure I can make it that far. Just let me sit right he—"

The gun cocked. "I said move!"

Olivia jumped a full foot across the tile floor. "All right! I'm going. Just…please calm down, okay, Shannon? You haven't done anything so far that can't be undone."

"Look, I really don't want to hurt you, Olivia, so if you know what's good for you, you'll stop trying to counsel me, shut your mouth and walk."

Olivia started walking, but she refused to shut her mouth. As long as she kept Shannon talking, there was still time to come up with an escape plan.

She was asleep, lying on her stomach with a pillow underneath her head and one knee bent, when he slid across the mattress toward her and covered her from head to toe from behind with his body. Her breathing was soft and even, rhythmic. She was completely unaware of his presence…until the moment that he reached down, gripped his cock in his fist and eased its head into her slick tunnel. She groaned and her walls contracted, sending his eyes rolling to the back of his head and his hips rocking forward to sink a few more inches of his flesh into her slick heat. He stroked her once, twice, three times and grit his teeth to keep from shattering the middle-of-the-night quiet with a savage battle cry.

It was late and pitch-black outside. In the wide shaft of moonlight that slanted across a portion of the bed, he reared back and braced himself on his palms on the mattress, watching his cock slowly glide in and out of her as if he were doing push-ups with just the lower half of his body.

Waking Olivia from her sleep just to take her a third time, which would ultimately only put her right back to sleep again, was selfishness at its finest. But Cooper couldn't get enough of her. Something happened to him when he was inside of her, something primal and raw, and like an addict he wanted to experience the high that making love with her gave him over and over again.

"I know you're awake," he leaned down and growled in her ear. "I can feel you coming around me." She was trying to come in silence and failing miserably, but he was too far gone to take pity on her. Lowering himself flush on top of her, he took her hands in his and stretched her arms out above her head on the mattress, while his legs rode the length of hers and his toes pointed her toes in the opposite direction. She turned her head and he rested the side of his face against the side of hers as he rocked his hips forward and gave her everything he had to give in one powerful stroke.

They cried out at the same time, and then his hips began dancing against her jiggling butt cheeks. Wildly, savagely, as if a live wire were streaming currents of electricity through his bucking body. A burst of semen shot out of his drilling cock before he realized that he was climaxing in earnest and his mouth went slack. "Aw, baby… I'm coming. I'm—"

Beep. Beep. Beep. Beep…

Cooper's head shot up from the pillow underneath it and his eyes slammed open. He looked around his hotel suite wildly. His cock was hard and lying against his abdomen like a felled log, a sure sign that he'd been in the middle of yet another erotic dream.

Beep. Beep. Beep. Beep…

His eyes flew to the bedside alarm clock. It was 3:30 a.m., which meant that he'd only been asleep for a couple of hours when the alarm—he frowned. No, wait, the noise that had awakened him hadn't come from the alarm. *Where was it coming from?*

Beep. Beep. Beep. Beep…

Spotting his vibrating cell phone on the dresser across from the bed, Cooper jumped up and caught the thing before it slid over the edge and fell to the floor. Flopping back across the bed with it, he touched a finger to the screen and put the phone to his ear. "This had better be good, Olivia," he growled into the phone. She was silent. "Olivia?" He was just about to hang up when something told him not to. Instead he switched on the mute function and put the phone back to his ear.

"If you're not going to put the gun away, Shannon, then could you at least stop pointing it at me?" he heard Olivia say. "It's making me nervous and I'm already an emotional mess as it is."

"Oh, *you're* nervous. First thing tomorrow morning, I'm supposed to stand trial for bank robbery, and *you're* nervous? That's rich, coming from someone like you, Olivia. That's really rich."

"I wasn't trying to offend you, Shannon. All I meant was that I want to *help* you, but I can't do it with a gun pointed at my head. Why do you even have a gun, anyway? And how did you get out of jail?"

"Stop asking so many questions!"

"I'm sorry. I'm just trying to *help*."

A whistle of fear curled out of Cooper's mouth. *I hear you, baby. Hold on. I'm coming.*

Already on the move, he tucked his cell between his head and shoulder while he got dressed and found his glasses. At the door to his suite, he slipped his wallet and room key card into his back pocket and checked to make sure that his holstered Glock was in safety mode. Then he swung the door open and hurried out.

In the lobby he leaned across the check-in counter and waved his badge and agency ID in the sleeping clerk's face. The young man's eyes cracked open and widened as he spotted the badge underneath his nose. He sat up so quickly in his chair that he almost fell out of it.

"Justin, is it?" Cooper asked, glancing at the other man's name tag. He couldn't have been a day over twenty-one. "Hi, Justin, my name is Cooper Talbot and I'm a special agent in charge with the FBI. I'm sorry to disturb your nap, but I need a car—preferably one with GPS—and I need it now."

Embarrassed at having been caught sleeping on the job, Justin scrambled to his feet and roughly scrubbed his hands back and forth across his reddened face. He looked slightly more alert when his eyes found Cooper's across the desk again and he cleared his throat. "Uh…yeah…okay. Let's see… would you like me to call you a taxi?"

"I don't have time to wait for a taxi to get here. What else can you do?"

"Uh… I could order a rental car for you but—"

"But I'd have to wait for it to be delivered," Cooper finished for him. "Not an option."

"Well, uh…"

"Fuck that. We're wasting time. What do you drive, Justin?"

"Um…a Ch-Chevy Camaro, sir, but—"

"Tell you what. I'll make a deal with you. You let me borrow your Camaro for a few hours and you get to keep your job."

Scared out of her mind, Olivia sent up a silent prayer that Cooper had answered his cell and was listening in right now. She hadn't had a chance to check her own cell because, as unpredictable as Shannon clearly was, she hadn't taken her eyes off Olivia for longer than five seconds at a time since the entire ordeal had begun. There was no way to know for sure if help was on the way or not, but she couldn't afford to think about what might happen if it wasn't. In just a few hours' time, Harriet would walk through the door and then Shannon would have two hostages. Another life would be in danger, and Olivia would never be able to live with herself if Harriet got hurt because of her.

Well, technically Shannon would soon have three hostages, if you counted the eight-week-old bun in Olivia's oven, but Olivia couldn't think about that right now, either. She couldn't think about the stash of parenting magazines that she'd hidden upstairs in her bedroom so Harriet wouldn't find them and make fun of her cluelessness; the crib and changing table that she'd picked out of a specialty catalog just this morning; or the fact that she had already decided to breastfeed, because it was better for the baby. She couldn't give in to the tidal wave of emotions that swept over her every time she let herself think about the new-mommy class that she had signed up for or the names that she'd already picked out.

She was hoping for a girl.

Stay focused, Olivia. Keep her talking.

Right. Focused. "How did you get out of jail, Shannon?"

"I made bail, Olivia. Are you surprised that I have other friends to bail me out?"

"Nothing surprises me anymore. I have to use the bathroom."

"You just went to the bathroom a few minutes ago."

"Well, I have to go again," Olivia said, grimacing when the knot on the back of her head thumped. "And I need a cold compress for my head. It's bleeding, remember? And food," she added and sighed forlornly. "I need something to eat, Shannon. I'm starving."

Shannon stopped pacing the floor in front of the sofa that Olivia was sitting on long enough to aim a disgusted look at her and shake her head sadly. "God, how did I never notice how much you talk? You haven't shut up since I got here. Why won't you shut up?"

"Because I'm your friend and I want to help you."

Shannon looked skeptical. "You're my friend?"

"Yes, I'm your friend. Wasn't I your friend when I bailed you out of jail and took you into my home?"

"Yes, you were and I'm returning the favor by not duct-taping your mouth shut and tying your ass to a chair. You see?" She spread her hands and smiled beseechingly at Olivia. "Now both of us have officially broken the rules of friendship."

"Broken the rules? What rules? What are you talking about?" The gash in her head hurt like hell, but thankfully the bleeding seemed to have slowed.

"I'm talking about you and that know-it-all FBI agent, sneaking around together behind my back and plotting to send me to prison!" Shannon exploded. "That's what I'm talking about! If I had done what I was supposed to do weeks ago, I'd be on a beach down in Mexico somewhere right now and none of this would be happening!"

"What were you supposed to do?"

"You have money," Shannon spat at her. "Lots of it. You've got this big, fancy house and loaded parents. And you're pretty loaded yourself, aren't you, Olivia?"

"Is that what this is about? Money?" Feigning surprise, Olivia lifted her hands and let them fall back to her lap noisily. "If so, then you're right. I do have money. I'll give you whatever you want. All you have to do is put the gun down."

"You must really think I'm an idiot."

"No…no, I don't. I think you're scared and that's okay, because I'm scared, too."

"Scared?" Shannon laughed hysterically, maniacally. "What's got you scared, Olivia? The gun? Is that why you're scared? You think I'm going to shoot you?"

"Are you?"

"Maybe. After I get what I want. You have to be punished for setting me up. That wasn't cool."

"Look, I don't know what you think you know, but whatever it is, it isn't true. I've been nothing but a friend to you."

"Oh, is that right? Well, I'll tell you what, *friend.* You and I are going to take a little trip to the ATM and you're going to withdraw money for me. I need money to repay some very scary people for bailing me out. I'm also going to need a couple of those shiny little credit cards in your purse and every piece of jewelry you own. Get up and let's go." She stepped back and pointed the gun at the center of Olivia's chest. "Now. Where are the keys to your car?"

"Um…" Think, Olivia! "M-my keys are in the k-kitchen but I need to change clothes first and get my shoes."

"What you're wearing is fine," Shannon said, eyeing Olivia's red tank top and flare-leg pajama pants critically. "Leave the robe, though."

"No."

Shannon's eyebrows shot up. "No?"

"No," Olivia repeated, hating the slight tremble in her voice. Scooting to the edge of the sofa cushion, she got to her feet slowly, wobbling only a little bit when the room tilted on its axis. Squinting against the pounding in her head, she pulled her robe tighter around her and met Shannon's cold glare as she shook her head. "Unless we're going to a flea market, I refuse to leave the house wearing pajamas, with my head bleeding and animal sounds coming from my stomach. I'll go to the ATM with you, but first I need to use the bathroom, change clothes, tend to the gash in my head and eat something, because if I don't I'm going to either pass out or throw up. Worst case scenario, I'll do both and then you'll never get the money you came here for."

"Pass out? When did you get so freaking fragile? Are you sick?"

"No, Shannon. I'm not sick. I'm eight weeks pregnant, and right now you're pointing that goddamn gun of yours at my unborn child. That makes me very nervous, so will you please put it away?"

Chapter 18

Cooper's eyes bugged. *Pregnant?*

Had Olivia just said what he thought he'd just heard her say? She was pregnant?

Pregnant? With his *child?*

Cooper's heart dropped into his stomach and he sucked in a shaky breath. Who was he kidding? Of course she was pregnant with his child. If he thought about it long enough, he could almost recall the first time that he had slipped inside of her unprotected, right down to the exact second. She'd been in the shower and he had sneaked up on her like a thief in the night, sucking on her engorged clitoris until her walls were pulsing so hard that she was coming, and then lifting her up and impaling her on his throbbing cock while she was still convulsing violently, so that she could take him to heaven with her.

The second time, she had gifted him with underwater fellatio in the pool and, in exchange, he had gifted her with a quick, hot and hard underwater fuck. After that he'd lost count, and now in hindsight he realized that he was really no better than the driver who had picked him up from the airport earlier. Neither of them could keep their hands off the women they loved.

But...damn, a baby?

The woman of his dreams was having a baby?

His fingers tightened around the Camaro's steering wheel. Easing his foot off the gas pedal, Cooper allowed himself a moment to let the fact that he was going to be a father sink in, and then he quickly changed lanes. According to the GPS, the turn-in for Olivia's subdivision was just up ahead, and he didn't want to risk missing it. There was too much at stake.

He found the street he was looking for and burned rubber turning the corner. The Camaro was powerful and fast, but it was also loud, which was why he parked it down the street from Olivia's house, switched his cell over to his Bluetooth earpiece and hurried the rest of the way to her house on foot. The last thing he wanted to do was alert Shannon to his presence and lose the element of surprise. He didn't want the gun that she was waving around to be anywhere near Olivia when he aimed his Glock at Shannon.

"This complicates things."

Olivia looked up from the heaping plate of food on

the table in front of her and caught Shannon's eyes. "What? The fact that I'm pregnant?" she said around a mouthful of pot roast. "Honey, you don't know the half of it." She bit into a roasted potato and moaned. "You really should have some pot roast. Either it truly is the best I've ever tasted or it just seems that way because it's my last meal. I'm not sure which, but either way, it's delicious."

"You're keeping the baby?"

"Of course. I mean, at first I was all like, what the hell? But after the shock wore off and I thought about it, I realized that not keeping it was never an option." Her gaze fell on the gun that Shannon was still holding. "I was going to tell Cooper later today and everyone else after that, but I guess my secret's out now, huh?"

"*Cooper?* The FBI agent with all the bow ties and pocket protectors? *That's* who knocked you up? How in the world did that happen? He's not even your type!"

"I know, right? But somehow I managed to fall in love with him anyway, so, okay, yes, you're right. There, I said it. I'm guilty. I was sneaking around with Cooper behind your back," Olivia said. Then she thought about the situation and set her fork down to show Shannon an inch of empty space between her thumb and forefinger. "Somewhat. But I wasn't plotting against you, Shannon. What I was doing was having the best sex of my life. The man's a beast in bed."

That's right, baby. Keep her talking.
"The man's a beast in bed," he heard Olivia say

and damn near swooned. If he was a beast, it was only because she brought it out of him.

Praying that none of her neighbors were peeking out of their windows just then, Cooper ducked into the shadows alongside Olivia's house and crept around to the backyard. The privacy fence was locked from the inside, so he backed up a few steps, got a running start, and climbed it as quickly and quietly as possible. Once he had cleared it, he flattened himself against the side of the house and slowly edged along the brick wall until he reached the kitchen.

A couple of months ago, he had lectured Olivia about her tendency not to close the blinds or draw the curtains at the tall bay windows in the kitchen. Now he was relieved to find that she hadn't listened to him about that any more than she'd listened to him about anything else. Both the curtains and the blinds were still standing open and he could see her clearly.

"Hurry up and finish eating," Shannon instructed. "It'll be daylight soon. I have to go."

"Where are you going and how are you planning to get there?"

"I thought you said you had to use the bathroom?"

"I do, but—"

"Then stop asking so many questions. You've eaten enough for three people already. Now let's go to the toilet." He watched Olivia push back from the kitchen table and stand. The gun pointed at her chest made her motions slow and deliberate, and caused his lungs to twist in his chest. One wrong move, one wrong word and his life would never be the same. "Leave the robe."

"Why? It's chilly—"

"I said take it off!"

Even with a gun trained on her, Olivia hesitated, and in that instant Cooper understood that that's where her cell phone was hidden. If she took off her robe, he would no longer be able to hear them. "Take it off, baby," he whispered to the chilly night air. "Just take it off."

She did, and a few seconds later, both she and Shannon disappeared from sight. Cooper uttered both a prayer and a curse.

Then he heard a gun cock behind his left ear and froze. "Turn around. Slowly."

He did, coming face-to-face with a muscle-bound, brown-skinned man with hard eyes and a snarl on his mouth. They stood eye-to-eye and nose-to-nose, but since his Glock was still holstered and the barrel of the other man's weapon was now hovering in the air mere inches away from his left temple, he kept his hands in plain sight and his gaze level.

"Who the fuck are you?" the man wanted to know.

"Cooper Talbot." He ran his tongue around his teeth and swallowed. "Who the fuck are you?"

"Broderick Cannon. Now you. Why are you skulking around my sister-in-law's house?"

For the first time in weeks, Cooper's mouth curved into a genuine smile. "You're Elise's husband."

Broderick sucked in a sharp breath. "You know my wife?"

Uh-oh. Careful, Cooper. "Only what I've heard about her from Liv."

"Liv?" For several tense seconds Broderick stared at Cooper as if he could see right through him, and then slowly the gun in his hand lowered and a smile took over his mouth. "You must be the FBI boyfriend," he drawled as he holstered his weapon, took a step back and visibly relaxed his massive shoulders. "What the hell took you so long to get here?"

Cooper's eyebrows shot up. *What?*

"Just kidding," Broderick quipped before Cooper could curse him out. "You have any ideas on how to get into this museum?"

"No, but—"

"Then I do," Broderick cut in briskly. "Follow me. There's a basement window up near the front of the house that we can climb through." Pivoting, he took off, walking back the way that Cooper had just come. "Once we're inside, we can take the back stairs up to the mudroom and move in through the kitchen. I disabled the alarm as soon as I got here and figured out what was up." He stopped walking and looked back at Cooper over his shoulder. "You packing?"

"Yes."

"Good, because if by some twist of fate I happen to miss when I pull the trigger, I'm counting on you to have my back. We need to gain control of this situation and rescue Olivia as quickly as possible."

"That's what I'm talking about. Let's go."

They worked together in the darkness for the next few minutes, breaking into Olivia's house through a seldom-used basement window that Broderick had apparently discovered during one of his regular security sweeps, as quickly and quietly as humanly possible. Impressed with Broderick's ability to move in silence, like a giant black cat, Cooper climbed through the window after him and dropped to the balls of his feet on the concrete floor. "They really ought to get that thing fixed," he murmured to Broderick as they started up the stairs.

"Shhh!" Broderick hissed and put up a hand for silence as he appeared to listen to something that only he could hear. "They're in the study."

"What are you, psychic?" Cooper hissed back.

"No. I updated the security system not long after Elise and I first got married. Part of the updates included hidden microphones in every room." He caught the look on Cooper's face and the meaning behind it, and grinned. "Don't worry. They can only be activated within so many feet of the house and, up until we got here a few minutes ago, I was the only one who knew they were there. Here." He took a small earpiece out of his pocket and pressed it into Cooper's hand. "I'm listening in with this. Congratulations, by the way."

"Thanks." Blushing to the roots of his hair, Cooper snatched his Bluetooth earpiece out of his ear and replaced it with the one that Broderick had given him. It took him a second to adjust to the enhanced sound quality, but when he did he swore that he could hear Olivia blink. "How did you know what was going on?"

"Elise wanted to surprise Olivia by coming home tonight. Guess which one of them ended up getting surprised, though?"

"Elise is here? Where is she?"

"She should be in the attic by now." Broderick reached up and touched a button on his earpiece. "Baby, are you there?"

There was a moment of silence and then Elise's husky voice filled his ear. "Yes, I'm here. I'm just... having a hard time right now."

"Why?" Broderick's eyebrows met in the middle of his forehead. "Is something wrong?"

"Yes, something is wrong, Broderick!" Elise hissed. "My sister is pregnant and I have to hear about it from a psychopath? Really? What kind of injustice is that?"

In the basement, Cooper and Broderick shared a look and then simultaneously rolled their eyes to the ceiling. Silently Cooper tapped his watch and Broderick nodded. "Later. Okay, baby? We'll deal with that later." She sobbed into their ears. "Do me a favor and take out your earpiece for a minute, so we can hear."

"We're going to talk about those microphones, too, Broderick."

"I know we are, baby. But we don't have to do it now, do we? Take out your earpiece, please. Put it back in and check in with me when you reach your bedroom." He then motioned for Cooper to follow him up the stairs. With Elise out of the mix, they tuned in once again to what was happening between the two women in the study.

"I think I might need stitches."

"You're fine," Shannon droned. "I didn't even hit you that hard. Let's go find your purse and shoes so we can get out of here."

"What if I refuse to go?"

"Then I'll sit here with you until that bitch who works for you gets here in a few hours, and then you'll be responsible for what happens next. Don't try me, Olivia. Right now I don't have very much to lose. If your baby's daddy has his way, I'll be an old woman when I get out of prison. When I think about it like that, death by lethal injection doesn't sound quite so bad."

"You're insane."

"And you're starting to get the picture now. Good. Now let's go find your purse and shoes before I change my mind and shoot you right now. Boy, that would certainly mess up your lovely little plans to get married and live happily-ever-after, wouldn't it?"

"I'm not getting married. I'm moving to London next month. Or, rather, I *was* moving to London next month. The only plan I had was to tell Cooper that I was pregnant and then call him from London, after I was already gone for good."

"They're in the hallway now," Broderick murmured. When Cooper only stared back at him blankly, he dropped a hand on Cooper's shoulder and squeezed. "You okay?"

From somewhere, Cooper managed to find his voice. "Yeah." He nodded to help convince himself that he was telling the truth. "Yeah... I'm okay. I'm just... London?"

"I chased Elise all the way to Florida," Broderick told him matter-of-factly. "The Carrington women are beautiful, but they're also stubborn."

"I heard that," Elise drawled.

"I love you, baby."

"Whatever. I'm in my bedroom. Now be quiet so I can hear."

Taking Broderick's cue, Cooper nudged him aside and took the lead, turning the doorknob and slowly opening the basement access door. Silently he stepped out into the mudroom, which was just off the kitchen, and after making sure that the coast was clear, motioned for Broderick to join him.

Chapter 19

It was nearly six o'clock in the morning and Cooper still hadn't come to save her. That either meant one of two things: that he'd missed her call altogether or that her hands had been shaking so badly when she'd placed the blind call in the first place that she had pressed the wrong button. For all she knew, the most that she had succeeded in contributing to her own rescue was to leave a confusing voice mail for her tax accountant to listen to when he arrived at work in a few hours. By then she could very well be dead already. Either way, she realized with a disgusted sigh, unless she suddenly had a stroke of genius and devised a master plan to escape— which was highly unlikely, since these days she could barely remember her own name—she was pretty much screwed. She had never stood a chance.

When Olivia thought about it like that, her predicament was kind of funny. Only kind of, because there was still the gun pointed at her chest to consider. But still. She wasn't above finding the humor in any situation, and this one was no exception.

The first giggle bubbled out of her mouth as she was forced back into the study at gunpoint, carrying a pair of leather Prada driving moccasins in one hand and her purse in the other, and ordered to sit down on the sofa. She plopped down in the center of it and set her purse on the cushion next to her, giving in to a second giggle because she was too nervous not to.

Shannon was incredulous. "Are you actually laughing right now?"

"Yes," Olivia said and did it again. "I'm s-sorry." Unable to continue speaking coherently, she dissolved into a fit of giggles that sounded hysterical even to her own ears. She had lost the ability to control herself, though, so she threw up her hands in defeat, let them fall back to her lap noisily and went with it.

"Shut up!"

"I'm s-sorry," she sputtered in between giggles. Noticing the fury on Shannon's face, she made a visible effort to sober up, sucking in a dramatic deep breath and releasing it slowly, complete with hand gestures and exaggerated facial expressions. "Okay," she huffed a few seconds later. "I'm back now. Where were we? Oh! That's right, I was just about to put on my shoes and drive you to the ATM so you can steal all of my hard-earned money and skip town."

"You think this is funny, Olivia?" Shannon snarled. "You think I'm funny?"

"No, of course not," Olivia said and burst out laughing. "N-not you—m-me," she said, almost panting the words out between giggling spells. "I'm what's f-funny. My life is wh-what's f-funny."

"Yeah, you've got it so hard around here," Shannon sniped as she looked around the sumptuously furnished room with disdain. "Put your shoes on and let's go. I forgot to dump out your jewelry box when we were upstairs, so we have to go back up there before we leave. Hurry up."

"No."

"I said hurry up, Olivia!"

Olivia giggled again. "Yeah, I'm not doing that, Shannon. You're probably going to kill me anyway, so just do it now and get it over with, okay?"

Shannon's gaze narrowed suspiciously. "What is this, more of your reverse-psychology bullshit?"

"Nope," Olivia chirped. "I think your insanity is starting to rub off on me, because sitting right here, just now, I experienced a startling moment of clarity. I saw the future, and do you know what it has in store for me?"

"No, and I don't ca—"

"I saw myself living halfway across the world, raising a child alone. A child who only gets to see its father during the summers and on alternate holidays, which by the way is *sooo* unfair. I saw myself going to weekly speed-dating sessions, hoping to meet another man who makes my heart skip a beat the way Cooper does and never quite succeeding. So I keep going and going, week after week, until I've earned myself one of those embarrassing nicknames.

You know the ones they give older single women, something ridiculous and hurtful like Speed-Dating Sally or Thirsty Thelma…" She trailed off, shaking her head incredulously. "After Cooper, nothing will ever be the same for me again. I'll compare every man I meet to him and they'll all fall short in one way or another, so I'll die alone.

"I saw myself wasting what's left of my life, pining away for a man who wants to marry a soccer mom—not someone like me. I'm not his type, Shannon, and knowing that no matter how much I love him, I could never pretend to be something that I'm not, well, that breaks my heart. And I don't think I've ever had my heart broken before. Can you believe that?"

Shannon snorted sarcastically. "What I can't believe is that the legendary man-whisperer, Olivia Carrington, is sitting here, whining about a damn man. That's what I can't believe. As interesting as that little tale that you just told was, you can stop stalling and get up now. Just for that we're going to stop by Elise's room and collect her diamonds, too."

"Yeah, I'm not doing that, either. I mean it, Shannon. You're going to have to shoot me."

The gun cocked.

"Wait!" Olivia cried, throwing up her hands like a human shield. "Just…give me a minute, will you? At least let me say a quick prayer or something."

"Take all the time you need, baby," Cooper said as he stepped through the partially closed, double pocket doors at the far side of the room. The Glock in his hand was pointed straight at the side of Shannon's head as he advanced into the study with measured, purposeful steps. His flat, unblinking stare was fixed on Shannon's profile. "She's not going anywhere and neither are you."

"Cooper!" His name on her lips was the sound of complete and utter relief. As if someone had flipped an invisible switch, tears sprang up and spilled over onto Olivia's suddenly flushed cheeks. "Please be careful. She has a gun."

"I can see that," Cooper said calmly.

"And so do I," Broderick said, easing into the room via the foyer. Both his gun and his eyes were fixed on the back of Shannon's head.

"One of us is going to have to lower our weapon, and I think you know that it's not going to be me, Karen," Cooper informed Shannon calmly. Her gun was still aimed at Olivia but her eyes were locked in a battle of wills with his. He refused to allow her to look away from his face. "That is your real name, isn't it? Karen Lewis?"

"Shut up," she said and then surprised them all with a burst of maniacal-sounding laughter. "Olivia, get up and come over here." Olivia didn't move. "Do it or I'll shoot your ass right now!"

"Don't move, Olivia," Cooper snapped. "Listen to me, Karen. I've had a long day and I'm tired. And after listening to my woman describe how delicious Harriet's pot roast is, I might just be a little hungry, too. So I won't be in the mood to play with you for much longer."

"Does it seem like I'm playing to you?"

"No, it doesn't, which means that we have a problem, don't we?" His eyes flicked over to Broderick's for the space of a heartbeat. "I can't just stand here and let you shoot the woman I love. Aside from the fact that it would absolutely destroy me, I couldn't help but overhear her tell you that she's pregnant with my child. How do you think that makes me feel? My woman is having a baby—*my baby*—and here you are, pointing a gun at the both of them. I don't want to kill you, Karen, but I will."

"You had this planned all along, didn't you?" Shannon spat at him. "You knew you were going to ruin my life when you came here to interview me the first time, didn't you?"

"No, I didn't. I didn't start to suspect that you were a sociopath until later," Cooper replied candidly, his gaze and his gun steady. "I didn't find out the extent of it until later still, and I never told Olivia. You've got approximately three seconds to put down your gun or I'm going to put *you* down."

Shannon had the nerve to look amused. "Wait, so we're all just going to start shooting on the count of three?"

Cooper cocked a brow, shrugged. "I guess so. One."

"You're bluffing."

"Two."

"Okay, so you're not bluff—"

A single gunshot fired into the room and everyone froze. Then Shannon began screaming in agony. Broderick was the first to spring into action, kicking the gun that fell to the floor at Shannon's feet clear across the room and then catching her slumping body midair before it could meet the same fate. With a flick of his wrist, he spun her around and, with little sympathy for the fact that she'd just been shot in the hand and was bleeding profusely from the resulting wound, handcuffed her. "Sit," he barked and dropped her into the nearest chair. "And be quiet," he snarled as he whipped out his cell phone and began dialing. "Elise?" he called out, seemingly as an afterthought.

"Right here," Elise Carrington said, rising from where she'd been crouched in a corner of the room, hidden behind a wing-backed side chair and a towering artificial tree. Per the plan they had worked out before moving in, she had crept down to the first floor and positioned herself in the study while Olivia and Shannon were upstairs in Olivia's bedroom. The pearl-handled .22 gun that she was never without was still smoking in the palm of her hand when she set it down on a side table and hurried over to Olivia.

"Oh, baby! Come here!" She folded Olivia into her arms and held on for dear life. Pulling back after several seconds of relieved sobbing, she smoothed Olivia's hair back from her face and searched her eyes. "I was worried sick! What were you thinking, goading her like that?"

"Ups-stairs," Olivia sputtered, clinging to her sister for dear life. "When w-we walked out of my bedroom, I looked down the hallway toward your bedroom and I s-saw the door open and the l-light on. I knew I hadn't left it on so I thought… I hoped…" She trailed off as she collapsed into Elise's arms and dissolved into tears again. "Oh my God, I was so scared." It didn't seem to occur to her until after she had cried herself empty that Elise was actually there with her in the flesh. She pulled back, wide-eyed and staring in disbelief. "Wait. What are you doing here?"

Clinging just as tightly, Elise smiled through her own tears. "I was going to surprise you," she said. "Surprise! Oh and apparently Broderick has our house bugged, so we've been listening in this whole time."

"What!"

"Never mind that right now, sweetie. Are you sure you're okay?"

"Yes, I'm fine. Just a little shaken up and my head hurts like hell. But I think I'll survive," Olivia said, reaching up to touch the lump on the back of her head gently and grimacing. Her gaze fell on the tall, muscle-bound man across the room just then and her bottom lip trembled. "Broderick," she whined piti-fully, pulling away from Elise and rushing over to him with tears in her eyes for a bear hug. "I'm going to kill you later but I'm so glad to see you right now! When did you two—"

"Uh, excuse me…"

All eyes swerved over to Cooper's ashen face. "I'm sorry to interrupt this touching little family reunion, but I'm not all right, in case anyone cares," he put in tightly.

"Um…babe, why don't we take Shannon and wait for the police outside, on the porch?" Elise suggested, shooting Broderick a meaningful look. "I think these two could use a little privacy."

Liking her immediately, Cooper nodded his thanks without taking his eyes off Olivia's face. As soon as they were gone and he was alone with her, he looked for her eyes and found them moist and brimming with possibility. His heart twisted in his chest as they stared at each other. "You are…" He trailed off as the full magnitude of what had just happened, of what could have just happened, slammed into him. Momentarily speechless, he lifted unsteady hands and dragged them down his face wearily, his breath whistling through his tense fingers forcefully. A moment later he sank down onto the arm of the couch and took a second to get himself together. "Do you have any idea how scared I was, listening to you goad her into shooting you? I thought… You don't even want to know what I thought. Are you all right?"

"Yes." She reached up and fingered the goose egg on her head and grimaced. "Mostly. I'm sorry you were worried."

"Worried?" He looked at her like she was crazy. "Olivia…you are everything to me. Worried doesn't even begin to scratch the surface. Baby, I was beside myself. I love you. I want to spend the rest of my life with you. It just occurred to me that I could've lost you tonight, and that would have devastated me. So I'm sorry, but after what happened here tonight, if you think that I'm going to just stand by and allow you to move to London, then you're out of your mind. Because—"

"I'm not," she cut in. "I won't."

As if in a trance, Cooper stared into Olivia's beautiful, watery eyes and released a long, shaky breath. "You're pregnant?" She nodded hesitantly and he thought that she'd never looked more beautiful. "How long have you known?"

"Only a few days. I was going to tell you today… when I called you back."

"At four o'clock."

"At four o'clock. But then everything happened and… Are you angry?"

"Angry?" Cooper sputtered incredulously, gaping at the love of his life. "How could I possibly be angry, Olivia? I just found out that the woman of my dreams is carrying my child, a child that we made together, while we were falling in love. I just found out that the woman I love is having my baby and you want to know if I'm angry? My God, Olivia, anger is the last thing I'm feeling right now. What I am is so in love with you that it scares the shit out of me. What about you? Are you angry? I hurt you and I never meant to do that. Can you ever forgive me?"

"I already have. I was going to tell you that today, too. I love you, Cooper."

"I'm glad to hear that because, while I was listening to you risk your life, I too experienced a moment of clarity, Olivia. I saw the future too, and there wasn't a goddamn soccer mom anywhere in it. There was only you, love. Marry me."

"Yes!" Olivia cried, racing across the room, toward Cooper. "Yes, yes, I will!" He opened his arms just in time to catch her when she leapt.

* * * * *

There was something about the slow way his gaze traveled up her body before meeting her eyes that made her take a deep breath. She shook her head, then quickly changed directions. "I mean, yes. Of course we do. Does anybody else need anything?" she asked as she walked around the table. Everyone said no.

Tracee dashed into the kitchen and found the steak sauce in the pantry. She couldn't believe that guy was sitting in their dining room. He'd recognized her, but he hadn't said anything about yesterday. Steak sauce in hand, she returned to the dining room.

When she set the bottle on the table, he thanked her with a self-satisfied grin on his face.

"I hope everything went all right yesterday," he added before she walked away.

Tracee placed her hands on her hips. So, he wanted to acknowledge what he'd done.

"Luckily yes, everything was fine. Thank you for asking."

Bridget Anderson writes provocative romance-filled stories about smart women and the men they love. She's written for Kensington, BET Books and Harlequin. *Rendezvous* (Kensington, 1999), a romantic suspense novel, was later adapted into a made-for-television movie by BET Books. Bridget always knew she'd be a writer. Her first book was made of construction paper, cardboard and pink yarn. In fact, she still has it.

While growing up in Louisville, Kentucky, Bridget penned several short stories, for her eyes only, which fueled the flames for a writing career. She is a member of Romance Writers of America, Georgia Romance Writers and The Authors Guild. When she's not writing, she loves to travel. She's fallen in love with Paris, France, and can't wait to get back to Ghana, West Africa.

Bridget currently resides north of metro Atlanta with her husband and a big dog that she swears is part human.

Books by Bridget Anderson

Harlequin Kimani Romance

When I Fall in Love
The Only One for Me
Something About You
The Sweetest Affair

Visit the Author Profile page
at Harlequin.com for more titles.

THE SWEETEST AFFAIR

Bridget Anderson

To Shirley Harrison, who's always there
to help me out of a tough spot.

Dear Reader,

Thank you for purchasing *The Sweetest Affair*, the fourth book in the Coleman House series. I hope you will enjoy reading it as much as I enjoyed writing it. This is the last book in the series, and I'm sad to see it end. I hope you'll also read the first three books in the series: *When I Fall in Love*, *The Only One for Me* and *Something About You*. I'm considering a spin-off series, so if you'd like to see that happen, drop me a note and let me know.

To learn more about past and future releases, sign up for my newsletter on my website at www.bridgetanderson.net. I love and appreciate reviews, so please take the time to leave one. You can find me on social media at Twitter: @Banders319; Facebook: Banders319; Instagram: bandersonbooks.

Thank you,

Bridget Anderson

Chapter 1

Tracee Coleman closed the barn door to the Coleman House's U-pick store. The Coleman House estate was part bed-and-breakfast and part organic farm. Tracee worked part-time in the kitchen with her aunt Rita, cooking breakfast and pastries for the guests and family members who worked there.

"Well, that's it. Another successful season comes to a close. And not one cookie or pastry left." Tracee walked over to the empty bin that had earlier held bags of pastries. Her heart swelled with pride thinking about how well her sweets had been received at the bed-and-breakfast over the years. She hoped that same success would follow her into her own shop.

Tracee's best friend and soon-to-be business partner, Mae Watts, helped her gather empty bins and stack them up against the wall. "Girl, this is just the beginning of great things to come. When are you going to tell Rollin you're leaving?" Mae asked.

Tracee shrugged. "I've been juggling both jobs pretty well so far. Besides, they know I'm trying to open my own store. That's not something I can keep from my family."

"Yeah, I guess not. Why would you even want to? If it wasn't for Rollin, you probably wouldn't be where you are. Girl, you've got the best family."

Tracee finished stacking all the bins on their shelf against the wall, thinking about how she'd gone from baking cakes and pies for the bed-and-breakfast to taking orders from customers all over town. If Rollin hadn't let her use the bed-and-breakfast kitchen on numerous occasions, Tracee's Cake World would still be a pipe dream.

"Ladies, thank you for everything."

Tracee turned around as her cousin Rollin and his wife, Tayler, walked into the barn. They were the cutest and most generous couple she'd ever met. When they hired her and her sister, Kyla, two years ago, she'd had no idea the experience would be such a rewarding one. At the time, she was only looking for a part-time job. Instead, she found her future.

"No need to thank us," Tracee said as she came around to meet them at the front of the store by the registers. "We're just tidying up so we can get out of here. My shift is up."

"He means thank you for hanging around while we helped settle up the church folk. They cleaned us out today. We don't have a lot of produce left to donate to the shelter this evening."

Mae walked over to join them. "Yeah, those ladies purchased everything that wasn't nailed down. You have such a supportive church community."

Mae lived over in Garrard County and attended a Presbyterian church in her neighborhood. However, she'd attended Shiloh Baptist with Tracee on enough occasions to know half the congregation. And it was those networking skills that Tracee counted on to help them in the future.

"Oh, Tracee, I almost forgot." Tayler pulled a piece of paper from her pocket and handed it to Tracee. "Mrs. Bond gave this to me for Kyla. She heard about the money Kyla's collecting to help with her African project. She doesn't get online, so she wrote a check made out to the nonprofit. Can you pass this on to Kyla?"

Tracee took the check and read the amount— twenty-five dollars. "That is so sweet of her. Didn't they just have some major work done on their house?"

Tayler nodded. "They did, but everyone's so proud of the work Kyla's doing they want to be a part of it." Tayler reached out and fluffed her hands through Tracee's hair. "Look at you, looking all like Tracee Ellis Ross on television with this big hair today."

Tracee shook her head, happy that her curls were popping today. "I know, huh." She folded the check and put it in her pocket. She was proud of her little sister, too. Kyla was a PhD candidate who'd started a small, local nonprofit program teaching people where their food came from. Now, with the help of her fiancé, she was expanding to several small communities in Africa, which was where she'd been for the last few weeks.

Mae cleared her throat. "You ready to go?"

Tracee shook the thoughts from her head. "Sure, let me run up to the house and get my purse. I'll meet you in the car."

"What are you guys up to tonight?" Tayler asked.

"First I'm taking Tracee to pick her car up from the shop, then we're going to stop and get Gavin and Donna a baby shower gift. What is this, Tracee? Baby number three?" Mae asked.

Tracee stopped at the door and turned around. "Oh, I almost forgot about that. That's right, I need a gift before Saturday."

"That little family of Gavin's is growing," Tayler stated.

"It sure is. I'll be right back." Tracee opened the door and hurried toward the house. Mae wasn't aware of what she'd just done, but by bringing up Gavin's coming baby, she'd only added to the feeling of failure that Tracee was battling. She wanted a family of her own one day.

She walked through the back door of the bed-and-breakfast so as not to disturb the guests enjoying the front porch. On this last day of September, they were at capacity. Once in the back office, she pulled her purse from a drawer before going to find her aunt Rita and cousin Corra in the kitchen discussing the evening's dinner preparations.

"You gone, baby?" her aunt Rita asked.

"Yes, ma'am. Mae's taking me to pick up my car."

Tracee's cell phone rang, and she excused herself and stepped away.

"Hello?"

"Hey, Tracee, this is Melanie—we spoke a few weeks ago regarding cakes for my upcoming wedding."

Tracee almost dropped the phone. Of course she remembered Melanie Jefferson. Her family owned the largest winery in the area, and she'd snagged herself one of the richest guys in the state. "Hi, Melanie. Yes, I remember our conversation. I baked a cake for your social club, I believe?" Tracee knew that was right, but she didn't want Melanie to know how excited she was to get this call.

"That's correct. Well, I've narrowed my search, and if you can fit us into your schedule, we'd love to sample your cakes."

Tracee thrust her fist into the air and waved it around. It took everything in her not to jump around and scream at the top of her lungs. "Of course I have room in my schedule for you and your fiancé, Melanie. How soon are we talking?"

"I was thinking about a week from now. My fiancé, Harry, is in France right now, but he'll be back on Sunday. How about Tuesday afternoon?"

"Sure, one moment, let me check my calendar." Tracee put her cell phone on mute and ran her hand through her hair, pulling it back as she caught her breath. Her excited fidgeting captured the attention of Corra and her aunt, who stared at her with raised brows. All she could do was smile as she checked a nonexistent calendar.

"Melanie, Tuesday at noon is perfect. I usually meet clients at the Rival Hotel, if that works for you guys?"

"That's perfect—they're in the middle of town."

"Great, now let's talk a little about what you have in mind." Tracee hurried around the kitchen looking for a piece of paper. As if she knew just what her cousin was doing, Corra opened a drawer and produced a notepad and a pen. Tracee took it, mouthed *thank you* and eased into a kitchen chair. While Melanie described what type of cake she had in mind, Tracee scribbled everything down. They spent the next few minutes discussing Tracee's specialties before she gave Melanie her Pinterest URL, where she could see more samples of her designs.

The ladies in the kitchen continued going over dinner plans until Tracee hung up. The minute she did, they stopped everything.

"Was that really Melanie Jefferson?" Corra asked.

Tracee smiled and set her phone down. "It most certainly was."

"I heard she was getting married. Did she ask you to do the cake?" Aunt Rita asked.

"She wants to have an official tasting—can you believe it? She might hire me to do her wedding cake."

"Tracee, that's wonderful!" Aunt Rita added. "You know that is going to be a huge wedding. And a huge opportunity for you."

Tracee stood up. "I know. I have to make sure we get this wedding. I did a cake for her aunt's social club a few months back, and everybody practically drooled over the cake."

"That's because your cakes are to die for. You see how fast they leave our shelves. I have all the faith in the world you'll get this order," Corra said.

Tracee sighed. "I know Melanie likes my cakes. We'll just have to hope her fiancé does, too. I've scheduled the cake tasting for Tuesday."

"Do you want to have it here?" Corra asked, excitement dancing in her eyes.

"No, I can't. I've infringed on you guys too much with my side business. I'm going to use the Rival Hotel. They have several small meeting rooms that I've used when I didn't want to meet clients at my apartment. I don't think I want to invite Melanie and her fiancé to my apartment—he'll wonder what type of ghetto cake lady she hired."

Corra walked over and opened the pantry. "Girl, there's nothing ghetto about you or your business. You and Mae are so professional in your approach. Why do you think so many people want to patronize you? And your Pinterest page, oh my God! That page makes my mouth water every time I check it out."

Tracee took the sheet of paper from the notepad and put it in her purse before returning the pad and pen to the drawer. "That's Mae's excellent photography skills. She's working on a website now."

"You guys are going to be such a huge success. Just wait until Melanie's wedding details hit the papers and the internet. Your phone is going to start blowing up. I hope you're ready for what's about to happen to you."

Tracee thought about all the success happening around her—she was beyond ready. "I've been waiting for a break like this ever since I moved to Danville. I didn't know the idea of opening my own place was even remotely possible, but with a little help, I may be able to pull it off. And Ms. Melanie offers the type of visibility I need."

"Go get what's yours, girl. We're going to have to start purchasing our treats from you from now on."

Tracee laughed. "Don't worry, you're not losing me just yet. I'm not going anywhere until we're able to open the doors on our own place."

Aunt Rita crossed her arms over her chest. "Well, I've been around you Colemans long enough to know that when you go after something you want, you get it. Melanie won't be able to say no."

Tracee hugged her aunt and cousin before running out to the car to share the news with Mae.

Laurent Martin pulled his Mercedes up to the valet station at Brandywine in Woodland Hills, California, got out and then tossed his keys to the young man with the restaurant's logo embossed on his black shirt. He was having lunch with his father, and Thomas Martin didn't like to be kept waiting. Time Is Money and Money Is Time was his father's motto. *If something is taking up too much of your time, it's eating into your bottom line. Get rid of it.* That was another of Thomas's sayings.

Inside the restaurant, Laurent spotted his father right away. Standing at six feet five inches, an inch taller than Laurent, his father had a way of commanding the room, even if he was sitting down. Thomas Martin had taught his boys to work hard for everything they had. Just because the family owned a chain of luxury hotels didn't mean they were guaranteed a piece of the business unless they earned it. And all three Martin boys worked their tails off.

Laurent briefly stopped at the hostess station, where he was pointed in his father's direction. He glanced down at his new Tom Ford suit, hoping it would meet his father's approval. Appearance was everything in the world of luxury, according to his father.

"Laurent, you're right on time." Thomas Martin looked up as Laurent reached the table.

Laurent glanced as his watch before pulling out the seat across from his father. Fifteen minutes early was on time, on time was late. He'd arrived fifteen minutes early.

Thomas smiled as Laurent took a seat. "So, how has your day been?"

A waiter hurried over to take Laurent's drink order. He thanked him. "So far so good. No fires to put out—yet anyway."

"That's good." Thomas took a sip of red wine, his preferred drink at lunch, then he set his glass down. "Well, now that the summer's over, it's time to prepare for the upcoming holiday season. Do you have any new developments you want to run by me?"

Laurent gave his father a questioning gaze. This wasn't the kind of conversation they usually had in public. The waiter came by, and Laurent glanced at the menu before ordering his favorite onion soup and petite filet mignon. "No new developments. Why? Are Marquis or Aubrey working on something new?" His oldest brother, Marquis, always had something in play, but Aubrey spent most of his time maintaining what they had.

"As a matter of fact, yes. Marquis is working on a renovation project for the Grand Cayman location. I initially thought he was only trying to get a vacation out of the deal, but if he can make some improvements at the same time, I'm not going to sweat him over it."

"That sounds like a sweet plan," Laurent added.

"If he finishes before the holiday rush, it will be. If not, and he causes us any cancellations, I might have to move him back to cover the US locations. You know how he can talk his way into just about anything."

Laurent laughed at the reference to Marquis. His father was correct—Marquis could talk his way into a royal wedding if he had to. In fact, he was so good he'd talked their father into letting him run all the Caribbean hotels by himself. Aubrey was just as persuasive and had talked himself into the European market. Trips to France and Italy were on his calendar frequently.

While his father continued to discuss a little family business, Laurent sat wondering what they were really here to discuss. Thomas Martin wasn't in the habit of calling a lunch meeting just to catch up. His father wanted something from him.

After their meal was served, and his father went

through another drink, he finally got around to the reason for the lunch.

"I don't think I ever told you how impressed I was with the way you handled that harassment situation at Abelle Toronto last month."

Laurent nodded. "Thank you."

"You're living up to your title as family trou-bleshooter. Whatever the situation, turn it over to Laurent—he can handle anything. I appreciate you, son. I can't be everywhere."

"It's not a problem. It's what I do best," Laurent said.

"Which brings me to another challenge for you."

Here it comes. Laurent lowered his fork and took a drink of water to clear his palate. He sat back and waited for his father to dump some project on him that neither of his brothers wanted.

"You're also an excellent negotiator. I've watched you over the years. And you're who I need to help close the deal on a small-town hotel chain I've been trying to purchase."

Laurent was surprised. Thomas Martin was a master negotiator. All of their hotels were in prime locations due to his father's stellar skills. Why would he need him to step in? "I don't understand. This is something you've been working on?"

Thomas nodded. "I have. From a distance, with very little luck."

Laurent squinted as he tried to read the truth from his father's eyes. "What's the real story?" he asked.

His father shrugged. "No story. Just a stubborn old man who can't see a good deal when it looks him right in the face. I need you to help him see the benefits of selling to us. Tonight I'll email you all the details. You should be able to wrap things within the next week or two."

Laurent shook his head. "I'm leaving for the Caribbean tomorrow for the next two weeks. I take vacations, too, you know."

"Laurent, this deal can't wait for you to come back from vacation. This is a simple acquisition that we should have closed already. Your gift of persuasion is required on this one. I need you to leave by this weekend at the latest."

Oh, no, you don't! "You want to hijack my vacation and send me off to some godforsaken place to negotiate a deal you couldn't get yourself? Why does that not sound so appealing to me?"

"Because that's not the situation. You're merely postponing your vacation for a couple of weeks to handle something for the family that, frankly, only *you* can do. Come on, you know your brothers. They're like bulls in a china shop. This deal is going to take a little more finesse. A more subtle approach, if you will."

Laurent was being fed a bowl of crap, but he nodded anyway. "And that's where I come in," he said, pointing to himself. "You know, something about this stinks. Where is this hotel?"

His father puffed up his chest and cleared his throat. "No deal I've ever tried to negotiate stinks! This is an opportunity for Martin Enterprises to own more than boutique hotels. We've talked about expanding into the medium-size hotel market for years, and that's what this chain will do for us."

"Where is the hotel?" Laurent asked with a little more bass in his voice this time.

Raising his chin and looking down his nose at his son, Thomas Martin let him know he didn't appreciate the tone. "It's in Danville, Kentucky. A short drive from Lexington."

Laurent tilted his head and blinked. "Where in the hell is that?"

"You've heard of the Kentucky Derby, haven't you?"

"Of course I have."

"Well, there's another horse track in Kentucky. Keeneland is in Lexington, and this place isn't too far from there. We can even relocate one of the hotels to Lexington to take advantage of the racing industry."

Laurent shook his head. "I knew it. So you're sending me to some little hick town while Marquis and Aubrey get the more appealing jobs. Why do I feel as if I'm being punished for my negotiating skills?"

The waiter returned to refresh Laurent's water. Thomas paused until he left to continue.

"You're not being punished. I've been watching you over the years, and I'm fully aware of the fact that you've wanted to put your own stamp on a property just as your brothers have done. So I'm going to offer you something better than what your brothers have. Son, you have a creative side to you that extends beyond the realm of business. I have no doubt that given the opportunity, any property you control will be a huge success. That's why I'm prepared to give you complete ownership of one of the hotels."

Everything inside Laurent's body screamed *yes*. His spine stiffened as he sat up straight and nodded. He needed to conceal his excitement until he heard all the details of his father's offer. The old man could be generous, but he could also be calculating.

"You don't have to thank me now, but a little show of appreciation wouldn't hurt. I'm giving you something both of your brothers would die to have."

"I do appreciate it. As a matter of fact, it sounds too good to be true, so I'm waiting for the other shoe to drop. What's the catch?"

Thomas shook his head. "None. You've earned this. All you have to do is return with a signed deal for the chain and you have your very own hotel to do with as you please. Of course, if you want input from me or your brothers, we're always here for you. Once it's yours, you can keep working with the current staff, or establish your own staff—it's up to you. But I need you in Danville next week."

Laurent couldn't contain the corners of his mouth as they turned up into a smile. How long had he expressed his desire to strike out on his own and establish something totally different from the luxury five-star hotels his family owned? Each hotel was a one-of-a-kind creation with its own personality based on the location. Abelle's, for example, with its French theme, served an elite clientele that demanded nothing but the best.

"Thank you. I think I'll be taking the first flight to

Danville on Monday morning." Laurent beamed with so much excitement he could hardly contain himself.

"You'll have to fly into Lexington and drive to Danville, but it's a short trip. When you arrive you can check in to the hotel like a regular guest. No need to alert anyone as to your intentions right away. Let's meet Monday morning to go over the current offer, then you can be on your way."

Laurent finished lunch with his father on a good note. This had to be the best lunch they'd ever shared.

Chapter 2

Laurent pulled up to the Rival Hotel in a rented, dark blue Hyundai Elantra. The car was a calculated choice for who he needed to be this weekend. His father had tried to work with Mr. Patel, the hotel's owner, with no success. No doubt it was his father's overconfidence, often mistaken for arrogance, that got in the way. Laurent had met with his father to go over all the particulars of the offer, which was very generous. However, after that meeting he postponed his departure until Friday, in order to do some of his own research. Mr. Patel had said he'd have to think it over and discuss it with his family, but he hadn't gotten back to Thomas.

Laurent's presence was to push those conversations along while making the family feel comfortable that they were getting the best deal possible.

He'd traveled in his athletic gear, another calculated choice, and left his Gucci luggage at home. He'd purchased a Samsonite duffel and an inexpensive suit bag especially for this trip. He got out of the car and looked up at the hotel, which was in need of a little TLC. The location in the middle of town was a plus, and probably what attracted his father in the first place. However, the building merely faded into the background, with very little curb appeal. Now he was curious as to the condition of the interior.

The front doors slid open as he carried his gear into the hotel lobby. The first thing that hit him was the overly perfumed smell. What were they trying to cover up? The hotel was about ten years old, but the choice of decor gave it a much older feel. For a Friday afternoon, things were kind of slow. There weren't very many cars in the parking lot, and only one person sat in the lobby reading a magazine. Laurent walked over to the front desk to check in.

"Good afternoon, sir, checking in?" A young, studious-looking Indian guy in thick wire-rimmed glasses greeted Laurent with a smile.

His plaid shirt didn't look like a hotel-issued uniform, which meant things were probably pretty lax at the Rival. Laurent returned the smile. "Yes, I am. Laurent Martin."

The young man glanced down at the computer, inputting information until he found Laurent's name. "I have you here, sir. Laurent Martin, a king room for a week. Is that correct?" he asked.

"It is," Laurent confirmed as he reached into his pocket for his license and credit card.

The clerk accepted his cards. "I'll be right back."

The minute he walked away, Laurent shook his head. The clerk shouldn't have to leave the front desk with the customer's information. That would have to change once he took over the hotel. He turned around and took another look at the uninviting lobby. Everything was square, with sharp edges and small bursts of colors. There seemed to be no theme at all, just some stiff furniture and a table that held what looked like brochures from local establishments.

"Hello, Mr. Martin!"

Laurent turned back around at the sound of his name spoken in a much deeper voice than the front desk clerk's. A taller man, also of Indian descent, with a thick mustache and eyebrows, greeted him with a huge smile on his face.

"I'm Raji Patel, but please call me Raji." He reached his arm across the counter to shake Laurent's hand. "My father informed me of your visit. He's looking forward to meeting with you."

Surprised, Laurent returned the handshake. "It's a pleasure to meet you, Raji. I'm looking forward to meeting with your father as well."

Raji reached back and took Laurent's identification from the desk clerk and handed the cards back to Laurent. "Here you go. I'm sorry, but our card reader out here isn't working at the moment."

Another situation Laurent would have to fix. He placed his cards back in his pocket. "No problem. I understand."

Raji finished checking Laurent in while the young

clerk moved over to help an older couple who'd just walked in.

"I'll get you your keys so you can check out your room. I'm sure you're tired after that long flight," he said as he smiled up at Laurent.

"It wasn't that bad. I practically live on airplanes, so I'm used to it," Laurent said as he accepted the room keys from Raji.

"Man, I couldn't take all that flying. I fly about two or three times a year because I have to check on our other hotels. Didn't experience any turbulence, did you?" he asked.

Laurent smiled and shook his head. "No, none."

"Good for you. My dad tells me your family owns a chain of hotels as well. Are you the head sales guy or something?"

"No, I'm VP of lifestyle brand management."

Laurent watched Raji's faraway look as he nodded his head. "In other words, I represent the company with regards to new developments, proposals and negotiations. I offer suggestions on brand and type best fit based on the proposed market and location. Along with managing guest satisfaction and a host of other responsibilities."

Raji nodded. "I started working for my dad right out of high school. Worked my way up to general manager."

Laurent smiled. "Will your father be around this evening?" he asked, wanting to get things started and over with as soon as possible.

"My dad probably won't be around until tomorrow afternoon. Along with my brother, Arjun. You'll meet them then. If you're up to it, I can give you a tour of the property once you've rested? All of the hotels have this same layout, but the decor is different."

"That would be great. Let me make a few phone calls and I'll be back down."

"Sure, take your time. I'll be in the office. Just ring the bell on the counter when you come back."

Laurent found his third-floor room and was pleasantly surprised by the clean design and decor. It wasn't fancy, but appropriate for the location. After checking out the room and making a few phone calls, he decided to return to the lobby for that tour. Before he could ring the bell, the younger desk clerk popped out from the back room.

"Raji will be right with you. He said to make yourself at home."

Laurent did just that and walked over to the couch and had a seat. He leafed through the current *People* magazine before Raji walked out to greet him.

"Well, that didn't take long at all," Raji pointed out.

Laurent stood up. "No, I'm kind of eager to check things out."

Raji began the tour by pointing out where breakfast was served every morning. There was a small gym down the hall, and a pool, which happened to be closed at the moment. Laurent made mental notes as Raji gave him an in-depth look at the property Thomas wanted so badly.

"This hall gets the most traffic." Raji pointed down a corridor with lots of closed doors. "Conference rooms. Almost every group in town meets here for one thing or another." He walked down the hall, calling out the names of the rooms.

Laurent looked at the well-traveled, outdated carpeting and wondered how any proprietor could let his property get this far out of hand.

"It might not be the Taj Mahal, but it's clean."

The irritated tone to Raji's voice let Laurent know he hadn't been able to hide the displeased look on his face. While he hadn't meant to insult, he was afraid he had just made a tactical error. Mistake number one.

After the tour, he found a pizzeria within walking distance of the hotel. He returned and settled in for the night. His cell phone rang while he was catching up on the news. He picked up the phone to see Marquis's name.

"So what do you think of the place?" Marquis asked, sounding as if he had a smile on his face.

"It's a dump. The location is perfect, but this place needs a major overhaul." Laurent adjusted the pillows against his back and grabbed the television remote to mute the sound.

"Of course. Once we take ownership, the entire chain will transform into something that's up to Martin Enterprises standards."

"You mean once I take ownership, don't you?" Laurent was certain his father had informed his brothers that he was giving him a hotel. He shared everything with them.

Marquis laughed. "That's right, this one's all yours. If you can pull it off, anyway. Have you seen your old fishing buddy yet?"

"What fishing buddy?" Laurent could count the number of times he'd been fishing on one hand.

"Sam Kane, your buddy from Berkeley? Didn't he used to take you guys out on a fishing boat all the time and come back empty-handed?"

Laurent laughed. "Yeah, we called it fishing, but every trip turned into a yacht party. It's hard to concentrate on fish with so many women on board." A brief picture of bikini-clad women dancing around the boat brought a smile to his face. "Man, I haven't seen Sam in years."

"When Dad told me you were going to Danville, I remembered running into Sam's father a couple of months ago. Sam met a girl from that area and moved to Kentucky. He's a professor at the local college in Danville. I wasn't sure if you knew that or not."

"I had no idea." He thought about how boring the town had looked on his drive in. "Why in the hell would he give up life in California for this place?"

"Hey, the love of a good woman will make you do some crazy things. I think he's married with kids and all. You should look him up."

Laurent shook his head. In college, Sam had had a different woman every semester. Sometimes more than one a semester. He loved to party and show everybody a good time. "I'm going to do that. But married with kids—man, I might not even recognize Sam."

"Tell him I said hello when you two hook up. Well, I just wanted to offer my assistance if you need anything. I know you've got these negotiations down pat, but I'm here for you if you need me."

"Thanks, Marquis, that means a lot." Marquis was a numbers man who could quickly provide Laurent with statistics on anything he needed in a matter of hours.

"No problem, bro. I'll be going back to Grand Cayman over the weekend, but I'm available by cell."

The Caribbean. Did he have to rub it in? "I don't think I'll have any problems, but if I need you, I'll reach out to you or your assistant."

"Oh, that would just make Lonnie's day. You know she has a crush on you. Every time you come to my office, it takes her several minutes to pull herself together after you leave."

Laurent laughed. "That is not the truth. But tell her I said hello anyway."

They shared playful laughter before Laurent ended the call and decided to call it a night. He'd skip looking over the hotel paperwork; he'd read enough on the plane. Instead, he'd hit the sack early and have a good run in the morning. That was the best way to see the surrounding area and survey what he was getting into. Then he'd have to look up his old buddy Sam. Hopefully, he hadn't changed too much and could still show him a good time while he was in town.

Tracee kept glancing in the rearview mirror at the boxes strapped into the back seat. She'd prepared a sample wedding cake along with a dozen cupcakes in various flavors for Melanie Jefferson's cake tasting this afternoon.

"Are you nervous?" Mae asked from the passenger's seat.

"As hell! I just hope he likes my cake. I know Melanie likes them, but if this fella of hers doesn't, we're sunk."

"Girl, don't worry—he'll probably like whatever she likes. I'm also eager to check out this space that you're wanting to lease."

"When the Rival Hotel first opened, my grandmother had a little coffee and pastry spot there. When she passed, my cousin Betty took over. The space grew into this small café, and she ran it until she passed a few years ago. So you can kind of say the space has been in my family for years. It has its own separate entrance and everything. After my cousin's passing, Mr. Patel closed the coffee shop's doors. I don't think it was ever very lucrative. I'd forgotten all about it until I was helping Corra and Tayler with one of their Color of Success events. The windows have this fancy paper on them so you can't tell what's inside. They opened the room to store some of the larger items for the event and I saw this space that would be perfect for our café—with a little remodeling, of course."

"And the location is perfect. We can take advantage of the hotel crowd as well as the downtown business community. I'm getting more and more excited about this venture."

"Me too," Tracee said after taking another glance at her precious cargo in the back seat. She pulled into the Rival Hotel's parking lot and found a space by the back door, which was closer to the hotel's small kitchen. She needed to store her baked goods in their refrigerator while she set up everything else for the meeting.

The front desk clerk unlocked the small meeting room she'd reserved and had the kitchen provide a side table with water and glasses. The room wasn't the most elegant of places to meet, but it did provide the privacy she needed and a backdrop for her to display her cakes without taking anything away from them. Within minutes, she and Mae had their brochures on display and had made sure the temperature in the room was just right.

Mae rubbed her palms together. "Time to bring in the cakes."

Tracee's heartbeat pounded in her chest. This was it. The moment she'd been waiting for. It was time to put her best foot forward. Mae's naturally flawless face and short curly hair always gave her a professional, polished look. She, however, had tried to tame her curls by pulling them back into a ponytail, but loose tendrils of hair were touching the sides of her face and neck.

They entered the kitchen and collected their cakes from the woman on staff. Tracee carried the sample wedding cake, while Mae followed her with the box of assorted cupcakes. Under her arm was a sleeve that held the cutting utensils Tracee liked.

The kitchen door opened into the corridor that led to the meeting rooms, the pool and the gym. Because her hands were full, Tracee turned around and, using her butt, pushed on the door. Immediately, something didn't feel right.

Chapter 3

Downtown Danville was about as slow as Laurent thought it would be. In some ways it reminded him of the small villages in Quebec he used to frequent with his mother when he was a child, only there were no French-speaking people here. He'd wanted to get up early for his run but overslept when he forgot to set his phone. His morning runs cleared his head and readied his mind for the work to come. Instead, he pulled on his running gear and went for a jog rather than eating breakfast.

With earbuds in, listening to his favorite playlist, he jogged his way back to the hotel. He wasn't sure what time Mr. Patel would be returning, but he planned to take a shower, dress and be ready for anything. Some community social group must have been having a meeting, because there were little old ladies mingling all around. Laurent caught the front desk clerk's attention and asked where he could find the closest vending machine. He needed a bottle of water. The clerk motioned down the hall, and said something about "toward the gym."

Switching the music on his cell phone to his cooldown playlist, he continued briskly down the hall toward the gym. There were several doors, but none of them had a vending sign. He started to say forget it and just go up to the vending machine on the third floor when he saw an unmarked door and a light coming from underneath it.

"This must be it," he said to himself. He reached for the doorknob and pulled it open, getting the surprise of his life.

A scream, followed by something flying over his head, ended with a pair of big, beautiful black eyes looking up at him. On reflex he'd grabbed the woman falling out of the door under her arms, just in time to keep her from hitting the floor. The light floral scent of her perfume tickled his nose, causing him to take a deep breath. Still inside the doorway, another woman stood with eyes bucked and mouth wide-open. That wasn't a good sign.

"Oh my God!" the woman in the doorway screamed.

As the woman in his arms struggled to right herself, Laurent tried to make sense of what had just happened. That wasn't the room with the vending machine. He helped her up before yanking the earbuds from his ears.

"Look at what you just did!" the woman yelled as she straightened to her full height.

When she set her eyes on Laurent, he stopped breathing for a second. She was beautiful. Her eyes could stop traffic, and those ruby-red lips were calling his name. Her hair was pulled back, but ringlets of curls had loosened as she'd fallen into his arms. His eyes followed her as she walked around him and over to something on the floor—a crushed white box. He needed to say something, but he was speechless.

"Oh, man, not my cake! Not now!" she screamed.

He found something of a voice. "I'm sorry, I didn't see you."

"Girl, is it okay?" Both women were in the hall now, as the beautiful one from his arms gingerly righted the box and examined the contents. A few of the older women from the lobby had come peeking down the hall to have a look.

Laurent had the sinking feeling he'd just ruined this beautiful woman's day.

She threw the top back. "It's ruined! My beautiful cake is ruined." She quickly turned to the other woman. "You have the cupcakes, don't you?"

"Right here." She held up a smaller, square box kept secure in her hands.

Both women took a deep breath before turning their fiery gazes on Laurent. He swallowed hard as he wrapped his earbuds around his cell phone. "Again, I apologize. I opened the door thinking I would find the vending machines."

The tall one with the red lips narrowed her eyes at

him, and he immediately felt worse. He had to offer to do something to fix the situation. He took a step toward them. "Let me buy you another cake," he offered. "Or two."

"You can't buy another one of those, son." The shorter, hippy sister tilted her head at him.

"Didn't you see the staff-only sign pasted above the door?" asked the tall woman, with her nostrils flared.

Laurent hadn't seen any sign on the door. But when he turned around and glanced up, sure enough there was a plaque just above the door that read Staff Only. Why in the hell wasn't it on the door instead of above the door? He quickly turned back to the women, who had "told you so" smirks on their faces.

"I'm sorry. I didn't see that. Just let me run upstairs and get my wallet—"

"This is a one-of-a-kind cake that can't be duplicated, you idiot. I have a meeting in less than fifteen minutes, and now I don't have a cake." She let out a nervous laugh. "This is crazy. The biggest meeting of my life, and you ruined it and my cake."

"Don't worry, girl, we still have the cupcakes." The shorter woman held up her box with a smile. "And even though the cake is smashed, maybe they can still taste it."

"I can't present that cake to anybody. Especially not Melanie."

Laurent wanted to return to his room and let these women resolve the situation themselves.

Then the taller one turned her wrath on him again, placing a hand on her hip. "Why are you walking through this place with those earphones on, anyway? You can't hear what's coming or going."

"I could ask why were you backing out of a room when you couldn't see what was on the other side. Like I said, I'm sorry, but I don't think I'm totally to blame here. Besides, I offered to purchase you another cake. I'm not sure what else I can do."

"You're right, you can't do anything else. You've already done enough." She turned to her friend. "I'm going to go in there and sell this, cake or no cake. Come on, Mae." Without another word they headed down the hall toward the conference rooms.

The minute she walked away, Laurent couldn't shake the feeling he should be going after her. Something about the look in those piercing eyes grabbed him by the throat and wouldn't let go. Who was she? He hadn't even gotten her name. Although at the moment, he doubted she'd want to give it to him. He stood there watching her confidently stride down the hall with a smile on his face.

Tracee's heart was pounding in her chest as she walked down the corridor. Her first official tasting was ruined unless she could quickly come up with something clever to save the day. Then again, she could just be honest with them and let them know how some jerk had caused her to lose her balance and ruin the sample cake. They still had a few minutes. When they reached the small conference room, Mae held the door open for her. Tracee took one look over her shoulder to see if that gym rat of a brother in shorts was still standing around. He wasn't.

"Girl, can you believe that dude," Mae said, following the direction of Tracee's gaze. "I bet he had that music blasting through his ears and wasn't paying attention to where he was going."

"That's obvious," Tracee said as she turned around and entered the room. "What I should have done was taken his money just on principle. If we don't get this gig, I'm going to find him and kick his butt."

Mae helped her display the cupcakes while they scrambled to come up with a story to save the day. Before they could agree on something, the door to the conference room opened, and a beautiful blonde followed by a shorter white guy entered the room.

"Melanie!" Tracee strode to the door to greet them.

"Hi, Tracee, it's so good to see you again."

"Same here." Tracee greeted Melanie with a cursory hug. They had gone to the same schools, although they hadn't been in the same classes, so Tracee felt as if they had something in common.

Melanie introduced her husband-to-be, and Tracee introduced Mae. Everyone had a seat at the round table full of brochures and cupcakes. Tracee couldn't help but notice the way Melanie's fiancé kept looking around the room. He made her nervous.

"So where's the cake?" he asked. "I thought this was going to be a cake tasting."

Tracee sighed and looked at Mae, who sat poised with her professional smile, leaving the explanation up to her. There was only one thing she could do. Tracee stood up and walked over to the side table where the smashed cake sat. In her book, honesty was the best policy.

* * *

When Laurent returned from his run, an envelope had been slipped under his door. Mr. Patel requested that he meet them at a nearby restaurant for lunch, which was just what Laurent had hoped for—a more relaxed atmosphere to discuss business. After he showered and changed into an outfit that made him look more like the average middle manager than a company VP, he was ready to meet with Mr. Patel and his sons. He grabbed his leather portfolio and set out to make magic happen.

He found the small Indian restaurant with no problem. Once inside, he was ushered to a back room, where a table filled with food, along with three men, waited for him. He assumed this was Mr. Patel and his sons.

The oldest of the three men walked toward Laurent with a slight limp in his gait. "Ah, you must be Laurent Martin?"

"Yes, sir. And you must be Mr. Patel." Laurent smiled and accepted the man's outstretched hand. Laurent towered over the shorter man, who was white headed with a salt-and-pepper mustache and beard. His face looked as if the years had taken a toll on him, but he smiled nonetheless. The tantalizing aromas and vibrant colors of the food on the table made Laurent's stomach growl. After his morning run, he was ready to eat, but he hoped they were also prepared to talk business.

"Call me Abeer. It's a pleasure to meet you after speaking with your father on so many occasions.

I'm sorry we could not come to an agreement, which would have saved you the trip."

"Well, let's hope you and I have better luck. My father has briefed me on everything, and I think we've included some incentives that you will find to your liking. Martin Enterprises is very interested in your properties, and in doing right by your family."

The older man had crossed his arms over his chest and glanced away, giving Laurent the impression that he wasn't interested in business. Mistake number two, Laurent said to himself. *He invited you to lunch—don't talk business yet. Let him lead the conversation.*

"Have you met my sons?" Mr. Patel asked as he waved them over. The two men at the other end of the table broke free of their conversation and joined them. "This is my son Raji, whom I believe you met yesterday."

Laurent nodded toward his tour guide and smiled. "Yes, I did. Thanks for the tour," he said as he shook Raji's hand.

"This is my eldest son, Arjun. He lives in Somerset and manages our hotel there."

Arjun was a slight man with a small frame. He offered Laurent a weak handshake with a closed-lip smile. He accepted the man's hand, to the sound of more people entering their private section of the restaurant. When Laurent turned around, a few women dressed in flowing saris, along with a few small children, entered the room. Arjun explained that the family would be joining them for lunch.

Mr. Patel patted Laurent on the back. "I hope you

like Indian food, and that you're hungry. A good friend of mine owns the restaurant, and he is an excellent cook. I didn't know what you'd like to eat so, as you see, we ordered a little bit of everything. Come on, let's eat."

Disappointed but not too surprised, Laurent smiled as he was introduced to the rest of the family before being told where to sit. He had truly been invited to lunch and not a business meeting, as he'd hoped. He understood now he had to gain Mr. Patel's trust before he'd speak numbers.

After a more than disappointing lunch with the Patels, where not a word of business was spoken, Laurent returned to his room and did a little digging to look up Sam Kane. Just as Marquis had said, he was a professor at Centre College. He got his old buddy on the phone.

"Man, I can't believe you're in Danville. Laurent, I haven't seen you since... I don't know man, when was the last time we were together?" Sam asked.

"Amsterdam, a year after graduation from Berkeley. We about shut the place down. That's why I almost fell out of my chair when Marquis told me you were married."

"A lot's changed since college, man. I met a woman who had the power to shut all that *partying* down. We've been married ten years now. Two kids, a boy, a girl, and a big-ass dog. Guess you can say I'm living the American dream."

Laurent shook his head. Happy for his friend, but surprised at the same time. "Man, that sounds wonderful, but somehow I thought you'd probably be practicing international law and living overseas. Thought you might follow in your old man's footsteps." *Like I did.*

"Law school really wasn't my thing. I thought about it, but after spending a few years studying abroad, I chose international relations instead. And now I'm teaching it."

"That's what I hear. Sam, the college professor. I'm proud of you, man. We have to sit down and get caught up while I'm in town."

"Definitely. How long are you going to be here?"

Laurent thought back to the lunch he'd assumed was going to be his first meeting. "A week or so, and then I'm taking a two-week vacation to someplace tropical."

"Man, we'll definitely have to get together. I want you to meet my wife. I used to tell her all about my old fishing buddies." They laughed together and went on to trade stories of fishing for women instead of fish. Sam's parties had been popular with all the beautiful women on campus.

"Say, I've got an idea. What are you doing tomorrow?" Sam asked.

It was Sunday and Laurent didn't know of a church to attend in the area. "Nothing. I'm all yours."

"My wife and I have reservations at this little bed-and-breakfast that does a wonderful Sunday brunch. It's kind of new, and we've been wanting to go for a while. Why don't you come and join us? That way we can catch up and you can meet my wife."

"Sure. Just let me know where to meet you."

"Great. I'll call and have them add one more. Is this your cell you're on? If so, I'll text you the address and time."

"Yep. You've got it."

"Fantastic! I can't wait to see my old fishing buddy."

"Me neither," Laurent said, chuckling at the way they used the term. He said goodbye, then pulled out his laptop. He was about to engage in the one thing he didn't like to do on a Saturday night—work.

Sunday brunch was another one of Tayler's ingenious ideas. Make it elegant, keep it simple and treat the guest like a VIP. Tayler knew how to take advantage of slow times and monopolize on them. Anyone who reserved a spot for Sunday brunch was offered a discounted rate for a midweek stay. Tracee was surprised by the number of folks who took advantage of the discounts. She especially liked the fact that she was able to grab a few more hours, since she hadn't been working Sundays.

This Sunday she was in a particularly good mood. Whoever said it doesn't pay to tell the truth was lying. After she'd confessed about her accident yesterday at the cake tasting, Melanie and her fiancé had still wanted to taste the smashed cake. They loved it so much that they looked through her portfolio of pictures and picked out the one they wanted. She had her first affluent client, which she hoped would lead to more business and greater revenue over time.

The kitchen was abuzz with Tayler, Corra and her aunt Rita all getting ready for the brunch crowd.

Tracee had baked a carrot cake and buttermilk panna cotta earlier that morning. Presently, there were only four guests staying at the bed-and-breakfast, with five reservations for brunch.

From the kitchen, Tracee could hear some of the guests had arrived and Tayler was welcoming them. Minutes later, Tayler entered the kitchen with orders of steak and eggs, breakfast pizza, French toast with berries, waffles and homemade jams. They also served a variety of cereals, muffins and other pastries.

Tracee backed out of the kitchen with a plate of French toast in one hand and a steak and eggs plate in the other. She turned toward the table full of handsome men and women with a smile.

"Who had the French toast?" she asked. A woman at the end of the table raised her hand. Tracee held the plates above their heads as she made her way to set the plate in front of a middle-aged black woman with beautiful salt-and-pepper hair. The hair was the first thing to catch her attention. She hoped as she grew older her hair would be so luscious.

"And how about the steak and eggs?" She held up the second plate.

"I believe that would be mine." A voice came from the other side of the table.

Tracee looked across the table and almost dropped the plate. The rude guy from the hotel yesterday looked up at her with raised brows. The corner of his lip turned up, and she realized he recognized her as well.

Chapter 4

Tracee shook the stupid look from her face and walked around the table to deposit his plate before him. "Your steak and eggs."

"Thank you. Would you happen to have any steak sauce?" he asked, glancing up at her.

There was something about the slow way his gaze traveled up her body before meeting her eyes that made her take a deep breath. She shook her head, then quickly changed directions. "I mean, yes. Of course we do. Does anybody else need anything?" she asked as she walked around the table. Everyone said no.

Tracee dashed into the kitchen and found the steak sauce in the pantry. She couldn't believe that guy was sitting in their dining room. He'd recognized her, but he hadn't said anything about yesterday. Steak sauce in hand, she returned to the dining room.

When she set the bottle on the table, he thanked her with a self-satisfied grin on his face.

"I hope everything went all right yesterday," he added before she walked away.

Tracee placed her hands on her hips. So, he wanted to acknowledge what he'd done.

"Luckily yes, everything was fine. Thank you for asking."

"Do you two know each other?" a man sitting across the table asked.

"I ran into her yesterday at the hotel. I believe you were on your way to a meeting?"

Mr. Rude had asked her that with squinted eyes. She gritted her teeth and smiled. "I was. A very successful meeting, I might add."

He smiled. "I'm glad to hear that. I don't believe I got your name?" he asked.

"And I don't believe I gave it." She let out a deep breath. "Tracee Coleman, and you're?"

"Laurent." He stood up halfway, holding the napkin in his lap, and offered his hand, knocking over his glass of iced tea at the same time.

Tracee jumped back as he quickly grabbed the glass before losing all of the contents. She wanted to laugh. He used his napkin to soak up the liquid from the table.

"I'm sorry about that," he said to the man sitting next to him, who'd managed to move his plate out of the way before any damage was done. Then Laurent turned his attention back to Tracee and extended his hand. "I'm clearly not making a good impression, but the name's Laurent Martin."

Tracee accepted his hand. "It's nice to meet you. Don't worry about that. I'll get you another tea. I don't believe I've seen you around here before. Do you live in the area?" she asked as she walked over to the sideboard for the pitcher of iced tea.

"No, I'm here on business."

"Laurent is an old fishing buddy of mine." The man next to Laurent put his arms around the woman sitting next to him. "I'm Sam Kane, and this is my wife, Janet."

Tracee nodded a hello to them.

"Laurent and I used to go fishing a lot in our college days."

Sam's wife elbowed him, while Laurent shook his head with a big smile on his face. Fishermen, huh? Tracee hated fishing. She ended this pleasant conversation by making sure everybody had everything they needed. She cleaned up the wet napkins and left the room to let the guests eat.

When she walked into the kitchen, her aunt Rita was pulling her carrot cake from the refrigerator and preparing to cut a few slices.

"How's it going out there?" she asked.

Tracee nodded. "Smooth as usual." She helped her aunt cut the cake and then started loading the dishwasher.

Tracee made a point not to return to the dining room for the rest of the brunch. Her aunt Rita handled the dessert, while Tayler cleared the table. Laurent Martin was an extremely handsome man. In his jogging clothes, or in casual attire, he had an unmistakable swag about himself. A swag that she wouldn't be able to resist, given the opportunity. Thankfully, she wasn't interested in somebody's old fishing buddy, no matter how hot he was.

Four days in town, and Laurent still hadn't been able to sit down with Mr. Patel to discuss business. In the meantime, he'd spent his days working remotely on projects that needed his attention, and looking over the Rival Hotel deal again. When he finally sat down with Mr. Patel, he would knock his socks off.

Meanwhile, he poured all his frustrations out on Sam as they sat at Nik's Place, drinking beer on a Tuesday evening.

"Thanks for coming out with me, man. Sitting in a hotel for the last couple of nights watching television is not what I had in mind when I flew over here."

Sam laughed. "Yeah, I know life in Danville is much slower than California, but I've gotten used to it. It's a pretty cool place actually. Great for raising a family." Sam cleared his throat. "You know, I have to admit that I'm surprised you're not married by now. Even though we all liked to party back then, you always struck me as the serious type. I mean, half the time you brought your girl on our fishing trips."

Laurent smiled and shrugged. "I don't know. I guess I just haven't found the right woman yet, or maybe I'm destined to be a bachelor—who knows. One day when the time is right, I'll slow down long enough to really get to know somebody."

Sam held up his beer bottle for a toast. "Well, enjoy the journey, my man."

They clinked bottles. The sound of women laughing from the other side of the restaurant caught Laurent's attention. The music was loud, but the women even louder. "Sounds like somebody's having a good time," he said. If Sam wasn't married, Laurent would suggest they check it out, but times had changed.

"It sure does," Sam replied as he turned in his seat to follow the ruckus with his eyes. Unfazed, he turned back around.

"So, how is married life?" Laurent asked. "Because man, I remember how you used to live for the weekends and parties. Remember how we used to drive up the coast partying with the girls up there? You were a beast, Sam!"

Sam smiled, but shook his head. "Man, I was searching for something and didn't even know it. Once I hooked up with my wife, I didn't even want to keep partying unless she was there with me. I'm telling you, man, she put something mighty powerful on me."

"Hell, I can see that. Look where she's got you. Not that this isn't a cool place, but Danville, Kentucky! Come on, Sam, you don't miss Cali at all? Or hanging out in the VIP room in Paris for a weekend?"

"Oh, I did at first. But I had my fill of a different woman every week. When you meet the right woman, your future will become crystal clear. Mark my words."

Laurent finished off his beer. "Okay, but what

does a single guy do around here for a good time? Because I haven't met that woman yet."

Sam shrugged. "He finds himself a good woman."

"Well, considering I'm going to be here for such a short time, that's not an option."

"Then how about a day at the racetrack? Keeneland's open all month for the fall meet. I don't have any classes on Wednesdays."

Laurent smiled. "Now that's what I'm talking about. A little horse racing while I'm here. Sure, let's make it happen." Laurent looked around. "Where's the men's room?"

Sam pointed. "Straight back on your left. Can't miss it."

"I'll be right back." Laurent walked through the restaurant toward the back. In a back corner, he found the group of loud women celebrating something. The table was decorated with balloons and gift bags everywhere. He only saw a few faces, but everyone seemed to be having a good time. He smiled to himself. He loved to see people enjoying life.

"Thank you all so much for remembering my birthday." Tracee gave Mae, who was sitting next to her, a hug. She was one of the true friends Tracee had since moving back into town. While Tracee was in Louisville learning how to become a pastry chef, Mae had been in business school. She'd met her husband and become a successful businesswoman before losing everything in their divorce. But with Tracee's help, she would bounce back.

"How could I not? The ladies of the book club wanted to surprise you."

Tracee looked around. "And you did. Great food, great friends—this was nice."

"And great liquor." Mae picked up her glass of wine.

"Don't talk about liquor. I need to run to the little girls' room." Tracee got up. "I'll be right back."

"Okay, but grab your jacket when you get back—we're taking our drinks up on the deck. The music's better up there."

Dinner and drinks with the girls was great. This wasn't the way Tracee usually celebrated her birthday, but money was tight now with Tracee's Cake World taking every dime she had. Every one of the women celebrating with her was a customer, and everyone in the restaurant potential customers, she thought as she walked to the restroom.

After checking her lipstick and washing her hands, she shouldered the door open. The corridor leading to the bathrooms was well lit, and a man had walked out of the men's room ahead of Tracee. Something about his body looked familiar.

He suddenly stopped and stepped back, stepping on her toe as two girls hurried past him headed for the bathroom.

"Ouch!" She jumped and pressed her hand against his back.

"Oh, excuse me."

Tracee hopped on one foot, while squeezing the other toes in her hand.

"I'm sorry, did I—?"

Mr. Rude. Tracee let go of her foot and straightened up. "Yes, you stepped on my toes." He smiled, and Tracee's heart fluttered. Why did he have to be so freaking handsome with those mesmerizing eyes and perfect lips?

"My apologies. I was trying to get out of the way. Looks like somebody had one drink too many the way they ran past." Then he gave her a quick head-to-toe glance.

He recognized her, but she'd bet he didn't remember her name. And she wasn't going to bail him out. Laurent Martin—she remembered his name. She tilted her head and smiled. *Either say something or get out of the way.*

"Tracee, we've got to stop meeting like this."

She crossed her arms. "So, you do remember my name. This is the third time in four days that I've seen you. Are you following me?"

His eyes widened, and he held his palms up. "No, ma'am. I'm just having a beer with a friend. I had no idea you'd be here." Then he raised a brow. "I might ask you the same thing. Are you following me?"

She laughed. "Absolutely not."

He lowered his hands. "If you say so."

The way he smiled at Tracee, slightly bobbing his head to the music in the bar, sent a shiver through her body. This brother had to know he was a head turner even in a casual black T-shirt, jeans and those fly boots. He was probably used to women tripping all over themselves to get to him. She was about to open her mouth to say something when he pointed toward her head.

"What's the occasion?"

She reached up and touched the crown she'd forgotten was pinned into the top of her hair. "Oh, it's my birthday. It's a book club thing. We pass the crown around for each person's birthday. Kind of silly, I know."

"That's not silly—it sounds fun. And happy birthday."

She nodded slowly. "Thank you."

"After you," he said, pointing back into the bar.

Tracee led the way out. After a few steps, she stopped and was just about to say goodbye and rejoin her friends when he leaned in closer to her.

"You'll have to let me buy you a birthday drink before you leave."

She held her chin up. "I just might do that." It would serve him right for ruining her cake if she ordered something expensive. "My friends and I are headed up on the deck if you'd like to join us. The music's better up there," she said, shocking herself. Why was she inviting this man to join her party when she didn't know anything about him other than he was fine as hell?

He glanced back at the bar, and for the first time she realized he might be with a woman.

"I'll see what Sam wants to do. You remember Professor Kane from Sunday brunch?" he asked.

Tracee looked around him and saw the professor sitting at the bar. His wife wasn't with him. "Oh, yeah. Your fishing buddy. Bring him, too. The more the merrier. But I'll warn you, my girls tend to get pretty lit up on the deck."

Laurent chuckled. "That sounds like the place to be." He glanced around him at the diners. "It's getting pretty dead around here."

"Then come on up," she said with a wave. *What the hell could it hurt? This little hen party is about to get turned up.*

His smile gave her life.

When she walked back into their section of the restaurant, some of the girls had already started packing things to go upstairs. Tracee had opened her presents and they'd finished dessert. This crew was ready to get their groove on, on a Tuesday night.

"Wasn't that the guy from the hotel Saturday morning?" Mae asked as Tracee reached the table.

Leave it to Mae not to miss a thing. "Yeah, that's him. The same guy that showed up at Sunday brunch."

"And he just happens to be in here tonight, too?" Mae asked, peeking around Tracee.

"Child, please, this makes the third time I've run into this guy. Coincidence, you think?" Tracee asked as she reached for her purse.

"Yeah, like maybe your paths were destined to cross. This is a small town, you know. Then again, he could be stalking you."

Tracee laughed. "Well, if he is, he's kind of cute, don't you think?"

"Kind of! Oh, he's very handsome. And he's got a certain sex appeal about himself. What were you guys talking about, anyway?"

Tracee shrugged. "Nothing really. He asked about the crown, so I invited him to join us on the deck."

Mae's head rocked back. "No, you didn't! The guy who ruined your cake?"

"Yep. Him and his professor friend. Come on, let's get up there."

Tracee slipped her jacket back on and followed the ladies to the deck, where there was music and an empty dance floor. Large heaters were placed around the perimeter to keep the chill away. Several tables were set up with a small bar and a DJ corner. One waiter sat talking to the DJ. All of Tracee's presents and the ladies' purses were deposited on one table while they hit the dance floor.

After a few minutes, more people from downstairs found their way up and joined in on the fun. Mr. Wood, who Tracee took all her dry cleaning to, even made it up with his wife. The middle-aged white couple were celebrating their tenth wedding anniversary. Then Tracee saw Laurent as he reached the top of the stairs nodding his head to the beat, and she lost all her rhythm.

Chapter 5

Tracee stumbled over her own feet and bumped into one of her friends.

"Tina, I'm so sorry," Tracee said with her hand over her mouth. She couldn't take her eyes off Laurent. Right behind him was his friend Sam, who was good-looking as well, but happily married. Together they looked like trouble—in a good way.

Afraid she'd stumble again and embarrass herself, she left the dance floor and walked over to Laurent and Sam. "I see you made it up."

Laurent gestured to his friend. "You remember Sam?"

Tracee accepted Sam's outstretched hand. "Yes, I do."

"Happy birthday," Sam said.

"Thank you."

A few more people came up the steps behind them.

"Maybe we should grab one of these tables before they're taken," Laurent said, as he walked over to the table next to Tracee's and pulled out a chair.

Was he pulling out a chair for her? Such a gentleman. She hesitated, because she didn't want her girls to think she was deserting them after all they'd done for her. Laurent merged the chairs, making one long table for six. She smiled and sat down.

One of her friends knew Sam, and they stood talking for a few minutes.

"What are you drinking?" Laurent asked as soon as Tracee sat down.

"I'll have a glass of white wine, thank you." She changed her mind about the most expensive thing on the menu.

"You're welcome." He walked over to the bar.

Two of her girlfriends came by to say good-night and give her another birthday hug. Tracee thanked them for everything.

Laurent returned with her glass of wine. "So, Tracee, tell me a little bit about yourself," he said as he set the glass in front of her.

"Well, you know I work at the Coleman House bed-and-breakfast."

"Yeah, Sam was telling me that's a family-run establishment. Did your parents own it?"

"No, my cousins' parents. Rollin and Corra, the owners, are my first cousins. I work there part-time, along with my younger sister, Kyla. As you've probably already guessed, I'm the pastry chef. I cook everything from desserts to side dishes."

Laurent lowered his head. "Yeah, about the cake. I know I've apologized numerous times, but I want to let you know how happy I was when you said it didn't ruin your presentation. How did you pull that off?"

"I told the truth. They thought it was funny and wanted to taste the cake anyway. Thank God it hadn't fallen out of the box. But all's well that ends well."

"So, you bake cakes for people outside the bed-and-breakfast?"

She reached into her purse, pulled out a business card and handed it to him. "Tracee's Cake World. I was on the way to my first 'official,'" she said, using air quotes, "cake tasting. And I needed that business. It's going to help me open my own store."

He read the card. "So you're a professional?"

"I'm a professional pastry chef, yes. But I can cook just about anything you want."

Laurent smiled at Tracee before turning up his beer bottle.

"So what do you do when you're not fishing?" Tracee asked Laurent.

Laurent lowered his head and chuckled. "I'm a hotel brand manager."

"What's so funny?" she wanted to know.

He shook his head. "Nothing, I was just thinking about how much Sam used to love to go fishing." Then he turned his seat around, facing her. "What do you do when you're not in the kitchen baking up something sweet?"

Tracee sipped her wine. "I'm always in the kitchen

baking something, or working on my business. But I also like to go to concerts in Lexington or Louisville."

"Really! Who do you like to see in concert?"

"Oh, I have really eclectic taste in music. You probably won't know anyone I name."

"Try me."

She set her wineglass down and gave him the side eye. She hadn't met a man yet who enjoyed her eclectic tastes in music. "Okay, how about Sabrina Claudio."

"Love her," he responded.

"Okay, that was easy—everybody loves her. How about Masego? Or French Kiwi Juice?"

Laurent leaned back in his seat, bringing his brows together. "What do you know about French Kiwi Juice?"

She smiled. "Oh, I know jazz. I know he's a multi-instrumentalist. I'm not too young to appreciate good music when I hear it."

"That's cool. Have you seen him perform live?"

"Unfortunately, no. Not yet, anyway. Have you?"

"I had the pleasure of catching his show in San Diego once. In a word, he's mesmerizing."

She smiled. "I can only imagine."

"I'm not as familiar with Masego, but I have heard the song 'Tadow,' featuring Masego. I like that one in particular."

"Oh, yeah, why?"

He shrugged. "I don't know—something about the groove reminds me of when my brothers and I used to play together. Growing up, we had ourselves a little band."

"Really! Where did you play?"

He laughed. "At home. We weren't actually good enough to leave the basement."

"Oh my God. I bet it was fun, though."

"It was. We listened to everybody and tried to mimic them. I'm particularly well versed in old-school music because my brothers are older than me. But I listen to a little bit of everything."

"What instrument did you play?"

"Guitar, a little bit of the keyboard."

"Wow that sounds fun. So, where are you from Laurent?"

"Palo Alto, California."

"What brought you to our little town?"

"I'm kind of working on the Rival Hotel's brand."

"Do you travel a lot, checking on hotels?"

He rocked his head from side to side before nodding. "I do, yeah."

"Well, you're staying in the second-best establishment in this town. The first one being the Coleman House bed-and-breakfast, of course," she said with a wink and smile.

Laurent rocked his head in time with the beat of the music and returned the smile. He was staring at her, which made her a tad uncomfortable.

"I like your hair," he finally said.

The compliment came out of the blue. On reflex she reached her hand up and touched the curls that couldn't be tamed today, so she'd just let them fly. "Thank you."

He pulled his chair closer and leaned in. "So, Tracee, why are you celebrating your birthday with your girlfriends and not your man?"

"If I had a man, do you think I would have invited you to join us?"

He straightened up. "No, I guess not. Or, I'd hope not."

She smiled and shook her head. "No, I wouldn't disrespect my man like that."

He grinned at her.

Sam joined them at the table. Two of Tracee's girlfriends had already grabbed chairs on the other side of her, while Mae hadn't stopped dancing.

"Lau, I'm gonna have to bounce. I'll give you a call tomorrow, bright and early," Sam said to Laurent as he turned up the rest of his beer.

"I'll be ready," Laurent said.

"You guys going fishing in October?" Tracee asked.

Sam almost choked on his beer and quickly jumped back to keep it from running down his shirt. He looked down at them, smiling. "I don't fish anymore."

"He's taking me golfing," Laurent said, before standing up and giving Sam some dap. "Get home safe, and tell the missus I hope to see her again before I leave."

Sam set his beer bottle on the table. "I'll do that. You guys enjoy your night."

Tracee checked her watch. It was only 9:00 p.m., and the restaurant wouldn't be closing until ten thirty.

"Would you like something else to drink?" Laurent asked after Sam left.

Tracee held her hand over her empty glass. "No, thank you. Maybe a glass of water."

"You got it." He stood up and returned to the bar.

Mae finally grabbed Sam's vacant seat. "I see you and Mr. Rude are hitting it off."

Tracee shrugged. "He's nice. And I'm just being friendly."

"Uh-huh. I know that seductive *friendly* look of yours."

Tracee shrugged. "What? He's cute."

Laurent returned with her water. They spent the next few minutes chatting it up about the new voices in R&B before Laurent asked Tracee if she wanted to dance.

"How about one dance with the birthday girl? Be forewarned, I'm not Fred Astaire, but I can hold my own."

She laughed. "Then maybe you can hold it for me, too. I'll try not to step on your feet."

Two more of Tracee's girlfriends danced over to her to say goodbye. They exchanged quick hugs before Tracee joined Laurent on the dance floor.

The DJ played a mix of pop and hip-hop, to Tracee's delight. Laurent moved out of one move into another with ease. He wasn't anything like her, black girl with no rhythm. "I thought you said you couldn't dance?" she asked him a few minutes later.

"I can't, but that doesn't stop me from trying."

After a few tracks, the DJ announced it was time to slow it down. Tracee thought she would scream when he played "Tender Love" by Force MDs, which was one of her favorites. But that was a slow jam, so she turned to walk away, but then Laurent took her hand.

"You're not leaving me, are you? This is a classic."

Her eyes widened. "I know, but I'm not really a slow dancer." She turned to walk away again, but he didn't let go of her hand. She glanced back at him.

"Let me teach you," he said.

The look in his eyes when he said that made her insides turn to jelly. He bit his bottom lip and raised a brow, waiting on her answer. She'd bet he could teach her a lot of things. The intensity of his gaze drew her like a bee to honey. "Okay, but don't blame me if I step on your feet."

He laughed and placed one arm around her waist while he kept holding her other hand. She tried to keep a little distance between them.

"How long did you say you were going to be in town?" she asked, merely to make conversation.

"Hopefully I'll be on a plane headed back to California by the weekend."

"Why do you say hopefully? What could stop you?"

"I have a business meeting this week that I should have had yesterday. If there's another delay, I could potentially be here a little longer."

She nodded, secretly hoping something trivial went wrong and she'd have another chance to see him. She closed her eyes and concentrated on the music for a minute when she felt Laurent pull her closer. They were really slow dancing now. She could feel the contours of his body pressed against hers, and she liked what she felt. The way he controlled her body and moved his hips said a lot about him. He could definitely hold his own, and yet she felt he was holding back.

"You're doing pretty damned good," he whispered in her ear. "I still have all my toes."

She whispered back, "Consider yourself lucky." Mr. Wood and his wife danced near them. He held his wife close, with her head on his chest. The love they had for one another came through in their dance. It was a beautiful thing to watch.

Tracee found herself wishing Laurent would wrap his arms around her body. She wanted him to run his hands up her back and grind into her like the boys used to do at high school basement parties. She could feel how hard and toned his body was, which made her weak in the knees. And his cologne smelled so masculine and tempting. Then the music slowly faded away. She opened her eyes and released her bottom lip that she hadn't realized she'd been squeezing.

Laurent let go of her hand and took a step back. He smiled down at her. "Thank you."

She sucked in a quick breath to keep from passing out—he was so fine. "No, thank *you*, that was nice." She spun around and wanted to shoot herself. Why did she have to say it was nice? As he followed her to the table, he placed his hand at the small of her back, and the muscles in her center contracted. Being around this man made her feel sexy.

Mae sat with an elbow on the table and her chin in

her palm, staring at them. "You guys looked great out there," she said as Laurent pulled out Tracee's chair.

Laurent held his chair back and looked down. "And she didn't step on my feet once." Everyone laughed as he sat down.

"While that was beautiful to watch, it reminded me that I need to go home and make a phone call before it's too late," Mae added, reaching for her purse. "Tracee, do you want me to help you put some of your gifts in the car?" she asked as she stood up.

It was time Mae called her boyfriend, John, before he went to sleep. Tracee looked at the gifts on the table and decided she only needed help with two of them. It was getting closer to closing for the restaurant and she should be leaving herself, but she wasn't ready to leave Laurent. "Uh, yeah. I guess it is getting late."

"Unless you want to finish your water and maybe Laurent can help you out?" Mae offered.

"Yeah, sure. When you get ready to go, I'll walk you to your car and help with anything you need. I was kind of hoping you'd stick around a bit. I'm enjoying your company."

Tracee looked from Mae's beaming face to Laurent, who held his bottom lip between his teeth, smiling. He was stunningly beautiful. "I think I will stick around for a bit. If you're sure you don't mind helping me out?"

"Not at all," he said, reassuring her with a smile.

Tracee stood and gave Mae a hug, thanking her for everything. Mae whispered in her ear, "Call me the second you get home." When Tracee released her, she winked at her. Tracee smiled at her best friend. "I'll do that."

When she sat back down, she noticed the party atmosphere they'd brought to the deck had vanished. Now there were only a few couples sitting close together enjoying the music and the ambience from the giant heaters, and the starlit sky.

"Thanks again for the dance, and sharing your birthday evening with me," Laurent said.

"I should be thanking you for livening up my night. Those are my book club sisters, and I love them, especially Mae, but they all have families or men to go home to. I take all my gifts to my lonely apartment." The minute she said that, she realized she'd just told a man she didn't know very well that she lived alone. How stupid of her.

"Well, good friends are hard to come by. Even harder than a man for some women, I'm sure. I can count the number of good friends I have on one hand. The men in this town are stupid if one of them is not at home waiting for you."

Tracee laughed. "You're right about having good friends. But I'm more focused on my business these days. I really don't have time for a man. Besides, I've been told my standards are too high."

"Ah, a woman with high standards," Laurent said.

"I think every woman should have high standards, don't you?"

He nodded. "I agree. So should a man."

"Is that why you're single? Or are you waiting for somebody who likes to go fishing with you?"

He laughed and tilted his head, staring at her. "How do you know I'm single?"

Tracee finished off her wine. "Because you're sitting here with me instead of lying across the bed in your hotel room talking to your girl on the phone."

He leaned forward and rested his forearms on the table. "You're right, there isn't a woman in my life right now. And I'm sitting here with you because I want to know more about you. I've never met a pastry chef who works at a bed-and-breakfast before. How do you like it?"

"I love it. I'm surrounded by my family all day, and people on vacation who are usually in a good mood. My cousin Rollin sets the example and goes the extra mile for his guests on a daily basis. He's very personable. And his wife, Tayler, she's the best. I've learned so much from her about business it's crazy. We have a U-pick store, where customers come out and pick their own organic vegetables. It was Tayler's idea to start selling some of my cakes and pies in there. And Tracee's Cake World grew from that."

"You sound very passionate about your work. I know that carrot cake on Sunday was the best I've ever had."

"Thank you." She hesitated a moment before posing a question. "Let me ask you something. Did you know I was going to be there on Sunday?"

He looked surprised. "No, why?"

She shrugged. "I don't know. The first thing that ran through my mind tonight when I saw you was how strange it seemed that I keep running into you in such a short time span. This town is not *that* small."

"If you're still questioning whether I'm following you, relax, I'm not. Sam suggested this place since it was close to the hotel, and I don't really know my way around. He also invited me to brunch Sunday with him and his wife. I had no idea you'd be at either place. But I'm glad you were. It gave me a chance to properly apologize for Saturday morning's incident."

Tracee waved him off. "Oh, let's not bring that up again. It's water under the bridge. Completely forgotten."

He nodded. "Thank you."

"Well, it looks like the DJ's ready to shut it down." The music had switched to piped-in jazz while the DJ started putting his equipment away. Only one other couple remained on the deck now. "I guess we'd better leave, unless we want to get locked up here."

Laurent stood up and helped Tracee with her chair. She started picking up gift bags and wrapping the balloons around her wrist. He grabbed the heavier bags and followed her downstairs and out of the restaurant. Tracee had backed her car in close to the front door. She reached in her purse and popped the trunk with her key fob.

After they placed the packages in her trunk, they walked around to the driver's door. She unlocked the door and leaned in to tie the balloons down so they would be out of her way. When she stood up, Laurent was standing there holding his car keys. "Where's your car?" she asked.

He pointed to a dark blue Elantra parked across the lot from hers. "It's a rental."

She nodded as they stood there awkwardly for a few seconds. She wondered if he was going to ask her out again before he left town. If he asked, she would definitely say yes.

Laurent held out his hand. "Well, Tracee, it was definitely a pleasure meeting you and celebrating your birthday with you. In fact, it was the highlight of my trip." He smiled, flashing his bright white teeth at her.

She shook his hand. "The pleasure was all mine." He held her hand a little too long, causing her to lose herself in his eyes. She hadn't even noticed him take a step closer to her until he leaned in. She smiled up at him. "Good night." The words sounded stifled coming out of her mouth.

"Good night," he said, slightly above a whisper.

He let go of her hand and eased his hand around her waist. Then he did it! He kissed her. A soft and gentle touch on the lips. She froze, so he came back for more. This time she closed her eyes and parted her lips, inviting his tongue inside. All the nerves in her body tingled with excitement. She needed to sit down. She could taste the beer on his breath and the desire in his mouth, and she didn't want him to stop.

When he released her lips and lowered his hand from her waist, she wanted to scream. Oh, God, she wanted more.

"A birthday present, from me to you," he said, arching a brow.

Be still, my beating heart! Her eyes fluttered. "And the best one I've received all night."

Laurent took a step back, laughing. "Get in the car. And do me a favor?"

She opened the car door. "Yes."

"Ring the hotel once you get home. I'm in room 319. Let me know you made it home safe."

"I'll do that." He held the door while she climbed inside. She closed the door and waved bye to the best-looking man she'd ever met. To a man who'd just kissed her and made her want to take her panties off right there in the parking lot.

Chapter 6

Laurent stood in the parking lot watching Tracee's car pull off. He wasn't ready to let her go, but he had no choice. When he licked his lips, he could still taste her. The smell of her perfume was still in his nostrils. Once her car was out of sight, he headed for his rental.

Inviting a woman back to his hotel didn't seem like the right thing to do, but the more he thought about it, the more he thought maybe he should have asked her up. It was her birthday and she'd probably be spending the rest of the night alone. He climbed in the car and started the motor. He shook his head, smiling to himself. If Tracee came anywhere near his room tonight, he'd make sure she wouldn't want to go home until tomorrow—if then.

His cell phone rang, interrupting the luscious thoughts he was having about Tracee Coleman. He glanced down at the caller ID. It was his father. He squeezed his eyebrows together and was tempted not to answer, but he put the phone to his ear as he pulled out of the parking lot.

"Hello, Dad."

"Laurent, imagine, if you will, me sitting in my den enjoying my afternoon cognac when I open this terribly disappointing report you sent me earlier."

Laurent shook his head. Time to get Tracee off the brain and talk business with his father, who had undoubtedly expected a miracle from him.

Thursday morning got off to a great start. Laurent went for a quick run before showering, then grabbed some breakfast. He'd dressed in a basic suit so as not to appear too overdressed for the clientele. This deal was sweeter than what his father had originally proposed, and according to their financials, the Patels would be fortunate to get what he offered. When Mr. Patel and his sons entered the room, Laurent was ready to do business. He'd waited long enough to lay his cards on the table.

Minutes into the meeting, however, something went wrong, and the entire mood shifted. Mr. Patel went from "I'm listening" to "now it's time for you to listen to me."

"Laurent, I understand everything you've shown me, and I appreciate the work you've put into this deal. However, the Rival Hotel is deeply rooted in the community of Danville. For starters, we're loyal to our employees, and in return they're loyal to us. I've only had to fire one person since the day we opened our doors. Do you know of another establishment that can say that after ten years in business?"

Laurent smiled. "No, sir, I don't."

"I've made one important promise to my employees. As long as they want to work here, I will have a job for them. And yet there is no mention at all of the existing staff in your deal."

Laurent licked his lips and sat a little taller, ready to address the older man's concern, when Mr. Patel started again.

"It's not just the staff I'm concerned about. We also host a number of community meetings, as well as social events, sometimes for free. Now, while we're not expecting you to promise us anything, we do want to sell this place to someone who understands its standing within the community, and who will continue the tradition we've set forth. I shared my concerns with your father earlier this year. I thought we had somewhat of an understanding in that regards." He pushed the papers Laurent had given him to Arjun, sitting next to him.

Laurent took a deep breath. "I understand your concerns and—"

"I don't think you do," Mr. Patel said, shaking his head. "Tell me what you know about our fair city."

Laurent had prepared for everything—except that question. He recited some information he'd read off the internet and talked about his experience over the last couple of days. It wasn't good enough.

Arjun spoke up. "My family owes a great deal to

this city. They have supported us and allowed us to flourish over the years. I believe what my father is trying to say is, he'd like to see a bid that's more inclusive with respect to the legacy we have built here. Not that you have an obligation to do so…but that is what he'd like to see."

Laurent nodded. "Anyone in the community will still be able to use the hotel in the same fashion as before."

Mr. Patel cleared his throat. "You mentioned that you had brunch at the Coleman House on Sunday. They're a small bed-and-breakfast that stays in business because of the great customer service and hospitality they provide. Everyone in the county and surrounding counties knows of their reputation. Well, the Rival Hotel has that same type of reputation in the community. We're not just a big-box hotel—we're a part of every family in this town. If you want to know how I know that, I'll tell you. Recently, I was diagnosed with cancer, and I don't know if we could have survived some of the rough times without the support of the people of Danville. When I walk away from this hotel, it will be to get some much-needed rest."

Laurent exchanged eye contact with every man sitting across from him before settling his gaze on Mr. Patel. He gave an understanding nod and used a gentler tone. "I'm truly sorry to hear about your diagnosis. I know that must have been a hard time for your family. I think I have a better perspective as to what you're looking for now. Give me a few days to talk this over with my family, and I'd love to sit down with you again."

The Patel men glanced at one another before Mr. Patel nodded.

Laurent hadn't fully understood what his father meant when he said they wanted someone a little more relatable. He'd assumed Martin Enterprises' power and wealth had gotten in the way of the deal, which was why he'd come dressed down. However, what Mr. Patel wanted was someone more in touch with the community they served, possibly on the same level as the community. What he'd anticipated to be a slam dunk seemed to have hit the rim and bounced off.

The oven buzzer sounded, and Tracee pulled herself from the chair and walked over to the stove. The kitchen of the bed-and-breakfast smelled of ginger and pumpkin as she pulled two tins of cupcakes from the oven and set them on a cooling rack. She'd spent the last two days baking and working on her business plan. Earlier when she detailed her time with Laurent to Mae, she told her she didn't expect to see him again, and that was the truth. The man could have left town by now for all she knew. Still, she couldn't believe she'd let him kiss her.

"Oh my God! Something smells good in here." Corra entered the kitchen with a couple of grocery bags in hand.

Tracee glanced over her shoulder while pulling containers from the cabinet for the muffins. "Cupcakes for dessert tonight."

"What are you still doing here? I thought you got off at noon today," Corra asked, setting the bags on the table.

"Aunt Rita's still a little under the weather, so I thought I'd hang out and help with dinner preparations." Two bags of candy slid from Corra's groceries as she began putting things away. "Isn't it kind of early to buy Halloween candy? It's three weeks away still." Tracee asked.

"Yeah but, we're having a party. Instead of letting the kids go door to door at home, I've decided to invite a few families out here, and we'll have a Coleman House bed-and-breakfast Halloween party."

"That's nice," Tracee said, as she found lids for her containers in another drawer.

"Is everything okay?" Corra asked.

Tracee nodded. "Yeah. Just fine, why?"

"Because you aren't your normal bubbly self. How was the party Tuesday night? I'm sorry I couldn't make it."

Tracee shrugged. "It was nice. We turned the deck up."

Corra stood by the counter and inhaled the aroma coming from the cupcakes. "Did you make enough for me to have one?" she asked.

"I made enough for everyone to have two." She popped one out and handed it to Corra, and then took another one for herself. She flopped down at the table to consume it. One thing Tracee had always prided herself on was not eating her own sweets. The more she baked, the less she ate. She missed her little sister, Kyla, who could eat her cupcakes and not gain a pound. She, on the other hand, was another story.

Corra sat down next to her. "Okay, what's up? Your sweets live on my hips, but it isn't often that you consume your own product. What's got you on the cupcake crack?" Corra asked.

Tracee smiled and shook her head. She loved her cousin. "Nothing, really. I was just thinking about this guy I met Tuesday night." She removed the paper from her cupcake.

"What about him?" Corra asked before biting into her treat.

Tracee shrugged, now wishing she'd never said anything. "He just seemed like a nice guy. He joined our little party on the deck."

"Did you get his number?"

Tracee shook her head. "No, he's from California. For all I know, he's probably gone back by now."

Corra shrugged while they sat in silence eating their cupcakes. Then Tracee's cell phone rang. She walked over and picked it up from the kitchen counter. The caller ID displayed a number she didn't recognize, but she answered it anyway.

"Hello," she said, with as much excitement as a slug.

"Hey, Tracee?"

Her eyes popped the minute she recognized Laurent's voice. "Yes."

"It's Laurent. I hope I didn't catch you at a bad time?"

"No, you didn't." She hadn't thought she'd ever see or hear from him again.

"Good. It looks like I'm going to be in town for a couple more days, so I thought maybe I could ask you for a tour of the city, and take you to dinner afterward?"

She smiled. He wanted to see her again. "I don't mind giving you a tour at all, but you've been here at least four days—haven't you gotten out?"

"Very little. But I'd like an insider's perspective. And if I'm being honest, I'd like to see you again."

She turned her back to Corra. "Sure, I'd like that, too. What day did you have in mind?"

"How about this afternoon when you get off work? Unless you have other plans."

Her hand immediately ran to her unruly hair. "I'm actually working late this evening, so how about tomorrow?"

"Great. When and where should I pick you up?" he asked.

"How about here at the bed-and-breakfast around 1:00 p.m. Do you remember how to get here?"

"It's in my GPS. So, I'll see you tomorrow?"

"I'll be waiting." Tracee set the phone down and turned back to Corra.

"Was that him?" Corra asked.

Tracee nodded. "He wants a tour of the town, from a local's perspective."

"Huh. Sounds like an excuse to ask you out. And I didn't mean to be listening, but did you say he's been here before?"

Tracee returned to the table. "He came to Sunday brunch with his friend Sam Kane and his wife.

Sam's one of a handful of black professors at Centre College."

"So, is your guy cute?" Corra asked with arched brows.

Tracee wrinkled up her nose and nodded fast. "Not to mention funny, and he's a gentleman. He walked me to my car at the end of the night and helped me with my packages." She stopped short of telling her about the kiss.

"Well, I can't wait to meet him. I'll be here tomorrow afternoon when he picks you up."

Tracee rolled her eyes. "You would be."

"Hey, I have to let Kyla know about this guy. We all know how picky you can be."

Tracee's mouth fell open. That old argument again. "I am not picky. I just have standards."

They debated Tracee's choice in men until Corra's daughter, Katie, burst into the kitchen to notify her mother that her brother, Jamie, had taken off on one of the bicycles the bed-and-breakfast had for guests—without asking permission.

Corra jumped up from the table. "That boy knows better." She turned back to Tracee before running out. "Well, maybe you didn't get his number, but I see he's got yours."

Tracee crossed her arms and poked out her bottom lip. *How did he get my number?*

As soon as Tracee finished working Friday afternoon, she went into the bathroom to freshen up before Laurent showed. A tour of the town wasn't exactly a date, but dinner afterward was. So, tonight she had a date with an attractive guy from California. In some ways, Laurent reminded her of her father. Before her parents lost their farm, her father had worn overalls most of the day, but when he took her mother out he had great taste in clothes. He never looked trendy, but he invested in classic pieces that never went out of style.

The bell over the front door jingled, and Tracee's hand froze in midstroke. That was Laurent. She quickly finished powdering her face and applied some lipstick. By her calculations, Tayler should be manning the front desk at this hour. She hurried into the back closet and grabbed her jacket. She turned down the hall and walked out into the lobby just as Corra walked through the front door.

Laurent turned from Tayler behind the reception counter to Tracee coming down the hall. She fought hard not to blush all over the place and give this guy a clue that she was excited to see him again.

"Oh, here she comes now," Tayler said as she gestured toward Tracee.

Not since Kyla was dating Jackson had Tracee seen such smiles on Tayler and Corra's faces. She introduced everyone before letting Tayler know she'd be returning later for her car. She was glad they got a good look at him in case he turned out to be some type of serial killer or something.

They walked out to Laurent's rental car, and he held the door open for her. He resembled the clean-cut, could-possibly-be-boring boy next door, but he was the finest boy next door she'd ever seen.

"This is a nice place, with a nice reputation," he said as he held the door.

"Looked us up, did you?"

"Before I came to brunch, I did a little research." He closed the door and walked around to the driver's side and climbed in.

"I'm glad you were impressed. My cousins have put a lot into the bed-and-breakfast and the organic farm. Their parents would be proud."

He started the car. "What happened to their parents?"

"They died years ago in a car accident. Rollin's sister, Corra, only joined the business two years ago. Now it's truly a family affair."

Laurent nodded as he drove down the long driveway from the bed-and-breakfast toward the main road. He stopped at the end of the driveway. "Which way?"

"Take a left. We'll start on Main Street."

"Near the hotel?" he asked.

"Unless you already know that area," she said.

"No, that's fine. I know very little about this town, other than what I found on the internet. But you know how that is—every city puts its best self on display. I'm looking for the inside scoop."

"What are you, an investigative reporter or something?" she asked, laughing.

He shook his head. "Nothing like that." Then he glanced over at her. "Like I said, my trip's been extended, and I wanted to see you again. What better excuse than to spend some time getting the lay of the land?"

She shrugged. "You could have just asked me out."

"I thought I did," he said.

"Not under the pretense of wanting a tour."

"But I really do want the tour. I'm interested in the town. So, show me everything."

Tracee laughed. "Okay, this should take all of a couple of hours."

Minutes later, Laurent drove down Main Street while Tracee pointed out important landmarks and fun places to dine and shop.

"I swear, your main street reminds me of a movie set—everything looks so pristine and quaint. The only things missing are the vintage cars. It's Norman Rockwellish, if you know what I mean."

She crossed her arms. "I do, but don't let the good looks fool you now."

"Oh, yeah?"

"Behind each and every one of these little shops, there's a story to tell. Some of the stories are scandalous, and some not so much. We have a lot of family-owned businesses in the area. And where there's family, there's drama."

"Intriguing! Family-owned businesses are pretty big in small towns, I'm starting to gather."

"In a lot of cases, there's not enough business for the big chains, so you're right. Then there's always a few people who don't want to stay in the family business. My brother, Gavin, used to work with my father on our small family farm. The way they lost the farm was dramatic for sure, but now Gavin's a technician at LSC Communications."

"How many brothers and sisters do you have?"

"One of each. Both younger than me."

"So, you're the big sister."

"That I am." She turned and glanced out the passenger side window. "Why don't you park along here somewhere? You can see downtown better on foot."

Laurent parallel parked in front of an antique-furniture store. They got out of the car and strolled leisurely along the quaint historic buildings. Tracee took him inside a shop that showcased works by local artists. It didn't take long to work their way up one side of the street and then down the other.

"I don't see a lot of us around here," he commented.

"And you won't. We do have an African American population, but probably nothing like what you're used to in California."

He nodded. "I see. So, what do you do around here for fun, other than hang at the pizza parlor?"

Tracee shrugged. "Around here we make our own fun. Then there's always Lexington or some of the other surrounding cities to visit."

"I guess Sam was right."

"About what?"

"I asked him the same thing. His reply was, find a good woman and settle down."

Tracee laughed. "It's not that bad. Small-town living is all about family. My parents live not far from me, and my brother and his family aren't that far, either. My little sister lives in Lexington. Do you live close to your family?"

"My brothers live in Santa Clara, which isn't far from me, but they travel a lot. My father lives in Palo

Alto, even closer to me, however, he recently remarried and, well, he's enjoying his new bride."

"Your parents are divorced?"

"No, my mom died when I was in high school."

Tracee stopped and looked at him. "I'm sorry."

"Thank you." Laurent looked up at the ice cream shop in front of them. "How about a scoop?"

Tracee looked into the window of the shop where one of her friends used to work. "Sure, come on. I've got a good story about this place."

Chapter 7

They sat and enjoyed ice cream while Tracee told him more stories about some of the people she knew who worked in downtown Danville. She hoped this was the type of inside scoop he wanted. After the ice cream shop, they finished the tour of downtown and made their way back to the car.

Tracee took him over to the Dr. Ephraim McDowell House for a guided tour of the home where the first American surgical procedure was performed. The little woman who led the tour was so sweet, and Tracee learned a thing or two herself. Then she walked him by Constitution Square and the original log post office that served as the first post office west of the Allegheny Mountains. By the time they finished with those spots, Tracee was starving.

Upon walking out of the little post office building, Laurent said, "As interesting as it all was, I think I've had about enough history for one day. I don't know about you, but I'm hungry."

"I'm famished," she replied.

"Cool, where can we grab a bite?"

"Do you like Cheddar's?" she asked.

He turned his head sideways. "I don't believe I've heard of it."

"It's American cuisine, with reasonable prices. I think you'll like it." If he enjoyed fish, he'd be able to get some there.

He smiled. "Okay, if you say so."

Within minutes, they were sitting in Cheddar's across the table from each other, enjoying an appetizer and a glass of iced tea.

"You know, from what I've seen so far, Danville seems like a quiet little town without a lot going on. Everybody's laid-back, and things move at a slower pace. So, how do businesses survive or even thrive at this pace?"

She shrugged. "We have something going on all the time. Out at the bed-and-breakfast, we celebrate every holiday, the change of seasons, harvest time—you name it. In town, they have a huge annual BBQ festival. And they have events for just about everything, as well."

The waiter arrived and took their dinner orders.

"Have you lived here all your life?" Laurent asked.

Tracee shook her head. "I was born and raised in Nicholasville, Kentucky, then I went to college in Louisville. I didn't move to Danville until years after I graduated."

"That's where the Kentucky Derby is, isn't it?"

"Yep, right up the road. I lived there for five years."

"If you don't mind me asking, what made you move to Danville? I mean, isn't Louisville a larger city?"

"It is. But sometimes even a big city can be too small for two people to live in."

He nodded. "I see. Man trouble?"

"Something like that." She lowered her gaze from his intense stare. She was not going down memory lane with this man. "But I don't regret moving here. I reconnected with my best friend, Mae, and I get to see my family every week. I have a niece and nephew that I adore, as well as another one on the way."

"Well, it's his loss, not yours. Every time I look at you, I'm amazed that you're single. I see an intelligent, sexy woman that some fool let get away."

She bit her bottom lip to keep from blushing. "I bet you say that to all the ladies," she said with a roll of her eyes.

He laughed. "No, I don't. And I consider myself very fortunate to have had you drop into my arms like you did."

Tracee held her chin up. What was he buttering her up for? "How long did you say you'd be in town?"

He shrugged. "A couple more days, at the most."

She smiled. "Well, we may have to extend this little tour. You're good for my ego. At one time, the Second Street area used to be a thriving African

American business district. We have some information at the bed-and-breakfast I'll get and show you tomorrow if you're interested?"

"Definitely."

"Great. Since my sister's out of town, I'm helping out at the farmers market in the morning. You can pick me up there."

After dinner, they climbed into Laurent's rental and headed back to the bed-and-breakfast.

"I'll say one thing, this countryside is beautiful. Especially with all the colorful foliage at this time of the year. And just look at that sunset."

Tracee glanced off in the distance at one of the things she truly appreciated—a perfect sunset. "If you don't have to be back at a certain time, there's a spot up the road where you have a perfect view of the sun setting."

"I've got nothing but time. Let's hit it."

Tracee had Laurent drive past the bed-and-breakfast entrance to a spot up the road where the tree line was lower and so the sun dropping off a cliff was visible.

"Nice… It's like a color explosion." Laurent turned the car off and opened his door.

Tracee got out as well and walked around to the front of the car. "This is the perfect time of year to witness the change in this spot. Is it like this in California as well?"

"Yes. But I'll have to admit, I'm hardly relaxed long enough to fully enjoy it." He leaned against the front of the car and crossed his legs at the ankle.

Tracee followed suit and cast her gaze out across the colorful foliage before her. Too bad Laurent wasn't sticking around—she could get used to him. He crossed his arms and turned his gaze to her.

"You come here often?"

She shook her head. "Not often, no."

He turned around to glance back over his shoulder. "This looks like what teenagers call a make-out spot. A policeman's not going to come along with a flashlight once it gets dark and tell us to move along, will he?"

Tracee laughed and reached out to punch Laurent on the arm. "Of course not. What kind of girl do you take me for?"

"One that knows how to have a good time. I enjoyed Tuesday night. I thought about it Wednesday night and I started to call you, but thought I'd better not."

"I was up to my elbows in sweet potato pies anyway. Two of my regular customers are nursing homes. They keep me pretty busy."

"I noticed there's a bakery in town. Isn't that competition for you?"

"Of course, but they can't duplicate my recipes. I've put my own spin on some of my grandmother's old recipes. I also modified recipes from the bakery I used to work for in Louisville. I've been told that my sweets are like crack. Once you get hooked, I've got you."

"From what I've tasted, I can believe that."

"Besides, I'm going to be leasing a prime spot downtown in the Rival Hotel."

Laurent turned toward her, resting his elbow on

the car hood. "You mean somewhere close to the hotel?" he asked.

"No, inside. There used to be a business connected to the hotel with an entrance from the inside and another from the outside. It's been closed for a while now, but I've been talking to the owner and I plan to reopen right there."

"Inside the Rival Hotel?"

"Yep."

He nodded. "Why not opt for your own spot downtown, or in a mall somewhere?"

"The hotel is kind of a special place for me. So it has to be there. Besides, I'm this close—" she held her index finger and thumb an inch apart "—to getting a small business loan."

He looked down at the car before turning back to the sunset, this time leaning his elbows back against the hood. She turned around and joined him, and they remained silent for a few minutes just enjoying the view.

"Can I ask you a question?" she said, breaking the silence.

"Sure," he responded.

"Why did you kiss me?"

He reached over for a lock of hair that had fallen across her face and tucked it behind her ear. "I don't know. Why does a guy kiss a girl? Because he wants to see what her lips taste like, or maybe because I didn't have a present for you and it was the only thing I could think of at that moment. Those red lips were calling my name." He cupped a hand around his mouth and called out to the wind. "Laurent, Laurent, kiss me."

"My lips said no such thing!" Tracee laughed.

He nodded. "Oh, yes, they did. They gave me that seductive pout that said, 'come hither, young man, and devour me. I've been waiting on you all night long.'"

Tracee held a hand over her mouth and laughed. If she'd given him that impression, maybe she'd had one glass of wine too many. "I don't pout," she said after she dropped her hand.

He pointed at her. "Yes, you do. Like now. Your lips are as beautiful as this sunset, far more inviting and begging to be kissed." He leaned in closer to her before reaching out and placing a hand behind her head.

Tracee's pulse quickened with the touch of Laurent's hand at the base of her neck. He gently pulled her closer and softly kissed her lips. Butterflies took flight inside her stomach, flying in every direction, as confused as she was. Should she return the kiss? She leaned against the car, letting him kiss her.

His lips were soft and moist, and she was having a fantasy of snuggling next to him in a warm bed. He released her and leaned back.

"Now this is officially a make-out spot," he said.

Saturday morning Laurent found the farmers market at the edge of town, just like Tracee said. After walking past booths of everything from organic produce to homemade soaps, he found the Coleman House Farm's booth. Tracee was in the middle of bagging a bunch of greens for two women who were trying their best to talk her down on the price. Laurent had tried to dress down in a pair of blue jeans, sneakers and a dark gray zip-up jacket, but he might have still been a little overdressed for this Saturday morning crowd. If he was going to be here much longer, he might have to do a little small-town clothes shopping.

The minute he made eye contact with Tracee, she checked her watch. He was early. It was eleven forty-five. After the ladies purchased their greens, they moved to the next booth.

"Ma'am, I wonder if you can help me pick out some greens," Laurent said as he picked up a bunch and water unexpectedly ran from the greens down his arm. He jumped back to keep the water from getting on his clothes.

Tracee grabbed a wad of paper towels and quickly exchanged them for the greens in his hand. He dried the water running up his sleeve. He couldn't believe the silly shit that happened to him when he was around this woman.

She came from behind the table, took the wadded paper towel from him and pitched it in a nearby garbage can. "I'm going to assume you wouldn't know how to cook those greens if I gave them to you."

"I wish you weren't right, but I'm afraid my skills in the kitchen could use a little work. I can make French toast, if that counts."

"Hey, not everybody can do that, so give yourself some credit. You have to get the proportion of egg and milk just right."

"Oh, I've perfected that. I also use a secret ingredient that just makes your mouth water."

She smiled. "I bet you do." Then she bit her bottom lip.

Laurent looked down at Tracee's snug jeans that stopped at her ankles and her white sneakers. Under a black vest, she wore a long-sleeved black T-shirt that hugged her hips. The Coleman House Farm logo was on the front in white letters. Her hair was pulled into a loose bun on the top of her head. And those silver hoop earrings were large enough they nearly touched her shoulders. Her casual appearance was sexy as hell.

"I know I'm a little early, but I didn't want to miss you."

"Not a problem. We were about to pack up. Just let me grab my purse."

"Laurent, I see you've found our farmers market."

He turned around at the familiar voice as Raji, Mr. Patel's youngest son, greeted him. Laurent didn't know why, but he hadn't expected to see him away from the hotel. They exchanged handshakes. A beautiful Indian woman stood beside him, smiling. "Don't tell me you sell vegetables, too?" Laurent asked.

Raji laughed. "No, but we do frequent the market. My wife likes to cook with fresh vegetables. This is my wife, Charmi."

Laurent nodded, and she nodded in exchange. "It's nice to meet you."

"So, what brings you to the market this morning?" Raji asked.

"I'm waiting for a friend. We're going to do a little sightseeing."

Raji grinned and nodded. "That's nice."

Laurent noticed him glancing toward the Coleman House truck.

"Miss Tracee is your friend?" Raji asked.

"Yes, she's my new friend, and my Danville tour guide."

"So, where are you two off to today?" he asked.

Laurent glanced over at Tracee. "I'm not sure yet. But I'm sure it will be something interesting."

"Well, you have beautiful weather for a tour. Enjoy your day."

"I will. You do the same." Laurent watched Raji and his wife as they strolled away.

"Okay, I'm ready," Tracee said as she walked up.

"Where are we off to?" Laurent asked.

"Yesterday I spoke to a member of the African American Historical Society who's going to be our guide for a brief tour of the African American business district and a few other historical landmarks I thought you might be interested in." Tracee looked down at her watch. "We're meeting him at the visitor's center in fifteen minutes."

"Sounds interesting. Have you taken the tour before?" Laurent asked.

Tracee shook her head. "No, believe it or not. I know Danville has an interesting African American history, but I've never felt compelled to take the tour. I guess I'll be learning right along with you."

Laurent was looking forward to his day with Tracee whether he learned anything to benefit him with the hotel deal or not. "Who knows—maybe before the day is over we'll teach each other something."

She smiled up at him in a way that weakened his knees, and he knew he was going to be in trouble today.

Chapter 8

After the African American historical tour, Laurent had gained more respect for the town of Danville, Kentucky. He'd learned some things that would serve as a marketing tool for him if they purchased the Rival Hotel.

"That was an amazing tour and a nice way to start the day," Laurent said to Tracee after they dropped off their tour guide and prepared for the next stop.

"It was, wasn't it? I'm surprised. To tell you the truth, I thought it was going to be a little boring, like yesterday, but it wasn't."

"Learning about your own culture's past is never boring," he said. "So, where to next?"

"You can't come to Kentucky without having a

horse-related experience, so I'm taking you horseback riding."

Laurent's eyes widened. "I've never been horseback riding."

"Well, you know what they say—there's a first time for everything. Come on, it's just a short ride up the road."

He was beginning to like this woman, but he didn't know if he liked her enough to climb on the back of some smelly horse. "You know, when I think of Kentucky I think of horses, but betting on them instead of riding atop one."

"Riding is better than betting, trust me. You never went horseback riding when you were young?" she asked.

"No, I didn't." The closest he'd come to a horse was dropping stacks of money at Belmont Park, a major Thoroughbred horse-racing track in New York, with a group of friends.

"Then this is going to be fun."

"If you say so."

On the way to the stables, they stopped at a farm-to-table restaurant for a quick lunch. Once they were back on the road, Laurent removed one hand from the steering wheel and placed it over his chest. "I know the tour's not over yet, but I want to say thank you. Your tour has turned into the best part of my trip. Who would have thought I'd find a beautiful woman to show me around and make me feel so welcome? I'm really enjoying your company." He glanced at her, watching her blush, before placing his hand back on the wheel.

"You might want to hold your compliments until after the horseback ride. If you've never ridden before, you might be walking a little bowlegged later."

He laughed, but she was the only person he wanted to see walking bowlegged. And he wanted to be the reason for that new stroll.

He drove the thirty minutes to the riding stables envisioning large stinky horses shooing flies with their tails and ears. Instead, he encountered a nice, clean stable with nothing but healthy-looking horses. He still wasn't sure this was something he wanted to do, but he was following Tracee's lead, and he'd enjoyed himself so far. Tracee introduced him to the woman who owned the stables, and she gave him a little tour of the facility before introducing him to his horse. A sickening feeling bubbled up in Laurent's stomach when the horse threw his head back and seemed to laugh at him.

"You're not scared, are you?" Tracee asked.

Laurent snorted and shook his head. "Of course not. I'm game for anything. Let's go." After a little instruction from the owner, Laurent stepped up onto the platform, hooked his foot into the stirrup and then swung his other leg over his horse.

"Okay, this here's Chester, and he's happy to meet you. Hold on to the reins there." The owner made sure Laurent was positioned correctly before she walked away.

Tracee and her horse trotted over to Laurent. Chester turned slightly to greet his buddy, and Laurent tightened his legs around the horse as he felt himself falling forward.

"You can sit up and relax. He's not gonna throw you," Tracee said as she and her horse circled around Laurent.

He inched himself up straighter but didn't like the feeling one bit.

Tracee laughed. "If you could see your face right now."

The instructor tapped Laurent on the knee. "You might want to ease up on your grip there, buddy. Your leg muscles will be sore for days gripping like that."

Laurent looked at Tracee and shook his head. He loosened his tense leg muscles. "Why did I let you talk me into this?"

"Oh, come on, I thought you were game for anything?"

His eyes widened. "So did I, until now."

Finally, they set off on a nice stroll following one of the young guides. Old Chester trotted right next to Tracee's horse, which Laurent was thankful for. Getting the hang of holding the reins and staying in the saddle wasn't really that difficult. After a few minutes, he fell into a steady rhythm.

"Did you grow up around horses?" Laurent asked Tracee once he could concentrate on something other than not falling off the horse.

"No, but my dad did, so he took us riding a couple of times a year."

Laurent enjoyed the view as they trotted along and he learned more about Tracee and her upbringing. Unfortunately, the saddle didn't get any more comfortable, and the smell of the horses as they used the open-air restroom made things worse. Chester had a fondness for grass, but the instructor asked Laurent not to let him eat grass. How he was supposed to keep this thousand-pound animal from doing so she didn't say.

As they headed back to the stable, the horses got a little happy and trotted over to the platform. Laurent didn't know what happened next, but Chester overshot the platform and kept going. He tried to stop him by pulling back on the reins, which obviously wasn't the thing to do. He could hear Tracee yelling his name and see the instructor running to catch up with him, but Chester had a mind of his own and tried to stand up on his hind legs.

Laurent leaned forward, determined to stay on the horse, but then old Chester came down and kicked out his back legs. The movement threw Laurent for a loop as he felt his body sliding off in one direction while trying to keep his grip on the reins.

A second later, he was lying on his back looking up at Tracee as she smiled down at him.

"Are you okay?" she asked.

He moved a little to make sure nothing was broken. "I don't think old Chester likes me," he said before coming to his feet.

"Something must have spooked him," the instructor said as she walked up with Chester. "You don't look none the worse for the wear, though," she said after looking Laurent up and down.

He brushed his pants and jacket off. "I'm fine. Maybe a little bruised ego, but I'll survive." To show he had no hard feelings toward the horse, he reached out and swatted old Chester on his hindquarter. The horse's tail swung up, and Laurent jumped back.

Tracee bent over laughing.

"Can we go now?" Laurent asked while biting his lip and trying not to laugh at himself. His ego couldn't take much more of this place. He thanked the owner and assured her again that he was all right. He couldn't wait to get back behind the wheel of the car—somewhere he felt as if he had control.

"Well, that was an interesting experience," Tracee said as she buckled her seat belt.

Laurent did the same, then started the car. "I like the horses at Belmont Park better," he said before glancing over at Tracee. She held a hand to her mouth, and they both opened up and laughed as loud as they could.

"I can't believe I actually fell off a damned horse and onto my ass out there."

"Oh, but you looked good up there. It's the dismount that was so entertaining." She started chuckling again.

As he pulled out of the parking lot, Tracee pointed him into the right direction.

"You're still laughing at me," he said playfully.

She put a hand over her mouth, shaking her head. "She said *old Chester*, like the most we'd get out of him was a trot."

"Yeah, that sucker almost broke out into a sprint with me on him. That was dangerous, you know. What if I'd been a kid who fell and hit their head?"

Tracee slowed her laughter until she stopped. "You're right, that was dangerous. I'm glad you didn't hurt yourself. Maybe old Chester needs to be retired."

"Or I need riding lessons, one or the other."

"Well, there's a little klutz in all of us," Tracee said.

He straightened his arms and gripped the wheel. "Not in Laurent Martin. I'm the most coordinated, balanced individual you'd ever want to meet."

"Uh-huh, like when you turned your drink over at brunch last Sunday?"

He nodded his head and sucked his teeth. "So, you wanna bring that up. How about you stumbling back into my arms?"

She turned in her seat and opened her mouth wide. "Ah! That wasn't my fault. You opened the door on me!"

He shook his head. "Yea, there's a little klutz in all of us."

After they enjoyed another good laugh, Laurent asked, "Okay, where to now?"

She sniffed the air. "Smells like we need a shower. Those horses rubbed off on us."

Laurent glanced over at her with nothing but explicit things on his mind. "That sounds like a good idea. Your place or mine?"

Tracee stepped out of the shower and reached for a towel to dry off. She had thirty minutes before Laurent returned. He'd gone to his hotel to shower and change, and then he'd be back for her. As she lotioned up, she thought about how much fun she'd had with Laurent in the last two days. If he lived in Danville, she'd have to give him a run for his money, but he was only in town for a short time. She couldn't remember what he said his business was, but whatever had delayed him, she hoped it kept him around a little longer. He was funny, good-looking and well educated—she could tell that from their conversations.

As she slipped into a fresh pair of jeans, the phone rang. She hoped it wasn't Laurent saying he wouldn't be able to make it back. She checked the caller ID before picking up her home phone.

"Hey, Mae, what's up?"

"I'm at the hospital, and I may have secured another corporate account for us. I'm going to check back with the director of food services later in the week."

"That's great! This afternoon I'm going to start on a few batches of cookies for the church. I volunteered to provide my lemon cookies for tomorrow's dinner service."

"Girl, you're going to get the church folk addicted to those cookies now. The last time I brought home a batch, John ate all but two and begged me to have you bake some more."

Tracee laughed. "And I did. Stop by tonight and I'll fix him a box."

"Thanks. So, what else you got up for today?"

Tracee held the phone between her ear and shoulder while she pulled a few tops from her closet, trying to decide on one. "Well, I have a dinner date with a very nice man."

"The guy from the hotel. What's his name?"

"Laurent," Tracee said in her best French accent.

"Yeah, him. You mean you've seen him since Tuesday night and didn't tell me?"

"I know how busy you've been. I was going to tell you. He called me yesterday for a tour of the town."

"Yesterday? I thought he was only in town for a couple of days."

"Whatever he's working on has been delayed, so he'll be here for a few more days. I'm not sure how long. I'll ask him tonight."

"It sounds like you're digging this guy."

"He's nice, and he makes me laugh," she said, settling on a thin black and white sweater.

"Well, enjoy him while you can. I'll drop by later to get those cookies."

Tracee said goodbye and ended the call, tossing the phone on her bed. She looked back at the clock on her nightstand. Laurent would be there any—

Her doorbell rang.

Laurent had changed into a dark gray sweater and black pants, which was perfect for where Tracee had in mind.

Minutes later, they entered Tracee's favorite pizzeria. "They have the best pizza in Danville," she told Laurent as they walked in. A little food, a little dancing and a little something to drink was what she had in mind. As the night rolled on, it seemed as if everyone in Danville had the same idea. The restaurant was so crowded they had to share tables, forcing Tracee to almost sit in Laurent's lap. His arm stretched around her shoulder, and his mouth was practically in her ear when he spoke.

"Any live music around here?" he asked.

She nodded. "Yeah, if you like country music," she said with her nose touching the lobe of his ear.

They were too close. The smell of his cologne made her whole body shiver.

He shook his head. "I'll pass."

The DJ at the pizzeria was going to have to do for tonight. He played top-forty pop, with a little hip-hop mixed in. Tracee managed to get Laurent to the dance floor a couple of times before they were afraid they'd lose their seat for good if they got up again. After the pizza, she was about to order some tiramisu when she remembered she had to whip up several batches of lemon cookies once she got home.

"Are you a dessert kind of man?" she asked.

He shrugged. "That depends. What did you have in mind?"

She put her lips as close to his ear as she could, again while resisting the urge to kiss his neck, and said slowly, "Rosemary-lemon shortbread cookies, from scratch."

He pulled back and stared down at her with wide eyes. "You're baking them?"

She nodded. "I need to bake four dozen before the night's over."

He tilted his head and put his lips to her ear. "Let's go."

Laurent paid the check, and they exited the noisy pizzeria and headed for the rental car.

On the ride to her condo, Tracee wondered if she was doing the right thing by inviting Laurent over. After spending so much time with him, she still didn't know very much about him. The one thing she did know was that she was extremely attracted to him, in a dangerous kind of way.

Chapter 9

The minute Tracee walked into her condo, she turned on the bright living room lights. She thought about texting Mae or somebody in her family to let them know Laurent was there, but she felt silly doing that. Besides, Mae would be swinging by later to pick up the cookies.

"Come on in." She tossed her purse and jacket on the couch before going into the kitchen, turning on all those lights as well.

Laurent walked in and followed her into the kitchen. "You have a nice place here."

"Thank you. I love to decorate."

He took a seat at the kitchen table. Tracee stepped into the powder room across from the kitchen and washed her hands. "Would you like something to drink?" she called out.

"Sure, if it's not too much trouble."

When she returned she noticed how relaxed he looked sitting there with his legs wide-open and his hands clasped in his lap. "Not a problem at all." From the cabinet she pulled down two wineglasses, holding them up. "Red or white?" she asked.

"White."

She set the glasses on the counter and opened the refrigerator. "The cookies won't take long to bake, and if you want you can turn on the television in the living room." She walked over to hand him a glass of wine.

"I'm cool right here. I'd like to watch the master at work."

She smiled and took a sip of wine. "Uh, if you stay in here, I might put you to work."

Laurent held his hands up. "Work me, baby. I'm all yours tonight."

Tracee glanced up at the ceiling for a brief moment. *If only.* Then she set her glass on the counter. "Okay, Mr. Martin, wash up and we'll get to baking."

Laurent jumped up and walked into the bathroom. Tracee proceeded to pull out her pans and the ingredients she needed from the refrigerator. She also started to preheat the oven.

"Okay, what do you need me to do?" Laurent asked when he returned.

"First, look inside that closet and get an apron out. You're going to get something on your sweater for sure."

He opened the closet door, pulled a large apron from the peg inside and tugged it over his head. Tracee watched him tie it in the back before joining her at the counter. He glanced down at the Eiffel Tower on the front and smiled.

"Nice apron," he said.

"Paris is my favorite place in the world."

"Have you ever been there?" he asked.

"Yes, I have. When I was in culinary school, I spent two weeks in Paris taking baking and cooking classes. It was wonderful. Isn't Laurent a French name?"

He nodded. "It is. My grandmother was French Canadian from Montreal. All the men in my family have French names."

"You want to lightly butter that pan for me?" she asked him. "You said you have two brothers, right?"

He pulled the paper back from the stick of butter and began working. "Yep, two older brothers. Marquis and Aubrey."

"Did you spend much time in Canada as a child?"

"Several holidays, but that's about it. My mother was happy to leave the cold for California, so my grandmother came to visit us more than we went there."

"Is your father from Canada, too?" she asked as she zested a lemon.

"No, Chicago. Evanston, Illinois, actually, north of Chicago."

Laurent reached over for a paper towel while Tracee turned on the food processor to pulse the lemon, sugar and rosemary. After wiping his hands, he walked over and picked up his wineglass. She continued to blend the butter, salt and vanilla.

"Ça sent bon," Laurent said while leaning against the counter. "That smells good."

Tracee smiled. "Um, that sounded good. French is such a beautiful language. Are you fluent?"

He shook his head. "No, but I remember some things. Do your neighbors ever come over looking for something sweet? Because with smells like this going on, I'd be knocking on your door all the damned time."

She laughed. "Occasionally a neighbor will say, 'it smells mighty good up in there,' but no, no one has ever asked for something to eat." She turned off the food processor. Laurent stared at her with those mesmerizing eyes, and she almost missed the pan when she turned the dough out.

He quickly set his glass down and caught the pan, preventing it from sliding off onto the floor.

"Thank you. Now we need to make as many round balls as we can to fill up these cookie sheets."

"How many are you making?" he asked.

She cleared her throat. "*We* are making four dozen. Don't be shy, get your hands in there. You did say you were all mine tonight," she said, lowering her voice.

Laurent smiled and took a step back. "I did say that, didn't I? Well, I'd better get comfortable." He turned around and removed the apron before pulling his sweater over his head.

The hairs on Tracee's arms rose and her heart thumped hard against her chest. But she was slightly disappointed, because he had on a black T-shirt under the sweater.

"I hope you don't mind, it's getting a little warm," he said, standing there with his sweater in one hand and the apron in the other.

A tingle ran through her body. "No…not at all. It, uh…it is a little warm in here. The oven heats up the house after a bit." His short-sleeved T-shirt showed off his muscular arms and the frame of his chest.

He draped his sweater over the back of a chair before putting the apron back on. "Okay, where was I?" he asked, rubbing his palms together.

"You were about to dip your hands into this bowl and start making some lemon balls. Just place them on the sheet, like those." She'd formed a few already for him to follow.

He picked up the spoon she'd been using and scooped a spoonful into his hand. "Believe it or not, this is the most time I've spent in the kitchen in a long time."

"I hope you don't eat a lot of frozen dinners."

"No, but I dine out more than I should. Something like this intimidates the hell out of me."

"And this is easy. Once we're finished, we'll bake two sheets first for twenty-five minutes. While we wait, you can make the icing."

He wiped his hands again while she placed the pans in the oven.

Next, she let him help her with the icing before setting it in the refrigerator to chill.

She walked over and picked up her wineglass.

"Laurent, exactly what is it you're doing at the hotel?" she asked before taking a sip.

"I'm meeting with people and kind of assessing the hotel's brand."

"Okay, so how do you do that?" she asked.

"For instance, I conduct thorough property visits, look into labor trends, resolve staffing issues and stuff like that. Then I report back to our executive team."

She nodded again. "I see… So, what happens when you find a problem?"

"Well, it might be time for some new operational policies."

Tracee tilted her head. "Who do you work for again?" His job sounded more important than what she'd initially thought he did. It sounded interesting.

Laurent laughed. "Martin Enterprises. You look like I've confused the hell out of you. I promise I didn't mean to."

"You should have just said you were a hotel spy. That's what it sounds like."

Laurent shook his head. "I'm not spying on anybody. I'm very out in the open with my questions and observations. You'd be surprised how much knowledge you can gain just by asking questions."

Laurent retrieved his glass of wine before turning to Tracee. "What now?" he asked once they were finished.

"Now we wait. We can go back into the living room, away from the heat." She'd said it, but she doubted she could avoid the heat her body was giving off by being in his presence.

* * *

After Laurent saw Tracee's CD collection on her bookshelf, they took each other down memory lane. Tracee played CDs, and Laurent pulled up some of his favorites from his cell phone. When the first batch of cookies was complete, they took them out and put another batch in the oven before returning to the living room.

"What's this section over here?" Laurent asked, picking up a stack of CDs Tracee had set aside.

"Oh, that's my UK invasion stack. Are you familiar with any of the artists?"

Laurent leafed through the stack, nodding his head, then stopped. "Who's this?"

He handed Tracee the CD. "That's Labrinth. You've never heard of him?"

"Don't think I have."

"Then you have to let me play you something." She jumped at every opportunity to play her favorite music for someone. She played "Beneath Your Beautiful," by Labrinth, featuring Emeli Sandé, one of her favorite artists. She sat cross-legged on the floor listening to the lyrics hoping he could appreciate the beauty of the song as well. Tracee cut her eyes at Laurent, who was staring down at her from his side chair. She glanced away, wishing the nasty thoughts running through her mind would go away.

"That was beautiful," Laurent said after the song ended. "I like songs like that. About stripping down to who you really are and not putting on airs for somebody."

"And I like the part about not being perfect. That's

deep." She set the CD aside and looked around for another one of her favorites.

He grabbed his cell phone from the side table and slid down on the floor across from Tracee. "I've got one I bet you'll like. It's old-school. You may not know this group."

A slow-tempo song started, and Tracee liked the tune. "Who is it?"

He smiled. "Atlantic Starr, 'Let's Get Closer.' It's a classic. My brothers and I used to sing it when we had our band. The music was real easy."

Tracee took note as to how close Laurent was sitting to her on the floor during the song. "I like the music, and it does scream *old-school*."

He laughed. "Yeah, I told you I'm pretty well versed in that area. How about this one." He sat with his back against the chair and placed his phone on the floor between them.

Tracee immediately recognized Maxwell's voice. She smiled and closed her eyes.

"That one's 'Till the Cops Come Knockin','" Laurent said.

"Oh, I know that one," she said. Her body rocked in time with the music. Then she heard Laurent singing. She opened her eyes, surprised that he had a really smooth voice.

He stopped singing and looked at her.

"You have great taste in music," she said.

He smiled. "So do you. Play me another one."

Tracee selected a couple more CDs and continued to entertain Laurent with more of her favorites. She didn't know how it happened, but somehow she and Laurent ended up next to one another when he pulled up "Burn Slow" by Ro James.

Tracee's body leaned back into Laurent's chest, and she closed her eyes as he wrapped his arms around her. Their bodies moved in time with the groove, and she lost herself in his arms. The moment put a smile on her face. This man wasn't hers, but she wanted him. Maybe if only for tonight.

Laurent brushed her hair away from the side of her face and leaned down to kiss her on the temple. His kiss was soft and suggestive. She fought to keep her hands to herself, but he was making it difficult for her. She ran her hand along his forearm that embraced her. His hairy, strong arm was warm to the touch.

The song went off too soon, but the one that followed turned Tracee on even more. "Permission," another Ro James tune, had Tracee turning around in Laurent's arms. He released his hold on her body and brought both hands to her face. He held her face while he kissed her long and hard.

Tracee's body was on fire with desire. She wrapped her arms around Laurent and kissed him back with an unabashed shame and thirst like she'd never had for any man before. Her head spun as he released her lips and kissed a trail down to her neck. She threw her head back and bit her lip—his kisses were driving her crazy. He reached around and pulled her legs toward him and rested her head in the palms of his hands. She relaxed as he lowered her to the floor. Her breath caught in her throat as he gently bit at her nipples through her sweater. She shuddered as she caressed the back of his head.

In one fast move, he stopped and pulled her sweater over her head, tossing it onto the chair. Tracee lay on the floor staring up at this beautiful man with fire in his eyes. He then pulled his T-shirt over his head and tossed it with her top. He came down on one elbow and ran a hand along the side of her cheek, down her breast and around her waist. The music switched to another slow R&B song, and she could have sworn he'd set that up.

Tracee was soaking wet.

Then the oven buzzer went off.

Laurent jumped. "Oh, man." He exhaled before dropping his head between her breasts.

It took everything Tracee had inside her to not just let those cookies burn.

Chapter 10

Laurent sat up on his elbow, and his eyes met Tracee's. "The cookies?" he asked.

She closed her eyes and nodded.

He inhaled a deep breath and fell over on his back. Tracee lay still for a moment, waiting for the nerve endings in her body to stop tingling. She finally sat up as the music on his phone changed to the next track.

"I'll be right back." She got up and walked off to the hall bathroom.

Laurent closed his eyes and tried to steer his thoughts to something other than Tracee for a minute. But it was useless. He could see her big smile, her beautiful eyes and her curvy body against his eyelids. Whenever she laughed, it warmed something deep inside him. He was so comfortable with her he could lie on the floor with her all night sharing something special to the both of them.

He heard her moving around in the kitchen and opened his eyes. She had cookies to pack up, and he was keeping her from that. He sat up, forcing himself to remember that baking was her livelihood and at this point, he might be in her way. He reached for his T-shirt and decided it was best to leave before they went too far. After pulling his T-shirt and sweater back on, he picked up his phone and stopped the music.

"What are you doing?"

He turned around, and Tracee walked across the room in her jeans and that black lace bra that had captivated him so much a few minutes ago. He swallowed hard and hoped she'd stop before she reached him. If she touched him, he'd have a hard time doing what he knew he needed to do. "I think I better go."

"Why?" she asked with an innocent look on her face.

"I've taken up enough of your time, and I know you have things you need to do."

She stood close enough for him to pull her into his arms, but he clenched his jaw and kept telling himself to leave now, before it was too late.

She put her hands in the back pockets of her jeans and shrugged. "I'm finished with what I needed to do tonight, but if you have to leave, I'll understand." She walked past him, bumping against him in the process, and put on another CD. When she turned around, she ran her hands up and down her crossed arms.

He was going to leave, but he couldn't get his feet

to move toward the door. Instead, he stood there holding his phone in one hand and his keys in the other. She reached for her sweater, and he decided he couldn't let this moment pass, so he beat her to it. "Are you cold?" he asked as he held out the sweater.

She smiled and turned up her lips. "Yes, I am."

He tossed the sweater, along with his keys and phone, over onto the couch, farther away. Her mouth widened in surprise. "Let me keep you warm." He pulled her close, wrapping his arms around her body, and then whispered in her ear, "How's that?"

She let out a deep breath. "Perfect." She returned the hug, wrapping her arms around him as well.

"Look, Tracee, I don't know how long I'm going to be in town—"

"You're not leaving tonight, are you?"

He bit his lip and loosened his hold enough to look down at her. She stared up into his eyes, and his need for her grew stronger. He didn't say another word. He shook his head. They understood the stakes, and they still wanted one another.

She pulled out of his embrace and grasped the hem of his sweater. He raised his arms, and she pulled the sweater up and over his head. His T-shirt was next. If there was a chill in the air, he didn't feel it. His body was on fire again. While his clothes lay in a pile on the floor, Tracee reached for his hand and led him to what was no doubt the staircase to heaven.

At the top of the stairs was a room fit for a queen. Her bed had a tall headboard that, like the rest of the room, was draped in rich, royal colors and gold tones. She turned around, facing him when he reached out and tugged at the waist of her jeans. For a moment, he stared at her beautiful body, noticing her shiver. He stroked his hands up and down her upper arms. The heat in his hands quickly doused her chills as their gazes collided and her body relaxed.

Her lips parted, and his breath quickened. She lowered her gaze and slid her hands up his chest, forcing him to let go of her arms. Her fingers slowly traveled up his chest, and his breath caught in his throat.

"You have protection, don't you?" she asked.

"Yeah, I do."

She smiled up at him with big eyes. "Great."

She went for his belt, and in a matter of seconds they'd stripped their clothes off and lowered themselves to her bed. He tried to kiss every square inch of her body while she giggled with delight. When he brushed his lips across her nipples, he felt them harden. Her breasts rose and fell as she drew in quick breaths. He sucked a breast into his mouth, and she squirmed and moaned underneath his touch, causing him to go weak with need. He was hungry for her and spread her legs with one hand before caressing the velvety softness beneath his fingers.

"Oh, God, Laurent." She slid her hand around to caress the back of his head, while holding his mouth to her breast.

When he released her, he looked down at her hardened nipple and licked it until the throbbing between his legs forced him to stop. Heart pounding, he moved up and looked down at her succulent lips. "You're so beautiful," he whispered before capturing her bottom lip between his teeth.

He brought his hands around to her firm butt cheeks and squeezed. She kissed him hard, with a hunger that set him on fire. They clung to each other, stroking and sucking, desperate to douse the fire that had consumed them. He reached a point when he was so hard he couldn't take it any longer. He had to have her.

Tracee straddled him, his erection mere inches from where he wanted to be. He thrust his hips up, letting her know what he was ready for.

"Wait." She leaned closer and placed her palms on his chest as she caught her breath.

He looked up and met her gaze. He prayed she wasn't changing her mind. Not now.

"Where's the condom?"

He breathed a sigh of relief. "In my wallet."

"Don't you think now would be a good time to get it?"

He smiled. "I didn't forget it. I just want to look at your beautiful body for as long as I can."

She leaned closer with her smoldering eyes and kissed his chest, which nearly took him over the edge. Before he could climb out of bed and pull the condom from his pocket, the doorbell rang.

She sat straight up.

He looked up at her and tried to hide his crushed feelings. "Expecting company?"

"You know you're wrong for that," Mae said through the phone.

"Wrong for what?" Tracee asked, giggling. She

was straightening up the CDs she hadn't been able to put away last night.

"Shoving that box of cookies out the door at me. You could have at least let me say hello to the man."

"Child, please, you're lucky I answered the door."

Mae laughed. "I know that's right. Girl, I can't say that I wouldn't have left your ass out there ringing the bell my damned self. What time did he leave?"

"I don't know, sometime this morning. It was still dark out."

"And you made it to church this morning, after all that fornicating last night?"

"Let she who is without sin on this phone cast the first stone. And what did you and John do when you got home last night?"

"Okay, the both of us need to go to Bible study this week. I got horny just sitting there watching the two of you look at each other like you hadn't eaten in years."

Tracee laughed. "Was it that bad?"

"Hell yeah. So, what's up for today?"

"I need to deliver these cookies and then stop by Corra's to—"

"That's not what I'm talking about. Are you going to see Laurent today?"

"Oh, I don't know, we didn't make any plans. He might be doing something with his friend Sam." Tracee had enjoyed Laurent's company so much last night, but she understood it was a temporary thing. Any day now he would be returning to California. Besides, she wasn't trying to set herself up for another heartbreak.

"Did he say when he's leaving?"

"No, but maybe I'll see him again before he does. If I don't, I at least have something wonderful to remember him by."

Mae laughed. "Sure, if you say so. Girl, I know you're trying to have this nonchalant attitude, but I see through that shit. You might like to have a good time and all, but you let that man stay the night! The Tracee I know only does that when she's really feeling somebody. Which hasn't happened in a while."

Tracee hated to admit even to herself that Mae was right, but she was. And she didn't want to address any feelings she was having for Laurent. She wanted to be able to have a fling with this guy if she wanted to. "Whatever, Mae. Girl, this isn't anything serious. I'm just going to enjoy myself for a minute. Any law against that?"

"None whatsoever, I'm only making sure you don't get hurt."

"Child, please, he can't hurt me. He's something to do for a week or so, that's all."

"Uh-huh. Well, keep telling yourself that. Anyway, I'm in the car now headed to Richmond for the day, but there's another reason for my call. I know we're scheduled to meet with Mr. Patel tomorrow morning, but I'm not going to make it."

Tracee let out a deep sigh. "Mae, you missed sitting down with him last time. I looked forward to you making this meeting so he'll know my partner is in this with me."

"I know, and I'm sorry. But my boss asked me to head up a customer visit on his behalf. I'm flying to St. Louis first thing Monday morning. You'll do great, but I'll be with you in spirit."

"It's not the same thing," Tracee said with no enthusiasm. "But I totally understand. You have to do what you have to do. I'll call and update you after the meeting."

"I want an update on Laurent, too."

Tracee laughed. "Sure. If I see him again." She hung up hoping deep down in her heart that last night wasn't a one-night stand. She also tried to shake the growing uneasy feeling about Mae canceling on her. She prayed her friend was still as invested in the business as she was.

Monday morning, Tracee pulled up to the Rival Hotel and immediately looked around for Laurent's dark blue Elantra, but it wasn't there. She hoped he hadn't left town without saying goodbye.

Once inside, she met up with Raji, who happened to be an old classmate of Kyla's. He was dressed in a suit today, which was unusual for him. Seconds later, his father, Mr. Patel, came out and escorted her into a small conference room that was set up banquet style.

"Would you like a cup of coffee?" he offered politely.

"Sure," she said, as she set her purse and folder on the table before joining him at the coffee station against the wall. "Thank you for giving me a little time on your schedule this morning."

"Not a problem." He handed her a cup. "Decaf?"

"Yes, please." While he poured the coffee, she gathered her sweetener and cream. Once prepared, they took their cups to the table and sat down. She could sense a change in the air. Mr. Patel was more relaxed than she'd ever seen him. With her he was always professional, but he'd never offered her coffee before.

"So, how is everything with Tracee's Cake World?" he asked. "I thought your partner would be joining us today?"

She blew on her coffee and chose her words carefully. "Business is good. Sales were up this summer, and now I'm getting ready for the holiday season. Unfortunately, Mae had an emergency out of town, so I'm flying solo today."

"Well, I'm happy to hear that business is good. The unexpected does happen, so I understand."

"Mr. Patel, I want to thank you for everything you've done in support of our business. If you hadn't let us use your refrigerator a couple of times, I probably would have lost some of my biggest orders. And I more than appreciate the free meeting rooms."

He sipped his coffee. "I'm happy to do whatever I can to support you. I didn't see any reason to charge you for use of the room when you only want it for an hour or two. Little things like that I love to do for the community. The relationship we've had with the Coleman House over the years has been a beautiful one. This whole community has been very good to me and my family. I'm sure your café will be a great asset to the hotel." Then he cleared his throat.

She opened her folder, ready to talk business.

"Before you do that, there is something we need to discuss."

He set his coffee cup down and clasped his hands together on the table in front of him. Tracee swallowed the knot in her throat. She didn't like the serious change in his tone of voice.

"The future of the Rival Hotel will be changing. At this point in my life, I've decided to retire from the hotel business. I'm selling all of the locations except one."

Tracee's eyes widened. "You're kidding."

He shook his head. "I'm afraid not. I'm currently in negotiations with two separate companies. I'm sorry I couldn't have shared this information with you sooner, but we weren't close enough to a deal."

"And you are now?" she asked, with a sinking feeling in her stomach.

He smiled. "Yes, we're closer. Nothing has been signed as of yet, but negotiations are going well."

She took another sip of coffee, then pushed the mug aside. "I think I already know the answer to this, but will Tracee's Cake World be a part of the deal?" she asked.

He chuckled. "If that were possible, I'd do it. However, I'm afraid it's not."

She pressed on. "So, who are you considering selling to?"

He raised his brows. "I'd rather not share that information, considering we're still in negotiations. But I will mention the café when discussing the sale."

Tracee took a deep breath before taking one last sip of the coffee she was sure he had hoped would soften the blow. "Once you make a decision, I hope you will let me know, so I can approach the new owners about the space before someone else does."

He smiled. "Of course. And I'm very sorry I didn't have better news for you today."

"So am I. But all's not lost. I know you, Mr. Patel, and I'm sure you'll keep me posted."

He promised to do just that as they walked out of the conference room through the hotel lobby. The thought of the Rival Hotel being taken over by new ownership saddened Tracee. The hotel was a staple in the community and the only place outside the Coleman House she liked enough to consider doing business. Contrary to what she'd told Mr. Patel, there was no guarantee he'd keep her posted like he'd said. If she wanted that space, she'd have to do everything in her power to find the prospective buyers and approach them herself. She needed Mae with her now to shoulder the news. Wasn't that what partners were supposed to do?

Chapter 11

Tracee had missed her baby sister's presence at the Coleman women's discussions over breakfast. This morning, Kyla was back to tell everyone about her trip to Africa with her fiancé, Miles Parker.

The minute Tracee and Kyla were alone, Tracee filled her in on her current business situation.

Kyla set down her cup of tea. "Didn't Mr. Patel say the space was yours once you came up with the money? He knows someone in our family has rented that space ever since he opened. We expected to keep that tradition in the family."

"That's what I'm trying to do." Tracee shrugged and leaned back in her seat.

"If he won't tell you who the prospective buyers are, have you tried Raji? You know that boy can't keep his mouth shut. He gossips more than any woman I know."

"No, I haven't, but I don't know Raji like you. You guys went to school together, so maybe the next time you see him, you can poke around for me."

Kyla ran her fingers through her ponytail. "I'll just come out and ask him. Raji's like a kid. If he knows you want something and he has the answer, he can't keep it to himself."

"Thanks, Kyla. Business is really picking up, but I can't do the type of marketing I want to do until I have a signed lease on the space. I'm already servicing several downtown businesses."

"And I heard you landed Melanie Jefferson's wedding. That's a major feather in your cap, girl. Your unique cakes are such a huge hit. I can't wait until you create one for my and Miles's wedding."

Tracee sat up and clasped her hands together. "Me neither! But I do wish you were getting married here, since the bed-and-breakfast is famous for our weddings, too."

"I know, and I'm sorry." Kyla stuck out her bottom lip. "But Miles and I talked it over, and we want the ceremony performed in church."

Tracee stood up and walked around the table to hug Kyla. "I understand, and I'm so happy for you."

"Thank you." After they embraced, Kyla placed her hands on her hips. "So, what are you doing to make sure you get that space in the hotel?"

Tracee sat back down. "I had an idea for the pot-luck this weekend, so I invited Mae's cousin who's a photographer and writer for the paper."

"So, he's going to cover the potluck, but how does that help you?" Kyla asked.

Tracee smiled. "Oh, you'll see."

If anyone had told Laurent that at any point in his life he'd be in Kentucky attending a potluck dinner, he would not have believed them. However, the Coleman House Farm had some of the best fresh organic vegetables he'd ever put in his mouth. Plus, Tracee had invited him, and he didn't want to miss an opportunity to see her again. He'd seen her twice over the last couple of days, and like teenagers who'd discovered sex for the first time, they couldn't get enough of each other.

Tracee met him as he approached the house with her hair pulled into a long poufy ponytail cascading down her back. She had on a low-cut white top with a matching jacket and a pair of distressed jeans with some cute flats. The first thing that came to his mind was how well she would fit in in California. She greeted him with a kiss.

"How has your day gone so far?" she asked.

"Great." He eagerly returned the kiss, tasting some sort of cherry lip gloss. He wished they could skip the potluck and go back to her place. "My morning started with a good run. Thanks to you, my run is more interesting now that I have a better lay of the land. After that, I had a great conference call, which set the tone of the day."

The potluck was being held in the U-pick barn. Tracee led the way down the path to the big barn.

She smiled. "A conference call on a Saturday morning. My, my, you are a busy man."

"And now I'm a hungry man," Laurent said as they strolled inside the barn full of colorful people and flavorful smells. The barn was a tad drafty, but huge heaters strategically hung about kept it from being too cold.

Once inside, Tracee gave him what she called the potluck tour. She grabbed a couple of plates and escorted him around the table as they filled their plates with food from every color of the rainbow. At the same time, she introduced him to several of their neighbors.

"What are those crackers there with bacon wrapped around them?" He could feel his stomach growling but had to question some of the dishes.

Tracee smiled and elbowed him. "That's Joyce Ann's famous goat cheese and bacon creation. She brings them every month. Want to try one?" she asked with a raised brow.

The way she cocked her brow at him said it all. He cleared his throat and glanced away. "I think I'll pass. I'm excited to try these dishes prepared by the Coleman House cooks."

With full plates, they walked over to sit down across from Corra and her husband, Chris. Laurent found the dinner conversation enlightening. Chris was a businessman much like himself. They shared a passion for golf and football. Later, Tracee left the table and Laurent noticed her talking to a young man who was taking pictures of the dessert table she said she'd worked on most of the day.

Laurent hadn't realized how caught up he was in watching them until Corra pointed it out. "That table is amazing, isn't it?"

He tore his eyes away from them and turned to Corra. "It is. Tracee's an amazing pastry chef."

"Oh, she's more than that. Tracee is an artist. The title pastry chef doesn't begin to describe the designs she comes up with for cakes. And her theme parties and weddings are off the chain. We're going to hate to lose her once she opens her own place."

Laurent nodded in agreement with Corra. "In the little time I've been here, I've definitely come to understand that Tracee is a very special woman. She told me how she helped build your line of baked goods."

"She actually started the line. My aunt Rita bakes desserts for dinner and afternoon tea, but nothing on the scale of what Tracee started. She had us serving two to three different desserts with every meal. I am, however, proud to say we'll be her first regular customer. She has some recipes she'll reserve just for us."

Laurent turned his attention back to Tracee and the young man, who now held a tape recorder to her mouth. After a few minutes, Tracee walked away with her chin held high and a smile on her face.

After dinner, Laurent spent some time talking to Rollin and Chris before Rollin gave him a quick tour of the organic farm. The property was impressive, and he'd never met a brother who owned a farm and a bed-and-breakfast. Although Rollin confessed the women ran most of the bed-and-breakfast. The story of their humble beginnings reminded him of his father's rise in the boutique hotel industry.

After the farm tour, and when most of the guests had left, Laurent found Tracee sitting at a table looking less than enthused. A stark contrast from the happiness she'd displayed not long ago.

"Hey, what's up? Why are you sitting over here all alone?" he asked before he noticed she was looking down at her cell phone.

She shrugged. "I don't know. I'm just hoping my little plan pays off."

He sat down beside her. "What plan is that?"

She took a deep breath, sat up straight and placed her cell phone on the table. "Monday I found out some bad news, and I've started putting a plan in place to help myself."

He frowned. "Is it something you want to talk about?" He had to acknowledge that he was developing feelings for this woman, and he didn't like to see her hurt and sad.

"Well, you know I'm trying to open my own café in the Rival Hotel. So, I met with Mr. Patel Monday and found out he's selling the hotel. He wouldn't say to whom, but I'm not going down without a fight. I'm determined to find out who the prospective buyer is and have that space for my café."

Laurent jabbed his jaw with his tongue. Mr. Patel had shared information that Laurent had hoped he'd keep close until the deal was announced. From experience, Laurent knew to keep his mouth shut until he achieved his goal. Sometimes, a simple slip of the tongue could set you back and destroy all you'd worked so hard for.

He took one of Tracee's hands in his, and massaged her knuckles. "How do you plan to do that?" he asked, eager to hear her answer.

"I can't say, but I was texting somebody about that when you walked up. I also arranged this whole photo shoot today. I need to position myself as a great tenant to the new buyer. Although I don't know who the potential buyer is, a front-page story about me can't hurt. You know what I mean?"

The determined eyes that looked up at him sent a chill through his body.

"The minute you think things are looking up, somebody throws a boomerang at you and you're back at square one." She rested an elbow on the table and her forehead in her palm.

He looked down and caressed her long slender fingers. "I know I've asked you this before, but have you considered another location?"

She shook her head. "Nope. Remember me telling you the location was special to me?"

"Yeah, I do."

"Someone in my family has leased that space from him for years."

"Really? There's a connection to the Coleman House?"

"No, that's my father's side of the family. My mother's mother opened a coffee stand in the hotel not long after Mr. Patel open his doors. After a few years, she expanded the space to the size it is now. When she became ill, my cousin took over. She ran it until she got married and moved away. Mr. Patel has used it as storage space ever since. It took me a couple of years to get my finances straight, but now that I'm ready, he's ready to sell it off. My mother's family has lost a lot over the years, so I wanted to at least keep this tradition going."

Laurent nodded. "I understand. It has more sentimental value to you than anything."

"I don't even want to consider another spot."

Laurent hoped what he was about to say would be understood. He cleared his throat.

Tracee felt as if something wasn't right. Laurent squeezed her hand so hard it hurt. His palms were warm, and he kept rubbing her knuckles.

"Remember when you asked me what my business was in Danville?" he asked with his head down.

"Yeah, and you said you're a brand manager. Don't tell me that wasn't true?" She hoped to God he wasn't about to tell her he'd lied or something like that. A queasy feeling started in the pit of her stomach.

He chuckled, but his focus stayed on her hand.

Before he looked up into her eyes. "No, that's true, I am a branding manager. One of the things I handle is acquisitions. So, the reason I'm here is…uh—" he stalled before clearing his throat again. "I'm here to purchase the Rival Hotel."

"What!"

"Yeah, we're negotiating to buy the hotel chain."

A sudden coldness hit Tracee to her core. Her eyes

widened, and in her head she could hear herself yelling, *uh-uh. He did not say that!*

"We've assessed the business and made them an offer. Right now, I'm waiting on a few more particulars to be worked out, but after that we'll own the chain."

She couldn't believe what she was hearing. "So, all this time I've been talking about opening my business, you knew you were purchasing the hotel, or trying to?"

"I did, but I couldn't talk about it until the deal was completed. However, I see how distressed you are about possibly losing the space, and I don't want you to feel that way. Once I close the deal, your problem will be solved. I've seen the space you're referring to, and I think it will be great for a café. I can lease it to you."

She slid her hand from his. He looked so pleased and satisfied with himself, as if he'd just solved her problem. "Laurent, you haven't purchased the hotel yet, so I think it's a little premature to think you're the answer to all my problems."

He clasped his hands together. "Tracee, under normal circumstances I would have never said anything. But I think this is a done deal that I can have wrapped up by the weekend."

She leaned back in her seat and crossed her arms over her chest. "What makes you so sure of that?" she asked, wondering if he knew about the other prospective buyer.

"Mr. Patel likes my deal. We're ironing a few kinks out, but I'm sure by our next meeting everything will be to his satisfaction and he'll sign the papers."

No, he didn't know about a second buyer, and Tracee didn't think it was her place to tell him. If Mr. Patel had wanted Laurent to know, he would have told him. She pursed her lips and acted as if she knew nothing.

Laurent reached out and pinched her chin. "That's better. I like to see you smile."

"Laurent, I know you think you're my solution, but what if Mr. Patel doesn't like your offer? If it's all the same to you, I'd rather not put all my eggs in your basket." She pulled her hand back.

His shoulders dropped, and he clasped his hands together again. "What choice do you really have?"

She jerked her head back. "I have choices, and just like you, I prefer to keep them close to my chest for now."

"Tracee, come on. That came out wrong. I'm just saying that—"

"I know, you're the only option I have. But, Laurent, if I'd known you were trying to purchase the hotel, our friendship would have taken a much different turn. I would have had a choice in that matter. And my meeting with Mr. Patel where I learned about a surprise sale wouldn't have thrown me for a loop." She stood up to leave.

He stood up as well. "Tracee, let me just say I'm confident things will work out. Give it a couple of days—you'll see."

"I hope you like surprises, because you might be in for a big one." With her chin held high, she turned and headed out of the barn.

Chapter 12

Bright and early Saturday morning, Laurent met Sam and a few of his buddies at the nine-hole Sweetbrier Golf Course in Danville. The weather was perfect, the crowds were nonexistent and the fall foliage was absolutely breathtaking. Since college, both Sam and Laurent had improved their golf games. Sam's coworkers, also professors at the local college, were avid golfers as well. The course wasn't the best Laurent had played on, but it was sufficient to get a good workout. After about five holes, the conversation began to pique his interest.

"The landscape of downtown will definitely change once the Rival Hotel has been sold," Danny, an economics professor, said.

"I just hope they don't tear the place down, or turn it into an eyesore," Paul, another professor, replied.

Laurent and Sam shared a glance. Sam was aware of his interest in the hotel but kept that between them. He hadn't shared any pertinent details about Laurent with his colleagues.

"I don't think we have anything to worry about. If, or rather when, the hotel is sold, I'm sure the new owners will keep it right where it is. I know I'd hate to see too drastic of a change," Sam said, glancing at Laurent.

Danny walked over to switch out clubs. "I don't know, from what I hear, these companies specialize in mergers and acquisitions, then they destroy anything that resembles the original."

That wasn't true of Martin Enterprises, so Laurent wondered where this guy got his information.

"Do you know who's trying to purchase the hotel?" Laurent asked Danny.

"The Stephenson Group out of Lexington, and some other company from California. That's all I know right now. And I'm sure old man Patel is trying to squeeze them for everything he can get. He's a shrewd businessman."

The rest of Laurent's game went downhill. All he could think about was how he needed to get off that course and to a computer. He needed to find out all the details he could regarding a second buyer. Did his father know this bit of information? If so, why hadn't he told him?

"So the old man didn't say a word about negotiating with anyone else?" Sam asked Laurent as he placed his clubs in the trunk of his car.

"Not a word." Laurent set the clubs Sam had

loaned him into the trunk as well. "How can I be expected to compete when I don't even know there's a competitor? That might explain one thing, though."

"What's that?" Sam asked as he closed the trunk.

"Why he's stalling. He told me he wanted to sell to someone who understood their connection to the community. So I've spent the last week getting a feel for the community and how the Rival Hotel fits into the landscape. Now I'm curious to know if he's asked my competitor the same thing." Laurent climbed into the passenger's seat.

"You think he's trying to play the both of you to get a better deal?" Sam asked.

"Without question," Laurent replied. "Aside from him not feeling comfortable with my knowledge of Danville, he threw in several other stipulations that I'm trying to work out. But now I feel like I've wasted my time." Laurent looked out the window as Sam pulled away. There was only one good thing that had come out of him being in Danville so far. That was Tracee. But unless he could seal this deal, his efforts wouldn't pay off for her, either.

"Thanks for the invite this morning. This has been a very enlightening day, and it's going to make for a very exciting Monday." Laurent pulled out his cell phone and searched for his father's number.

Laurent realized Tracee was a little upset with him when he tried to make dinner plans with her for Saturday night. She was baking and meeting with Mae to work on their business plan. And Sunday after church, she would be busy working, as well.

He had to admit he was beginning to crave Tracee Coleman. Just hearing her voice made a difference in his day.

After he hung up with Tracee, he dialed Marquis. It was time to find out who his competition was and how to beat them.

"Hey, bro, I thought you'd be back here by now," Marquis said.

"I thought so, too. But this deal is taking a little longer. I found out some information today that you might be able to help me with."

"Sure, whatever you need."

"Do you still have that research team that works on a twenty-four-hour turnaround?"

"I do, what do you need?"

"Some dirt. I found out we're not the only one trying to purchase the hotel. What can you get me on the Stephenson Group out of Lexington, Kentucky?"

"How soon do you need it?"

"Is Monday morning too soon?"

"Not at all. Leave it to me. I'll need some information from you, so stick by the phone and I'll have someone call you in a minute."

"Thanks, and do me a favor. Don't mention this to anyone. Especially not Dad."

"Man, you know I wouldn't do that. I'll get back with you."

Laurent wasn't proud of himself for calling Marquis, but he knew his big brother could be discreet and get any information he needed. Laurent never asked where the information came from, and he didn't want to know now.

* * *

While Laurent patiently awaited the results from Marquis, he decided to see if Tracee was really working on her Sunday evening. From the driver's seat of the Elantra, he started to dial her number but quickly ended the call before it rang. If she was mad at him, she might tell him she was busy and hang up on him. But if he just showed up, he had a feeling he'd be welcomed. He decided to take a chance and cranked the engine.

During the less than fifteen-minute drive, he chastised himself for what he was about to do. He'd never been the type of guy to just show up on a woman's doorstep, but he couldn't stay away from Tracee. When he was around her, he forgot all about business and focused on her laugh and her arresting beauty.

He pulled up to her condo, and the lights were on inside. He hesitated after killing the engine. The last thing he wanted was for her to think his visit was all about sex. It wasn't. Although they had been doing a lot of that lately. He just needed to see her, to smell her and to have her voice put his mind at ease.

After he climbed out of the car, he turned the collar up on his coat. The brisk cold wind blew through his coat as if he didn't even have it on. He rang the bell while nibbling on his bottom lip. He didn't know what type of reception he was about to get, but he hoped it would be a warm one. After he rang the bell for a second time, the door opened.

A skeptical-looking Tracee, with a hand on her hip, took a step back and let him in. At least she didn't close the door in his face.

"I just happened to be in the neighborhood, so I thought I'd drop in to see if you were still mad at me." Laurent said with trepidation as he walked in behind her.

"I was never mad at you." She closed and locked the door behind him. "Just disappointed." She turned around and walked toward the kitchen. "I was about to eat dinner."

He turned down the collar of his jacket and shook off a chill. "I thought maybe you'd let me take you out for a bite."

"Take your jacket off. I made chicken marsala." She continued into the kitchen.

Laurent shrugged out of his jacket but couldn't take his eyes off her long legs or her curvy backside that, in black yoga pants, commanded his full attention. He realized now that he should have kept driving. He tossed his jacket on the couch and followed Tracee into the kitchen.

She pulled a second plate from the cabinet and set it on the table.

She'd left the Sunday paper on the counter, and he glanced down to see her beautiful face smiling back up at him. "Hey, I see that guy from the potluck got you in the paper," he said as he picked it up to read the article.

"Yep, that's what he was there for."

Laurent ignored her attitude and finished reading the article. The story covered the monthly potluck dinners the bed-and-breakfast put on and highlighted Tracee's Cake World. When he finished he returned the paper to the counter.

"Wash your hands."

Her harsh tone in Tracee's voice caught him off guard. She was more than disappointed. He let it go and stepped into her powder room to wash up. When he returned, she was sitting at the table with a glass of wine in her hand, swirling the white liquid around. His eyes transfixed on her glass. He'd dated enough women to know that look. He was in trouble. He pulled out a chair and sat down. "Are you okay?" he asked.

"Yeah, help yourself." She pointed to the platters of chicken and green beans on the table.

She'd already fixed her plate, and obviously waited on him. He fixed his plate, then poured himself a glass of wine. He reached for her hand to say the blessing, and to his surprise, she obliged.

They started eating in silence. A thick cloak of tension hung in the air like a rain cloud. Tracee kept her focus on her plate. After a couple of bites, Laurent braced himself for the shoe to drop.

"When were you going to tell me?" she asked.

He looked up at the stony expression on her face. "Tell you what?" He had no idea what she was talking about.

"That Martin Enterprises isn't just the name of the company you work for, but your family's business. That you aren't just a branding manager, but the VP of branding and an heir, along with your two brothers, to a multimillion-dollar business. That you're the much sought after son of Thomas Martin, founder of the exclusive Abelle hotel chain. For Christ's sake, Laurent, your hotels have butler service, spas and art galleries in the lobby!"

Laurent set his fork down and let her get it all out of her system.

"You're riding around town in an Elantra and eating at the pizzeria like it's something you do everyday. Martin is such a common name I never put two and two together. I thought you worked *for* Martin Enterprises, not that you *are* Martin Enterprises. You carry yourself more like a middle manager than a millionaire. This isn't your life. You're here pretending to be somebody you're not. But this is my life, Laurent, and that café is my future. You can play games with the Rival Hotel, but don't play games with me!"

"Tracee—"

She held out her palm to stop him. "I'm not done!"

Chapter 13

From across the conference table, Laurent studied the crease in Mr. Patel's brow as he read over the proposal Laurent had handed him. His rival, the Stephenson Group, wasn't who Mr. Patel thought they were, and Laurent hoped he could see that. Martin Enterprises, on the other hand, had a stellar reputation.

Mr. Patel slid the document to his son Arjun, on his left, while lifting his chin in Laurent's direction. In a smooth, placating voice, he said, "I see you've done your homework."

Laurent pulled his shoulders back and felt taller and stronger than he had during their last meeting. "A good businessman always does."

Raji, who was sitting to Mr. Patel's right, leaned

over and whispered something in his father's ear. Something that Laurent wished he could hear.

"Laurent, I don't know how you came upon this information, and I don't think I want to know." A stony expression took over Mr. Patel's face. "I've looked into the Stephenson Group myself, and I've heard nothing but good things about the company. They are very familiar with Danville and our commitment to the community." He paused and cleared his throat. "That's not to say I don't have a few reservations about them, or you wouldn't be here. However, this—" the older man broke eye contact with Laurent and tapped his index finger against the paper in front of his son "—is not California, and not the way we do business."

Laurent shook his head and leaned into the table. "Sir, I'm very aware of where I am. I've spent the last week getting to know your quaint little town and the wonderful people who live here. I've also gained a better understanding of what the Rival Hotel means to the community."

Mr. Patel pushed his chair back and slowly came to his feet. "Laurent, I have no doubt you put a lot into digging up this information, however, I feel like we're still not on the same page. I expressed interest in a few key areas during our last meeting that I don't think you picked up on. Getting in touch with key members of the *business* community would be more beneficial to you than with young women in the community."

Laurent exchanged eye contact with Raji, the only family member he was aware of who'd seen him with

Tracee. "Sir, I assure you that any *friendship* I've developed since being here has helped me to see Danville from an insider's perspective."

"I'm sure it has," Mr. Patel said with a forced smile before placing a hand on Arjun's shoulder. "Excuse me, but I'm not feeling so well right now, so Arjun here will have to conclude the meeting for me. If everything goes well, we may be ready to make a decision later in the week."

Laurent pressed his lips together in an attempt to hide the disappointment from his face. He'd hoped they'd complete the deal today. "Mr. Patel, I'm a very patient man, and I understand how important this negotiation process is to you. However, I think I've provided you with more than enough information to make a decision today. I would love to do business with you, but I am prepared to leave without a deal by the end of the week. You're not the only small chain hotel we have our eyes on. Martin Enterprises is in the hotel business and only the hotel business. Unlike my competition." As Laurent's grandmother used to say, it was time to crap or get off the pot.

"So he just left the room without another word?" Thomas Martin's voice came through the phone in a rushed tone.

Laurent had dreaded this phone call all afternoon. After last week's report back to his father that he hadn't completed the deal, he'd wanted the next call to be a reason for celebration. Instead, he had to report yet another delay.

"I made it clear that we're prepared to walk away

if a decision isn't made soon, but Mr. Patel wasn't feeling well, so I finished up the meeting with his sons." Although Laurent had issued the threat, he didn't want to walk away from this deal. This was his opportunity to have something for himself—and possibly help Tracee at the same time.

"You played your cards correctly. Although I want that chain, I'm prepared to walk away if he wants more than the twenty percent increase we've offered. We've made an effort, and that's all we can do."

Laurent had been throwing his dirty clothes in a laundry bag for the cleaners but stopped midtoss. "You're not serious, are you?" He had been bluffing, like he'd done numerous times before. And his father seldom walked away from anything.

"Laurent, you've been there for how many weeks now? I sent you because I had faith that you could work with Mr. Patel when I couldn't. However, it seems as if the man doesn't really want to sell his property. We've negotiated in good faith and had patience with him. Sometimes deals fall apart—that's part of doing business. You can't get too attached. Just walk away."

Laurent shook his head and sat down on the edge of the bed. "You can't be serious about walking away from this one. You dangled the ownership carrot in my face and now you want to take it back? I've done everything within my powers to get this deal. Believe me, after he fully looks over everything I provided, he'll be ready to sign the papers."

"Son, I hope so. I want this for you just as much as you want it for yourself."

Laurent hung up with his father and finished gathering his laundry. This trip wasn't going as smoothly as he'd expected. Forget his Caribbean vacation—now more than anything he wanted this hotel. Although his father had told him to pack it up, he wasn't a quitter. There was something about this deal and this town that he couldn't walk away from. Or maybe there was a certain woman who was the reason he couldn't walk away.

Tracee relaxed back into her father's broken-in recliner, kicking the footboard out. He'd brought the chair from their old home on the farm to their newer home in the city. The seat, which had contoured to his body, always gave her a safe and comforting feeling.

"You know Ernie says he can tell when you've been sitting in his chair." Paula Coleman, Tracee's mom, walked into the family room and sat in her chair next to Tracee and opposite the television.

Tracee ran her hands down the arms of the soft leather chair and inhaled. "How can he tell?"

"You leave your perfume behind. He says he can smell it a mile away."

Tracee's eyes widened. "What's he trying to say? My perfume's that strong?"

Paula shook her head and chuckled. "No, honey. I think it's more that he can tell the smell of each one of his children. So, what's going on with you?"

"Nothing, I just got off work so I thought I'd stop by to see how you guys were doing."

"Well, it's Tuesday, so your daddy's at the brotherhood meeting at church."

"Oh, I forgot all about that. What time does he come home?"

"Usually by four. So, what did you want to talk to him about?"

Tracee glanced over at her beautiful, brilliant mother, whom she could never put anything past. "Mama, what do you do when what you thought was the beginning to a bright future starts slipping through your fingers?"

"Baby, what's yours is yours. If it's meant for you, nothing can stop you from getting it. All you need is faith and patience."

Tracee let out a loud breath and sat up in the seat. "I've been patient for a long time. I want what's mine. I'm thirty-four years old with nothing but a part-time job and a side hustle."

Paula tilted her head and took a deep breath. "Tracee, you have a talent for creating and decorating cakes unlike anything I've ever seen. Be patient, baby. Maybe God has something bigger and better in store for you. But until that day comes, stay ready."

"I'm trying, Mama, but Satan keeps putting up roadblocks."

The doorbell rang.

Paula stood up to answer the door. "A roadblock is not a closed door. Remember that, baby."

Tracee's little sister, Kyla, joined them for a late lunch. Tracee was excited to know if Kyla had been able to get any information from Raji, but she held on to her excitement until after lunch.

"Don't worry about the dishes, Mom, I'll put them in the dishwasher." Kyla stood up and grabbed her mother's plate. "Tracee, you can get your own."

"Well, isn't that nice of you," Tracee said as she grabbed her plate and followed her sister into the kitchen. Once they were inside, Tracee handed Kyla her plate. "One more plate would have killed you?"

"Girl, I was trying to get you alone." After placing the saucers in the dishwasher, Kyla reached into her pants pocket. "I ran into Raji yesterday. I didn't know if you wanted Mama to know about this or not."

Tracee took the folded piece of paper from her and opened it up. "The Stephenson Group in Lexington," she read aloud.

"Ever heard of them?" Kyla asked.

Tracee shook her head. "No, but you'd better bet I'll know everything there is to know about them come tomorrow morning."

Tracee sat on her living room floor between the coffee table and the couch, staring into her computer screen. Beside her was a tablet with numerous notes she'd taken over the last couple of hours. After leaving her mom's, she couldn't wait to get home and start her research. The Stephenson Group was a holding company with a diverse portfolio including hotel real estate investments, financial services, automobile dealerships and asset management companies. Tracee gathered some names and switched to LinkedIn to do a more in-depth search.

She was deep in thought when the doorbell rang. *That has to be Mae.* She glanced at the clock on her computer before tearing herself away to answer the door. It was five thirty, and Mae had said she'd be over right after work.

Mae walked through the door like a business-woman on a mission. Today was going to be a good meeting. She hadn't gotten in good before Tracee started rambling about her findings.

"You won't believe what I found out this afternoon," she said.

"What's that?" Mae asked.

"The Stephenson Group. That's the name of one of the Rival Hotel's prospective buyers." Tracee closed the door and motioned Mae over to the couch, where her laptop sat on the coffee table.

"How did you find out?" Mae asked as she sat on the edge of the couch, still holding her purse.

"I didn't, Kyla did. She's been friends with Raji since high school. I think he had a crush on her at one time." Tracee resumed her seat on the floor with her back against the couch. "Anyway, I've been digging into this company all afternoon. They're a holding company and they own multiple businesses. I'm try-ing to narrow it down to who's in charge of the hotel acquisitions, but that's hard. I might have to make a few phone calls."

"Tracee, I need to talk to you about something."

Tracee snapped her fingers. "Oh, and I don't think I've told you about Martin Enterprises. That's going to blow your socks off." So much had happened in the last couple of days, Tracee was on information overload.

"Tracee, I need you to stop and listen to me."

Her friend's voice was shaky. Tracee glanced up at her—she was sitting as if she was about to leave. "What? Why are you sitting there like that? Take your coat off."

Mae cleared her throat. "I can't stay. But I didn't want to do this over the phone."

The hair on the back of Tracee's neck stood up. She put her pen down and got up from the floor to sit on the couch. "Girl, you're scaring me."

Mae lowered her shoulders. "I'm gonna have to bow out of the business."

Tracee's eyes widened. *I didn't hear that right.* She shook her head before studying her best friend and business partner. "What are you talking about?"

"I was offered the position of director of marketing this morning, and, Tracee, I can't turn that down. It's the position of a lifetime. I'll be the first African American female director with the company. That's the career path I was on before my divorce, when I had to put everything on hold."

Tracee was listening but felt a pain developing in the pit of her stomach at the same time. First the café itself, now her business partner. It seemed like the harder she tried, the more things fell apart.

"You've helped me get my head back in the game," Mae continued, "and I'm so grateful for that. I wanted to tell you the minute he made the offer, but I knew this was news I had to deliver in person."

Tracee nodded. "I understand—honestly, I do. I know it might not look like it, with my damp eyes and all, but I do. I'm just a little bummed right now, that's all. But I know what this position means to you, so I'm happy for you. Congratulations."

Tracee leaned over to give her friend a big hug. Mae deserved that job. As much as she hated to lose her as a partner, Tracee couldn't help but be happy for her. "Are you sure there isn't a way you can swing the job and be my part-time partner?" Tracee asked with a big smile after the embrace.

Mae frowned. "The job's in Memphis, Tennessee."

Tracee flinched, and her mouth fell open. She was on the verge of tears. "You really are leaving me, aren't you?"

"Not for a couple of weeks. I don't start until after Thanksgiving. Maybe until then I can help you find a new partner."

A wave of nausea found its way up the back of Tracee's throat. She moved back over to the couch and sat down. "I appreciate that, but get yourself ready to move. I'll find somebody, or I'll go it alone. Either way, I can't be stopped now." She wiped at her tears that threatened to spill over.

A huge smile broke out on Mae's face. "Girl, I've known you since junior high, and believe me, I know you'll find a way to open that café. Don't stop reaching for it. Never give up."

Tracee ran her hands through her hair and reminded herself to breathe. She blinked back tears as she quoted her friend. "Never give up! That's exactly what I plan to do."

Chapter 14

After Mae left, Tracee turned off the computer, turned on the television and balled up on the couch. She didn't care what was on the screen—she just wanted something to take her mind off her troubles for a few minutes. She needed to regroup and get herself together. The minute her head hit the couch, Laurent came to mind. Sunday night he'd surprised her by stopping by, and she'd surprised him by asking him to leave. Why hadn't he told her about his family's wealth? She'd thought he was just a fishing buddy of Sam's. Where was he right now? Would she ever see him again? She shut her eyes and fought the urge to reach for her cell phone.

In two weeks, Tracee had developed an unexpected fondness for Laurent. Now she needed to put some distance between them. If he became the new owner of the Rival Hotel, would he stay in town and run the hotel, or hire someone else and return to California? What about their friendship, which was turning into a relationship? She enjoyed having sex with him, but what if their intimacy had affected him leasing her the space like he said he would? Had she known about his pursuit of the hotel, she never would have gotten involved with him. Everything was so complicated right now she felt overwhelmed.

Her cell phone buzzed from the coffee table. She stared at it but didn't move. *Not now. I don't want to talk to anybody right now.* Maybe it was Mae calling to see if she was okay? She was, so there was no reason to answer the phone. Then she thought about the way she'd kicked Laurent out Sunday night and the fact that he might be leaving any day now. She reached for the phone and turned it over. The display read Laurent Martin, so she answered it.

"Hello."

"Hey…it's Laurent, were you busy?"

She swung her legs off the couch and sat up. "I know who it is, and no, I'm not." Her tone was void of enthusiasm, and he probably thought it was all about him.

"Feel like some company?"

She hesitated, covering her face with her hand. What had she just thought about putting some distance between them? If he came over, no doubt they would end up in her bed; she couldn't help herself. She could see the strong structure of Laurent's jawline, his perfect nose and the beautiful bow of his top lip that made her want to kiss him every time she was with him.

"Hello? You didn't hang up on me, did you?"

Her eyes popped open. "No, I'm here. Sure, come on over. We need to talk anyway." Her thoughts went from losing the space to Laurent's deception, and now the loss of her business partner. She might be down, but she wasn't out. She was just as determined to have her café as Laurent was to own the hotel. Instead of being mad at him, maybe she needed to take him up on his offer and work with him.

It took fifteen minutes for Laurent to get there, walk in and pull Tracee into his arms. She closed her eyes and inhaled. What she needed right now was a hug, and Laurent's hello hugs were everything. She didn't want him to let go, but he did.

Laurent held her at arm's length, clasping her forearms. "I'm sorry. If there was a way I could have told you more about me without discussing the deal, I would have. I could have handled Sunday night a little better as well. I have so much pressure on me right now to finalize this deal that—"

Tracee let out a loud sigh. "I accept your apology. We do need to talk, though, because now I feel like I don't know who you are."

He held one hand to his chest. "You know me, Tracee. I just didn't give you all of my background, but I wasn't pretending to be somebody I'm not. I'm just a guy from California who loves music and my work. My family's French Canadian and African American. You know I have two brothers, Aubrey and Marquis, a father, Thomas Martin, and a stepmother who thinks she's Marie Antoinette. I have family in Evanston, all over California and in Montreal that I don't see that often because of my work. I have an MBA from Berkeley. My blood type is O positive, and—"

"Stop it!" she said, laughing. "TMI. Nobody asked for all that."

"Well, I want you to know who I am and what I'm about." He let go of her other arm. "In more ways than one, I'm a musician trapped in a businessman's body. You know my love for music is real."

She nodded as he spoke. "I know that."

He smiled. "Thank you for letting me come over. You said we need to talk, and I agree with you."

Tracee reached for Laurent's jacket and placed it on the arm of the chair before walking back over to the couch to reclaim her spot. He followed and sat next to her.

"Would you like anything to drink?" she offered.

"Naw, I'm good."

She felt like she could use a bottle of wine, but she knew what one glass would do to her on an empty stomach, so she let the wine stay where it was.

Laurent leaned forward, resting his forearms on his thighs. "What did you want to talk about?"

She crossed her legs. "I received some pretty bad news today, so I need to know what you think your chances are with Mr. Patel."

He took a deep breath. "What kind of bad news?"

"Mae came by earlier, and she's pulling out of the business."

Laurent sat up and frowned. "Why?"

"She's moving to Memphis." Tracee told him everything she knew about Mae's promotion and how she was going to miss her business partner and best friend.

He leaned over, scooting closer to her, and pulled her into his arms. "Baby, I'm sorry. I know you two had big plans for the future," he said softly in her ear.

She closed her eyes and allowed herself to be comforted for about a nanosecond, then she pulled back out of his embrace. "So, I'm back to square one." She held her hands up and started counting off. "I don't have enough money. I have no partner and no location. But that's not going to stop me. I'll find a new partner." With her elbows bowed out, she placed her palms on her thighs and gave Laurent a serious look. "What I don't want to do is find another location."

He nodded. "I know you don't. I can't say what's going to happen, but either I'll have a deal or I'll be going home by the weekend. That's why I wanted to see you."

Tracee's chest tightened as Laurent gazed over at her with a dismal expression on his face. She'd known this day was coming sooner rather than later, but she hadn't realized the impact those words would have on her. It felt as if someone had punched her in the gut. She couldn't respond. They sat staring at one another while the television blared on, unnoticed.

She controlled the quiver in her voice long enough to ask, "So you came to say goodbye?" His eyes squinted, and her insides began to melt.

"I have to get back or my family might start looking for a new brand manager."

"Don't leave yet. I'm not ready to let you go." Tracee couldn't control the trembling of her bottom lip as she placed a hand against Laurent's chest, feeling the loss already.

The corners of his mouth slowly turned up, and he arched a brow. "You're not?"

She bit the inside of her cheek, feeling vulnerable for a moment, but wanting him to know how she felt. "No. Right now I'm thinking about how bad I want you to kiss me."

"Funny, I was thinking the same thing." His head lowered, and his lips met hers.

The softness of his lips warmed Tracee down to the bone. She snuggled closer to him. He wrapped his arms around her, and the thought of him taking his hugs away saddened her.

He backed up slightly and glanced down at her before planting a soft kiss on the tip of her nose. She closed her eyes and experienced the most gentle, sensual thing he'd ever done to her.

His voice lowered to a whisper when he pressed his lips against her ear. "I need to hold on to you."

She hardly recognized the thick voice coming from Laurent. His words and lips were coated with desire as he planted kisses from her earlobe down her neck. His kisses sent hot, sensual flames throughout her body. She needed more air. She leaned her head back on the couch, still holding on to Laurent's shirt. He slid a hand around her back and lowered her down to the couch. His lips branded her neck and her chest before making their way back up to her lips.

The need to touch and explore Laurent's body again was so overwhelming for Tracee. She'd never wanted a man as much as she wanted this man right here. She couldn't control when he left, if he left or if he ever came back, but she could control tonight. He was hers tonight.

The cologne Laurent wore was enough to send her over the edge any day, but tonight his scent tickled her senses and made her want to come out of her panties. He ran his hand down her body, and she ached to feel him against her skin. She let go of his shirt and pushed hard until he sprang back and stared down at her. His brows furrowed, and she watched him try to bring his breathing under control.

"You're not leaving me tonight," she whispered.

He stood up, bringing Tracee to stand with him. He stared down into her eyes before pressing his palm lightly against her cheek. She closed her eyes and leaned into his hand.

"Tu es si belle," he whispered.

Tracee opened her eyes before narrowing them at him.

"You are so beautiful," he said in a soft voice.

She smiled. "I love it when you speak French." Then she took his hand and led him to her bedroom.

Laurent's hand trembled slightly as he unhooked Tracee's bra and slid the straps down her shoulders. He leaned down and kissed her there. She dropped her head back into his chest, wanting to savor every moment of his touch. He brought his arms around her stomach and squeezed tight.

There was something different about the connection between them tonight. Tracee didn't know if Laurent could feel it or not, but she wasn't her usual playful self. He wasn't her man, and she knew it, but tonight she needed him to make love to her as if he was. When he released her, she finished removing her bra and tossed it on the chair before leading him to her bed.

When they reached the bed, he turned her around and took her face between his palms. She waited for him to say something, but he never did. Those big brown eyes were talking to her, telling her how much he wanted and needed her, but nothing came out of his mouth. She could say *I love you*, but it was too soon. She didn't want to scare him away. If he left her tonight before making love to her, she'd cry herself to sleep.

Laurent lowered his head and kissed her forehead, the tip of her nose and then her lips. She wanted a man to look at her the way he was gazing into her eyes right now for the rest of her life.

Without warning, he bent down and picked her up. She wrapped her legs around his waist and her arms around his neck. He walked across the room until her back was above her bed, and then he bent over and tossed her onto the bed. He smiled down at her as he stripped off his shirt, then unbuckled his belt.

She watched him look at her, and her body began to tremble with anticipation. She knew what was coming, but still she bubbled over with excitement.

Chapter 15

Laurent took his time when he made love to Tracee, and expressed with his body what he wanted to say but hadn't. Something was different about Tracee tonight. After two weeks he'd begun to fall in love with this woman. There was strong chemistry between them that he couldn't deny.

In the warm afterglow of lovemaking, Laurent's body was still on fire. He pulled her closer as she snuggled against him. She'd ignited every part of him, and yet he wanted more. Her curls brushed against his neck and chest, and he could feel his erection returning. With his arms wrapped around her, he cupped her breast in the palm of his hand and squeezed.

"Where's your phone?" Tracee asked him.

"Downstairs, why?"

"I wanted to play you a song."

He smiled. "How about I sing for you instead." He cleared his throat. "Let me take you back to some old-school." The song Laurent knew she would recognize was "I'll Make Love to You," by Boyz II Men.

He squeezed her a little tighter and serenaded her with his best rendition of the Boyz II Men vocals.

Laurent had sung that song so many times when he and his brothers performed at family and friends' weddings that he usually went into autopilot mode. But not tonight. Tonight, for the first time, the song meant something to him. When he finished, he kissed the top of her head.

"That was beautiful," she said in a soft voice.

"Thank you."

"I'm surprised you didn't pursue singing as a full-time career."

"We played around growing up, but we were never serious musicians. It was fun, and I guess a way for my parents to keep us out of trouble. My mom loved to hear us perform. Then I went off to college and kind of lost interest in music for a little bit."

"Don't tell me that's when you met Sam and turned into a fisherman?"

Laurent laughed and released Tracee's breast while still holding her close to him. "I'm going to let you in on a little secret. I've never held a fishing pole in my life."

Tracee pulled away from him and turned around, grimacing. "So, why all the joking about fishing?"

"Sam's dad had a yacht. So we called it 'going

fishing' whenever he threw a party and invited a lot of women. The yacht was our bait."

Her mouth fell open. "So you were fishing for women?"

Laurent held his palms up. "Sam was, not me. I was just along for the ride."

She twisted her lips. "Sure you were."

He laughed and pulled her back into his arms.

"I didn't think you, nor Sam, looked like the out-doorsy type. I bet you guys were a couple of play-boys in college."

Laurent cupped her breast and gently massaged. "I've never been the playboy type. I had a lot of fe-male friends, but strictly platonic relationships. Plus, I work too hard to have time for that type of lifestyle. Besides, I'm a one-woman man."

"Oh, yeah! Then you need to buy that hotel so you can stay right here in Danville. As a matter of fact, I'm thinking about locking you in. Have you ever been kidnapped before?"

Laurent threw his head back laughing. "No, I haven't. But I promise I won't put up a fight. I might even enjoy it."

"You would." She laughed and turned in his arms, resting her cheek against his chest.

"You could make me your love slave. Force me to have sex with you every hour."

Tracee pushed herself up and flashed him an openmouthed smile. "You're enjoying this, aren't you?"

"Immensely." The anticipation of making love to her was enough to get him hard again. He reached down and pulled her up until she straddled him. He wanted to feel her warm flesh.

Tracee settled snugly against him, placing her arms around his neck and kissing his face. Her sweet lips against his skin made him smile. He closed his eyes and grasped her hips as she rocked back and forth against him.

"Laurent, what if I pay Mr. Patel a visit and try to persuade him to go with your deal? He likes me—he might listen to reason."

Laurent opened his eyes. "Thank you, baby, but I can't let you do that."

"But if you don't get it, I'll be forced to deal with somebody else."

He smiled at her sheer dogged determination. She would have her café in that spot no matter who owned the hotel. Her ambition was inspiring, and he had no doubt she'd succeed. But so would he.

He brushed her hair back from her cheek and pulled her forward to kiss her tempting lips. "He's retiring, so yes, he's going to sell to somebody. But he won't get a better deal than the one I gave him. For two weeks he's had me jumping through hoops, only to find out he's been playing me this whole time."

"You didn't know another company was trying to purchase the hotel?"

"No, I didn't. He didn't like the initial deal my father proposed, so I was sent to negotiate a better deal. Then he tells me he wants to sell to someone who understands the hotel's place in the community. He led me to believe that if I made an effort to understand Danville and the people who live here, we'd have a deal. But that wasn't good enough. We negotiated a few more points that I had no problem with, but then I learned that I have some competition. This whole time he's been juggling both companies to see who he could get the best deal from."

"So what do you know about the competition?" she asked.

"I did a little digging around, and they are not the type of company he wants to deal with. He didn't like the fact that I researched my competition, but I'm sure once he checks into everything I said, he'll thank me. After all, I've jumped through all his hoops, and I doubt that the other company has."

"So, was calling me for a tour a part of jumping through his hoops?"

He pondered her question for a few seconds. She had a confused look on her face. "In a way, but you helped me get a perspective I couldn't have gotten otherwise. And in the process, I got to know you."

She sat back and stared at him a moment before swinging her leg around and shifting her body until she sat next to him on the bed, reaching for the covers. What the hell had he said wrong?

"Did you use me?" she asked, her voice a pitch higher than before.

Laurent faced her, leaning on one elbow. "Of course not." He didn't like the way she put that, but had it not been for Mr. Patel's request, he might not be lying here with her right now.

"I'll send him a thank-you card. But if he hadn't asked you to learn more about the community, you still would have called me?"

"I like to think that I would have, but I can't say. Initially, I'd only planned to stay in town for a couple of days. I told you that."

She turned and regarded him with puzzled eyes. "In other words, no. I did introduce you to a lot of people and give you that 'insider's perspective' you were looking for. Was this a perspective you wanted to get as well?" She pointed between herself and him. "All a part of becoming one with the community?"

He reached out and pulled her back into his arms. "Of course not." A cool breeze sailed through the room, as if someone had opened a refrigerator door. All the warmth between them vanished, along with his erection. Laurent could feel her slipping away from him. "You already know the answer to that. You've been on my mind ever since I ran into you at the hotel. Then, when we kept bumping into each other, I knew I was supposed to connect with you."

She chuckled as she threw the covers back, swinging her long legs over the edge of the bed. "I hear what you're saying and I know you're right, but somehow I still feel a little used."

"Tracee, don't feel that way. Those tours, and you, are the best thing that's happened to me in a long time. It may look as if I used you in some form, but I didn't."

"How about the potluck? You met my whole family and got to meet a lot of the people who live out here. What do you call that?"

"I called it spending time with a beautiful young lady who *invited* me to the bed-and-breakfast's potluck dinner. She introduced me to her family and I had a great time. The next day, she had me do something I'd never done before. I went horseback riding."

"I'm not saying you didn't enjoy yourself. Hell, I enjoyed myself. I'm just saying maybe you were attracted to me for some manufactured reason, not because you were interested in me. Then the sex got good, and here we are."

He shook his head. "If it wasn't for Mr. Patel, I wouldn't have had the pleasure of learning more about this town, or you. Maybe I should thank him instead of being upset with him. Because whether he sells to us or not, I walk away with something more valuable than just good sex."

She shrugged and stared at him as if trying to detect if he was being truthful or not, which he was. If nothing else came out of this trip, he'd found a woman he wanted to be with. He didn't know how, but he wanted to be with Tracee. He reached out to stroke her cheek, but she turned her head.

"I'm gonna need to think about this. Yeah, I thought we were having a great time, and then I started falling for you, but now I don't know how I feel." She stood up.

Laurent threw back his covers. "Tracee, where you goin'? Come back to bed." He looked around at the glowing clock on her nightstand. It was 2:35 in the morning.

"I'll be back. I need to use the bathroom," she muttered before disappearing behind the bathroom door.

He lay back on the pillows and ran his hands over his face. Tonight couldn't end like this—he wouldn't let it. She'd admitted she was falling for him, and the feeling was mutual. Which was why he wanted to be up front with her. He didn't play games with women.

When Tracee returned, Laurent patted her side of the bed. "Come here, let me talk to you for a minute."

She stared at him, leery of his motives. He patted her side of the bed again, and she walked over to join him.

"You're not really upset over this, are you?"

Tracee snorted. "I know I shouldn't be, but I can't help thinking that if Mr. Patel hadn't played you against the Stephenson Group this whole time, we wouldn't be having this conversation right now. It's not like you would have reached out to me anyway."

To hear that name come out of Tracee's mouth made the hair on the back of Laurent's neck take notice. He'd been careful *not* to mention the name of his competition, but somehow she already knew. "How did you know who the other company was? I never mentioned them."

"I have my resources."

"How long have you known?" he asked, curious now that maybe *she* was trying to play him, too. Had she known from the moment he met her?

"Why? That's not important."

"It's important to me," he said, with a little more bass in his voice than he'd intended. Had she contacted anyone from that company?

She got out of bed again. "It's important to me that I get my lease. You're not the only one who knows how to do a little research. I'm going to take a shower."

Laurent sat there thinking. Could she be in contact with someone from the Stephenson Group? Was that why she had such an attitude? To what lengths would she go to secure that lease?

He climbed out of bed and reached for his clothes.

The next morning, Laurent threw on his running gear and grabbed his earbuds. When he opened the door to his hotel room, he got the shock of his life. Standing on the other side of the door with his fist up, poised to knock, was his father, Thomas Martin.

"What are you doing here?" The words spewed out of Laurent's mouth at a speed that made his father blink his eyes. He frowned and pushed past Laurent.

"I might ask you the same thing. What the hell's going on?" he asked as he walked in.

In his signature Ralph Lauren business suit, his father looked around the room as if he expected someone else to be there. Laurent closed the door and removed the earbuds. "I told you what's going on. You've gotten my reports. The deal is taking longer than I anticipated. Now I've discovered there's another buyer in line."

Thomas Martin shook his head. "So what? You've never let something like that stop you before." He walked over and put his hand on Laurent's shoulder. "This isn't like you, Laurent. You're a shrewd negotiator, or you used to be. What's happened to you, son? I thought you wanted this deal."

Laurent pulled away from his father's condescending tone. "I do! But you need to give me a little more time."

His father walked over and looked out the window at the city below. He stood there shaking his head before turning back around to face Laurent. "I gave you a few days, which is all it should have taken. So I'll meet with Mr. Patel myself and discuss this new discovery. Go for your run. I'll fill you in when you get back."

Like hell you will. Thomas Martin was a fair man, but if you squandered an opportunity he'd given you, there might not be another one. Laurent saw the disappointment in his father's slack face and heard it in his lifeless words. He'd let him down. The family's troubleshooter and master negotiator wasn't living up to his reputation.

He dropped his phone and earbuds on the table. "Wait a minute. I'm getting dressed. This is still my deal."

Chapter 16

Standing in front of a mirror in what used to be Kyla's room the summer she lived at the bed-and-breakfast, Kyla helped Tracee try on a Wonder Woman costume. "I think this thing is too tight, don't you?" Tracee asked as she studied the strapless one-piece that showed off her curvy figure, but might be too much for a kids' party.

"No tighter than this stupid jester costume you talked me into. Now be still while I get all this damned hair under your headband."

"I'm glad Corra decided to throw a Halloween party this year. I prefer partying over waiting on some kids to ring my bell so I can toss them a few pieces of candy. Besides, the kids don't come by like they used to anymore."

"Yeah, I know." Kyla took a step back and looked at her handiwork. "Wait until they get a look at you, superhero, in your over-the-knee boots and bright red lipstick. That shade matches the top of the suit perfect."

"I look like a hooker," Tracee said, glaring back at herself.

"No you don't. Wonder Woman's an Amazonian warrior. That's what you look like."

Tracee didn't agree with her little sister, but since she'd gone to all the trouble of bringing the costume from Lexington, she appeased her. "So, is Miles coming to the party next week?"

"I think so. He said he would be in Lexington on the thirty-first, so I'm sure he'll come. If he does, I might not wear this lame costume—we'll get matching ones."

"Oh, that's so cute. I love to see couples all matchie-matchie."

"Why don't you and Laurent get matching outfits?" Kyla asked.

"Please, Laurent and I aren't a couple. Besides, he'll probably be gone by then."

"Didn't you say he was trying to purchase the hotel?"

"Yeah, but he might finish his deal and be out of here before Halloween."

"But if he does purchase the hotel, won't he be in town a lot more? I mean, if he's going to run it, maybe he'll relocate here."

Tracee shook her head. "I don't think Laurent has any intention of moving to Danville."

Kyla placed her hands on her hips. "Did he say he wasn't?"

Tracee shrugged and realized something for the first time. They'd never talked about what would happen once, or if, he purchased the hotel. He never said who would run it or if he'd be back in town to do anything. "He didn't, but it's not something I think will happen."

"And you're okay with that? Don't try to tell me you don't have feelings for that man, because I know you do. It's not just a sex thing like you want me to believe."

You could fool some of the people some of the time, but she could never fool Kyla. "So what if I like him. When his business is over here, he'll go back to California. I'm just hoping he buys the hotel and leases me the space. I'm working on lining up a new partner."

Kyla stood next to Tracee and started laughing as they looked at themselves in the mirror.

Tracee grabbed Kyla's hand. "Come on, let's go show Corra."

Kyla snatched her hand away. "I'm not going out there like this. I look like a clown. We have guests."

"Girl, nobody's hanging out in the lobby. Who's going to see us but Corra? Come on, she's working on the computer at the front desk."

Tracee took Kyla by the hand and pulled her out of the spare bedroom, down the hall and out into the lobby. Kyla begged her not to and laughed all the way. The minute they walked through the lobby entrance, a tall, distinguished older black man who stood at the counter turned toward them.

Tracee heard Corra say, "Ah, here's Tracee now. Ladies, uh…this is Mr. Thomas Martin. He's looking for Tracee."

She dropped Kyla's hand as a rush of adrenaline tingled through her body. Did Corra say Thomas Martin, as in Laurent's father? Kyla turned around and retreated back into the family quarters. Tracee wanted to run away as well, but he'd already seen her.

Mr. Martin stared at her boots and worked his way up to her red lips, with raised brows. "Tracee Coleman?" he asked.

"Yes, I'm Tracee. You'll have to forgive the costume—we're getting ready for our first big Halloween party." The suffocating suit made her breasts look as if they were ready to pop. And from the disapproving look on Mr. Martin's face, she was sure he thought the same thing.

He offered his hand. "I'm Thomas Martin, Laurent's father. Would it be possible to speak with you alone for a moment?"

His grip was firm, and the words in her mouth froze. She did not want to meet Laurent's father dressed like this. Costume or not, he might get the wrong impression of her.

Corra came from behind the counter. "Tracee, you might want to step into the library for a little privacy." She motioned them in that direction before turning the opposite way. "I'll be in the office if you need anything, okay, Tracee?"

Tracee nodded, unable to verbalize a response. What was Laurent's father doing in Danville? And how did he know to come looking for her at the bed-and-breakfast? Mr. Martin took a step back, and Tracee pulled herself out of the daze she'd sunken into. She smiled as she walked into the library. "We can talk in here."

He walked in behind her, and she closed the pocket doors. She turned around to find his focus on the books. She breathed a sigh of relief.

"You're probably wondering why I'm here," he said as he turned around to set his disapproving gaze on her again.

She crossed her arms over her chest, feeling the coldness in his eyes. She sensed that this man did not like her. "Are you looking for Laurent?"

"No. I've come to speak to you."

She uncrossed her arms and placed a hand over her heart. "Me!"

"Yes. I believe you're the young lady who's been occupying my son's time since he's been in town." That wasn't a question, but more of a statement, which he followed up with a curt smile.

She shivered. There was something not so nice about this man. "I gave him a tour of the town and we've spent some time together, yes."

"And there lies the problem." He walked away and ran his fingers across some of the books. No doubt looking for dust, the way he had his nose all up in the air. "You see, Laurent was tasked with closing a very important deal. It should have taken him a couple of days at the most." He stopped and turned back to Tracee. "However, he's been here for over two weeks."

Tracee dropped her smile. "Yes, I know. He told me about it."

"Well, you see, Tracee…may I call you Tracee?" She nodded. "Sure."

"Tracee, I know my son. He's never let anything get in the way of negotiating a deal. He's a Martin—it's what he does. But he's young, and the only thing I can think of that would distract him from taking care of business is a beautiful young lady such as yourself."

Tracee wanted to smile, but the quick head-to-toe glance he gave her Wonder Woman costume let her know that wasn't exactly a compliment. He'd come to insult her.

"I'm sorry, but are you trying to insinuate that I'm the reason Laurent couldn't close that deal?" It was insane, she knew, but that sounded like what he was saying.

"On the contrary. I'm sure you helped him in numerous ways, and I thank you for that. Unfortunately, Laurent has a fondness for beautiful women. So when I received his report about a delay, I knew a woman was involved somewhere."

"And you came to Danville to tell me that?"

He left the bookshelf and strode closer to her. "I came into town to finish the deal. Once I learned of your existence, I wanted to meet you myself. I wanted to see the woman who could cost my company millions of dollars. The woman who'd stolen my son's heart."

Was that what she'd done? "Mr. Martin, your son has stolen my heart also. In the short amount of time

Laurent has been here, I have to admit I've grown very fond of him."

He smiled down at the floor before glancing back up at her. "Of course you have. Laurent is a very sought-after bachelor. A young woman would be lucky to be seen with any of my sons. Laurent didn't come to Danville looking for a woman. He had a job to do, and I thank you for helping him. But in a few days the deal will be complete and Laurent will return to California. I wanted to make sure you understood that."

She bit her bottom lip. Laurent's daddy was telling her to back off his son. "Sir, I'm well aware that Laurent won't be staying in Danville."

Mr. Martin smiled and clasped his hands together. "Good, we have an understanding. In the next couple of days we'll be closing this deal, and I'd appreciate it if you could manage to stay away from Laurent during that time. He works better without the distraction."

He walked toward the library door, and Tracee was too flabbergasted to open her mouth. She just stood there with her arms crossed and her heart breaking.

Mr. Martin opened the doors before turning back to Tracee. "Ms. Coleman, it was a pleasure meeting you. As I said, you are a lovely young lady, and I hope we have an understanding?" He smiled like a Cheshire cat, waiting on her to answer him.

All Tracee could do was nod her head.

"Good, and I'll see myself out, thank you."

He left, and she wanted to run and slam the door behind him. She wanted him to get the hell out of there and never come back.

Tracee still stood in the same spot minutes later when Kyla and Corra walked into the library. She couldn't move. Her conversation with Mr. Martin had stunned her.

"Tracee, you okay?" Kyla asked as she touched Tracee's shoulder.

"What did he want?" Corra asked.

Tracee closed her eyes; she could see Laurent lying in her bed and feel his arms around her as she cuddled up next to him. He always kissed the top of her head, and she thought that was the most romantic thing. But did he do that with every woman? His father said he was sought after. Did that mean he had lots of girlfriends in California?

"Snap out of it, girl," Kyla said with a snap of her fingers in Tracee's face.

Tracee blinked and looked at her little sister, who'd taken off her costume and put her khakis and polo shirt back on, the Coleman House Farm uniform. She was waving her hand in Tracee's face. Tracee swatted at Kyla's hand. "Get your hand out of my face."

"Well, what the hell happened? You're standing here looking crazy and he just took off. What did he say? What did he want?" Kyla asked.

"He wants me to stay away from his son, that's what he wants."

"Say what?" Corra asked.

The stunned looks on her family's faces summed up Tracee's own feelings. She still couldn't believe that man came into town, then drove out there, all to ask her to stay away from Laurent. He could have done that shit over the phone. How did he even know they had been seeing one another? Had Laurent told him about her?

"Who does he think his son is?" Kyla asked.

Tracee took a few steps back and sat on the couch behind her. "He's Laurent Martin, son of millionaire Thomas Martin, who's the owner of Abelle, a five-star boutique hotel chain that caters to the wealthy. They have hotels in Canada, France, the US and Italy, too, I think."

Kyla and Corra came to sit on the couch on either side of Tracee.

"No shit!" Corra said.

"Tracee, how long have you known that?" Kyla asked.

Tracee shrugged. "I found out when I was doing research on the Stephenson Group. I researched Martin Enterprises, too. Laurent never told me he worked in the family business. Not that it makes a difference, because now I'm in love with the guy. But after what his father just said to me, I don't know that I'll ever see him again."

Corra leaned back and crossed her arms. "Okay, tell us everything he said. Nobody comes into my home and insults my family."

Tracee fell back onto the couch and covered her

eyes with her hands. "I should have taken off this suit before coming out into the lobby. He probably thinks I'm some type of a floozy or something. I made a bad first impression."

Kyla pulled Tracee's arms down. "Tracee, what did the man say?"

Tracee relived the worse fifteen minutes of her life to her family members. Afterward, Corra and Kyla were ready to find out where Mr. Martin was staying and ride over to give him a piece of their minds.

"I was right. Laurent used me. He can have any woman he wants—why would he be interested in me?" Tracee dropped her face into her palms again and felt sorry for herself for a few seconds.

"You mean, why wouldn't he be interested in you?" Corra stood up. "Tracee, Laurent was lucky to have met you, and he knows it. Don't listen to his father. I've seen you guys together, and believe me, he has strong feelings for you as well. And I don't for one minute believe he used you."

Kyla stood up, too. "Come on, Tracee, don't let him get you down on yourself."

Tracee dropped her hands and leaned back into the couch again. She took a deep breath and shook her head. "It's not just him. Mae had to pull out of the business, I don't know who Mr. Patel is going to sell the hotel to and Laurent and I had something like a fight the other night. I might not see him again anyway. Nothing is going right. Things should be coming together instead of falling apart."

Kyla and Corra flopped back down on the couch opposite Tracee for a group hug.

"I wish I'd known he was Laurent's father when he walked in," Corra said. "I'd have told him we were closed until hell freezes over."

Tracee looked at Corra, who rolled her eyes, and the three of them burst out laughing.

Chapter 17

Laurent spent most of Thursday morning on his cell phone. He'd neglected a few of his ongoing projects and had to put in the time to make sure they weren't totally going south. Through conference calls, his direct reports had kept him on top of anything critical, but some issues he had to attend to himself. For now, a phone call would have to suffice, but soon he'd have to get back to his life and his job.

He was deep in thought when his brother Marquis called.

"The old man told me he was going to Lexington on business, but I know a line when I hear one. How's it going?" Marquis asked.

"He has his way of doing things, and I have mine. He's getting in my way. Yesterday he insisted on a meeting with Mr. Patel, only to make me look like a fool. I had to sit there while he went on and on about Martin Enterprises' esteemed reputation."

Marquis's robust laughter came through the phone and Laurent shook his head, smiling to himself. "Man, you should have been here. He put on a show."

"Relax, little bro, you know that's how he is. I can see him with his chest poked out now. Martin Enterprises hotels have been awarded five stars by *Forbes Travel Guide*, *Business Insider* and every other important publication in the world. We offer experiences, not just a room to sleep in."

Laurent sat back in his hotel chair, laughing at the way Marquis had his father down to a tee. "Man, I think you *were* there."

"I've been there enough," Marquis answered.

"Well, for what it's worth, I believe he impressed Mr. Patel's sons, if no one else. He's staying in Lexington, thank goodness. After the meeting he said his wife is dragging him to some function there."

"Maybe that's the business he had to attend to. If you're lucky he'll stay in Lexington and let you handle your business. What happened with the information I gave you?"

"Yeah, we need to talk about that. I'm gonna need someone who can corroborate those findings."

Marquis made a sucking-air-through-his-teeth sound. "Not sure if I can do that, little bro."

"Yes, you can. You're a Martin, and we make the impossible possible. And I need contact information before tomorrow."

"What?" Marquis asked, raising his voice.

"This deal is mine, and it's going down tomorrow. The old man wants me to play hardball, so that's what I'm going to do. You've got about eighteen hours to get back with me."

Marquis let out a deep breath. "Stay by the phone. I'll see what I can do."

"Thanks, bro. I'm nothing without you—you know that, don't you?"

"Yeah, yeah, whatever. Butter me up. You know I've got your back."

Laurent hung up, eager to add an addendum to his deal before his last meeting with Mr. Patel. He needed a yes from the old man. He had big plans for the hotel that he hadn't shared with anyone, and walking away wasn't a part of his plan.

Laurent worked until his eyes blurred from staring at his laptop screen. He sat back to take a break when he realized he hadn't eaten anything since breakfast and it was past dinnertime. He leaned back and stretched, trying to figure out what he wanted to eat tonight. He could go for anything besides pizza. He closed his computer, disconnected his cell phone from the charger and grabbed the Elantra's keys.

He drove through town trying to decide on a restaurant. The urge to pick up the phone and ask Tracee to have dinner with him was strong, but he fought it. She was upset with him, and he knew he needed to give her a little time. He'd have to pick something out himself. He pulled into the nearest Speedway gas station to fill the tank. About the only thing he did like about the rental was the gas mileage. This was his first fill-up since arriving.

His mind wandered back to Tracee as he pumped the gas. He hadn't noticed a truck pulling up across from him until he heard someone call his name.

"Laurent?"

He turned to see a young woman close the truck door and walk over toward him. A sign on the side of the truck read Coleman House Farm. Then he recognized the face. "Hey, you're Tracee's sister, Kyla, right?"

She stopped at the trunk of his rental. "Yes, I am."

The gas handle clicked, and Laurent turned around to top it off at an even amount. The way Tracee's sister's eyes were narrowed and she crossed her arms over her chest, he had a feeling this wasn't going to be a pleasant conversation.

"It's nice to see you again," he said as he waited for his receipt.

"When's the last time you spoke to Tracee?" she asked.

Laurent pocketed his receipt and joined her at the trunk of his car. She looked like she was about to drill him about something.

"Tuesday night, why?"

"Did you know your father stopped by the bed-and-breakfast yesterday?" she asked as she leaned against the trunk of the Elantra.

Laurent's brows rose as he took a step back. *Impossible.* "My father?" he asked in disbelief.

She nodded. "Yes, Mr. Thomas Martin."

Laurent felt his heartbeat increase along with

a ripple of anger that ran through him. *No, Dad wouldn't do that. Why would he do that?* His father had returned to Lexington after the meeting yesterday, or so he thought. "Did he say what he wanted?"

"He came to speak to Tracee."

His chest muscles tightened. His father had spoken to Mr. Patel and his sons, who'd undoubtedly told him about his relationship with Tracee.

"What did he say to her?" Now he leaned against the Elantra.

"Let's just say he wasn't so nice. He accused her of costing you a deal that stood to be worth millions, I believe."

Laurent lowered and shook his head. *Damn, how could he!* He didn't know what had gotten into his father lately. It wasn't like him to show up and interfere with Laurent's deal, and it definitely wasn't like him to seek out Tracee in that way. "That's not true, you know?"

"I didn't think so. But he tried to sell it. Right before he asked her to stay away from you in order for you to complete the deal."

What the hell! His father was sticking his nose somewhere it didn't belong.

"I'm sorry. I don't know what's gotten into him. He flew in yesterday for a quick meeting. He had no business bringing Tracee into this. I guess she's upset with me now, huh?"

Kyla nodded. "I'd say so. I didn't hear what your father said, but he upset my sister something awful."

"Damn." Laurent had to get that man on the next flight back to California. "I'll talk to him, and I promise you it won't ever happen again. I apologize on his behalf. He's just a little hyped about this deal, that's all. I'll reach out to Tracee."

Kyla pulled away from the car. "I don't know you, really, but do know that Tracee has strong feelings for you. So strong that your dad really got under her skin."

Laurent's heartbeat pounded in his chest as he also pushed away from the car. The anger inside him was building so, he wanted to strangle his father. "Thank you, Kyla."

Another car pulled up behind Laurent, waiting for him to move since all the other pumps were full.

Kyla took a few steps backward. "Whatever you do, don't hurt my sister. She deserves a good man."

He nodded. "I know, and I have no intentions of hurting her."

Kyla turned around and went to fill up the truck. Laurent climbed in the car and took off. Now he wanted to see Tracee. He needed to talk to her and make everything all right again. He pulled out his cell phone and dialed her number. The call went straight to voice mail. He didn't want to, but he left a message asking her to call him as soon as she could. But something told him he wouldn't get a call back. Then he dialed his father. He answered on the first ring.

"Hello, and I know why you're calling," Thomas Martin said in a commanding tone.

Laurent ignored his father's "you know I'm the father" voice. "What kind of game are you playing with me? You give me this deal, then you interfere in the worst way possible. What did you say to Tracee?"

"See, I was right. She is the problem. Son, don't let a woman open your nose so wide you can't focus on the business at hand. I sent you down here to close a very important deal."

"Where are you?" Laurent didn't want to hear another word from his father. He only wanted him gone.

"We're in Lexington."

"At what hotel?"

"Laurent, I'll be back in the morning."

"No, you won't. I'm on my way there now. We need to talk."

Instead of finding a local dinner spot, Laurent hit the highway headed to Lexington, thirty minutes away. He needed to sit down with his father and put an end to his meddling. Having Thomas Martin step in at closing for any other deal would be a feather in his cap, but not this one. His father had promised him this hotel if he could close the deal, and that was exactly what he was going to do. After handling his father, he would have to make amends with Tracee. He wasn't about to let her, and the deal, slip from his grasp.

Friday morning after his run, Laurent showered and dressed for his 11:00 a.m. meeting with the Patels. Thomas Martin and his wife were on a flight back to California. Marquis had come through late yesterday with the name and number of a businessman who could corroborate his findings regarding the Stephenson Group. Before Laurent left Lexington, he'd met a gentleman eager to provide all the information he needed.

He placed a quick call to a local florist and had a dozen red roses sent to Tracee at the Coleman House, where he knew she'd be this morning. Then he sat down to send her a text message and attached the perfect song, "Get You" by Daniel Caesar. Music was how he expressed himself, and with this song she'd know how he felt.

He needed to talk to her, and he would after he'd taken care of his business. He hadn't gotten much sleep last night, unable to get Tracee off his mind. Whatever move he made next, he wanted her to be a part of it. Whether he purchased the hotel or not, he didn't want his relationship with her to end. He wanted them to take it to the next level.

At 11:00 a.m. Laurent walked into the conference room at the Rival Hotel with the confidence of his father, his brothers and the entire Martin Enterprises team at his back. No matter what, he was his father's son, and this was what he did best.

Thirty minutes into the meeting, Laurent had Mr. Patel eating out of his hand. He detailed his assurances that the current staff could stay on after renovations, if they so desired. He'd noted that the established community involvement aspect of the hotel was intact, along with an added outreach to the local college offering a place for returning graduates and visiting parents, as well as people doing business locally.

"I'm also aware that before you decided to sell,

you were going to lease the space downstairs to Tracee's Cake World. I want to give her that lease alongside a small jazz café that I plan to open."

For once, Mr. Patel didn't look at his sons with dissatisfaction. Instead, he smiled at Laurent and gave him an assuring nod. "I think time has shown you what this place means to me. And I appreciate you going the extra mile."

"Thank you, sir. I also have someone I'd like you to speak with." He pulled out his cell phone. "You were skeptical about the information I gave you regarding the Stephenson Group, so I reached out to the former owner of Hotel VanDee in Lexington. Mr. Robert VanDee would like to share some information with you."

"Didn't they sell that property a few years ago and reopen under another name?" Raji asked.

Laurent shook his head. "No, but I'll let Mr. VanDee explain why." He FaceTimed with Mr. VanDee, who explained how the Stephenson Group had purchased his hotel, only to tear it down and build another business—after promising to renovate and keep him on as a consultant. Laurent let Mr. Patel and Mr. VanDee talk before ending the call.

Afterward, he left the family to talk among themselves. While he waited, he walked down to the lobby and dialed Tracee's number. The call went straight to voice mail again, and he left another message. "Hey, Tracee, I need to talk to you when you have a few minutes. I ran into your sister yesterday and... I'm real sorry about what happened. I don't know how to explain my father's behavior, but I'm going to try. I hope you got the song I sent you. I'll talk to you later." He hung up, shaking his head.

"Excuse me, Laurent?"

He looked up at the sound of Raji's voice. "Yes?"

Raji stood against the rail from the mezzanine level looking down at Laurent with a smile on his face. "We're ready to resume."

Laurent bit his lip and tried not to read anything into that smile. He slipped his phone into his pocket and headed back to the conference room.

Chapter 18

Friday night Tracee wanted to let her hair down and get Laurent off her mind. She hadn't answered any of his calls, nor listened to his voice mail. His father had helped her realize how hard she'd fallen for him in such a short time. She'd even admitted it to Kyla and Corra, something she wished she hadn't done. Now the three of them sat in the pizzeria, eating, drinking and doing whatever she could to get Laurent off the brain.

"Would you like to dance?" A voice came from behind Tracee.

She turned around, and a young man all in black with a mustard-colored jacket and an array of heavy chains around his neck smiled at her. A college student. She smiled back. "Sure."

Before getting up, she turned to Kyla and Corra, who'd been nursing the same drink for the last hour. "It's time to have some fun, ladies." When she turned around, the college guy took her hand and led her to the pizzeria's small dance floor.

As it turned out, he was a pretty good dancer, and the DJ's selection of hip-hop music was good as well. But neither one could keep Tracee from thinking back to her birthday night when she'd danced with Laurent. He invaded her every thought while she fought hard to concentrate on her dancing partner. It was time to turn it up.

Laurent rang Tracee's doorbell a couple of times before giving up and getting back into his car to head for the bed-and-breakfast. Since she wouldn't answer his calls, he'd have to track her down. He hit his second strike when Tayler informed him that Tracee had gone with Corra and Kyla to their favorite Friday night spot—the pizzeria.

Minutes later, he walked into the pizzeria and found Corra and Kyla sitting at a pub table with a half-eaten pizza propped in the middle.

"Did you save me some?" he asked as he approached the table.

Surprise! Corra looked up at Laurent with her mouth wide-open. Kyla, on the other hand, slowly turned up the corners of her mouth, as if she'd expected him to show up.

"If you like veggie pizza, help yourself," Kyla said as she pointed to the leftover slices.

"Mind if I join you?" he asked.

"Please do." Corra turned her stunned expression into a soft smile.

Laurent pulled out a chair and sat down.

"I'll pass on the veggie pizza, but I will take a look at the menu." He hadn't eaten since breakfast, because he hadn't really had an appetite. "Where's Tracee?"

The women gave each other wide-eyed looks before Kyla turned her gaze to the dance floor.

Laurent followed her gaze, and that's when he spotted Tracee. She was working up a sweat with what looked like a group of young college kids on the small dance floor of the pizzeria. He could tell she was enjoying herself. Her curls were loose, big and bouncing freely all over the place.

"Here you go." Kyla handed him a menu. "Their calzone's good."

Laurent looked the menu over but couldn't concentrate on anything he read. When he glanced up at the dance floor, the music had changed, and Tracee was still dancing.

"So, Laurent, Tracee said you may be leaving soon. Is that true?" Corra asked.

"Yes, in a few days. But I'll be back soon, though."

"Oh! Good news?" Kyla asked.

Laurent gave the ladies a little smile. "Yeah, that's actually what I want to talk to Tracee about. If she's not too upset with me."

As if on cue, Tracee danced her way over to the table without making eye contact with Laurent. "Ladies, you have to get out there—the music is good and there are plenty of dance partners. Those guys belong to a fraternity at Centre College."

Laurent looked at Tracee and wondered how long she was going to keep pretending she didn't see him. After a few beats, he concluded she was going to be stubborn.

"Hello, Tracee," he said, above the music.

She turned to him with cold eyes, clenching her jaw. He wanted to walk over and put his arms around her. He wanted to take away any pain that he or his father had caused.

"Hi. I thought you'd be on your way back to California by now," she said before picking up her drink and playing with the straw.

He slowly shook his head. "No, not yet."

"Uh-huh," she muttered before turning away. "So, ladies, why so quiet? Let's order another drink. Where's the waiter?"

"None for me," Corra said.

"Me neither," Kyla added.

Laurent forgot about eating and focused on what he'd come here for. He set the menu down and stood up. "Tracee, can I talk to you a minute?"

She looked up with a polite smile on her face. "I think your father said enough for the both of you." With her drink in hand, she turned her back to him, giving her attention to the dance floor.

He leaned into the table and said, "Excuse me, ladies," to Corra and Kyla before walking around to get Tracee's attention. She sipped her drink, and her gaze wandered everywhere but on him.

Laurent leaned into her, placing his hand on the

table behind her and his mouth close to her ear. "I'm sorry. I didn't know he was coming, but give me a minute to explain what happened."

Tracee threw a hand up, palm out. "There's nothing to explain. I totally understand and I won't interfere with your business."

He wrapped his hands around hers, getting her attention. "Can you follow me, please, so we can talk?"

"Tracee."

The both of them turned at the sound of Kyla's voice.

She held out Tracee's jacket. "It's kind of loud in here," she said with a wink.

Laurent let go of Tracee's hand in order for her to put her drink down and accept the jacket from her sister. He wanted to thank Kyla. When Tracee turned to him, he stifled a smile and gestured toward the door. He placed his hand at the small of her back as they exited the restaurant.

Once outside and a few steps away from the door, Tracee whirled around on Laurent. "I'm not supposed to be distracting you," she said with her hands on her hips. "Your father and I have an understanding, or didn't he tell you?"

Laurent rolled his shoulders and let out a heavy sigh. "That was an asshole move by my father, but he doesn't speak for me."

"He seems to think he does. Or maybe it's the business's best interest he had in mind." She shoved her hands into her jacket pockets.

Laurent reached out to touch her, but she pulled away. "Okay, I'm so sorry my dad showed up and showed out like that. His presence here surprised the hell out of me, too. He wanted to meet with Mr. Patel, and as far as I knew, after the meeting on Wednesday he went back to Lexington, which is where he was staying. I had no idea he even knew who you were, let alone that he came out to the bed-and-breakfast. He's gone now. He and my stepmother took a flight back to California this morning."

Tracee zipped her jacket up all the way and turned up the collar. "Your father's a grown man—no need to apologize for him. He spoke his mind. Did he tell you he came to see me?"

"No. I ran into Kyla yesterday at a gas station."

"She shouldn't go around telling my business."

"Well, I'm glad she told me, since neither you nor my father were likely to say anything. Tracee, I know he didn't mean it."

"No, maybe he was right, and I was right. Maybe you did use me and it backfired on you. The same way your research backfired on you." She crossed her arms and stared him down.

Laurent wanted to pull her into his arms, but he didn't want to get smacked, so he kept his hands in his pockets. He hoped the good news he was about to share with her would turn her attitude around.

"Tracee, it's cold out here. Let's get in the car and talk?"

She looked over her shoulder toward the parking lot, and then back at him. He could see the conflict going on in her head. She wanted to be with him, but she wanted to continue to be mad at the same time.

"Please. I have something I need to tell you."

Surprisingly, she didn't protest. They walked over to the Elantra, and he opened her door. She held on to the door and looked up at him. "This won't take long, will it?"

He shook his head and grinned. She was stubborn. "Get in the car, Tracee."

Again she complied without an argument. He closed the door and walked around to the driver's side to climb in. She sat there with her arms crossed looking straight ahead. As much as Tracee tried to put on a brave front, Laurent knew she was hurt. He'd seen it in her eyes, and it was killing him. He started the engine.

"What are you doing?" she asked, unfolding her arms.

"Turning on the heat. You're cold." He reached over and stroked her arm while taking a deep, calming breath. "Tracee, I want you to pay close attention to everything I'm about to say. I never intentionally used you. I don't care who says otherwise. From the moment you fell into my arms at the hotel, I was eager to meet you and find out who you were. Yes, I called you for a tour *after* my discussion with Mr. Patel, but I could have chosen another route to get information on the town. I chose to call you because I wanted an excuse to see you again."

He reached over and placed his hand under her chin, turning her head to face him. "I kept calling because I wanted to be with you. You inspire me. You're a talented, determined, beautiful woman with a bright future. And if you let me, I want to be a part of your growth. I want to lift you up and support you in any way that I can. Not that you actually need my help, because the fire you have inside you will take you wherever you want to go, I'm sure of that."

She unzipped her jacket, and he reached over to turn the heat down. She looked like she wanted to say something, but he stopped her. He had a lot to say before he told her the outcome of his deal.

"Tracee, I want you to be that special woman in my life. Maybe I wasn't looking for a woman on this trip, but I thank the Lord that I found you. You brighten my day, and I think we're good together."

Her posture had relaxed, and her hands rested in her lap. He had her full attention now. A need to touch her and make love to her again consumed him. The sexy way she bit her lip and glanced up at him was more than enough to make him want to take her back to his hotel room and make love to her, but he had news to deliver.

"You know, when my father offered me this deal I jumped at it. I admit I wasn't excited about it being in Danville because I didn't think there was anything here. But I was wrong. My future is here."

Tracee let go of her lip and shook her head. "Laurent, don't do this to me. I know you're going back to California."

The look on her face was squeezing his heart. "Hey, I don't know how we're going to work this out, but we will. Tracee, if our love is meant to be, and I think it is, I know we'll find a way."

"So, you're not going back?"

"I am, but I'll be back real soon. I closed the deal

with Mr. Patel this morning. Martin Enterprises just purchased all four of the Rival Hotels."

Tracee's mouth fell open, transforming her sad face into a beautiful smile. "Wow! That's wonderful, Laurent."

She must have forgotten all about being mad at him, because she leaned over and gave him a big hug. He didn't want to let her go, but he did.

"Despite my father's interfering ways, Mr. Patel said yes to my deal. So you're looking at the new owner of the Rival Hotels."

She brought a hand to her mouth. "Oh my God, does that mean what I think it does?"

He nodded. "It means more than you think it does. I've planned for a café in the new hotel."

She blinked several times and looked confused. "You're doing what?"

"When I agreed to broker this deal, my father promised me sole ownership of a single hotel of my choosing. This is fulfillment of a lifelong dream for me. I get to have my jazz club, and you can have your café. I'm renovating and I've planned on space for your café. Or, how about a café by day and a music spot by night? That is, if you're still interested in working with me?"

Laurent thought Tracee was going to pull him from the driver's seat, she reached out and wrapped her arms around his neck so hard. He heard her crying before he felt the tears against the side of his face. "I guess that's a yes!" he said.

She released him and sat back, wiping her eyes. "That's a hell yes! The minute it seemed as if everything in my life was falling apart, I got down on my knees and prayed. I prayed you'd get the hotel and that everything would work out between us. Lord knows I wasn't ready for you to walk out of my life."

"Tracee, we're just getting started."

She cleared her throat. "What will your father say?"

Laurent laughed. "My father won't be a problem, you'll see."

"I don't know, Laurent. He did ask me to stay away from you."

"And I'm asking you to stay with me. To become my partner in business, and in life, so we can fulfill our dreams together."

"Laurent, this is more than I could have ever imagined. Are you sure you want to do this?"

"I wrote it into my proposal. I'm sure."

Someone tapped on the window, startling the both of them. Laurent looked behind Tracee to see Kyla and Corra peering into the car.

"Is everything okay in there?" Corra asked.

Tracee released his neck. "Can I tell them?" she asked.

He nodded. "Sure."

The car door flew open, and Tracee jumped out. "I've found my new partner!" she screamed.

Epilogue

Six months after Thomas Martin had asked Tracee to stay away from his son, he was now sitting at the dining room table of the Coleman House bed-and-breakfast with his wife and son enjoying Sunday brunch. Today's brunch was reserved for family. Rollin had added a leaf to the dining room table in order to accommodate Tracee's parents as well as her siblings. She looked around the table and couldn't keep the smile off her face. They were like one big happy family—husbands, wives and children.

Laurent's parents had flown into town for the grand opening of their son's new hotel, Hotel Nicholas. With the opening of the hotel, Laurent had found another way to honor his mother, who'd given all of her boys the same middle name—Nicholas.

After the deal closed, he'd spent the last six months renovating the old Rival Hotel into a piece of artwork that the whole town was excited about. He'd had a soft opening two weeks ago in order to make sure everything was perfect for the grand opening. But first, Laurent had insisted his father spend some time getting to know Tracee and her family.

"Laurent, did I ever tell you my parents had a little garden out back when I was growing up?" Thomas Martin asked.

Laurent arched a brow and turned to wink at Tracee before answering. "No, that's news to me."

"Yeah, my old man liked to grow his own food as well. I guess you could say we had our own organic farm. He grew lettuce, tomatoes, onions, cucumbers, potatoes and some other vegetables. I'd almost forgotten about that."

"Everybody had some type of garden back in the day," Tracee's father added.

Tracee felt Laurent squeeze her thigh under the table. She reached over and found his hand. They held on to one another, expressing how happy they were at the moment. In a few hours, they would be celebrating the achievement of dreams come true.

The kitchen door swung open, and Rita, followed by Tayler, entered the room carrying with them platters of what smelled like heaven on earth.

"Um, something smells wonderful," Laurent said.

"That would be my multigrain blueberry pancakes," Rita said as she placed two platters in the middle of the table. "This here's family style, so help yourself. We got more coming." She returned to the kitchen for more food.

Rollin said the blessing, and then everybody dug in as Tayler and Rita returned with more plates. Tayler came around with pitchers of iced tea and water.

"Sir, would you like tea, water, or can I fix you a mimosa?" Tayler asked, standing next to Mr. Martin.

Tracee sat directly across the table from Laurent's father, who when he glanced up at her looked embarrassed and a little ashamed. They'd spoken once since the last time he entered the bed-and-breakfast, and all he said then was, "Hello, it's nice to see you again." Laurent told her he'd had numerous conversations with his father about her over the last six months. His father had apologized to Laurent for his behavior and promised to make it up to Tracee. She was waiting on that apology.

"I'll have some sweet tea, thank you," Thomas Martin said to Tayler, before flashing a smile toward Tracee.

Plates were clinking and glasses were being thumped against the table. Then silence filled the room while everyone enjoyed their food too much to engage in conversation.

Minutes later, Thomas Martin broke the silence. "These are the best pancakes I've ever had. And I don't know the last time I've had grits, but they're wonderful as well. I need to fly a few of my chefs in for cooking lessons. We might need to add a little southern flair to the menu."

The fact that Laurent's father had eaten in some of the best restaurants in the world, yet he praised

Rita's cooking, pleased everyone on the Coleman staff. Tracee loved the beaming smiles on Rollin, Corra and Tayler's faces.

Corra responded by adding, "Aunt Rita is the best cook in Boyle County."

"And don't forget about Tracee," Tayler added. "You know she's the best pastry chef in the county and we're going to hate to see her go. But I'm more than happy for her at the same time." Tayler held a glass of orange juice up to salute Tracee.

Tracee held her glass up in return, blushing, and winked at Tayler.

"So I've heard," Thomas Martin said, smiling at Tracee. "I hope we get to sample some of your work today."

Tracee was surprised that he spoke directly to her. Laurent squeezed her hand under the table again. "As a matter of fact, I baked a carrot cake and a golden cake with buttercream frosting for today's brunch."

"And her cakes are to die for," Rollin added. "At least that's what the girls say, right?" He gestured to Tayler and Corra before Tayler blew him a kiss.

"That's right. When the U-pick store was open, we couldn't keep Tracee's desserts on the shelf. And I'm sure that will continue now that we'll be your number-one customer," Corra said to Tracee.

"As long as you pay your bill every month, you'll always be my number one," Tracee replied.

Everyone at the table got a good laugh out of Tracee's response.

Finally, Rollin stood up and tapped his fork

against his glass. "Folks, I'd like to make a toast before we all get scattered around."

Tracee gave Laurent a thin-lipped smile, not sure what her cousin was about to say.

"First of all, I want to say thank you to Laurent for building such a nice hotel that is likely to steal some of my customers."

Everyone laughed again, and Laurent shook his head.

Rollin continued. "No, really. Hotel Nicholas is going to be a tremendous asset to the community. The whole town is excited about what you're doing. And we're excited about you making Tracee's Cake World a part of that excitement. I see nothing but good things in the future for you two. Here's to a successful grand opening celebration tonight. Oh, and don't forget to take a stack of our brochures to keep in your lobby."

Tayler yanked at Rollin's shirt, laughing, while he held his glass high. "To Hotel Nicholas."

The minute everyone took a sip, Laurent pushed his chair back and came to his feet.

"Keep your glasses up. I'd like to say a few words also." He cleared his throat and glanced around the room at everyone, stopping at his father. "I'd like to thank my parents for taking the time out of their schedules to fly down for the grand opening." He nodded at his parents.

"Wouldn't miss it for the world," his father said.

Laurent continued, "And for coming a day early in order to join this Sunday brunch. I told you it was going to be some of the best food you'd ever put in your mouth."

Thomas Martin nodded first to Laurent, then in Rollin's direction.

"And Rollin, you keep doing what you're doing. I don't think you'll have a thing to worry about as far as customers are concerned. If there's one thing I learned in researching Danville and its residents, is that the Coleman House farm and bed-and-breakfast has a stellar reputation. If anything, you might want to send your overflow my way."

Rollin gave Laurent a wide-eyed look before nodding.

"Seriously, I want to thank everyone for the hospitality you've shown me from that first Sunday brunch I attended here over six months ago, to assisting me with making some choices in regards to the grand opening. I've bragged about you to everyone I know, and I'm happy to call you friends. I look forward to entertaining you tonight, so here's to having a good time."

After the last toast, everyone finished their meals and Tracee helped Rita and Tayler serve dessert. Rollin had started a conversation with Laurent's father when Rita reentered the room with a camera.

"Mr. and Mrs. Martin, if you don't mind, may I have a picture for my wall?" She pointed to the pictures above the sideboard of the celebrities and local heroes who'd eaten or stayed at the bed-and-breakfast.

Laurent's father stood up, smoothing his tie down

the front of his chest before helping his wife up. "Of course, we're honored that you asked."

"Well, it's not every day that we have the president of a five-star hotel chain dining with us. Tracee showed me your hotels on the internet. Very impressive!"

Thomas Martin grinned as if he'd been complimented by the queen of England.

After pictures and dessert, Rollin offered Laurent's parents a tour of the property. Thomas Martin said he hadn't spent time on a farm since his childhood growing up in Evanston, Illinois. A fact that he repeated a few times before the day was over.

Tracee stepped out on the front porch and took a seat in one of the white rockers to get some air and to pinch herself. She couldn't believe everything that was going on inside. Everyone was happy, peaceful and enjoying one another. This was turning into the perfect day. The front door opened, and Laurent's father stepped outside.

"Here you are, Ms. Tracee." He walked over and took a seat in the rocker a table away from her. "I owe you an apology. The first time we met, I was an obnoxious blowhard. I said some unkind things to you, and I hope you've forgiven me for my bad behavior."

Tracee had been scared of Laurent's father, thinking he'd never apologize to her because he might have thought it beneath him. But he was just a man like every other man in there. "Thank you, sir. I was scared to talk to Laurent after you left. But we talked it over, and I think I understood the pressure you were under. So, you're more than forgiven."

Mr. Martin smiled. "Well, we're lucky that Laurent never listens to me. He's headstrong and capable of making his own decisions. What frightened me was the fact that he hadn't settled the deal, and I knew this was his future. All of my hotels will be left to my sons when I pass on. But an Abelle hotel isn't what Laurent wants for himself. I know him. Don't tell my other sons, but he's the most creative and talented of the three of them. He needs to express himself in his own way, with his own property. He's young, but Laurent is ready for ownership, and I hope you are as well. He shared his plans for Café Amour with me."

She tried not to show every tooth in her mouth as she smiled. "Yes, sir, I'm more than ready. You see, having my own business is a lifelong dream for me. My grandmother opened a coffee stand in the Rival Hotel years ago, and my cousin carried on the tradition until she passed. Now in that same spot I want to take her dream to the next level. I want to make my family proud as well."

Mr. Martin smiled. "I admire your drive, and I see why my son has fallen in love with you. You're not just a pretty face."

Tracee tried her best not to blush. "No, sir. I'm not."

"Sometimes It Snows in April," according to Prince, but not today. The weather was perfect, and the trees and flowers had begun to bloom.

Laurent's original plan had been to purchase the Rival Hotel, return to California and hire a project manager to oversee the renovations. However, after developing a relationship with Tracee, he'd decided to take up residency in Danville and handle the renovations himself. After all, Hotel Nicholas was his!

For the grand opening, he'd hired a local DJ to play old-school music all night. All of the hotel's staff played a part, from serving hors d'oeuvres to giving tours and greeting guests with gift bags that included samples from Tracee's Cake World. Local business owners and event planners, along with newspaper and magazine people from the surrounding counties, were in attendance. Everybody wanted to see what the new hotel looked like.

Laurent walked through the crowd greeting and welcoming everyone. In the corridor leading to the gym he ran into Sam and his wife, Janet.

"Laurent, this place is absolutely magnificent. Man, you've created a unique brand experience with the new hotel, and we love it."

"Thanks, man." Laurent pumped shoulders with Sam, before kissing Janet on the cheek. "I appreciate that, really I do."

"So we see you've found something to do around here for fun," Janet said.

Laurent laughed at her reference to him being bored when he first arrived in Danville. "Yeah, I found something and someone. Like Sam said—" he reached out and grasped Sam by the shoulder "—find a good woman and settle down. And I've been having nothing but fun ever since."

"Looks like we spoke her up. Here comes Tracee now," Sam said.

Laurent turned around as the woman who'd completely turned his world upside down sashayed toward them. Tracee looked stunning with her hair swept back from her face into a long ponytail running down her back. Her little black cocktail dress was a traffic stopper. It hugged every curve of her body, showing off her beautiful figure. When she smiled at him, his heart filled with warmth and nothing but love for her. Before leaving California, he'd made sure his father knew that one day Tracee would be a part of their family.

Walking alongside her was her best friend, Mae. They might not be business partners, but their friendship remained intact.

"Hey, guys, what are you doing standing out here? Café Amour is open and Tracee's Cake World is serving up dessert." Tracee hugged and kissed Sam and Janet before motioning them toward the café.

"Now this I'm looking forward to," Sam said. "You've created a sweet spot and a jazz spot under one roof. I think I'm going to have a new hangout."

"That's right, we have all your pastry needs during the day, then stick around for some smooth jazz in the evenings from Thursday through Sunday. I might even play a little something from time to time," Laurent added.

"Now you're talking. Thank you both for sharing your gifts with us. We'll be customers for sure," Sam said, smiling at his wife.

"And you know I've already reserved a table for John and me for this Friday night," Mae added before reaching out to give Laurent a hug.

After all the well wishes, Sam, his wife and Mae left them and went to check out the café.

Laurent took the moment they were alone to pull Tracee into his arms and kiss her inviting red lips. "You look so beautiful tonight—ready for the red carpet."

She snapped her fingers. "That's what we should have done. Rolled out the red carpet. Everyone from the local press is here. We're going to be on the front page tomorrow, you know."

He smiled. "I know. I've given a few interviews, but I have a feeling we'll be giving a few more before the night's over. I just want to take this moment to say thank you for entering my life and being there when I needed you most. Tracee Coleman, I love you so much."

She smiled. "I should be thanking you. Remember, I was the one who had the boring life until this good-looking guy from California showed up. A couple of days turned into a couple of weeks, and I was hooked. I love you back, Laurent Martin."

The hotel lights began to flicker, indicating it was time for everyone to assemble in the lobby for a speech from the new owner.

Laurent walked into the circle his staff had assembled for him and looked around at everyone in attendance with awe. Tracee's entire family was there. His parents were there, and his brother Marquis had arrived just in time for the reception. His other brother, Aubrey, sent his well wishes and apologized for not being able to get back from Hong Kong for the opening.

Butterflies were dancing in Laurent's stomach as he delivered his thank-you speech. He wasn't nervous about the speaking, but the little box in his jacket pocket had his heart beating double time. After he thanked everyone, he asked Tracee to join him. He introduced her to anyone who didn't already know who she was. Then, as if on cue, the DJ played her favorite song, "Why I Love You" by Major.

Tracee turned and smiled at the DJ, who was posted up in the corner. When the crowd gasped, she turned back around—Laurent had pulled the box from his pocket and gotten down on one knee. Her hand flew over her mouth.

Laurent reached out for her hand. "Tracee, I feel as if the stars have all aligned and God brought you to me. I love you with everything inside me, and I want to be there for you until the end of time. I want us to grow this thing together. I love you, I need you and I want you to be my partner in life. What do you say? Will you marry me?"

Tears streamed down Tracee's cheeks as she looked down at Laurent smiling up at her with wide eyes, waiting for her answer. She closed her eyes, wanting to savor the moment for just a second longer. This man was everything she'd ever wanted, even when she didn't know it. She loved him more than anything and couldn't bear to be without him. She opened her eyes and removed her hand from her mouth. *"Yes!"* she screamed and held up her shaking hand for Laurent to slide a beautiful engagement ring on her finger.

The applause sounded like thunder in her ears

while Laurent stood up and kissed her before wrapping his arms around her and giving her the best hug yet. She cried some more, thankful that she'd never have to go without his hugs ever again.

* * * * *

**Soulful and sensual romance featuring
multicultural characters.**

Look for brand-new Kimani stories
in special 2-in-1 volumes starting March 2019.

Available May 7, 2019

Forever with You & *The Sweet Taste of Seduction*
by Kianna Alexander and Joy Avery

Seductive Melody & *Capture My Heart*
by J.M. Jeffries

Road to Forever & *A Love of My Own*
by Sherelle Green and Sheryl Lister

The Billionaire's Baby & *The Wrong Fiancé*
by Niobia Bryant and Lindsay Evans

www.Harlequin.com

Get 4 FREE REWARDS!

We'll send you 2 FREE Books
plus 2 FREE Mystery Gifts.

Harlequin® Desire books feature heroes who have it all: wealth, status, incredible good looks... everything but the right woman.

FREE Value Over **$20**

YES! Please send me 2 FREE Harlequin® Desire novels and my 2 FREE gifts (gifts are worth about $10 retail). After receiving them, if I don't wish to receive any more books, I can return the shipping statement marked "cancel." If I don't cancel, I will receive 6 brand-new novels every month and be billed just $4.55 per book in the U.S. or $5.24 per book in Canada. That's a savings of at least 13% off the cover price! It's quite a bargain! Shipping and handling is just 50¢ per book in the U.S. and 75¢ per book in Canada.* I understand that accepting the 2 free books and gifts places me under no obligation to buy anything. I can always return a shipment and cancel at any time. The free books and gifts are mine to keep no matter what I decide.

225/326 HDN GMYU

Name (please print)

Address   Apt. #

City   State/Province   Zip/Postal Code

Mail to the **Reader Service:**
IN U.S.A.: P.O. Box 1341, Buffalo, NY 14240-8531
IN CANADA: P.O. Box 603, Fort Erie, Ontario L2A 5X3

Want to try 2 free books from another series? Call 1-800-873-8635 or visit www.ReaderService.com.

*Terms and prices subject to change without notice. Prices do not include sales taxes, which will be charged (if applicable) based on your state or country of residence. Canadian residents will be charged applicable taxes. Offer not valid in Quebec. This offer is limited to one order per household. Books received may not be as shown. Not valid for current subscribers to Harlequin Desire books. All orders subject to approval. Credit or debit balances in a customer's account(s) may be offset by any other outstanding balance owed by or to the customer. Please allow 4 to 6 weeks for delivery. Offer available while quantities last.

Your Privacy—The Reader Service is committed to protecting your privacy. Our Privacy Policy is available online at www.ReaderService.com or upon request from the Reader Service. We make a portion of our mailing list available to reputable third parties that offer products we believe may interest you. If you prefer that we not exchange your name with third parties, or if you wish to clarify or modify your communication preferences, please visit us at www.ReaderService.com/consumerschoice or write to us at Reader Service Preference Service, P.O. Box 9062, Buffalo, NY 14240-9062. Include your complete name and address.

HD19R

SPECIAL EXCERPT FROM

Savion Monroe's serious business exterior hides his creative spirit—and only Jazmin Boyd has access. Beautiful, sophisticated and guarding a secret of her own, the television producer evokes a fiery passion that dares the guarded CEO to pursue his dream. But when she accidentally exposes Savion's hidden talent on air for all the world to see, will he turn his back on stardom and the woman he loves?

Read on for a sneak peek at
Forever with You,
*the next exciting installment in
the Sapphire Shores series by Kianna Alexander!*

Savion held on to Jazmin's hands, feeling the trembling subside. He hadn't expected her to react that way to his question about her past. Now that he knew his query had made her uncomfortable, he kicked himself inwardly. *I shouldn't have asked her that. What was I thinking?* While his own past had been filled with frivolous encounters with the opposite sex, that didn't mean she'd had similar experiences.

"I'm okay, Savion. You can stop looking so concerned." A soft smile tilted her lips.

He chuckled. "Good to know. Now, what can you tell me about the exciting world of television production?"

One expertly arched eyebrow rose. "Seriously? You want to talk about work?"

KPEXP0319

He shrugged. "It might be boring to you, but remember, I don't know the first thing about what goes on behind the scenes at a TV show."

She opened her mouth, but before she could say anything, the waiter appeared again, this time with their dessert. He released her hands, and they moved to free up the tabletop.

"Here's the cheesecake with key lime ice cream you ordered, sir." The waiter placed down the two plates, as well as two gleaming silver spoons.

"Thank you." Savion picked up his spoon. "I hope you don't mind that I ordered dessert ahead. They didn't have key lime cheesecake, but I thought this would be the next best thing."

Her smile brightened. "I don't mind at all. It looks delicious." She picked up her spoon and scooped up a small piece of cheesecake and a dollop of the ice cream.

When she brought it to her lips and slid the spoon into her mouth, she made a sound indicative of pleasure. "It's just as good as it looks."

His groin tightened. *I wonder if the same is true about you, Jazmin Boyd.* "I'm glad you like it."

A few bites in, she seemed to remember their conversation. "Sorry, what was I gonna say?"

He laughed. "You were going to tell me about all the exciting parts of your job."

"I don't know if any of what I do is necessarily 'exciting,' but I'll tell you about it. Basically, my team and I are the last people to interact with and make changes to the show footage before it goes to the network to be aired. We're responsible for taking all that raw footage and turning it into something cohesive, appealing and screen ready."

"I see. You said something about the opening and closing sequences when we were on the beach." He polished off the last of his dessert. "How's that going?"

She looked surprised. "You remember me saying that?"

"Of course. I always remember the important things."

Her cheeks darkened, and she looked away for a moment, then continued. "We've got the opening sequence done, and it's approved by the higher-ups. But we're still going back and forth over that closing sequence. It just needs a few more tweaks."

"How long do you have to get it done?"

She twirled a lock of glossy hair around her index finger. "Three weeks at most. The sooner, the better." She finished the last bite of her cheesecake and set down her spoon. "What about you? How's the project going with the park?"

He leaned back in his chair. "We're in that limbo stage between planning and execution. Everything is tied up right now until we get the last few permits from the state and the town commissioner. I can't submit the local request until the state approval comes in, so…" He shrugged. "For now, it's the waiting game."

"When do you hope to break ground?"

"By the first of June. That way we can have everything in place and properly protected before the peak of hurricane season." He hated to even think of Gram's memory park being damaged or flooded during a storm, but with the island being where it was, the team had been forced to make contingency plans. "We're doing as much as we can to keep the whole place intact should a bad storm hit—that's all by design. Dad insisted on it and wouldn't even entertain landscaping plans that didn't offer that kind of protection."

She nodded. "I think that's a smart approach. It's pretty similar to the way buildings are constructed in California, to protect them from collapse during an earthquake. Gotta work with what you're given."

He blew out a breath. "I don't know about you, but I need this vacation."

Don't miss Forever with You
by Kianna Alexander, available May 2019
wherever Harlequin® Kimani Romance™
books and ebooks are sold.

Copyright © 2019 Kianna Alexander

KPEXP0319

Want to give in to temptation with
steamy tales of irresistible desire?

Check out **Harlequin® Presents®**,
Harlequin® Desire and
Harlequin® Kimani™ Romance books!

New books available every month!

CONNECT WITH US AT:

Facebook.com/groups/HarlequinConnection

Facebook.com/HarlequinBooks

Twitter.com/HarlequinBooks

Instagram.com/HarlequinBooks

Pinterest.com/HarlequinBooks

ReaderService.com

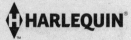

**ROMANCE WHEN
YOU NEED IT**

PGENRE2018

Love Harlequin romance?

DISCOVER.

Be the first to find out about promotions,
news and exclusive content!

Facebook.com/HarlequinBooks

Twitter.com/HarlequinBooks

Instagram.com/HarlequinBooks

Pinterest.com/HarlequinBooks

ReaderService.com

EXPLORE.

Sign up for the Harlequin e-newsletter and
download a free book from any series at
TryHarlequin.com.

CONNECT.

Join our Harlequin community to share
your thoughts and connect with other
romance readers!
Facebook.com/groups/HarlequinConnection

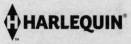

HARLEQUIN®

**ROMANCE WHEN
YOU NEED IT**

HSOCIAL2018